ALWAYS PRACTICE
SAFE HEX

JULIETTE CROSS

*Cover Design by Jennifer Zemanek

*Editing by Gemma Brocato

For Krys Kruse—
I don't know what I did so right for the angels to drop you into my life, but I'm so damn grateful.

Thank you for being an amazing friend as well as the best work buddy ever. XO

PROLOGUE

~LIVVY~

I COULDN'T CONTROL MYSELF. THE SECOND I LAID EYES ON THAT damn grim reaper, I bee-lined through the party, pretending my final destination wouldn't be right by his side. There was something perversely compelling in my lust/hate roller coaster ride of emotions for this man.

He'd been annoyingly arrogant from the first day of the contest when we'd met. The second time we met at our semi-final interviews, he both complimented and cut me in the same breath with that icy tongue of his. Finally, he'd been dominant and pushy on the way out of that last interview, then he had the audacity to accuse me of using my magic as an Influencer to roll over the judges in this PR contest we were both competing for.

To say he rubbed me wrong was an understatement. The fact that he also rubbed me so ridiculously right was absolutely maddening.

And the way he looked at me. *Jesus, take the wheel.*

No. *Jesus, look away.*

Because there was nothing but delicious, dark sin in those

obsidian eyes currently tracking me with such intensity across the room.

Gareth Blackwater was a pleasurable and maddening shock to my senses. From his always-in-place coal-black hair to his fair complexion to his razor-edged jaw and prominent brow, he was a feast for the eyes. Also, he was a cocky, annoying know-it-all.

People were mingling, eating, and drinking, but mostly waiting for the big announcement of who the three finalists would be.

Victor Garrison, President of Garrison Media Corporation, lingered toward the front of the reception room near the microphone, talking to his Chief Operation Officer, Marianne Mixon.

I grabbed a glass of Merlot at the bar then meandered over to stand right next to Gareth.

I'd gotten my sister Clara to give me one of her super-spells to block his powerful aura that was basically a concoction of sex-clenching, mind-buzzing lust. So far, so good.

Smiling at the holiday song piping out of the speakers, I kept my gaze on the stage, eagerly awaiting the announcement. But also, wanting to pretend nonchalance and see if Clara's shielding spell could really block the effect Gareth's aura had on me.

I smiled. "They're playing your song, Mr. Blackwater."

Of course, the slow, sultry rendition of "You're a Mean One, Mr. Grinch" reeked of sex and suggestive innuendo, which made me grimace. I didn't want him to think I found him sexy. Which I so did. Despite my best instincts.

Then I felt it. A powerful pulse of magic followed by a wave of dizzying desire that made my thighs sweat and my nipples tingle. So much for Clara's aura-blocking shield. He cracked it without even seeming to try. Just standing there with his ice man demeanor and aura of I-don't-give-a-fuck, like he wasn't slaying me with his insane sex mojo.

"Are you alright, Lavinia?"

Why did he always use my full name? Nobody else did. And

why did it sound so carnal and lascivious dripping from his overly full lips and rumbling out of his lusciously wide mouth? I was distracted for a second, imagining what those beautiful lips would feel like whispering something naughty against my skin.

He stepped closer. "You seem upset."

I snapped my gaze back to the dais at the front. "Just something I thought would work and didn't."

I was about to walk away, needing space from the grim whose wicked aura was breaking me into little, sweaty pieces when Victor Garrison stepped in front of the mic. He welcomed everyone, drawing us all into silence. After all, the party-goers were here for one and only one reason—to find out the names of the three finalists who would compete for the big prize.

"I won't make you all wait any longer," said Victor. "This was a very tight competition. As you may recall, we had you interview in groups of three. After analyzing your portfolios and interviews, we grouped you according to whom we thought you'd work with best."

Gareth cocked a haughty, black brow down at me.

"Don't look at me," I told him, knowing that arrogant look he was giving me was because we, along with another warlock, were grouped together. "I can't help it if their grouping skills suck."

Then, he laughed.

Goddess have mercy!

Gareth in his usual broody, austere state was disturbingly attractive. But when he laughed? Damnation and hellfire. He was like a dark angel showering us lowly humans with a glimpse of heaven.

I turned away abruptly, shielding myself from his hypnotic allure and trying to focus on Victor who was in the process of announcing the winners. *This* was what I was here for. Not to get tied up in knots over this enigmatic, cocky grim who happened to be my rival and who unfortunately set my body on fire.

"Without further ado," said Victor, smiling across the small gathering in the reception room, "the team we've selected as the finalists for the Garrison PR Competition are…Gareth Blackwater, Livvy Savoie, and Willard Thompson."

First, a wash of pure joy zapped through me as I beamed and nodded nicely at those giving us applause. Second, I realized I'd be spending a hell of a lot more time with the man standing stiff as a board next to me.

Gareth lifted his glass to the room then turned to me. The sharp angles of his cheeks and jaw seemed sharper. "Cheers, darling. You're stuck with me now."

Victor led the room in his own toast, congratulating all of us again, but my brain and body were both buzzing. Gareth wasn't happy about this news either. Seems I wasn't the only one feeling the nerves that we'd have to get along to some extent for the sake of the contest.

It was a competition, but we'd be required to work cohesively as a team on the public relations project.

"You don't seem very happy about it," I said, watching him gulp down bourbon like it was water. "Is it because you have to share the spotlight with two others? I'm sure that's difficult for you." I couldn't help teasing him. Something about him made me want to poke and pull and fucking misbehave.

"I suppose you're right," he agreed, holding my gaze. "I prefer to work alone."

"Oh, I see." I smiled lightly, taking a sip of my wine. "Never had a menage, have you?"

Poke, poke.

His jaw clenched before he replied coolly, "No."

"I'm surprised," I said with exaggerated glee. "You should give it a try, Gareth."

He didn't flinch. His dark gaze held tight to mine. "Why's that?"

"It might loosen you up. It's fun to let loose and lose control sometimes."

I realized a split second too late that Gareth Blackwater should not be poked.

"During sex," he said in that low, deep baritone of his, leaning close and giving me a whiff of his clean, masculine scent, "being in control is the only way I get off."

Suddenly, a tendril of magic wrapped around me, like a silken scarf. The hair on the back of my neck rose, then a vision popped into my head.

I was naked and bound and bending over black, silk sheets on a large bed. I couldn't move, then a large, gentle hand wrapped around my nape. It was Gareth standing behind me. The fiendish look of lust in his gaze turned me on as he reared his hand back and spanked my ass. I flinched, then I moaned with pleasure.

Gasping, I came out of the vision, my pulse pounding, blood racing. That wasn't my vision. That was *his*. I stared at Gareth in shock for two reasons. One was that he'd had a deliciously filthy fantasy of me. The second was a secret I'd just learned about grim reapers.

I cleared my throat and whispered, "You're a telepath?"

Knowing he'd get the message, I faced him fully and telepathed a message while holding his cold gaze. Our minds linked with a buzzing snap.

Dream on, grim. It'll never happen. You aren't the only one who prefers control. And I'd never hand the reins over to you.

His nostrils flared as he stepped even closer, mouth partly open as if trying to figure out what to say. For several seconds, he said nothing at all, devouring me from head to toe with those predatory, black eyes. Then he gave me a stiff nod.

"Congratulations, Lavinia." He upended his tumbler, downing the last of his bourbon, drawing my attention to the muscles working in his pale throat. "I suppose I'll be seeing you very soon."

Then he abruptly turned and stormed toward the exit. For a minute or two, I simply stood there, still in shock at that vision.

I then circulated the room in a daze, receiving congratulations from the other semi-finalists and Mr. Garrison as well as the Director of Marketing who would be overseeing the competition, Richard Davis.

But I couldn't remember a thing anyone even said to me. My mind was wholly distracted with thoughts of black silk sheets, pale skin, and the distinct, sharp rap of a hand smacking flesh.

Buckle up, I warned myself. This was going to be one hell of a ride.

CHAPTER ONE

~GARETH~

Outwardly, I was cool as ice. Dressed in black slacks and a gray dress shirt, I rotated my wrist, feeling the comforting weight of the Smart watch I custom designed. Everything was in its place. But inwardly, I was a fucking inferno of emotions.

Today, I'd finally see Lavinia again.

Since the party last month when it was announced that we'd be two of the three finalists in the PR contest sponsored by Garrison Media Corporation, I'd been spending the majority of my time trying not to think about her. So of course, I'd done nothing but.

She was an Influencer and one of the Savoie sisters' coven, so her magic had to be to blame. That's what I kept telling myself anyway. That the gut-ripping attraction I felt for her was nothing more than Warper magic. Influencers, also known as Warpers, typically earned the name.

They could warp a person's sense of control and willpower to do whatever they wanted. That's all this was, I repeated to myself as the elevator dinged, announcing my arrival on the top floor.

I stepped into the lobby and stopped at the desk of the receptionist who I'd met at the semi-finalist interview.

"I'm Gareth Blackwater."

She smiled. "I'm Cynthia. Yes, I remember you." A blush colored her cheeks. "This way, Mr. Blackwater."

I was well aware that my grim aura had a certain effect on people. Human and supernaturals. Her blush could mean a number of things. Perhaps my aura had her thinking about a secret sin she'd like to be acting on right at that moment. Grim auras pushed others to want to do their darkest desires. The ugly or carnal ones they kept hidden away from the world.

So I was used to the pink cheeks and eye averting thing.

Of course, her blush might also mean she was attracted to me. It was always hard for a grim to know. Either way, it didn't matter. The pretty receptionist wasn't on my radar, and this contest was business. I was determined to win this contest, and not for reasons others might think.

I didn't need the prize money. I'd be donating it any way to my cause that needed a dire influx of cash. It was what money couldn't buy that this contest offered my cause. I had to convince my other opponents, Lavinia and Willard, that mine was the best option.

I followed the receptionist down a long corridor where she took a left, leading us past several offices buzzing with activity. Finally, we reached the last door on the right which stood open. She gestured for me to enter.

"Mr. Davis will be joining you all soon."

I cringed at his name, wishing he wasn't the liaison for our project. I hated the man on sight at the semi-final interviews. For one, he emitted a dangerous kind of energy only grims could detect. Dark magic coursed through our blood. *Like knew like.*

The second reason was the way he looked at Lavinia. Not like the average man looked at an attractive woman, but like a predator sighting his prey. Something base and violent stirred inside my chest at the memory of the way he stared at her.

"Thank you," I told the receptionist calmly then walked into the large workroom.

My pulse catapulted faster at the sight of her. I thanked the supernatural gods that witches didn't have the heightened senses that the rest of us had. Until I reined myself under control over this woman, I would pretend she had no effect on me. At least, that was the current plan.

She sat across from Willard at a long table. The rest of the large workspace was filled with three desks, including desktops, and a lounge area with two sofas arranged in an L-shape, and a coffee table. There was also a small kitchenette station with a mini-fridge and microwave. This would be ideal for working through meals on our campaign.

Now, to discover what our campaign would actually be.

"Good morning," I greeted them both as I strode toward the table.

They both turned, Lavinia's eyes widening at the sight of me. A small tell. The sudden increase in her heart rate was more of one.

I knew that I'd annoyed the fuck out of her on more than one occasion. But I also knew that when I'd slipped up and let her see my little fantasy of her tied up in my bedroom, she had a very different reaction than I'd expected. Arousal.

This little working relationship might get complicated really fast if she continued to react to me that way. Because I sure as hell wasn't one to deny my urges. If she was on board, then so was I. Rivals or not.

"Morning," said Willard, standing and shaking my hand a little awkwardly.

"What's your designation again?" I asked as I took a seat on Lavinia's other side. "Healer?"

"Uh… yeah," he said, frowning. "Are you psychic?"

Lavinia arched a brow at me, wanting to know the answer. I gave her a smile.

"No. That is one thing I am not."

She narrowed those midnight-blue eyes at me. Now that she knew I was telepathic, it was likely eating her alive at what else I could do. If she only knew.

"Good morning to you, Lavinia," I said a little more intimately since I was now seated right next to her.

She turned to her notepad and scribbled something. "Nice of you to join us."

Her irritated tone skated right over me. At the moment, I was taking her all in. Wearing black tights with tiny white skulls, a red corduroy miniskirt, and a white, fuzzy sweater that made my fingers itch, she looked utterly delicious. Better than I remembered.

And her scent. Goddamn, she smelled heavenly. Like lavender fields and spiced apple, some cool combination of spring and fall.

After satisfying my starving senses with a nice long drink of her, I finally said, "I'm right on time. As always."

"We've been here since six thirty," she snapped, writing my name at the top of her memo pad then underlining it.

"Actually, I got here at six forty-eight," said Willard robotically.

"And I arrived at seven. Right on time." I turned in my seat, angling my upper body toward her. "Does it bother you that I don't arrive when you do? If you'd like more of my company, just say the word and I'll arrive however early you want me."

Her gaze snapped to mine, sapphire eyes sparking with fire.

God, she was so fucking beautiful.

"I was not implying that I wanted to spend more time with you."

"Seemed that way to me."

She tapped her pen on the memo pad. "While you weren't

here, we made some preliminary notes on the campaigns we want to propose."

"Great. I'd like to hear what you two are proposing."

"Why don't you tell us about your campaign?"

"No," I answered firmly. "I want to hear yours first."

She opened her mouth to object or agree, I wasn't sure, because at that moment, in walked Richard Davis.

He was tall, about my height. Moderately handsome, I suppose. I disliked him. Perhaps more than disliked. The expensive suit and polished veneer barely masked the sinister gleam in his gray eyes, hidden away behind his expensive suit and polished veneer. When he smiled, he reminded me of a snake opening his maw to eat something. Or someone.

"Good morning, everyone. I hope you all like your workspace." He gestured wide to the room with one hand, a portfolio in the other and then took the seat opposite Lavinia. Of course.

"It's lovely," she said amiably.

Willard looked around the room. "It's big."

"I haven't checked out the computers yet," I added, "so I'll let you know."

He chuckled like I'd made a joke. I hadn't. If they dumped some low-tech, shoddy PCs on us, I'd be bringing in my own. Who was I kidding? I'd be bringing in my own anyway or simply using mine at home. I didn't like my work on other computers that could be accessed for information.

"Well, if there's anything you're missing, just let me know." Richard opened the leather portfolio and removed three electronic key cards and passed one to each of us. "This will give you access to the building after hours if you decide to work late or on weekends. Security downstairs has been given your names and copies of your IDs, so whoever is on duty will let you up. And this key gets you past the lobby and into this office."

We took the keys which were white, rectangular plastic attached to a GMC lanyard.

He then took out three packets of paper, bound with paper-clips, and slid one in front of each of us.

"A couple of things in here. As stated in the contest guidelines, you'll be paid for your time. We know that you all are stepping away from your regular jobs to spend time on this campaign, and GMC wants you to be adequately compensated. After all, whatever cause the three of you decide to back will benefit from your work and from the backing of GMC."

He aimed his snake-like smile at each of us, lingering on Lavinia, then added, "You'll need to fill out the W2 in there before you leave today and drop it off with Cynthia at front reception."

"Thank you." Lavinia returned his smile politely.

She seemed to be our spokesperson since Willard wasn't quite socially equipped for civilized society, and I wasn't about to thank this prick for anything. I'd give my thanks to Victor Garrison when I saw him, because this was all coming from him anyway.

"So!" Richard clapped his hands together. "Seems you all have what you need. In your packets, there's also an itinerary and a copy of the contest guidelines for you."

Lavinia started flipping, looking for it. I couldn't help but watch the viper in the room. It was always wise to keep your enemies in your line of sight.

What kind of warlock was he?

That would be my first mission when I got home tonight. Finding out the extent of his capabilities.

"Let me help." Richard reached across the table and flipped her to the right page then patted her hand. "Right there."

He was lucky he withdrew and sat back down, because I was about to break off that fucking hand. I could do it with little effort. But then there would be an inquiry.

Of course, that would obviously ruin my chances of winning this contest. And it might be a little off-putting with the blood and all. Perhaps an overreaction. But I could barely contain the monster inside me wanting to maim this mother fucker.

And I did mean *monster*.

I fucking hated this guy. He was wrong on multiple levels. The first being the fact that he kept flirting with Lavinia and ogling her when she wasn't watching. I *was* watching this asshole though.

I quickly scanned all of the contest guidelines, which took me about forty-five seconds.

"I know that the first thing on your agenda is to decide on your cause for the PR campaign." Richard smiled with superiority. "Why don't you let me hear your ideas?"

So that he could try to persuade us to choose Lavinia's, since he was so intent on getting on her good side? Not a chance.

"Oh, sure," she said. "We could—"

"No, I think not," I interrupted.

For the first time, Richard's gaze swiveled to me. Yes, fucker. Look at me.

"The guidelines also state that the campaign is to be decided by the three of us alone. As stated, we're to *mutually decide upon both the cause and our course of action as a team*." I held his gaze, tapping the guidelines with my index finger. "*Of three*."

Yes, I'd memorized the guidelines that fast, asshole.

"As your liaison, I'd be interested to hear your ideas." His gray eyes narrowed with annoyance.

Like I cared.

Lavinia opened her mouth to say something, but I stepped in again quickly.

"I'm sure you would. But I think it best we follow the rules set forth by Mr. Garrison. After all, this is his company and his contest."

His lips thinned, his jaw hardened. Touched a nerve there. He didn't like that reminder. I went on in my casual manner.

"Anything you might say, good or otherwise, might be construed as undue influence."

For a moment, he simply glared at me, obviously trying to intimidate since his smile had slipped altogether. The very edge of magic laced the room. It wasn't mine or Lavinia's. And certainly not Willard's. This magic was…menacing.

Right when the awkward silence became almost unbearable, Richard's face cracked into that wide smile.

"Perhaps you're right, Mr. Blackwater."

I gave him a stiff nod, not dropping his gaze for a millisecond. Of course I was right. And he fucking knew it.

Richard stood and smoothed his tie. "I suppose I'll let you all get started then. I'll check back in later today to see how you're progressing." He nodded to Willard. "Mr. Thompson." Then he smiled wider at Lavinia. "Miss Livvy."

Lavinia's eyes narrowed as he turned and strode out the door.

"What a dick," I mumbled.

"What was that all about? Do you know him or something?" asked Lavinia.

"Did you see what a misogynistic asshole he is?" When she turned to me with raised brows, I added, "He used mine and Willard's last names properly but called you Miss Livvy. Like you're a little girl or something."

Her confused expression morphed into a radiant smile that punched me right through the chest.

"You're defending my womanhood?"

I suppose I was. Among other things.

She let out a little laugh, and that small, sweet sound eased the tension tightening every muscle in my body since *Dick* had walked through the door.

"That's kind of you, Gareth, but I'm used to it."

"Used to it?" I couldn't hide my disgust.

She laughed again and stacked her papers. "If I got angry every time a man was condescending to me with sweetie, honey, baby, or any number of belittling names to knock a woman down a peg, I'd be nothing but a ball of rage. Now let's get back to business."

The fact that she could brush his behavior off and return to our task so easily told me two things. First, men who treated women this way were pigs and should be taken to slaughter. And second, she was more bewitching than I ever realized.

CHAPTER TWO

~LIVVY~

IN ADDITION TO TELEPATHY AND HIS DARK-AND-BROODY, HOT-AS-fuck aura, I could now add photographic memory to my list about Gareth Blackwater. He'd flipped through the guidelines and knew them by rote. I had no doubt that if I asked him to recite the rules, he could. Word for word.

What I found even more fascinating, and humorous, was him getting bent out of shape over Richard Davis. Yes, the man was attracted to me, and yes, he was a chauvinistic prick. I'd dealt with men like him before. Still, I could barely suppress my smile with the way Gareth got his panties in a bunch and then got rid of him.

"Let's get more comfortable." Gareth rose from the table and walked over to the lounge area then sprawled on one, arm across the back of the sofa.

Willard followed. I sighed, picked up my memo pad and contest guidelines then did the same.

"Since you won't share first," I told Gareth, taking a seat on the other sofa where Willard had, "I will." Placing my notes in my lap, I said, "My proposal for our campaign is that we bring awareness to the werewolf problem."

A frown pinched Gareth's brow. "Go on."

"You remember what happened with my sister Violet a few weeks ago and the Blood Moon pack?"

He nodded. He and his cousin Henry had accompanied Mateo and Nico to find and save Violet when she'd been kidnapped by the pack. Of course, there was no need to save her, because apparently she had decided that the werewolves' demand for ransom was reasonable. Also, she was fully capable of saving herself with her telekinetic abilities.

"Violet has made us all aware that it isn't just the Blood Moon Pack who need her charmed tattoos to help them control their werewolves. And it goes beyond that. There's a negative stigma attached to the werewolf clans because of their tendency toward violence, which again isn't fully in their control. This stigma has prevented them from being accepted among the supernatural guilds, which is just wrong. I want to change that. They should be included with their own guild like the rest of us."

Willard had already heard my spiel so I turned to Gareth for a response. But there was none, at first.

Then finally, "Willard, what's your cause?"

"Wait, don't you want to respond or debate me on this?"

"No," he answered coolly. "I want to know Willard's cause first then I'll share mine and we'll discuss."

I wasn't going to argue for argument's sake. He was right. That was the best way to do it. So I sat back as Willard leaned forward.

"My idea is that we regulate vampire dens."

When he didn't go on, just like the first time we had this discussion, I turned to Gareth, "Before you got here—"

"Right on time," Gareth interrupted irritatingly.

Glaring for a second, which only made his lips twitch in amusement, I continued, "Willard explained that he doesn't think the vampire blood dens are regulated or policed enough. He had a friend who nearly bled to death when she consented to be a blood host, and there were hardly any repercussions for the vampire who did it."

"Where? Here?" Gareth's voice had dropped into a deeper, dangerous register tinged with anger.

I knew what he was thinking, and there's no way Ruben Dubois would allow any vampire to get away with that shit under his watch. As overlord of vampires here in New Orleans, he would never let it happen.

"No," said Willard. "It was in Baton Rouge actually. But the vampires have such free rein because of the power structure that if their overlord isn't an honorable man, or if he's lazy, they can get away with whatever they want."

What he said about the power structure was true. Next to Enforcers—witches and warlocks who had the ability to completely wipe any supernatural of all magical gifts—the vampires were the most powerful. This was why my sister Jules, an Enforcer, was head of the NOLA supernatural covens and given the duty to keep the peace, rather than Ruben.

Since the population of vampires greatly outnumbered the Enforcers among us, vampires held the most power of the supernaturals. Willard's proposition wasn't a bad one. The blood dens where vampires brought human and supernatural hosts to drink their fill were also run by vampires. So if the over-lord in charge was a dick, he or she could easily look away when their kind was misbehaving.

Still, I thought my cause was more immediate. Willard's issue should be addressed through the coven guilds, but the werewolf problem was bigger and needed serious attention.

That was one key purpose of this PR campaign. Mr. Garrison had directed us to choose a supernatural cause that needed awareness and funding, one that could make a difference.

Gareth seemed to let everything sink in, then his demeanor shifted from calm and cool to grave and serious.

"My proposition is to develop a foster program for supernatural orphans."

I have no idea what I was expecting, but this wasn't it.

He went on, dark eyes watchful. "Supernatural orphans are a grossly neglected population."

"There's a foster system—" started Willard.

"For humans," Gareth interrupted. He didn't seem angry at Willard's easy dismissal, but he was adamant. "This is the problem. No one sees the need, but I can tell you definitively that a supernatural in human foster care is a living hell for a child. And that's assuming the child is paired with a family that actually gives a shit and wants a child at all, as opposed to the government check that comes with them. If not, it can be even worse."

For the first time since I'd met this man, an emotion of vulnerability broke across his expression. It was fleeting. There and gone in a millisecond. But I knew without a shadow of doubt that he had suffered in foster care personally.

I jotted down his cause on my pad. "I can't believe there isn't a foster care program for supernaturals already in place."

"There's no fleshed-out program but there's an agency led by the High Witch Guild that places orphans via the SuperNet. However, nine times out of ten, there aren't enough families willing to take an orphan into their home. Or the case agent is overloaded, so they farm them out to the human foster program just to get them placed."

"We have that many supernatural orphans who can't be placed in our communities?" I asked.

"A witch and warlock couple may not want to take on a werewolf. A vampire couple may not want to take on a grim." He said this matter-of-factly but there was sharpness to his tone. "Besides, supernatural couples on the very short list looking for children who even find a match in their own designation don't always want a child who's *too old* or *troubled* or who has a history of violence. For werewolf children, that's basically a given."

"I'm ashamed to say that I never thought about this before," I confessed.

His steely expression softened the barest fraction. "Most don't. Unless you've lived it. Can you imagine being the only witch in a human family, unable to talk to anyone about your magic? About what you're thinking and feeling or how to hide this secret while not even knowing the extent of your abilities? Can you imagine puberty among humans?"

Willard made a choking sound. "That...that would not be good."

Understatement of the year. Puberty for supernaturals was a nightmare cocktail of hormones and exploding magical abilities. I remember Violet and I getting into a hormonal rage-fest when I was sixteen. She'd nearly thrown a TV through the window with her TK because I'd borrowed her favorite boots without asking her. It had taken Dad's very expert mediator skills to calm us down before we tore the house to the ground.

"Wow," I whispered to myself, trying to do exactly what Gareth said. Imagine a lonely child of our kind among people who not only may not want him but may not understand him on the most important level for a super.

The thought of Gareth suffering this way cut me to the heart. But in true Gareth fashion, he made sure I didn't pity him for long.

"Sympathy is an unnecessary emotion, Lavinia," he stated with a little bite and a lot of arrogance, tapping his pants leg with his forefinger. "Especially for someone like me. But what you can do is circle my cause on your little memo pad there, because it's the most urgent of the three."

How did the man make me feel sorry for him *and* want to punch his pretty face all in the span of one minute?

"I realize that you think you're always right, but I think we should debate whether or not your cause is the best for our campaign."

"Well, actually," said Willard, "I think it's pretty obvious that kids should come before misbehaving vampires."

"Thank you, Willard."

Gareth smiled brightly. He rarely did, and on this occasion, I noted his canines were sharper than the average person's. Not like a vampire, mind you, but still, it made me stare and wonder.

"I knew you'd see things my way. As for your cause, Lavinia." His smile slipped, brow furrowing in concentration. "The werewolf issue is a serious problem. I'll agree with you."

"Miracles do happen," I grumbled.

"*But...*" he grinned, "there's already a campaign under way. I've been informed that Ruben and your sister Jules are currently forming a plan of attack to bring the werewolves into the guilds."

Agitated that of course he already knew this, I replied, "True. But they haven't even gotten started. And it'll take more than my sister and Ruben to bring international awareness to the issue."

"I disagree. Jules and Ruben are both in places of high power in leadership. Ruben has connections around the globe and Jules has the ability to rally several higher-ups in the High Witch Guild to their cause. They could make this happen without our help. Also, your sister Violet is reaching out to other Seer witches to apprentice them specifically with the intent to tattoo charmed spells on werewolves across the country and even internationally to give them better control over their inner wolves."

I frowned. "How do you know all that?"

Violet had just decided to start reaching out via the SuperNet two nights ago. I wasn't aware that she'd made any of this public.

"Meanwhile," he continued, ignoring my question, "there are thousands of orphan supernaturals in the human foster care program or orphanages abroad. Orphans who are suffering without the guidance and care of their own kind."

His last sentence rang like a death knell to my cause.

He was right. Ruben and Jules were already on the case for the werewolf issue. Or at least, they were in the planning phase. And Violet was taking her own steps to help them.

Also, we were talking about innocent children here. Supernatural children who needed help, and I'd never even known this was a problem before today. Obviously, his cause was the direst of the three.

Clearing my throat, I tapped my pen on the pad, staring down at what I'd written. I'd planned on us each giving substantial arguments, jotting notes, then weighing the pros and cons of taking each issue on as our campaign. Then finally, we'd vote as a group.

I liked everything to be thorough and orderly. But apparently, with a few sound words from Gareth, my plan was summarily tossed out the window The man was annoyingly right.

"Okay," I finally said. "I agree. My vote is for the children."

"Your vote is for my cause." Gareth grinned maniacally. "So you're saying I'm right."

He was enjoying watching me squirm and concede to him. I hated that he'd won the argument, but come on, these were little kids we were talking about. I'd been fortunate enough to grow up in a whole and loving household. Every child deserved the same.

Rolling my eyes, I flipped to a new sheet on my memo pad then skimmed page two of the contest guidelines.

"Next on the agenda is to establish a course of action, ensuring all three of us have equal input and job responsibility in the plan."

"Awesome." Gareth leaned back, linking his hands behind his head, and relaxing like the lion lounging on his plain, waiting for the lionesses to bring him his next meal. "Let's get started."

Before I could respond, my phone buzzed on the coffee table. I picked it up to see a text from Evie begging me to take her shift at the Cauldron tonight. She wanted to go out to dinner with Mateo. Of course she did. It was Valentine's Day.

Irritated, because I didn't want to work a busy night like I knew tonight would be, I texted back, agreeing to do it anyway. I was going to be mentally exhausted after battling Gareth all day, but Evie deserved to go out and have a nice night with her Valentine. After all, I didn't even have one, so why shouldn't I help out?

"Got a hot date tonight?" Gareth's smile was entirely too lascivious if he actually thought I had a date, his gaze tracking my phone as I set it on the coffee table.

"Wouldn't you like to know?"

"That's why I asked."

He was flirting with me to distract me. Or torment me. Or both.

Huffing out a breath of exasperation, I crossed my legs—pretending not to notice the way his dark eyes skated up the length of them with slow precision—and tapped on my pad.

"Let's get to work."

CHAPTER THREE

~GARETH~

THIS WAS A BAD DECISION, BUT I COULDN'T FUCKING HELP myself. After I'd seen Lavinia's text from her sister, I knew exactly where I'd be eating dinner tonight.

"It's packed," said Henry as we made our way into the Cauldron.

"That couple is leaving." I nodded to a booth in the corner.

The Cauldron was a *seat yourself* pub owned by the Savoie sisters. While it was well known in the neighborhood of the Lower Garden District, I'd never been here before. Of course I knew it was owned and run by the head coven of witches in New Orleans, but I'd never been interested enough to check it out. Not much caught my interest. But Lavinia most definitely had.

As Henry and I slid into the booth, a busboy quickly cleared the plates and glasses away, then wiped the table clean. They were busy tonight. It was Valentine's so lots of couples filled the booths and four-top high tables.

The werewolf, Nico, was onstage and had just dedicated a

song to his woman, Violet—the one we'd helped him save from the Blood Moon pack a few weeks ago but who didn't need saving at all.

While he sang, I couldn't help seeking out Lavinia, finding her chatting with her sisters Violet, Clara, and Evie near the bar. The bartender, JJ, and his boyfriend Charlie were also among the group, talking and laughing together.

Yes, I knew basically everyone here. I made it my business to know all supernaturals in our territory and their human friends who were aware of our existence. For grims, information was everything.

My newest information about Richard Davis had me clenching my jaw. I hated for a prick like him to have that kind of power. I'd told myself that I came tonight to inform Lavinia. To warn her about him outside the workplace. But in truth, I just needed to see her, to drink in the luscious dark beauty of her a little while longer.

The fact that I'd been with her for eight hours today should've satisfied my senses. But it hadn't. I needed more. So much more.

And that had me tapping my index finger on the table, glancing around the bar to note every person here. It was an old habit to catalog all possible threats in my vicinity.

Having been tossed to and from four foster homes until one fateful night had forced my Uncle Silas to do the responsible thing and take me in, I had developed an ingrained paranoia and distrust of most people.

However, it was what had happened with that asshole Dennis at my last home that had my hackles rising and my mind on full alert around Richard.

Dennis had been sixteen to my eleven. We were two of five foster children in the Wexler home. The Wexlers weren't abusers, but they weren't exactly protectors either. They were somewhat apathetic about the children under their roof, keeping us fed and within the parameters of providing a "healthy home environment" in case Child Protective Services checked in on them.

I remember feeling a moment of warmth and happiness when I first met Dennis, realizing right away that he was a vampire. I'd thought the two of us could bond over being supernaturals in a human home, perhaps be friends if not brothers.

I was so fucking wrong. Dennis was the first person I'd met who seemed to enjoy wielding his power over others with brute force. The one thing he taught me, and taught me well, was that using strength and fear to dominate doesn't make you more powerful. It makes you a tyrant. I remembered that later when I came into my own power.

Something about Richard Davis this morning and the subtly menacing gleam in his gray eyes had me thinking about Dennis. So I'd decided that I'd warn Lavinia. Even if we barely got along for a few minutes at a time, I wouldn't deny that my attraction for her was deep and disturbingly real.

Regardless of my annoying fascination, I wouldn't allow an oppressor like Richard to go unchecked and catch her off guard. I knew what that felt like, and I wouldn't wish it on anyone.

Henry had his Zippo out, the one with the pink butterfly etched onto it. He was flicking the top on and off, on and off. His anxiety somehow eased mine.

I stopped tapping my finger and leaned back against the bench seat. "Nervous?"

His dark gaze narrowed on me. "Why'd we have to come here?"

"I thought you'd be glad to come with me. Get your Clara fix for the night."

"Look, dick. Don't pretend you aren't here to drool all over that witch, Livvy."

His ire didn't even phase me.

Nico finished his song and left the stage to join Violet and the others. I noticed Evie run to the bathroom, while Lavinia asked Mateo a question.

"I came to see her, yes, but not for that reason."

He leaned forward, both elbows on the table. "You're going to sit there and lie and tell me you don't want her?"

"I didn't say that." I smiled. His usual calm veneer fractured into minute pieces whenever Clara was around. "I'm just saying I did have some business to discuss with her tonight, and we need to eat so why not here?"

Well, it was business-*related* anyway.

"Sure. You keep telling yourself that."

"Hi, Henry!" Clara suddenly appeared next to our booth, beaming down at my cousin with the brightest smile.

I tried not to laugh at the way his eyes rounded in shock. He swallowed hard against her surprising appearance at our table like a fairy blinking into existence.

"Hi," he whispered low and gruff.

She turned to me. "I'm Clara Savoie," she said sweetly, offering her hand. "I don't think we've formally met, though Nico told me how you helped them out with that whole were-wolf fiasco."

Like I didn't know who she was, when she was born, who her parents were, her designation and level of magical powers, where she lived, where she worked, and what her favorite pastry was from the bakery, Queen of Tarts, across the street. I knew all of that except the last from my own shallow dive into the Savoie sisters. The tidbit about her favorite pastry was from my silent and staring cousin seated across from me.

I shook her hand. "Gareth Blackwater. Nice to meet you."

Goddamn. Henry wasn't lying. Her aura was a wash of drugging serenity.

I actually stared at my hand where her aura had seeped through my skin and poured through my veins with cool tranquility. Like a shot of the best bourbon. If she could do that to me, I couldn't imagine how it felt to someone like Henry.

Her magic was the perfect balance to ours; her light wanted to temper our darkness. We were in fact made of opposite mettle and magic. Now I understood Henry's obsession, though I also knew it was more than her Aura magic he was obsessed with.

According to his current murderous glare, he thought the expression on my face meant I might have designs on her now.

Smothering my smile, I said, "Your aura is quite lovely, Clara."

Her sea-blue eyes rounded. "You can see auras?" she asked excitedly.

"Not in color like you can. But we grims can feel them." I nodded to Henry.

His scowl deepened. A low growl rumbled up his throat, sounding like a fucking werewolf. I ignored his foul temper and misguided warning.

"Really?" she asked, all sweetness as her gaze moved back to Henry. "I didn't know that about grims." Then she laughed—a pleasant, sweet sound. "Of course, I really don't know *anything* about grims. Except that you're all rather handsome in an unconventional way."

"Unconventional?" I asked, absolutely relishing the blush staining the high cheekbones on Henry's pale face. "How do you mean?" I asked amiably, giving her my full attention.

"You're all quite fair-skinned, but I'm sure you knew that already. But it isn't that. Your bone structure is rather unusual."

"Is it? I hadn't noticed," I lied.

"Oh, yes. You all are so sharp-edged." Her gaze moved back to Henry who was hanging on her every word, his fidgeting with his Zippo came to an abrupt stop. "Reminds me of Russians I've seen in movies and such. Like the romance, *Anna Karenina?*"

"Mmm." I nodded.

She wasn't far off. It was the blood of our Varangian ancestry that gave us our sharp-edged bone structure as she called it. The Eastern Romans called them Varangians, the Vikings descending out of what was now Norway in the ninth century.

It was one of these ancestors who settled in the medieval state of Kievan Rus'—modern Russia—and became a Byzantine Varangian Guard. There, he met our ancestral foremother. When he took her by force as his wife, she had no idea she would be the first mother of a grim reaper.

"Have you seen that movie, Henry?" I asked. "*Anna Karenina?*"

He shook his head, a fierce scowl in place. He likely had no idea that he looked like he was on the verge of losing his shit. It didn't seem to bother Clara at all.

"Well, I could loan you my copy if you want to see it some time," she offered.

This was more comical and entertaining than I could've possibly imagined. If I'd known this would be my reward for dragging Henry here, I would've done it weeks ago.

"I'm sure Henry would love to borrow your copy," I interjected. "Or better yet, watch it with you instead."

His feral gaze sliced to me. Clara caught his expression, her smile dimming a little as she took a step back from the table.

"No, I wouldn't want to impose like that." She fingered a lock of her waist-length, platinum-blonde hair. "Can I get you both something to drink?"

"You're waiting tables?" Henry asked brusquely and irritated.

"No. But Livvy was talking to Evie and them, so I decided to pop over and help her out."

Clara's cheeks flushed bright pink after admitting she just wanted to come over to see this fool of a grim who was acting like she had the plague.

"Thank you, Clara. That's kind of you." I smiled, trying to ease her embarrassment over Henry's rude behavior. "I'll have a Maker's Mark on ice."

"Whatever you have on draft is fine," Henry told her, his voice and expression softening somewhat.

"I'll get that order right over to you." She blinked sweetly but was obviously not as joyful as she was when she'd walked over here.

As soon as she walked away, Henry collapsed forward, sliding both hands into his hair, he lowered his head, pressing his forehead to the table. Then he banged it lightly three times.

"Wow. You've got serious game," I observed. "I mean, between the frowning and growling and making her feel like a leper when I suggested you watch the movie together, she's practically in love with you."

"I hate you."

"No, you hate yourself. What the hell is wrong with you?"

He sat up and then slouched back in the booth.

"I don't know. I just can't function when she's around. There's never been anyone who…"

He broke off and looked away, eyes glazing. I sobered quickly at that despondent glimmer in his dark eyes, his jaw hardening.

Without looking back at me, he rumbled low, "She makes it all better."

For Henry to even remotely admit that he had an affliction that needed soothing was a miracle in itself. We rarely, if ever, talked about his problem. Because he didn't want to talk about it, let alone face it.

"Isn't that reason enough to go for her?" I suggested encouragingly. "Maybe she could help you."

His gaze shifted to Clara over at the bar talking to JJ. Mateo had his arm around Evie as they left the bar. Must be heading out on their date. Lavinia now stood next to Clara, listening in before swiveling to where we sat. Her expression morphed into shock, not unlike Henry's when Clara popped up out of nowhere. I smiled and nodded at her.

"Just look at her." Henry started flicking his Zippo lighter again. "She's a goddamn angel. Why would she want to be a part of my fucked-up mess?"

I tore my eyes away from Lavinia who was taking our drinks

from JJ to focus on Henry. Leaning forward, I clasped my hands together on the table and enunciated very clearly. Very carefully.

"Because she makes it all better."

His gaze snapped to mine, dark eyes haunted. As always. "I think I hurt her feelings just now."

"I'd agree."

"I should apologize."

"You should."

Lavinia plunked our drinks on the table right at that moment. "Well, well, well. Can't get enough of me during our workday that you had to stalk me here?"

"Something like that," I agreed, relishing this close-up view of her in a dark purple mini-dress that zipped all the way up the side.

She planted a hand on her hip. I loved it when she did that. For one, it accentuated the dramatic dip of her waist which flared out into generous hips. And for another, it meant her blood was up. Even now, I could feel her pulse thrumming faster, heating her skin, making me want to lick her all over.

Henry took three large gulps of his draft beer then slid out of the booth. "Excuse me."

Lavinia frowned at his sudden departure, watching him go. I didn't bother. I knew where he was going. My eyes remained on her.

"I needed to talk to you away from GMC." I lifted the glass to my lips.

She watched me sip my drink. "I think you just wanted an excuse to come and see me."

"There's a lot worth seeing."

Her pulse tripped faster at that, and she simply stared at me. I stared back.

I liked this game. Where she tried to figure out if I was lying to her or not. I always told her the truth. Except that one time.

But it was necessary. I lied to her when I accused her of using her Influencer magic to warp the judges at the semi-finals.

That was a ruse to distract her from the fact that I wanted to tear her clothes off and fuck her on the lobby floor. Still did, actually.

"Have a seat." I nodded to where Henry sat a moment before. "There's something I wanted to talk to you about."

"I have a lot of tables."

"This won't take long. It's important."

With a little huff, she slid into Henry's seat, mimicking my posture with her hands clasped on the table. "What can I do for you, Mr. Blackwater?"

Fucking hell. What couldn't she do for me?

Her midnight eyes narrowed at my devious smile. "That's not what I meant."

"Right." I cleared my throat and sat forward, remembering my purpose tonight. "I wanted to talk to you about Richard Davis."

"What about him?"

"If you're not aware, you've caught his eye."

"I'm aware."

"He's dangerous."

"Men in powerful positions have flirted with me before. I won't let him interfere with the judging of the contest if that's what you're worried about."

"That's not what I'm concerned about. I'm fairly positive he"—how to say this delicately without frightening her— "he intends this to go *beyond* flirting with you."

Her brow pinched, and I immediately wanted to make that look go away. "Has he said something to you?"

"No." I tapped my index finger on the table. "He wouldn't dare say a word to me." Unless coerced. Which I would when I had the chance.

"Yeah, after the way you dressed him down today, I guess not." She glanced over at one of her tables. "Look, Gareth. I don't know what this is all about, but Richard is a liaison for the judge panel as well as a judge himself on the overall contest. If you're implying that I'd use his attraction to me to try and gain points, I—"

"*No!* That's not what I meant at all," I admitted. "I know you wouldn't do that."

She arched one of those slender, black brows. "Oh, really? Because you accused me of using my magic on them before if you recall."

Fuck. Time to come clean. Otherwise, she wouldn't listen to me on this.

"I never believed you'd use your magic to influence them."

Her frown deepened. "You said—" she paused, measuring me, then asked, "But you think I'll use my body?"

"That's not what I'm saying either."

"Then what are you saying, Gareth?"

A tendril of fury swept through my blood, stirring the darkness always waiting there, wanting to be used. It wasn't for her. It was for Richard fucking Davis.

My voice was rough and aggressive when I leaned forward and spoke. "He's dangerous, Lavinia. He's an Enforcer, and he's got an evil streak a fucking mile long."

She blinked back the shock. Enforcers were a rare designation for witches and warlocks. The most powerful of their kind.

But not the most powerful supernatural of all.

Her voice was soft and tentative, drawing my gaze to those pillowy lips when she asked, "How do you know he's…he's evil?"

Clenching my jaw at the answer I knew I was going to tell her, I took a moment to calm myself and catalogued her beauty —the brightness of her wide eyes, the silky texture of her skin, the fullness of her mouth.

I didn't want to be honest this time. I didn't want to have her look at me with disgust or fear, but she needed to know.

"Grims always know where true evil lies. Because it lives inside of us. It's in our blood."

She didn't flinch away or curl her lip like I thought she

might. And she didn't disbelieve what I was saying I didn't think. She simply stared back with curiosity.

"So hear me now when I tell you, beware of him. Don't get caught alone with him." I wanted to add, if you do, call me immediately. But she wasn't mine to protect.

Not yet, a voice whispered.

Where the hell did that thought come from?

She might not be using her magic to influence the judges, but it sure was working a number on me. Leaning back, I swallowed a gulp of whiskey, finding Henry near the bar. He had both hands in his pockets, leaning down to hear something Clara was saying. She was back to smiling. The crowd was getting bigger and my nerves were fracturing.

I'd had my fill of people for the day. I needed to get home and find some peace and quiet. Especially after heavy doses of Lavinia for the past eight hours.

"Thank you." Her soft words pulled my attention back to her, the sight of her always a punch to the gut.

Henry stalked toward the exit, pulling a pack of cigarettes from his back pocket and lifting one to show me where he was headed. On a nod, I pulled my wallet out and dropped a couple of bills, making sure to cover the drinks and a good tip.

"I wasn't aware you had a thoughtful side." The snark was back in her voice and her mouth had returned to a teasing angle. "To come down here and warn me about him."

This, I could handle. Not the softness and sweetness of Lavinia. That side of her I could hardly bear. She was already battering against my walls with the rest of her charms. And I didn't fucking like it. Time to shore them up.

Standing, I slipped my wallet back into my pocket. "Perhaps, I have selfish reasons to keep him away from you."

She caught my roaming gaze. "You can't be serious."

Even so, her heart pumped faster, pupils dilating as she let her own gaze wander down my frame.

"We're rivals," she stated flatly, obviously trying to keep me at bay against her body's own will.

She might not realize it, but I could smell her arousal from here.

I leaned closer, planting one hand on the booth above her head, the other on the table, caging her in. She didn't move, even while her pulse quickened. I eased my lips close to her ear, inhaling her painfully hypnotic scent.

"We may be rivals, Lavinia. But it doesn't make me want to fuck your brains out any less."

Easing back a few inches, I drank in the view of her stunning face, mouth partly open in shock. That fucking *mouth*.

Licking my lips, I watched her eyes dilate to nearly full black. She wanted me to kiss her, and if that didn't make me rock hard.

"Happy Valentine's Day, Lavinia."

Then I straightened and got the hell out of there before I did something stupid. Like drag her home and tie her to my bed.

Because she was right. We might be working together on this campaign project, but in the end we were opponents for the grand prize. And I couldn't let this beguiling, brain-muddling witch get the best of me. My cock needed to stay in my pants.

I did my duty. I warned her about Dickless Davis. Now I needed to get my other head in the game, stop thinking and fantasizing about pale skin, endless curves, and long, black hair and win this contest.

I punched open the door of the pub, finding Henry leaning against the brick wall right outside, dragging on a cigarette.

"All good?" he asked, falling into step with me.

Shaking off the effects of being within her magnetic radius, I inhaled a deep breath of cold February air. Relieved to feel free again.

"Right as rain."

CHAPTER FOUR

~LIVVY~

"Don't forget your book, Ms. LeBlanc."

Clara picked up the copy of Lisa Kleypas's *Marrying Winter-borne* left on our coffee table in the den and carried it to the older woman at the doorway. Ms. LeBlanc was the last book club member to leave.

"Thank you, Clara." The eighty-eight-year-old widow who always had a smile in her eyes patted Clara's hand when she took it. "I can't wait till next week to see what Rhys will do next."

My sister smiled a little devilishly, helping Ms. LeBlanc into her coat. "He's aggressive wherever Helen is concerned."

"Reminds me of someone I used to know." The older lady sighed with a wistful smile.

Clara beamed with excitement. "Mr. LeBlanc was like Mr. Winterborne?"

"Not him." Ms. LeBlanc leaned in and whispered loud enough I could still hear. "Another man in my life once upon a time." Then she winked and pulled open the front door.

"Ms. LeBlanc," I stepped toward the foyer right off the den, "Are you sure you don't need a ride?"

She glanced out the open front door then back to me. "No thank you, dear. My Uber is already waiting."

Then Clara watched her get safely to the car and shut the door.

I shook my head, smiling. "Ms. LeBlanc uses Uber?"

"She's very resourceful." Clara walked past me and back into the den where she always set up her High Tea Book Club. "Did you get enough pictures?"

I turned back to face the room. "Actually, no. I need some still close-ups. Where's your copy of the book?"

Clara picked hers up from the club chair she'd been sitting in during their book discussion. I'd popped in at the tail end to get pics for her that she wanted for her book blog.

Our formal den was rarely used. Our mom would often have her morning coffee in this room, because the light was so pretty early in the day and she could have a few moments of peace before handling her six energetic daughters. I missed Mom and Dad.

I was happy they'd found a peaceful life in retirement in the Swiss Alps, but I missed hearing my dad's laugh and my mom giving us a hundred pieces of maternal advice. They promised to visit this year, perhaps for Christmas. And I couldn't wait. My dad gave the best bear hugs in the whole world.

My mind drifted back to Gareth and the fact that he grew up in foster homes. Apparently homes that didn't care for him the way they should have. I wondered if he remembered his parents before then, if they were loving parents like mine. I was curious to know more but doubted he'd tell me. He wasn't the type of guy to open himself up. And definitely not to the woman he seemed to consider his enemy.

Then again, what he had told me at the Cauldron two nights ago wasn't exactly something you'd say to your enemy. I wondered if—

"Are you okay?"

I snapped out of my reverie to find Clara sitting in her chair, watching me with a curious expression.

Taking the lens cap off my camera again, I set her book on the coffee table next to the tray of raspberry tarts and lemon squares. I fiddled with placing the book just right.

"You're good with emotions," I said as I snapped a few shots. "Tell me, can someone really desire their enemy? Enough to want to have sex with them?"

"Of course," said Clara. "*The Viscount Who Loved Me.*"

"Excuse me?" I moved the book to another position and took a few more shots at different angles.

"That was our book last month. Anthony and Kate hated each other. Still, they wanted to tear each other's clothes off every time they were in the same room together. Sometimes, animosity and anger is the perfect aphrodisiac."

"Why do you think that is?" I slid Clara's open notebook close to the tea tray and kept clicking my camera.

"Hatred and hostility are strong emotions," she continued matter-of-factly. "They get your heart rate up, heat the blood, make you sweat, drawing your focus solely to the one giving you these emotions. It's very similar to desire. So, wanting to have sex with Gareth is perfectly normal."

I dropped the camera from in front of my face. "Who says I'm talking about me and Gareth?"

Clara grinned, transforming her expression into a naughty impish look. "For one, your aura is red and pulsing and giving me all the sex vibes. And second," she rolled her eyes, "I mean, please."

Laughing, I asked, "No, don't give me that 'obviously' Clara look. Tell me what you're thinking."

She picked up a lemon square and took a dainty bite, folding her legs underneath her. "You've been angry at him from the first time you met him in this contest. You won't shut up about how much you *loathe* Gareth Blackwater." Her grin returned. "He also happens to be extremely smart, which I know is a big turn-on for you. And now that I've met him, I know that he's alarmingly attractive."

"Alarmingly?" I snapped two more shots then put my lens cap back on, setting it on the coffee table and then picking up a tart.

"Yes. As in, five-alarm fire. And he's got that dark and broody thing going that you're so obsessed with."

I considered what my youngest, and possibly wisest, sister was telling me. It's true, I liked the smart ones. My last girlfriend Mary was a professor of English literature at Tulane. I was drawn to her intelligence the first day I met her at French Truck Coffee. While she didn't disappoint as a conversationalist and bed partner, the chemistry and attraction simply sort of fizzled out.

That was typical of the people I was attracted to—male or female. I'd be intensely drawn to them then, inevitably, the fire would slowly die. I'd lose interest because I'd discovered everything new I possibly could about them then the attraction would fade before disappearing altogether.

Struck with a horrifying thought, I wondered if I was the kind of person who needed to be constantly thrilled and entertained to be attracted to someone.

I suppose she was right. I was stimulated by my brain first. So no matter how beautiful my partner was, if the cerebral stimulation wasn't there, or if it waned, so did the chemistry.

"I'm not saying you're a sapiosexual," added Clara, picking up her notebook and pen.

"A what?"

"Someone who's sexually attracted to intelligent people, meaning their brilliance is the most important trait to draw your interest." She doodled something in the top margin of her notebook. "I mean, you might be, but I think it's more that you're a high-energy Leo and a powerful Influencer. You're driven by excitement, the thrill of the hunt. Which is why your relationships usually die once you've caught them."

Still holding half a tart I stared at her, bewildered. "Since when did you analyze my entire dating life?"

She looked up from her doodling with a smile. "I know all of my sisters' psychological and sexual preferences as well as their emotional and spiritual needs. It's part of what I do."

Surprised, I asked, "How so?"

"Emotions tell me *everything*," she answered cryptically, still sketching. "So anyway, you should totally have sex with Gareth if you want. I know you want to."

Frowning, I stuffed the rest of the tart in my mouth, immediately wanting to grab another and feed my feelings rather than engage on this topic anymore. She was making too much damn sense, and I just wasn't prepared to be confronted with all this today. I asked a simple question which shined this eye-opening and not-so-pleasant spotlight on my dating history.

Still, she had a point. I resisted grabbing another tart and replied, "You're not wrong."

"I know." She shrugged. "So have sex with him then."

"Clara, I *can't*. I'm competing against him in the contest. It would be a conflict of interest. And distracting from the campaign."

"Are there rules in the contest guidelines that say contestants can't have sex with each other?"

I snorted. "I do believe they left that rule out."

"Good. Then you should totally fuck him."

I burst out laughing. The way Clara was so casual when she talked about fucking was hilarious to me. She still wore that endearing, sweet-as-pie expression, but she was totally serious.

"I'm not sure that would be such a good idea." I took her notebook to have something to do with my hands, suddenly fidgety.

"Well, I think it would be the best sex of your life."

"Why's that?" I pretended I wasn't that interested, while I read her notes and held my breath for an answer.

Clara was the most intuitive of all my sisters. Even more than Violet who was the Seer. Somehow, Clara's gift of being an Aura and tapping into emotions made her better at reading human beings than anyone.

"Because he's so buttoned-up and serious and intense. I'll bet when he lets loose in the bedroom, it's explosive." She gestured a bomb exploding with her hands.

The mere thought of being in his bedroom—tied up on black silk sheets—had my heart hammering. Time to change the subject.

Clara had been doodling a black heart in one corner. I skimmed down her list of discussion topics for her book club, stopping on the words *number one fan book blogger gift*.

"What's this about your number one blogger fan?"

"Oh! So my blog doesn't have a big following right now, but I do have this one blogger, RavenOne, who comments on *every* single blog. Always something interesting and intellectual. We've chatted not just about romance but about history and travel and even baking. A real reader, not just a random nice-post commenter, you know?"

"Mmhmm"

"Anyway, I was asking the ladies what they thought about giving her a gift, whoever she is."

"That should be easy enough. A gift card to Amazon would do, I think. That way, she can use it to buy books you recommend on the blog. Or whatever she wants."

"I wanted it to be more personal, but I suppose that would be easiest. She may not want to give out her mailing address for a gift from a stranger." She stood and started to gather the teacups and saucers stacked on the end tables. "Anyway, I appreciate your help with pics for the blog. I know you're really busy."

"Of course! What are sisters for if not for free services," I teased.

"Speaking of services, are you going to let Gareth service you?"

Everyone thought Clara was this sweet and innocent little thing, but underneath all the soft prettiness was a wildcat.

"No," I answered emphatically even while my body screamed *why fucking not?*

"I saw him getting kind of cozy with you at the Cauldron the other night."

"Speaking of…I saw you getting kind of cozy with his cousin, Henry. What's going on there?"

"I don't know what you mean," she said, her voice all honeyed innocence.

She carried the tray out of the den toward the kitchen, but I followed her after grabbing the tray of leftover pastries. Now look who was avoiding.

"Don't be coy. You flirt with him every chance you get."

"I talk to him, yes. I'm not sure that counts as flirting."

"And you always stare at him whenever he's around."

"He's very pleasant to look at," she said quietly, hand-washing the teacups carefully. Mom had given the delicate set with hand-painted lavender rims to her last Christmas.

"He's very…rough around the edges. Doesn't seem your type."

She smiled as she set a cup onto the drying rack. "You don't know my type." Then she gave me a superior look. "Just like you don't know your own."

"I most certainly do know my own."

"If that were the case, then you'd be in a serious relationship by now. Not hightailing it after a couple months with every partner you've had."

"My relationship with Christopher lasted eight and a half months," I protested.

"That's because it was long distance. It prolonged the inevitable. Since you were only able to see him on weekends when you went to Baton Rouge or he came here, it extended the regular timeline."

Was she right? Holy fuck, was I shallow?

"I'm not saying you're shallow or there's something wrong with you."

"I did not telepath my thoughts to you." Did I?

"It doesn't matter." She placed a saucer carefully on the drying rack. "I know what you're thinking anyway."

"What you're doing is making me wonder about my entire two decades of adult-ish dating."

She turned to face me, leaning a hip against the sink, and wiping her hands on a dishtowel.

"Livvy, try something new. *Someone* new. You tend to go for the emo and interesting pacifists. Or the wild and unique extroverts." She held out both hands like weights of a scale. "Either someone you can dominate," she lifted one hand, "or a mirror image of yourself." She gestured with the other., then toggled her hands up and down. "Neither are right for you."

I gaped at what she was telling me, silent as I took it all in. She was one hundred percent right. Shockingly so.

Clearing my throat, I crossed my arms, feeling rather raw at this realization. An unusual sensation with Clara. She and I were always so easily open to each other. But this was not an attractive depiction of me she'd just illustrated.

"So, you're saying I need a dominant introvert in an opposites attract sort of relationship?"

Her bright gaze held mine hard as she tilted her head to the side, eyes tracing me up and down like she did when she was reading my aura.

"What do you think?"

I thought she was horrifyingly correct. But the idea of stepping into any arena, even a sex-only relationship with a partner of that description sent a shiver tickling down my spine. A tingle of magic responded to that thought, whispering in the air.

Clara's eyes widened ever so slightly. Then she smiled. "I think you have your answer."

"From whom?" I played dumb.

Then she laughed, her grave expression brightening with her usual mirth. She stepped closer and squeezed my cheeks like I was a child. "Mother Spirit knows best. You better listen to her."

Then she waltzed out of the kitchen and through the back door to cross to the carriage house where she shared a loft apartment with Violet. Well, when Violet decided to sleep at the house. Nowadays, she spent all her time shacking up at Nico's place. Not that I blamed her.

I opened the wine fridge and uncorked a bottle of Jules's Merlot then poured a glass to the rim. I needed a long, hot bath and lots of time to ruminate.

Clara had dealt me a heavy dose of truth. Maybe I did need to change my dating course. I hadn't found Mr. or Ms. Right yet by following my instincts.

But was I truly following my instincts? Or simply who I thought I should be falling for? Clara said I needed someone I couldn't dominate and who wasn't a carbon copy of me, someone whose brain turned me on as much as his or her appearance. There was no denying that I was attracted to big brains.

A flash of memory struck me as I walked into the bathroom. Gareth leaning over me in the booth at the Cauldron. His dark eyes pinning me in place, even more than his arms on either side of me were. And when he told me he wanted to fuck my brains out, there was an immediate pulsating response between my legs. I had to wait a full minute after he left before I could stand and get back to work.

The thought of being vulnerable with Gareth—because I'd

always found sex to be the most intimate and open activities between two people—sent a cavalcade of warning flags flying.

He was a grim. An unknown. And his aura made me want to be very, very naughty. With him. My desire was so blood-burning, throat-choking intense that I feared what would be left after that kind of love affair was all over.

What was left of me, that is.

CHAPTER FIVE

~GARETH~

Her sweet scent hit me before I'd rounded the corner into our office. But that wasn't what had my mouth fighting a smile. It was her choice of music this morning.

She was an eighties lover I'd discovered. When I'd seen her at The Brat Pack with her sisters and cousins last month, I thought it a strange anomaly. But no, her playlists proved otherwise.

Yesterday, she'd asked Willard if he minded if she played music while we worked. She asked me much less politely, which only stoked my deep yearning for the woman. Every time she tossed me a defiant look or a snarky word, my dick got harder for her.

She stood at the long worktable with papers strewn all over, dressed in a form-fitting black dress that dropped straight at the hips to her knees. Patent leather, heeled boots encased her legs to an inch below the dress's hemline. There was nothing overtly seductive about her clothes, but *fucking hell...* the woman knew how to dress her body.

Depeche Mode's "People Are People" filled the workspace with that eighties mantra for equality. Interesting that the song still had quite a bit of relevance several decades later.

Today was our third workday, the day we'd map out our first promotional event. Apparently, Lavinia had gotten a head start on the planning. This wasn't surprising. The woman was a workaholic. Yet another similarity we shared.

"Are you going to allow me some choice in music selection or must we listen to Dave Gahan's melancholy voice all day?"

Her head came up, brows arched, as if surprised I knew the lead vocalist's name. Then she fell back quickly into the warrior queen veneer that made my pulse quicken.

"His voice is soulful," she argued, "not melancholy."

"Difference of opinion." I stopped on the opposite side of the table, glancing down at her lists and charts with the heading Pin-up Photo Shoot. It was the fundraiser she'd mentioned in the semi-finalist interview.

"*Music for the Masses* was the best album of new wave alternative in the eighties," she added, shuffling a few papers around, "no matter what your opinion is."

"Again, disagree." I kept my hands in my pockets and held her gaze. "*Pumped Full of Drugs* by New Order was far superior. However, they would've been even greater if their original vocalist hadn't killed himself when they were Joy Division. Ian Curtis was a genius."

I fought a smile as her expression softened in wonder before she blinked it away.

"You know your eighties music." She frowned, seeming to admit that despite herself.

"Among many other things."

She rolled her eyes, and again, I found myself fighting a smile. She was so easy to rile. And her lovely features only heightened with color and hardened with a goddess-like façade whenever she was annoyed. To have a proud, intelligent beauty like her submit to me would probably scramble my brains, not to mention other parts of my anatomy.

Willard walked in and mumbled "Morning."

"Great. We're all here. Why don't you tell us what you had in mind for your first promotion event."

Lavinia's back stiffened, probably thinking I might be mocking her or luring her into another verbal duel. But when I took a seat and clasped my hands loosely over my midsection and stared patiently, she seemed to realize I wasn't.

Willard popped open his laptop. "If you don't mind, I'd like to get both of your opinions on the website I've gotten started first."

As mentioned in our semi-finalist interview, Willard's proposal was to develop a website for our cause and campaign, and to develop promo ads to drive traffic to the website. It wasn't a bad idea, I'd admitted. Though to myself, I knew it would take more, which I was working on.

Willard punched in a few keys then swiveled his laptop around for us to see. I was sitting to the left of Lavinia who had a seat at the head of the conference table.

The design was clean, mostly in monochromatic earth tones except for a pop of vibrant green for headings and the buttons on the side.

"I'm still building it, but as you can see we have donation buttons as well as upcoming fundraising events in bold in the margins. I'll have links directly to the social media pages we set up for the fundraising events and the YouTube Live exclusives."

It was good. Really good.

"What's this down here?" I asked, pointing to a block of words that literally repeated the word text over and over halfway down the page.

"That's where the explanation of our cause will go. I figured you could write that," he explained. "Since it's your cause and you seem to have the background knowledge."

He scrolled farther down to a moving picture gallery of

people. Their names overlaying the black and white photos in the same bold, green font of the headings.

"What's that?" asked Lavinia, leaning forward.

Her lavender and spice scent teased me, making me inhale deeply and hold my breath.

"Testimonies," said Willard, clicking on one of the pictures. "These are just dummy pics and no text yet as you can see, but I figured we could interview some supernaturals who've gone through the human foster care program and share some of their experiences."

I stiffened, remembering some of my own. One in particular.

Lavinia's gaze was intent on me when she said, "I don't know if we want a list of horror stories as a way to get people excited about donating money."

"It doesn't have to read that way." I turned to her. "We can write the copy so that it isn't offensive but is also persuasive. And truthful." Looking at Willard's website, I was struck by how effective this could be. "Your design is perfect for what we want. Awareness and empathy. Nice job, Thompson."

The warlock's expression cracked from his usual indifference to relief.

"Thanks."

"Your Seer abilities helped you out?" I asked.

"It seems so," he agreed. "I wasn't sure if this was exactly right."

"It's perfect, really." Lavinia jotted something down on her notepad. "I'll start looking for people to interview. Jules can get me in touch with whoever is in charge of the agency in the High Witch Guild."

"Her name is Serenity Bowers," I told her. "I'll send you her contact information. Why don't you give me your phone number?"

That tiny line formed between her brows as she seemed to be wondering if this was my way of trying to get her phone number. I already had her number. But yes, I was also trying to see if she'd give it to me willingly.

She could've easily given me her work email instead, but she lifted her hand. "Give me your phone."

Holding her gaze, I lifted it from the table and passed it to her. Mesmerized by her expression of both satisfied and devious female, I waited for her to punch in her contact info and pass it back.

When I read *Boss Ass Bitch* above her number, I let out a bark of laughter. Willard jumped. Lavinia's smile spread wide as she stared at me.

"Don't change the name," she ordered when I looked back down at my phone screen.

"Don't plan to."

"So you don't mind writing the content for the landing page?" asked Willard. "After all, this is your cause so I thought it would be easier for you."

"Not at all. I'll take that duty."

"Awesome," said Lavinia, noting that down as well. "We'll need to make the website live by this weekend. I've got the photo shoot set up for early next week. So we'll also need to get this spread on the SuperNet pretty quickly."

"Sooner than that would be better," I added, "I'll write the copy today and don't worry about the SuperNet. Willard, send me the website URL, and I'll take care of the rest."

Lavinia gave me a quizzical look. "How do you plan to spread the word?"

"Don't worry about it. This is why you're lucky to have a grim on board."

Especially me, I thought but didn't say that aloud. Most grims were techies, but they didn't have access to the data that I'd amassed in my tech bunker at home. I could manipulate the algorithms to spread our link everywhere across the SuperNet, making it visible in ninety percent of the population's social media feeds.

"Is it legal?" she asked.

"Why is it that everyone thinks grims are criminals?"

Of course, it kind of was illegal, but it wasn't like I was spreading offensive ideals or advertising snuff films. I was spreading the awareness of a charity fundraiser to help supernatural orphans. So I didn't feel bad about it at all.

"You didn't answer my question."

Such a smart girl, Lavinia.

I smiled. "We better all get to work so we can get this website up immediately. We can break down the Pin-up Shoot this afternoon or tomorrow."

Rather than argue, Lavinia nodded. Willard closed his laptop and went to his desktop. "Lavinia, if you could send me the social media links for the campaign, I can get those loaded onto the site."

"Sure thing." She stood and walked over to her desk to work as well.

I couldn't help but watch her walk away, chastising myself for the self-torture before I pulled my own customized laptop out of my satchel. I logged on, using my hotspot, not the GMC WiFi. I never trusted anyone's WiFi access but my own.

By the time Willard left to pick up sandwiches for lunch from the deli on the corner, I'd finished perfecting the copy for the landing page as well as wrote a testimonial from myself. I figured if I was all in for this cause—which I wholeheartedly was—then I needed to be vulnerable as well. It might help Lavinia get others to open up if they knew one of our charity team had a personal connection.

I was emailing the copy to Willard when I felt her staring at me. Such a lovely feeling to know she might be transfixed like me.

"So," I spun in my chair to face her, still at the worktable, "why do you want to win this contest?"

She didn't glance away or pretend that she hadn't been

watching me. "I think that's pretty obvious. The prize speaks for itself."

"You want money and your name in the limelight, then?"

That annoyed expression returned. "No."

"Those are the prizes. One hundred thousand and the fame of the winning title spread by Garrison Media Corp."

"You say that like money and popularity are dirty words. It's everything I need to start my own business."

"There you go. That's the real reason. Was that so hard to admit? What business is that, exactly?"

"I think that's pretty obvious. My own public relations company, catering to supernaturals. Winning this could catapult my small business launch into the stratosphere."

I'd steepled my fingers, considering her words. She was right. But winning GMC's contest wasn't the only way to launch a successful business.

"I need this win more than you," I stated emphatically.

She made a disgruntled noise in her throat. "From what I've heard, you've already created a few apps that are very lucrative. Why would you need the money or the limelight, as you put it? Why do you want to win this contest?"

Rather than answer that question, because though I was willing to write a few vulnerable words down for the website, I wasn't ready to vocalize them to Lavinia.

"I think there's another reason," I taunted.

She turned completely away from her computer and crossed her arms and legs. "I can't wait to hear this."

A dizzying sort of excitement raced through my blood at her challenging stance. I don't know why but her defiance made my whole body harder than marble.

"You're a winner, Lavinia. You like to be on top." I let that innuendo sink in, which it apparently did, judging by the flush of pink crawling up her neck. "I think it's a fair assessment that you have a need to dominate in all facets of life."

Her eyes rounded, almost as if surprised by something I

said. Those full lips compressed together as she seemed to refrain from saying whatever she wanted to say. I mimicked her stance, crossing my arms and leaning back in my chair.

"The next thing you'll be saying," she said with a little bite, "is that my needs are too masculine or that I have penis envy or some other kind of toxic crap."

"Not at all. Women should be on top just as much as men. I can certainly enjoy that fact." Especially if she were on top of me. "As for penis envy, I don't believe or advocate for that misogynistic, fucked-up Freudian bullshit." I tilted my head, observing her powerful defiance. "However, I bet you would enjoy having a penis of your own."

"I wouldn't mind," she agreed casually. "Dicks are awesome. I wouldn't want to give up my pussy—because let's face it, it's *glorious*—but if I could have both, that would be amazing."

All saliva had dried up in my mouth, and I couldn't speak a word, my thoughts wandering to how glorious her pussy was and how I'd give my left testicle to discover it for myself.

That superior brow of hers arched as her mouth slid into a satisfied smirk. "Why don't you let me borrow yours, Blackwater?" she asked sweetly, her gaze dropping to my crotch conspicuously. "But only if it's big enough. I wonder if it would meet my standards."

"Why don't you come on over and find out." The words flew out of my mouth without me thinking twice.

Her smile slipped, then we were back to that trance-like staring contest we liked to engage in from time to time. There was no way she didn't notice how hard my dick was in my slacks, and I sure as hell wasn't hiding it from her.

I wasn't lying. If she wanted to find out if my dick met her standards, I was more than willing to show her.

She remained frozen in her desk chair, her chest rising and falling faster, her full breasts pushing against the thin material of her dress, as the thickness of desire tightened the room. It was always there between us. I knew that she felt it too. Especially right now.

Even when Willard walked in with our lunch, my senses were ensnared only by her ripe arousal filling my nostrils and my lungs. I blinked slowly, savoring her scent, then thanked my ancestors for giving me heightened senses.

CHAPTER SIX

~LIVVY~

THANK HEAVEN GRIMS DIDN'T HAVE VAMPIRE OR WEREWOLF senses. My heartrate was going ninety miles an hour and the needy throbbing between my thighs told me he'd know exactly what I was feeling if he possessed those traits.

He was confident enough already, and I was still on the fence about whether or not *trying someone new* like Clara suggested was a wise idea. I needed to keep my head in the game and on this campaign.

So that's what I did the rest of the day. I could barely eat my turkey sandwich after that conversation. My tummy was in knots. Gareth was so... so direct. And intense. He made me nervous, but he also made me want to engage and play with him.

Distracting, that's what he truly was. Knowing that, I settled into my work, found the contact info I needed from Jules and located three supernatural adults—a witch, a warlock, and a werewolf—who'd gone through the human foster care program and agreed to phone interviews about their experiences. We needed these testimonials quickly so we could get the website up and start spreading the word for our first fundraiser next week—the Pin-up Photo Shoot.

By the time I wrapped up my third interview and typed up the copy for Willard, I was more than ready to jet. The three of us left together, and I was glad we didn't bump into Richard. Gareth's warning about him had me on edge.

I didn't get any vibes from him that he was any different than other men who'd ogled my body in the workplace. Still, Gareth was so adamant about it, I wasn't keen on running into him. Especially with Gareth next to me.

Gareth let me go ahead of him as we exited the elevator.

"Goodnight, Perry," I said, waving to the nice security guard in the lobby.

"Night, Miss Savoie. Gentlemen."

I smirked that Perry knew me by name but not the guys. Of course, I'd brought him donuts on the first day. Sure, I wanted to butter him up, but also, his job was a lonely one without proper breaks all day. And if I ever worked late, I figured he wouldn't mind watching the polite lady who brought him donuts periodically as she went to her car.

We took the garage elevator, separate from the elevator leading to the main floors and stepped out into the garage parking lot together. I noticed that Gareth waited until I was in my car before he reversed his Audi. The kind of Audi that reeked of money. I didn't know cars, but I knew that his was shiny and fancy and expensive.

That perturbed me again thinking about the fact that he didn't need the damn prize money for this contest. Today had rattled me on multiple levels.

First, the sheer shock that the three of us worked so well together, despite Gareth typically being an antagonistic asshat. Then the whole penis envy conversation which only had me thinking about Gareth's penis. A lot. And finally, interviewing those supernaturals about their foster care experiences.

It wasn't that they were paired with neglectful or abusive parents. It was that all three of them expressed heightened anxiety having to hide their supernatural abilities and not having anyone to talk to at a young age, or when their magic was amplifying during their teen years.

It was an emotional roller coaster of a day, so what else could I do but bee-line my ass to Daisy Dukes on Carondelet for some greasy comfort food. It was after five, so I was able to find a parking spot right around the block, and it was before six so there were quite a few booths open when I walked in.

As I headed toward the first empty booth, a figure sitting at the bar caught my eye. And apparently, I caught his.

"Seriously? Are you stalking me now?"

Gareth's mouth ticked up into a smile as he slid off the stool, picked up his beer, and strode toward me. Even after a long-ass workday, he still looked like utter perfection. Not a hair out of place. His dress shirt still remarkably crisp and wrinkle-free. He'd rolled up his sleeves, which had me checking out his forearms with prominent veins roping up the muscles.

"I was here first, so you'd have to be the one stalking me."

"As if." I shimmied out of my red pea coat and dropped it into the booth before I plopped my ass on the bench seat.

Gareth slid into the other side.

"I didn't ask you to sit with me," I pointed out.

"But you wanted to."

I opened my mouth to snap something back at him when the waitress stepped up and handed us two menus.

"Can I get you something to drink?" she asked.

"Iced tea, please."

"I'm good." Gareth tapped his index finger on the glass his hand was wrapped around.

"I'll just give you guys a few minutes."

My gaze went to the tattoo covering most of the back of his hand. I'd been trying to get a good look at that one for ages now. The back of his left hand was covered in a blooming rose, which

I'd seen before, but the right hand was all about magic. It was a stylized Eye of Medusa—a protection symbol—the iris a deep blue, the rest in black ink swirling with offshoots of little stars, moons, and witch sign.

"Witch sign? Since when do grims tattoo themselves with witch sign?"

Our symbols looked similar to Celtic runes with slight differences, more delicate lines. Witch sign was often used when we needed to cast a strong spell. I recognized the one for door or gateway repeated on either side of a crescent moon near his knuckles. And the one for warrior.

"It's a powerful language." He kept his hand still, allowing me to observe closely. "They carry strong magic."

Frowning, because that didn't explain why a grim would want witch sign on his body. It was odd. But Gareth was odd, so why not?

He also had a thick cuff tattooed on the wrist of the same right hand. No, not a cuff. Those were scales. Without thinking, I reached across the table and flipped his arm, wrist up.

The muscle of his forearm tightened beneath my hand, a flare of heat hitting my chest as I slid my hand back into my lap. But he let me look my fill at his ink.

"A snake eating its tail?"

"It's the ouroboros. The ancient symbol of the cycle of life. Life, death, eternal renewal."

"I know the ouroboros sign." I grinned. "In some religions, the snake is a phallic symbol. A fertility sign."

His mouth quirked on one side. "Thinking about my penis again, Lavinia?"

Rolling my eyes, I replied much too quickly, "You wish."

His mouth widened, but he didn't keep teasing. He added, "It's also a symbol for the transmigration of the soul."

"Reincarnation?"

"Metempsychosis. But essentially the same thing."

I couldn't help but smile and tease him. "Isn't the renewal of the soul a rather optimistic belief for a broody cynic such as yourself?"

His irises, warmer brown in this light, flushed black, lending an ethereal fathomless quality to them. For a second, I was caught by them, feeling as if I was slipping into an abyss.

"A man can dream, can't he?" There was a somber tone to his question. As if he wondered if it was possible. In that single sentence, loneliness radiated from him. Quickly following, I sensed a brighter emotion in the grave set of his eyes and mouth.

Hope. My breath faltered. His tattoos reflected quite the tortured soul, one who was seeking some sort of salvation. Or perhaps simply another life altogether. My stomach twisted into a knot.

There were other small tattoos on his fingers—a compass rose, a skull, a chalice, more witch sign. Gareth was a mystery wrapped in mystery. One I longed to uncover.

Sighing, I picked up the menu and scanned. I realized this might be a good opportunity to pick his brain a little. Find out what made the man tick. Feeling his gaze on me, I looked up.

"Aren't you going to order something to eat?"

"I already know what I want." He took a sip of beer, his eyes never leaving me.

And just like that, the air sizzled between us. I'd started to get used to this fierce attraction whenever I got too close to him. I'd blamed it all on his aura, but now I was beginning to face the truth.

After all, I knew about grim auras. They nurtured and breathed fire into desires that were already there. They didn't create ones that weren't already brewing underneath the surface.

We were in one of our staring contests again, but this time I wasn't giving him my battle-ready death-glare. This time, I simply looked, observing his sharp features and his typically relaxed, but aloof expression. He wore the kind of cold beauty that couldn't be touched. Like nothing would shake the austere, haughty mask he wore so well.

Not long after I first met him, I thought how he wasn't what one might call classically handsome. His features were too stark and severe. But also, he'd probably melt my camera lens with his sculpted jaw and cheekbones and model-perfect shadows.

And those eyes. I'd once called them soulless. In reality, they were dark, endless pools that sparked with inner fire. All of him along with his somber yet watchful demeanor gave the impression of a cold, distant but very alert predator.

Yet, I had seen vulnerability crack his cool veneer before. It was fleeting and gone, but I'd seen it.

"You never answered my question today."

His obsidian eyes narrowed before his deep voice rumbled, "Which question was that?"

"Why do you want to win this contest?"

His jaw clenched, but he still didn't answer me.

"Is it because you were in the foster care program once too?" I asked softly. Gently.

The server stepped up to the table and set down my tea. "Are y'all ready to order?"

Gareth gestured to me. I glanced down at the menu.

"I'll take the Cajun Philly Cheese Steak and some cheese fries. Can you add jalapeños to those?"

"Sure thing. And for you, sir?"

Gareth's gaze didn't move from me as he ordered a Double D burger with fries.

"No cheese fries? They're so good here."

He shook his head to the waitress and handed over his menu. "Never tried them actually."

"What?" I laughed. "Blackwater, you don't know what you're missing. I'll let you taste mine."

As I sipped my iced tea from the straw, I glanced over the rim to find the tiniest smirk quirking his lips. Then I realized what I'd said.

"My fries, dipweed."

He settled back into the booth. "I'll taste anything of yours that you'll let me."

"What is this?"

"What do you mean?"

"This heavy flirting thing you've got going on."

"I apologize. I wasn't aware that you weren't aware of what flirting means."

"That's not what I meant."

"Then explain more clearly."

I moved my tea to the side so I could lean both my forearms on the table and asked in a low voice, "Why are you constantly implying that you'd like to have sex with me? To distract me from the campaign?"

He mirrored my posture, easing his forearms onto the table and clasping his hands together. My gaze drifted to his badass ink.

"Not at all. I was implying I'd like to have sex with you because I do in fact want to fuck you senseless. I'm glad to know that it was distracting though. Added bonus."

Narrowing my eyes, I sputtered, "Um, no. Never. We are not fucking each other, Gareth."

His smirk widened into a smile.

"Methinks she doth protest too much."

A burning flare crawled up my neck. "That's not how the quote goes. It's 'The lady doth protest too much, methinks.'"

Now he was full-on grinning like the devil himself. I wondered if they were related. "My way sounds better."

"Better than Shakespeare?"

"Better than Hamlet. A bit too loquacious for me. And now you're wandering away from the subject. Let's get back to the discussion on enjoying fucking each other."

A wave of blistering heat blazed into my cheeks and sweat beaded on my forehead. I didn't embarrass easily, for heaven's sake, but his directness was off-putting and rude and sending wayward, welcome messages to my vagina. She had fully perked up at this topic of conversation.

"Also, *loquacious?*" I arched a brow. "Trying to impress me with your big vocabulary?"

"Since you're unwilling to check out my big cock, I thought it second best."

Yes, I do believe he was the devil himself. I should've been insulted he was being so insanely forward, but for some reason it only made him more intriguing.

"Is this how you woo all the girls, Blackwater?"

His smile dimmed but didn't disappear, his dark eyes glinting with mischief and glee. "No, Lavinia. You seem to bring out the best in me."

I burst out laughing. "This is your best? I'd hate to see your worst."

He didn't answer, continuing his perusal of me. His gaze drifted from my eyes down to my mouth then to my neck and breasts then back to my eyes.

"You blush easily, Lavinia." His voice rolled like a silken caress, his gaze fixed on my neckline.

I didn't have to imagine what he was thinking about because it was clear as day in his dark, hungry gaze.

The fact was I did not blush easily. It was him. But I sure as hell wasn't about to admit that he got to me more than any man or woman I'd ever had a crush on. Yes, I had a stupid ass infatuation with this annoying, fine as fuck, grim reaper.

"Why do you want to win the contest?" I asked again, trying to regain a modicum of control on this conversation.

He shifted back in the booth, his mask back in place. The server dropped off our meals at the same moment.

"Here we are. Can I get you anything else?"

"Water, please," said Gareth.

After she left, I thought he'd make another evasive move and dodge my question. Instead, after taking a bite of his burger, chewing, and swallowing, he said with open frankness, "Because

I was an orphan in the system, and I know what hell truly feels like."

I paused from taking a second bite of my sandwich, which was saying something, because it was the greasy, meaty goodness I needed after such a long day. He continued eating.

"How old were you when you went into the system?"

A jarring stab in my chest reminded me that if he was an orphan, that meant both of his parents died at a young age. As if reading my thoughts, he went on steadily like we were discussing the weather.

"My parents died in a car accident. The drunk driver who hit them also died. At the time, we were living on Long Island. My father worked for a tech company in the city. He was rarely around. My mother stayed at home. I remember her the most." He took a minute to take a few more bites of his burger.

While his voice had little inflection at all while he recited this childhood tragedy, his gaze remained downcast at the table as he told it to me.

"How old were you?" I asked softly.

"I was seven. It was the week of Christmas." He ate a few fries. "Needless to say, I've never cared for the holiday much. Lost its magic for me that day."

Goddess above. A supernatural child of seven, losing his parents and then hating Christmas for the rest of his life because it reminded him of their deaths.

"And then the foster care program."

A dark laugh huffed from his throat and he shook his head, finally meeting my gaze across the table.

"Losing my parents was tragic, yes, but being sent to those homes nearly drove me mad. I realize that there are plenty of kind, caring foster parents in the system. But for some unholy reason, I wasn't sent to any of them." He finished his burger, and we ate quietly before he went on. "I bounced around to a couple of homes. No one abused me or anything. None of the foster parents anyway."

Cold dread trickled through my veins, and I couldn't take another bite.

"Who did?" fell from my mouth before I could think that maybe he didn't want to tell me about it.

Again, he surprised me by being frank, direct, and completely open. "When puberty hit, I was in the home of a rather neglectful family. They had several foster kids in and out of rotation in the home. They made sure we were fed and went to school, but there was no kindness or affection. Or very little that I remember. Of course, I was a withdrawn boy, still grieving my parents and feeling more than a little different from other human children in the home."

He tapped his forefinger on the table, watching the movement. I waited, barely breathing, not saying a word.

"One day, a new kid arrived. Dennis." His mouth thinned into a tight line as he paused on the name. "He was a supernatural. I knew he was the moment I set eyes on him."

Gareth finished eating, tossed his napkin on the plate, and slid it aside. He leaned back in the booth, his steady gaze on me as he finished the story.

"I was so happy to have another supernatural in the house. Someone that I could perhaps talk to about what was happening to me. My own magic was starting to build and make itself known."

"Your telepathy?"

A curt nod. "Among other things."

He didn't elaborate, and I realized I wasn't completely in his confidence yet. Grims always kept their magical abilities to themselves. Everyone knew about their giftedness in using technology, but I'd come to realize there was a lot more to them after he'd accidentally telepathed the vision of us in his bedroom.

Wiping that thought away, I asked, "Can I ask what Dennis did?"

"He was a vampire. I was eleven, he was sixteen." His voice

had gone glacial, his eyes black ice. I shivered, knowing the cold fury vibrating off him was about Dennis.

"He fed from you," I guessed.

Another stiff nod. "Frequently. Brutally. In the middle of the night when I was sound asleep. It's rather horrifying to wake up in the dark with someone eighty pounds heavier and a hundred times stronger than you, holding you down and drinking your blood with vicious, agonizing bites." He tapped his index finger on the table again, glancing around the room. "It's also rather odd for an eleven-year-old to take to wearing turtlenecks year-round."

"Year round?" I nearly shrieked, forcing myself to calm as my heart rate sped erratically. Nausea swirled in my stomach. "How long did this go on?"

Gareth's steady gaze held me fast, never wavering from anything but his regal, aloof façade.

"Ten and a half months."

I gulped hard at that thought. Brutalized for almost a year by this asshole of a vampire. And while Gareth remained calm in telling the tale, there seemed to be more details he was omitting. Either for my sake or for his own, not wanting to let horrors too dark or skeletons too old to fall out onto the table between us during a cordial Monday night dinner.

"What happened to stop it? Was he sent away?"

"My magic fully manifested one night unexpectedly." He watched me, observing carefully for something though I wasn't sure what. Then he added, "He didn't bother me after that."

A cool finality in the way his words left his lips. I wanted to know what magic came to him to assist him. I also wasn't sure I did want to know, because there was malice and vengeance in his voice.

What was he forced to do to save himself from Dennis? If so, what kind of toll would that take on the soul of a magical child all alone in the world? How did that form him into this adult sitting before me? This seductive, yet secretive, seemingly apathetic man.

"After that night, my Uncle Silas, Henry's father, was contacted. Uncle Silas had been estranged from my father and wasn't particularly concerned when Dad died, leaving behind an orphaned son."

"What changed his mind to take you in?"

"I changed his mind," he answered coolly without any explanation.

I couldn't help but ask, "How did you manage that?"

"Uncle Silas is a collector of power. He realized my abilities were an asset." He gave a small shrug, almost subconsciously it seemed. "After I'd"—he paused— "demonstrated my magical abilities, he took me in."

There was definitely something he was omitting. Specifically what those magical abilities were. What was this grim truly capable of?

"So you can see," he added, reaching across the table and pinching off three fries covered in melted cheese and jalapeños, "no supernatural should be fostered by humans. The dangers are endless."

He took a bite of the fries then his mouth quirked up into a lopsided smile. "Mmm. Good. You were right."

Ignoring his change of subject, I added, "And the media behind winning a contest run by the international Garrison Media Corporation could help the press push the supernatural community into action for the orphans."

He wiped his fingers on the napkin, all humor and lightness gone from his voice. "For many righteous causes, it takes a hell of a lot more than money to resolve them, Lavinia."

What else could I do but nod in agreement. Money can't right all the wrongs in the world. But awareness of injustice could pull on the heartstrings of many and launch a movement that money can't buy.

I suddenly found myself realizing I'd rather he win this

contest instead of me. My involvement in this was solely selfish. His was altruistic. Self-driven from his own experiences, yes, but still.

"You're right," I agreed. His eyes widened in surprise, which had me smiling again. "Hopefully, our campaign will bring the awareness it deserves."

"I think we're off to a good start." He tilted his head, still observing me with that calculating expression. "And we make a terrific team."

The way he said it implied that he meant me and him rather than our business trio.

"Can I get you any dessert?" asked the waitress, stepping up to our table.

"No, thank you." I broke from his heated stare. "Can I get a to-go box, please?"

I hadn't eaten even half my meal, so absorbed in the conversation. And quite frankly, the man sitting across from me.

"Sure thing. Be right back."

"I apologize." A frown marred Gareth's usually smooth expression. "I'm afraid my topic of conversation killed your appetite."

"Don't be sorry." I swallowed hard, because this was the first time he and I had talked without throwing snarky jabs or backhanded barbs at one another. "I'm glad you told me."

Yet again, we fell into looking at each other, both of us silent till the bill came. I reached for it, but it slipped from beneath my fingers and flew through the air into his hand.

I glanced around to make sure no one saw him using magic, but apparently none had.

"I can pay my bill," I said.

His lips twitched as he pulled out a credit card and held it up for the waitress who flitted over and took it.

"I'm not trying to malign your independence, Lavinia. You can pick up the bill next time."

"Well, thank you, Mr. Blackwater." Shoving my arms into

my coat, I huffed a laugh under my breath before standing and glancing down at him, looking regal and superior as ever. "But that's only *if* there is a next time," I teased.

I leaned over to pick up my to-go box and purse, knowing full well I wasn't ready to start going out with Gareth for regular meals. Sex was one thing, and that was *if* I decided to give into that urge. But dating was quite another. While I could be grown up enough to admit that he would be a catch for anyone else, the two of us would kill each other within the first month. Week, even.

When I turned from the booth, he was standing directly in front of me, mere inches between us. The violent assault of his nearness buckled my knees. I focused on not falling and steadying my breath, while he eased even closer, his hands coming up toward my chest.

Just when I'd managed to corral my wits and put my libido in check, he did something like this. Like stand so close I could see that his eyes weren't black anymore. The deepest coffee-brown surrounded dilated pupils.

I refused to back away as his hands—large with slender fingers, and tattoos that drew my eye—went to my oversized black buttons and began fastening my pea coat.

"Oh, Lavinia," he purred, smoothing the lapels of my collar after finishing the last button, dark eyes glinting. Then with a lascivious smile, he opened an intimate link and messaged me mind to mind.

There will most definitely be a next time.

CHAPTER SEVEN

~GARETH~

As I pulled my car into the garage of my home on Prytania Street, I was still reeling from dinner with Lavinia. I'd never intended to confess my sordid past as an orphan. I'd never meant to tell her about Dennis. And though I hadn't told her everything, I nearly thought she was using one of her persuasion charms as an Influencer to get the truth out of me.

But she hadn't. I'd never detected one spark of magic in the air between us. Unless I counted the ever-present lust burning through my veins whenever she was near. That wasn't her using magic on me, however. That was fate laughing in my fucking face.

Up to this point, my relationships with women had been calculated and brief. As I preferred them. A few nights together for sexual release then move on. Emotional dependency was uncomfortable, inconvenient, and unnecessary in my life.

I wasn't sure if it was because I'd lost my parents so young, and avoiding attachments kept that kind of brutal, gutting pain out of my life. Or if I'd simply learned remaining single was the best choice after living around Uncle Silas—the cold, hard-hearted bachelor after he divorced Henry's mother. Not that I would ever model myself after my asshole of an uncle, but he was successful. And I'd yearned for that more than anything after being a poverty-stricken orphan with nobody and nothing to call my own.

Either way, I'd not once considered taking a woman for more than a month at a time. There simply wasn't any need beyond pleasuring each other in the bedroom. That's what had always worked for me.

But now... Lavinia. It wasn't just her body that I desired. I wanted her mind, her heart, and her soul as well.

What was this obsession about, and how could I get rid of it?

The click-click of tiny toenails on the wood floors greeted me as I walked down the short hallway from the garage and into the kitchen. Queenie, my three-legged Maltese, yipped excitedly and danced in circles.

"And how was your day, my dear?"

She yipped again in that tiny bark she had, the white fluff around her eyes falling to the side as she wagged her tail. I grabbed her treat box from the cabinet.

"Here you are, darling." I dropped a few dog biscuits in her bowl and kept walking toward the stairs leading down to the first floor.

There were no basements in Louisiana. The soft soil would never allow it. But this house had been built on a slight incline where the second floor was actually the main living space. The third where the bedrooms were. I'd bought it, because the first was a wide, enclosed space with few windows that the first owner had used as a home theater. It served perfectly for my elaborate computer system with multiple monitors.

Right now, I needed my bunker. I needed to ground myself in what gave me comfort and put my mind at ease. I wanted to check in with Peonie at Obsidian, see if she found anything new on Dick Davis.

Perhaps my fascination with Lavinia didn't stem from desire but empathy. A need to protect. I knew what it felt like to be hunted. And whether she took me seriously or not, she was being hunted.

My instincts were never wrong about the evil of other men. Darkness swirled in my chest, whispering and wanting to climb to the surface. I banked the feeling back down, locking it tight behind the wall I'd built to keep it at bay.

All grims learned how to do this at a young age. Or at least, they were supposed to learn. Considering I had no teacher when it first manifested, I couldn't blame myself for what had happened to Dennis. A vision of his rounded eyes and twisted limbs flashed to mind.

I shut that away too and sat in my chair, swiveling toward the main monitor. Nothing new from Peonie via email, so I decided to call. Putting my phone on speaker, I dialed, while also running a diagnostic on MIMIC, the app I'd created to track FaceBook activity on the SuperNet. I created it specifically to find the target audience for our campaign.

While data was being generated and popping on screen in bar-graph form, a chipper voice answered the phone.

"Good evening, Mr. Blackwater. Twice in one week? I'm starting to wonder if you're flirting with me."

Grinning, because Peonie and I had always been strictly professional friends and would never be anything else, I teased, "Just wanted to hear your lovely voice again."

"Liar. You want something."

"Anything new on Richard Davis?"

The click of keys on a keyboard filled a short pause before she answered, "No. Like I told you before, we have records of everything you asked for. Other than his wild success in PR on the West Coast and a few model-perfect girlfriends who seemed to worship him, there was nothing in the system."

That was because he was deviously good at not getting

caught. Not because there wasn't anything to find. The certainty of it hummed bone-deep.

"There was one odd thing though when I did a background check into his family."

"What's that?"

"About ten years ago, his sister's teenage daughter Priscilla went missing. They live on the East Coast and he doesn't see them often. Richard brought several Seers to the case to try to find her, but the family never found out what happened."

Of course, if he'd brought the Seers, he'd have made damn sure they were glamoured not to point the finger in his direction. If the family had access to grims, they might've had more luck.

A dark stirring from that deep chasm swirled. A primal rumble rose from the caged depths, weaving to the surface.

Killer, the demon told me.

My entire body went rigid, understanding that my demon recognized monsters like himself.

"You still there?" Concern dominated Peonie's voice.

"Yeah. Thank you, Peonie. I appreciate your help."

An alert on my Smart watch buzzed, telling me someone had entered my front door. I tapped the security monitor to see Henry scooping up Queenie in the foyer. Even though my little rescue dog was perfectly capable of making it around on three legs just as well as if she had four, Henry made it his personal agenda to cart her around as her personal wheelchair when he visited.

"Anytime, Gareth. If something else pops up, I'll let you know."

"Thanks." I clicked off the call, contemplating the truth my demon had whispered to me.

The problem was, I couldn't go around calling people murderers without definitive proof. Especially not a powerful man like Davis.

And I certainly wasn't going to Victor Garrison and telling

him, *you see, this demon that lives inside me told me he's a murderer. That's how I know.*

Grims were already considered odd to most witches and warlocks. Plus, I couldn't make a confession like that on a whim, knowing I'd be breaking the almighty grim code to keep our secrets secret.

While Henry made his way through the house, I noted the data my app, MIMIC, had tabulated, locking in on the demographics for our campaign. But my mind was elsewhere, wondering how I could discover the truth of Davis's past. Because he was no fucking Cub Scout, that was for damn sure.

Henry clomped down the stairs still holding Queenie and strode to the gray sofa, plopping onto his back. He let out a heavy sigh, chomping his gum obnoxiously. Queenie curled up on his abdomen.

"What's wrong?" I asked, my gaze flitting back to the data on my screen.

He stroked Queenie absently. "Sean got suspended again."

"Shit."

"Yeah."

My cousin Sean, Henry's brother, was always getting into trouble.

"What was it this time?"

"Not for what he actually did." He continued to stare at the ceiling. "He was suspended because he was found with some Oxycontin pills in his locker."

Frowning, I spun away from my monitor to look at him. "Sean doesn't do pills. Smokes a little weed now and then but that's it."

"I know." Henry sat up and leaned back against the sofa, clenching his jaw. Queenie curled back up in his lap.

"Why did someone frame him?" My blood simmered with fury, luring my darkness for a second time in under an hour. I wondered who I'd have to teach a hard lesson to.

"He deserved it actually." Henry started chewing his gum

again in that annoying way. "One of the football players had been messing with him, taunting him. Typical bully bullshit."

Swallowing down the vibration of rage, I crossed my arms, tilting back in my chair. "Sean wouldn't tolerate that."

"No. He didn't. He pushed the asshole down the stairs with his TK."

I winced. "Fuck."

"Pushed him so hard, the kid broke his arm and fractured his wrist. Right before he fell, Sean told him to 'have a nice trip'."

"Sean told you?" He was a cocky little shit sometimes, but he wouldn't be proud to admit something like that to his brother.

"No. I pulled it telepathically."

"I'm sure he loved that."

Grims weren't supposed to use telepathy to invade minds. No supernatural was. It was a violation. As much as I'd wanted to take a peek into Lavinia's, I'd kept out. Now if she invited me in, that would be a different story.

"He was pissed as fucking hell," Henry broke into my thoughts. "But I didn't trust him to tell me the whole story, and I was right. He'd left that part out." His expression hardened. "His TK is strong, Gareth. Like yours. And it's growing stronger."

What he was really saying hit me hard, like a punch to the sternum. I considered before asking, "Do you think he's a grimlock?"

Like me.

Henry seemed to deliberate for a few seconds, then gave a stiff nod. "His abilities remind me of when you first got yours. When you first came to live with us."

Sean was quite a bit younger than both of us by decades. When Sean told Uncle Silas he was moving out to live with Henry last year, their father didn't even put up a fight, considering both of his offspring ungrateful. But if Sean was like me,

Uncle Silas would change his mind about his youngest son and try to bring him back into the fold.

"You're worried." Henry's fear skated into the room like a line of red streaking into the air.

"He doesn't have the control that you have." His voice was low and soft. "I'm afraid he'll do something terrible that he can't take back. Something worse than breaking arms."

"He could just be a top tier TK. Not necessarily a grimlock."

"Possibly," Henry agreed. "But my senses tell me otherwise."

And we both knew that Henry's senses were better than even mine.

He went on. "He doesn't seem to want to hold the smoke. He wants to let it out. He relishes it."

The smoke was what grims sometimes called the dark essence that lived in all of us. I never called it something as benign as that. Because mine was truly a monster.

We'd been taught how to cage it and keep it under control. Our Aunt Lucille, Uncle Silas's sister, had taught us Blackwater boys at a young age. For me, it was almost the day I came to live here. Uncle Silas knew better than to neglect this teaching I needed so much.

But some grims preferred not to cage it. Some opted to let it run wild, to lead them on dangerous paths. Those grims would eventually lose their humanity, bathing in dark pursuits and evil pathways.

"Sean isn't evil." My voice vibrated a little loudly in the room.

"No," agreed Henry. "But he enjoys being bad. And he's playing with fire."

"I'll talk to him."

"Good. He listens to you better than me."

Henry was chewing that gum like mad again. It was annoying.

"What else is bothering you?"

75

He moved Queenie off his lap and paced along the sofa, running his hands through his hair. "Those fucking werewolves are all over the place. Hanging out at the Cauldron all the damn time."

"Ah." I grinned.

He didn't notice as he went on. "And if that fucking redhead doesn't stop staring at Clara, I'm going to rip his eyeballs out."

"No harm in looking," I said evenly. "She's pretty to look at."

Now, he was pacing and grumbling. "I know she's fucking pretty." He rubbed his palms along the sides of his jeans, like they were sweaty.

"Are you okay? What's with chewing your gum like it's an Olympic sport?"

"It's nicotine gum. I'm trying to quit smoking, okay?" he snapped angrily.

"That seems to be going well."

"I need to quit."

"Why exactly? Not that I've ever cared for your habit, but it does help you with your nerves."

And by nerves, I meant the repercussions of him going against his grim nature.

"She—" he paused then, "it's bad for you."

"You can't die from lung cancer." Grims weren't affected by diseases like cancer. He was pacing nervously like an expectant father on six cups of coffee. "Mm. I think I liked you better as a smoker."

He rounded on me, furious, his eyes blacker than normal. "It's bad for you!" he bellowed before storming toward the staircase. "Come on, Queenie!"

She yipped and obediently followed her favorite person. He stopped at the stairs and picked up Queenie, cuddling her to his chest as he stomped up to the first floor.

Unperturbed by Henry's outburst since I knew why his emotions were explosive at the moment, I went back to my data and printed out the information to bring to Willard and Lavinia tomorrow.

Lavinia. A flash of her in that pea coat, a red that matched her lips, electric blue eyes, and soft expression crossed my mind. Something twisted in my chest, a yearning that felt different than the ravenous lust I typically associated with her.

Frowning, I tucked that away for now and focused on my work. Or as best I could with a beautiful, black-haired witch haunting my every waking—and sleeping—moment.

CHAPTER EIGHT

~GARETH~

I was starting to get déjà vu whenever I walked into our workspace at GMC. First, her scent would hit me like a sledgehammer from down the hall, then I'd walk through the door and find her curvy frame bent over a desk or table in a body-hugging dress that had my cock at attention in three seconds flat. If I thought jerking off would help ease my dick's reaction to her every morning, I'd make it part of my daily wake-up routine.

But it wouldn't change. I knew that now. The only thing that would quench this burn was to be buried balls-deep inside of her. Quite frankly, I wasn't sure if that would even do it. I sure as fuck planned to try. It was just a matter of time until she agreed to let me come aboard.

"Good morning." I joined her at the table and set down my folder with the data from MIMIC to share with her and Willard. "I'd like to share some stats with you both before we get started today."

Willard popped up from behind the desktop he was seated

at, chewing on a donut, half of which was in his other hand. I cringed over his untidy workspace, littered with empty to-go cups and snack wrappers.

"I'm ready." Lavinia picked up her pen and notepad and joined me at the conference table.

Willard took a seat, still eating his donut. Opening the folder, I pulled out the multi-page copies and slid them to each of them.

"What you're looking at is the footprint of our core demographic on the SuperNet. This lists the Facebook profiles of every supernatural who's donated to fundraising campaigns on social media this past year. It also breaks it down by the types of fundraisers they prefer."

Lavinia's brows furrowed. "How in the hell did you get actual profiles?"

Shrugging a shoulder, I continued, "That doesn't mean we won't also target those who haven't donated online. If you turn to the fifth page, you'll see another set of data that provides us with a list of profiles where FB bots have delivered targeted ads on local fundraising to those most likely to engage."

I was enjoying Lavinia's small smile of amazement when Richard walked in. My mood plummeted.

"Good morning, everyone." He swept the room with a too-bright smile, wearing an expensive gray suit and an entire bottle of cologne.

Lavinia and Willard greeted him, but I didn't. Especially when he rounded the table to lean over Lavinia's shoulder.

"What are we looking at?"

Lavinia huffed out an uncomfortable laugh. "Gareth has provided us with the data he promised on our targeted audience for advertising. It's far more detailed than I imagined."

She stiffened when Richard dropped his arm into her personal space to grab the handout in front of her, brushing the bare curve of her neck with the back of his hand. On fucking purpose.

The smoky essence twisted out of its home deep in the cavern where I kept it, stirred to life by Richard's nefarious presence. There was no doubt that my darkness recognized something evil inside this man. And if he didn't keep his hands off Lavinia, I was going to fucking kill him.

"Interesting," he murmured, frowning down at the data as he flipped the pages.

Like I gave a fuck if he found it interesting. He could move along any time now.

"How'd you get this kind of information?" he asked accusingly. "We've mentioned to you that you can't use criminal hacking skills for this project."

I was sitting back in my chair, one arm draped on the table, tapping a finger on the table in a slow, rhythmic tempo. I was also trying to calm the burning desire to throw Richard through the wall of windows and listen to the pleasant sound of his terrified yell as he plummeted to the street far below.

Murder was a bit much this early in the morning. Even for this prick. Time to set him straight.

"And as I swore when I signed the contract, I'm not a criminal." I kept the edge of threat out of my voice by some surprising miracle as I casually nodded to the packet in his hand. "The data I collect is procured from my own software. It isn't illegal."

Not at this point anyway.

"You created the software to get this information?" Richard's brows rose in shock and interest. "I'm sure Victor would be interested in purchasing it for the company."

"It's not for sale."

A flare of menacing magic slithered into the room and skated over my skin. I knew exactly where it came from. Richard wasn't dumb enough to try to use his nulling powers without a judge or jury present. Simply because I'd pissed him off? I didn't think so.

I smiled at him condescendingly. I'd love to see him fucking try. Even if he attempted to use his powers against me, it would come to nothing. They wouldn't work on me.

After a long, uncomfortable staring contest, he dropped the packet in front of Lavinia. "What else is on the agenda for today?"

"Um," Lavinia pulled her phone in front of her and opened her online calendar. "I was going to share the time and date of our first fundraiser, the Pin-up Photo Shoot. I've confirmed with the photographer Jackson at the studio. And we were going to hammer down details for promoting the event."

"Excellent." Richard pulled his phone from his pocket and peered over her shoulder. "I'll put it in my calendar as well. Can't wait to see you in action."

Though he said the last to the table, his gaze flitting to Willard who'd remained mute as usual, Richard's hand landed on her shoulder for a quick squeeze. Lavinia stood suddenly with her packet in hand, stepping away to face Richard.

It took everything for me to keep my seat while Lavinia vibrated with tension.

Richard smiled. "I'll leave you all to your work." Then he marched toward the door.

Surprisingly, Lavinia followed and stopped him with a soft, "Mr. Davis, just a minute" right outside the office in the hallway.

Though she whispered, I could hear every word. While I kept my eyes on the packet that I wasn't reading, my entire body was rigid and waiting.

"Mr. Davis, I just wanted to let you know I'm not comfortable with people touching me like that in the workplace."

"Oh. It was meant as a friendly gesture." He sounded like the excuse-making asshat that he was.

"I'm sure. But I wanted to be clear how I feel about it."

"Of course." I glanced up to catch him smiling like he thought her adorable. "It won't happen again."

When she strode back in, she took her seat back at the table and then pierced me with a wide-eyed gaze. "You need to bring it down a notch."

"What do you mean?" I asked casually, feeling the swirling darkness retreat back into its cave as Richard walked away, taking his loathsome aura with him.

"You know, stop giving Richard murderous looks like you're about to choke him."

She was close, I'll give her that. I'd been contemplating something more bloody, like dismemberment. But choking was a pleasant thought.

"Let's get to promotion. Is the ad ready to go?" I asked. "I can plug it into my software this afternoon."

"Not yet." She rose from the table. "Still working on the graphic."

"I'll get back to the website," mumbled Willard, returning to his desk.

She stepped closer to me, her sweet scent easing the strain that had been tightening my chest with Richard in the room. "Are you all right?" Her concern was etched in her brow and the softness of her voice.

"Fine," I assured her. "Let's get to work."

And that's what we did. The rest of the day went by without interference from the dickhead. It was getting close to closing time, and I wanted to copy some of Willard's handwritten notes on the website to check against MIMIC at home, to see if we were aligned.

"Do you mind if I make a quick copy?"

"Go right ahead." He kept tapping away at the keyboard.

I caught Lavinia checking me out as I passed by her desk. There was a distinct difference in her eyes when she was contemplating strangling me or fucking me. I winked as I passed and headed into the copy room next door to our office.

Almost as soon as I'd walked in, the door opened and someone walked in behind me. Lavinia. Her hypnotic scent was so embedded in me, I could detect her from a mile away. The meaning behind that had me swallowing hard and hoping for something I hadn't dared to hope before.

"Can I help you, Lavinia?" I asked, while copying Willard's notes.

"You know, it's not a good idea that we get involved."

I couldn't suppress the grin from my face as I twisted to face her. "I realize you believe this."

"But you don't?"

"That's obvious." I crossed my arms, leaning back against the copier. "You know I want you. It won't affect the competition."

She had a hand propped on her hip and her serious thinking face on. She didn't respond.

"What are you thinking?" I asked her.

She dropped her arm and sashayed closer. I clenched my jaw as my whole body went stiff.

I'm considering what it would be like to kiss you right now, she telepathed to me.

Fuck. Now I was *really* stiff all over.

Not only had she opened a mind-to-mind link, which felt magnificently intimate, but she was flirting. Quite aggressively. She was making me harder by the second.

You're more than welcome to come find out, I told her.

Not at work. She arched a brow, stopping only a foot away from me now.

Anywhere you want me, I'll be there.

Maybe. She cocked her head, giving me a sultry smile. *We'll see.*

Then she turned and walked out, leaving me in a befuddled, hard-as-rock mess. Combing both hands through my hair, I laughed.

When I returned to the office, she was studiously working at something on her computer, making a point not to look my way. But that tilted smile told me she knew good and well what state she'd put me in.

At the end of the day, the three of us walked out and took the elevator down to the garage together.

"Care to grab a bite at Daisy Dukes?" I asked, wanting to explore our earlier conversation in the copy room. Truth be known, I also wanted to stoke her fire the way she'd done mine.

I liked her games. I wanted to play with her.

I hadn't intended to ask her to dinner, but I didn't want her to leave, even after a full day of work in the same room. I was aware that my obsession was borderline neurotic. Still, I couldn't control myself. A very uncomfortable feeling for me.

She turned at the door of her car and smiled. "Not tonight. Grabbing dinner with a friend then heading to that eighties club."

I tempered my instant reaction to grin. "Partying on a weeknight?"

"Not really. Kaya is obsessed with a bartender who works there, so I'm playing wing-girl."

"Mm." I wondered which bartender. Probably Martell. He was a charmer.

"So," she emphasized dramatically, "you created a software that legally tracks movements on Facebook?"

"I did." Hands in my pockets. "You don't believe me?"

"No, I do. I just——" she shrugged a shoulder and bit her bottom lip to stop a smile.

"What does that look mean, Lavinia?"

She laughed and the sound twisted sweetly inside my chest. I wanted to hear that sound over and over. "I'm embarrassed to admit it but..." She sighed dramatically.

"But?"

"It's impressive, okay?" she spat with a touch of fire.

I didn't hold back my grin that time. "Difficult for you to admit, isn't it? That I'm impressive."

"Don't let it get to your head. Anyway, isn't it a given that all grims are tech savvy? Maybe you're just average for a grim and not that impressive at all." Her brow rose haughtily.

I'd never wanted to fuck her more.

I eased a step closer. "If you'd let me, I'd show you how non-average I am."

She stared, considering, then shook her head, glossy black waves sliding over her shoulders. "Maybe some other time."

Hands still in my pockets, I watched her nervously find the door, open it, and toss her purse onto the passenger seat. "Goodnight, Gareth."

"Have fun at the club tonight."

I turned and strode toward my car, exhaling a heavy breath, knowing exactly what my plans were for the evening.

CHAPTER NINE

~LIVVY~

THE BARTENDER WHO WE NOW KNEW AS MARTELL WAS A warlock, an Influencer like me. His charms were dialed all the way up when we took a seat at the bar. He recognized Kaya who'd come in with another friend last weekend.

"Is it always this crowded on a Wednesday night?" Kaya asked him, sipping on her draft beer.

"The only time we aren't hopping is when we're closed."

He gave her a wink and flashed a bright smile before heading down the bar to tend to another customer.

"Damn," I marveled, checking out the eighties design of the club yet again.

I'd been wowed by this place, The Brat Club, last time I was here when our cousins from Lafayette were in town. There was cool eighties memorabilia everywhere. The best was Ducky's shoes from *Pretty in Pink* in a shadow box on the wall above the bar. Quotes from all my favorite eighties movies were scripted in neon lighting across the brick walls. I was still stunned at the stellar branding.

But in addition to the OG eighties vibes, there were still high-tech additions. Like the charging stations at each booth for phones and the song request tablets spread about. I'd requested a Depeche Mode song and was waiting for it to make its way through the wait list before I dragged Kaya to the dance floor.

"Damn is right," she said, swishing her sleek black ponytail when she dragged her eyes away from Martell. "That man is fine."

Martell leaned closer to hear a customer's order, his dread-locks sliding forward. Then he flicked them back with a shake of his head as he turned to grab a tumbler, but not before sliding a knowing smile back to Kaya.

"He is well aware of what you think about him. But I'll agree. He is quite pretty to look at. He's rocking that Lenny Kravitz look for sure." I sipped on my second Molly Ringwald, which was the club's version of a cosmo. "But I was actually talking about this club."

"Yes, your greatest wet dream come to life."

"This is not my greatest wet dream." Instantly, black silk sheets and a cool, controlled man standing behind me flashed to mind.

Kaya arched a black brow. "Oh? And what might that be?"

I bit the cocktail straw between my teeth trying to decide if I should confess to her.

Instantly, Kaya belted out a laugh, her pretty brown eyes sparkling with glee. "You don't even have to say a word. It's that grim."

I let my forehead fall to the bar top. "Kaya," I mumbled. "Why is this happening to me?" I straightened.

"Pfft. Because you need a good, hard fuck, Livvy."

"What?" I snapped my head to face her.

But her gaze was back on Martell down the bar. She answered without looking at me. "You know it's true. You always choose partners who are meek and mild. Tender and sweet."

"I like tender and sweet," I mumbled defensively, frowning down into my empty glass.

"Mm."

"What does that mean? Would you look at me and stop ogling Martell, please? I need your undivided attention when you insult me."

She laughed again, twisting on her stool and draping her arm on the back of mine. Her full sleeve of colorful orchids with a snake slithering between seemed more menacing than usual at the moment.

"I didn't mean it as an insult. Of course you like tender and sweet. Who doesn't? What I mean is, you tend to choose men and women you can dominate. And from what you've told me about Gareth, he does *not* fit into that category."

This whole conversation felt very reminiscent to the one I'd had with Clara.

"You're captivated because he won't bow down and do your bidding. I think you need a challenge," Kaya added gently, "someone who can take the reins for a while. Don't you ever get tired of being the one in control all the time?"

Like a rock falling to the river bottom, I felt the answer resonate deep inside. It wasn't something I ever thought about. I was used to being the woman out front, leading in everything that I did. In business, friendships, relationships. I was the go-to girl for plans, for leadership, even entertainment as the life of the party. For everything really.

Would it be nice to let someone else take the reins?

Fuck yes, it would.

But...

"Gareth is just so... so..."

I couldn't wrangle my thoughts to coalesce into one single word that described the man. He was pushy and arrogant, but also brilliant and pragmatic. He was fine as fuck. Not to mention the off-the-charts magical signature that nearly punched me across the room the few times I felt him vibrating with his own power. Like when Richard was around.

And finally, there was that soft spot of vulnerability he showed when speaking of supernatural orphans. There was just no possible way I could hate a man who fought for the rights and safety of children. Belatedly, I realized he had slid out of the enemies category after our dinner at Daisy Duke's.

"I see," said Kaya, gloating over my inability to form a complete sentence about him.

"Hey, ladies. Can I get you a drink?" A hot guy with longish hair, a great smile, and a cool neck tattoo beamed down at me, then Kaya.

"We're all good. Thank you," I told him.

I could see that look of determination in his eyes as he leaned heavier into myspace. "How about a dance then?"

"That's nice of you to ask," I told him, then pushed out a pulse of magical persuasion. "You can go flirt with someone else now though."

Immediately, he stood straight and wandered over to a pretty blonde a few feet over.

"Well, well," said Kaya before taking a sip of her drink. "Now you're using magic to push away guys you'd normally be dragging to the dance floor."

Raising a haughty brow, I said, "I just wasn't interested."

"Because there's only one man who interests you."

Suddenly, the opening notes of "Strangelove" pumped through the club.

"Yes!" I popped off the stool and grabbed Kaya, thankful for the distraction. "This is the one I requested. Let's go dance!"

I glanced up toward the upstairs balcony as we wound toward the dance floor, lights pulsing. My heart skittered to a halt to find none other than Gareth Blackwater watching me, hands set wide and wrapped around the railing.

"Holy fuck," I muttered toward my feet to avoid his gaze, yanking Kaya closer. "He's here!"

The music was loud and pounding.

"Who is?" she asked, leaning toward me.

"The grim." I gave her a wide-eyed toss of my head upward. "But don't look!"

She looked up immediately. Of course. "Where?"

Trying not to be so obvious, I kept dancing and glanced quickly toward the balcony but he was gone.

Though we'd just been talking about him, I hadn't conjured him out of my fantasies or something. I hadn't imagined him. *Had I?* I shrugged, exhaling a deep, agitated breath to focus on the music.

We continued to dance, letting the music and the two-cosmo buzz carry me away a little. Still, I searched every corner of the room for him until I finally found him.

He was now leaning against a pillar next to the dais where the DJ was. While the DJ wasn't putting on a grand show like he did the weekend I was last here, he was saying a word or two between some of the songs. But it wasn't the DJ holding my attention.

It was most definitely the man in black slacks and starched, dove-gray dress shirt, soaking up the deep blue lighting pulsing overhead. He'd rolled his sleeves up to his forearms, his tattoos accented by his casually crossed arms. The simple sight of his exposed forearms and all that sexy ink had me sweating.

I couldn't keep my eyes off of him as everyone danced around me. Apparently, the feeling was mutual. His dark gaze, hooded in shadows, remained absorbed on me. Not a smile on his face. Completely stoic and seemingly indifferent as usual.

But he so wasn't. Not at all. Even from here and around the bodies who kept disrupting our eye contact, I sensed the smoldering gaze beneath that cool façade.

Finally, I looked away, down at the floor as I moved to the beat, realizing what I was wearing. I'd dressed in a black corset that overlay a red silk slip dress. Even though the dress hit right above my knees and covered most of my cleavage above the bodice of my corset, I was aware what this outfit did to my figure.

My thighs were sweating and not from the dancing. It was from the fact that Gareth was only about twenty feet away, devouring me with his intense gaze and I knew he was enjoying what he saw.

You just going to stand there and stare all night? I asked him, mind to mind.

He didn't answer, but I caught a quirk of his lips.

Someone is shy? And I thought you were a man of action, I teased.

Closing my eyes and leaning my head back, I started singing the lyrics, thinking of the man across the room. Kaya danced close, moving to the beat. This was our favorite way to cut loose.

When I dared to peer over at Gareth again, he was leaning over and talking to the DJ who'd removed his headphones to listen and nod. How did Gareth know the DJ?

I'd requested another song right after this one, "I Melt with You" by Modern English. But that wasn't what melded into the final notes of "Strangelove." The crowd slowed its rhythm to move to the sensual tempo of "Lullaby" by the Cure.

Kaya laughed beside me, pulling me close and whispering into my ear. "I'm going to take a break at the bar. Looks like you're about to have company."

Sure enough, Gareth had moved off the wall and was stalking me with steady, slow steps through the crowd. They parted for him automatically, like even the humans grinding on each other knew the power of the man moving like a force all his own toward me.

I held his gaze and smiled at his song choice, swaying and moving my hips seductively, singing the words. This was a super creepy tune. Robert Smith crooned about a spiderman capturing his prey and eating him for dinner tonight.

Gareth was mouthing the words, too, as he cut through the crowd, coming closer and closer. The blue lights pulsed softly over his coal-black hair and pale-white skin, making him look like a dark angel. A dark angel intensely focused on his target. I shivered pleasantly.

By the time he reached me, my chest was heaving and my thighs were slick with sweat, my panties damp with arousal. I couldn't help it. The way this man moved and looked and watched. He tied me in knots, and it was all I could do not to bite his full bottom lip the second he stood in front of me.

He didn't say a word as he started swaying in perfect counterpoint to me, his long-fingered hands sliding to grip my waist. Then his knees bent and shoulders moved forward alternately, perfectly mirroring my sensual movements to the music. His hands slid to my hips, exerting just the slightest pressure to lead me.

Holy fuck. Gareth could dance.

I hadn't prepared for that. I hadn't ever thought the ice man could move his body in the most erotic slow dance I'd ever experienced. The only place we were touching was where he had a firm grip on my hips, guiding me to move the way he wanted.

My arms were still at my sides, and he was unraveling me with nothing more than his beautifully clenched jaw and piercing gaze. I didn't want him to have all of the control, so I lifted my arms to encircle his neck, letting my fingertips trail along his nape.

His grip tightened, pulling me closer till my breasts were against his chest and our hips grazed with each sway back and forth, back and forth.

Those black eyes glittered with primal fire, and I was the one who'd sparked the flame. A burning warmth filled my chest, winding its way lower. His nostrils flared.

He started mouthing the lyrics again, drawing a wicked smile from me.

"Are you the spiderman?" I asked, our breaths mingling, mouths inches apart.

"No, Lavinia." He shook his head then dipped closer to me. I was sure he would kiss me, but he skimmed his nose along my jaw until his lips brushed my ear. "You are," he grated, biting my lobe. "And I'm so fucking caught in your web."

Then I felt the heavenly sensation of his warm mouth on my skin. And teeth. Oh, his fucking teeth. He was scraping and sucking at the same time, and I couldn't recall one stupid reason why we shouldn't be fucking each other's brains out.

I dug my nails into his neck and pressed my body tighter to his, clinging to him. All the while he kept us moving to the music, a wicked rhythm that now had his hard dick pressed tortuously against my abdomen.

His mouth coasted higher with light nips and tiny flicks of his tongue. It was like he was tasting me, not kissing me. Like a predator determining if his prey was good enough to eat.

"Gareth," I whispered. No, it was part moan and part plea, but I didn't care. I wanted more. I wanted *him*.

One of his hands skated up the side of my body, fingers spreading into my thick hair which he fisted and then tugged my head back, arching my neck so that I was looking directly up into his dark gaze. Still keeping us in a semblance of the dance, though I'd long since lost track of the song, of the crowd, of everything but my stealthy, patient hunter.

He dipped lower, his tongue tracing my bottom lip, his eyes slipping closed on a groan.

"Stop teasing," I whispered.

A sensuous quirk of his lips. Then he angled his mouth and moaned into our first kiss, consuming me with luxurious laps of his tongue against mine, sucking on my tongue when I retreated. Like he couldn't get enough of my taste. His other hand slid to the small of my back, then to my ass over the silk of my dress.

"Fucking hell," he rasped against my lips, breaking the kiss.

When I opened my eyes, I thought I'd spontaneously combust at the feral lust in his expression. Something else there too. I don't know. His magic buzzed along my skin, making me want to rub up against him. Actually, I *was* rubbing against him.

"Do you want to go somewhere more private?" he asked,

voice deep and dangerous. No mistaking the intent with that question.

When I nodded, done with any more pretenses, he immediately stepped back, grabbed my hand, and tugged me through the crowd toward a hallway. I didn't think to ask where we were going or consider if this was the right decision or not. I didn't care anymore. I needed to quench the fire burning between my legs and sizzling along my skin. The one Gareth had started the first day I laid eyes on him.

CHAPTER TEN

~GARETH~

Taking Lavinia by the hand and leading her to my office was the last thing I had in mind for tonight, and yet it was the first thing I thought once she'd whispered my name in a soft, raspy plea. I needed more than what I could do to her on the dance floor of my own club. Since she'd agreed to find a more discreet spot, it seemed she was of the same mind.

My office was the closest place for privacy. But not ideal for sex, especially not the kind of sex I wanted to have with Lavinia. The all-night-sweat-soaked-sheets kind. But right now, I'd take whatever I could get, my body rigid and feverish with need.

Pulling her into my office, I closed and locked the door. The music still played through the many monitors on the wall, my desk facing them. The only other furniture in the room was a black-felt sofa and a scarlet rug. Thankfully, the sofa was big and plush. I'd ordered it knowing I'd end up sleeping on it if I worked late some nights.

Before the club opening, I oversaw installation of the expensive memorabilia I'd acquired and the tech as well as making sure the construction workers got the design correct. I wanted to be on-hand, so I worked out of my office and often slept here. Right now, I was so fucking glad I'd bought this big ass couch. Because that's where I corralled Lavinia with slow, determined steps.

She moved backward, not to get away, but to tease, her sinful smile luring me closer. "You know the owner of this place or something?"

"Or something."

Her legs hit the sofa and she plopped down, that torture-device of a corset pushing her delectable breasts higher. I made note of the hooks lining the front.

"He or she won't mind you using their office?"

"Not at all." I pushed her back onto the sofa and then settled on top of her.

Pure. Fucking. Heaven.

I couldn't even imagine how good it would feel to be inside her.

"Lavinia," I whispered against the silken skin of her neck, nuzzling before licking and kissing a line up to her mouth.

She squirmed beneath me and pressed her breasts against my chest, her delicate fingers tangling in the back of my hair.

"Kiss me," she begged.

Immediately, my mouth was on hers, a groan slipping from my throat at her intoxicating taste. My vision hazed when she parted her thighs and welcomed me against her hot pussy.

"Fuck," I murmured against her lips, inhaling the sharp scent of her arousal.

In the club, my DJ, Bentley, had put on the second song I'd asked him to, disrupting whatever was on the wait list. I'd planned to be singing this one to her on the dance floor, not realizing I'd have her on my sofa. "I Wanna Be Your Slave" by Maneskin pumped through the monitors and the walls. And fuck if it wasn't so sadly true.

Bracing my weight on one forearm, I mounded her breast

with one hand and used my TK to unhook the top three loops of her corset. She didn't seem to notice, moaning louder as I drank deep at her mouth. When her top eased open, I slid the red silky top down, exposing a see-through black lace bra.

"You're trying to fucking kill me, aren't you?" I whispered.

She smiled, eyes half-black with arousal, her pupils swallowing the blue. "Go on, Blackwater," she teased, her hands wandering over my ass and then working between us to my crotch. "Don't be shy."

Growling, I wrapped up her wrists and pressed them above her head, watching as my TK tugged the cup of her bra down till her full breast popped free.

She gasped, eyes wide as she glanced down then back at me. "You can do that?"

Grinning, I let her wrists go and rose to my knees to straddle her, but I held her arms in place with my TK. She tugged but couldn't move.

"Holy shit." Her expression tightened in wonder and more arousal.

Telekinetics of the supernatural world were known for their abilities to move and crush objects with TK. But my talents were much more fine-tuned. I could use the power with whisper-soft delicacy and intricate manipulation, like unbuttoning corsets and holding the slender wrists of my woman to keep her firmly but gently in place.

"Scared?" I asked, for that was the last thing I wanted.

This wasn't something I'd planned to reveal, but I also couldn't control my instincts to overpower her using all of my skills and assets. But only if she wanted me to.

Her breath quickened, her chest rising and falling, her dusky nipple tightening beneath my gaze.

"No," she finally answered.

"Good."

I tightened my jaw, remaining on my knees as I eased the other side of her dress down with one hand. Once both of her beautiful breasts were exposed to me, I licked the pads of my thumbs and circled her nipples till they were tight, her hips coming off the sofa seeking friction.

"Gareth." She pulled at her arms, but I kept them pinned with invisible force.

Using TK, I slid the hem of her dress higher until I could see the triangle of black lace right below where I straddled her, my legs spread wide so I could reach her breasts from this height. Again, the hypnotic scent that was Lavinia's alone punched me with another wave of burning desire.

"You smell so fucking good," I murmured, watching her squirm and pant, her eyes dark with lust. "I want to eat you whole, Lavinia."

Her gaze dropped to my tented pants. Pinching her nipples with a little force, I let them go on her flinch and a gasp. Slowly, I unbuckled my belt and whipped it out of its loops then dropped it to the floor.

She was entranced, watching my hands, her hips coming off the sofa, her milk-pale, rounded thighs squeezing together. If I'd let her go to touch me and do what she wanted, I'd come within seconds and that just wasn't going to happen.

After unzipping and pushing my pants and briefs down enough to pull out my cock, I gave it a heavy stroke.

Her lips parted on a slight gasp, then she licked them on a whimper. "Gareth," she moaned, her pupils dilating further.

"So fucking beautiful," I murmured more to myself as I watched her tongue travel over her lips.

Bracing one hand on the arm of the sofa in between her TK-bound wrists, I planted my knees higher. She was already opening her mouth, and I had to squeeze my eyes closed at the erotic sight of her eagerly parting her lips to take my cock.

"Good girl," I praised, pushing the crown past her lips.

She moaned and sucked at the same time, my body flooding with adrenaline at the sound of her in ecstasy while she swallowed me. I reached down with my free hand and cupped the back of her neck, cradling her gently as I fucked her sweet mouth. I swept my thumb to the corner of her mouth and along her bottom lip, wanting to feel her take me.

"So perfect."

Her hips writhed as she clenched her legs together. I reached behind me, still pumping my hips in slow, measured strokes. When I skimmed my fingers between her thighs, she opened them for me. Her easy surrender made me harder.

Sliding her panties aside, I glided my middle finger through the slick folds of her pussy. She immediately bucked up, her eyes pleading for what she needed as she swallowed my dick.

Smiling, I circled her entrance, dragging her cream back to circle and stroke her swollen clit. "I want you to take me deeper."

She nodded, whimpering, and sucked harder as I rocked my hips a little farther, tapping the back of her throat.

"Fuck, Lavinia."

I slid two fingers inside her, and her hips came off the couch, trying to fuck my fingers faster than I'd wanted.

"No topping from the bottom," I warned, pulling my fingers free and giving her clit a light tap of warning.

She flinched, her lips clamping hard on my dick, grazing the sensitive flesh with her teeth.

"Goddamn," I laughed, sliding out of her mouth. "Dangerous woman."

She panted, her eyes glazed with desperate need. "I wasn't finished," she said.

She was aggressive. It turned me the fuck on, but I also needed her submission. Although I was unlikely to get it this first time, there was no doubt in my mind that there would be another. And another.

Shifting down her body, I maneuvered my shoulders between her legs. Gripping her thighs, I spread her wider, righting her panties and then opened my mouth on her pussy. Pulling the panties tight, I sucked her through the lace.

Her eyes rolled back and her hips rocked up with frantic thrusts, the spikes of her heels digging into my back. The pleasure-pain had me groaning and grazing my teeth over her lace-covered clit.

"Please, Gareth, please, please, please." She chanted and moaned, her breasts heaving as she climbed higher, her arms straining against the invisible bonds.

Pressing her thighs higher, I sucked at her entrance, knowing the fabric barrier was torture.

"Goddess save me," she whispered louder.

I nipped her inner thigh and laughed against her milky skin, sliding the lace off of her slit, swollen and wet from my attentions. She moaned.

"You are the goddess," I rumbled against her skin, scraping my jaw against the silken softness, then I captured her gaze, "And I am your slave."

What the hell had come over me? I never said things like that to a woman. If anything at all, it was things such as *just like that* or *harder* or *open wider*. Never words of worship. But this woman was unraveling me, second by second. Moan by moan.

And for the record, I never used my own ability of persuasion with a woman in bed. It just wasn't as satisfying if she was compelled to do my will. Which is why watching Lavinia writhe and squirm and whimper with need, slowly coming undone at my touch, spoke to some primal part of me. I had to focus to keep from letting the darkness out. That demon wanted to wrap her up and keep her for fucking ever.

She panted, spreading her knees wider for me. "Please Gareth, I can't take it." She pressed her hips up again, begging me for more.

I flicked her clit with my tongue. She groaned.

"Just pull out a condom and fuck me. I need it so bad." Then in a whisper that was almost inaudible as if she didn't mean to say it, "I need you."

I stopped and sat up, staring at her in disbelief for two

reasons. One, I never thought to hear her say something like those last three words to me. But the other had my gut clenching.

"What's wrong? Why'd you stop?" she whined.

"I don't have a condom," I admitted through gritted teeth and disbelief. I tried to come to grips with this tragic turn of events, but I couldn't.

"Wait. A grim, who seems to be always so prepared, doesn't have a condom?" Her head fell back on a deep exhale. "I can't believe you weren't packing several, waiting around for this opportunity."

My gaze trailed from her soaked panties up to her full breasts, tight nipples, ending on her lips, swollen from sucking my cock.

"I can't either." I hadn't wanted a quick fuck in my office anyway. Not for our first time. "Plan B it is, beautiful."

Looping my fingers into the outside edge of her panties, I slid them off and tucked them in my pocket. I released her from the TK and pulled her to her feet, admiring the heels and decided to still leave those on.

"What are—?"

Before she could wonder too long, I laid down on the sofa, propping my head on the arm. Taking her hand, I tugged her back toward me. But before she fell onto my chest, I used TK to lift her in the air, horizontal above me, and swiveled her around to face the other direction then lowered her pussy to my waiting mouth.

She jerked and moaned, but I held her hard, the taste of her so overwhelming, I groaned with ecstasy as I lapped her up.

"Oh, God, Gareth," she moaned, rocking gently against my mouth.

While I was barely coherent enough to pull away for even a second, I slapped her ass and nipped her inner thigh. "Put my dick in your mouth and suck me hard. I want to feel those teeth again."

She laughed while gripping the base of my cock, a gust of her warm breath on my head tightening my balls.

"Kinky bastard," she said before swiping her tongue around the crown.

Hissing, I cracked my palm across her cheek again, hard enough to sting then tight to her round flesh and squeezed. "No teasing, Lavinia," I commanded. "I want to come down your throat. Right fucking now."

I pumped two fingers inside her with a deep thrust and opened my mouth over her clit, groaning again at the heavenly taste of her. She immediately did as I said and swallowed me deep, pumping her mouth as I thrust my hips upward and groaned at her whimpering and gagging noises.

Relentlessly, I worked her clit while her muscles tightened around my fingers. She was so soaked, my fingers fucking her made that wet sex sound that drove me nearly insane. To think I had her dripping and I was drinking her down while she deep-throated my cock.

At the first sign of her orgasm fluttering around my fingers, she hummed a deep moan around my dick. That was it. I gripped her ass and spread her so I could fuck her with my tongue, kissing her hard and deep.

I groaned when I came.

"Good girl," I praised and lapped at her, savoring her taste while she savored mine

She was still sucking when I finally stopped throbbing. Before I was remotely down from the high, I used my TK to lift her and spin her around.

She squealed and laughed, hovering in the air above me. Smiling, I lowered her to me and spread my fingers into her hair, cradling her skull. I kissed her deep and long. She made that sweet, soft noise in the back of her throat as she kissed me back, the tilted smile of a satisfied woman spread across her beautiful face at the same time.

I broke the kiss. "Next time, I'll have a box of condoms ready for your pleasure."

She smiled, her fingers combing through my hair. "I love how you're so sure of a next time, Blackwater."

"I don't need to be psychic to know that we both want more than this."

"So cocky."

I grinned.

She rolled her eyes. "I meant, conceited." She leaned closer, capturing my gaze and whispered, "Though I did quite enjoy the cocky side of you." She emphasized it with a thrust of her hips.

"Fucking hell, woman." With a hand at her nape, I pulled her mouth back to mine so I could taste her a little longer. I couldn't seem to keep my mouth off her body. She was driving me to delicious madness.

She was unraveling every part of me with slow kisses, delicate fingers, and insanely soft skin. I wanted to inhale her like a drug and stay high forever.

We kissed a while longer, but she parted us first. I wasn't about to. Then she climbed off of me and righted her top. "So, you think it's wise that we let this happen again?"

I stood and started hooking her corset closed, with my hands not my TK.

"Wise or not, I want to do it again."

She didn't comment, but her smile tipped up as we both continued putting her clothes back in order.

I didn't want to frighten her with the thoughts going round in my head. There was no fucking way that our affair ended after this. This was just the beginning.

"Can all grims use telekinesis like you?" she asked, watching me notch the last hook between her breasts.

I smoothed her straps over her shoulders, wondering why I felt so compelled to share information with her. It wasn't something grims did with anyone outside our own race.

"No. Only some."

She peered up at me, looking perfectly sex-rumpled, but her gaze was clear, observing me closely. "Are you different than most grims in other ways?"

Sliding my palms to cradle her slender neck, I eased closer. "I am."

"How? Tell me."

I couldn't help the grin cracking my normally cool façade. I think I'd smiled more in the last hour than I had all of last month.

"So curious." I stroked my thumbs across the base of her throat, over her delicate collarbone then back to feel her pulse.

"Why won't you tell me? What's up with grims that they're so secretive?"

Now that, I could and would answer. Well, partly anyway.

"Grims have a strong core belief that information is everything. More powerful than money or fame or anything else. We also prefer to keep ourselves in check."

Because only grims understood what it felt like to fight and hold back a living, breathing darkness that wanted to propel us toward wickedness every day of our lives.

"Is there something you're hiding from other supernaturals?"

She was so smart, my Lavinia. My palms drifted up to cup her jaw. "Yes. We are."

"Is it dangerous?"

Her magic hummed to life, trying to wield her influence over me so that I'd answer her question.

Grinning yet again, I brushed a light kiss across her lips, savoring the sensation of her pillowy mouth yielding to my firmer one.

"Yes. Very," I admitted, but not because of her bewitching persuasion.

In truth, she couldn't overpower me with her magic if she tried. Few who walked this earth could.

"Are *you* dangerous?" she whispered, eyes dark as midnight as she clasped her slender white fingers around my wrists.

"To you?" I brushed my mouth against hers again, holding her gaze. "Never."

Couldn't say the same for everyone else.

A vision of glassy eyes, tears of blood, and twisted limbs flashed to mind. I shook it off and took her hand.

"Come on. Let me get you back to your friend."

She glanced around. "Wait. My panties. Where'd they go?"

"I'm keeping them."

"What? I can't walk out there without panties."

"Sure you can." I unlocked the door, looking at her over my shoulder, marveling that she still let me hold her hand. "Every time you realize they're gone, you can remember what we did together in here."

Her brow pinched. "It's weird you want to keep my panties."

"Since when did you ever think I was normal?"

She laughed. "Pervert."

"Only for you," I mumbled as I guided her out the door and back into the loud pumping music.

"So you know the owner of the club?" she shouted.

"I do."

"It's a really cool club. Perfect branding. Tell them for me."

I turned then and backed her to the wall, hands at her hips. "Tell him yourself. Right now."

Realization dawned and she lifted her chin and laughed, leaning her head against the wall. "No. Now your ego will be unbearable to deal with."

"It always has been," I whispered into her ear, sliding my hand between her thighs and gliding softly through her hot wetness. "So soft. I want to taste you again."

"Gareth." She clenched her fists in my shirt. "I don't know if this is a good idea." Despite her words, she pulled me closer till my chest brushed hers. "Us messing around during the campaign."

Right as her hips rocked forward against my palm, I gave her another petting stroke and then removed my hand back to her hip.

"Take the time you need to settle this in your mind, Lavinia," I told her with sincere earnest. "But know this. I won't stop until I have you in my bed."

And then I'd never let her leave. She had me utterly bewitched. Body and soul. I couldn't walk away.

The darkness purred in agreement, whispering to me, telling me she was mine whether she accepted it or not. The monster wanted her at all costs, twisting my will. The jarring sensation of the black rattling its cage pierced a stabbing pain into my chest. It was demanding to take over.

I flinched back, letting her go, staring at the floor while mentally pushing the well of sinister essence back where it belonged.

The fuck?

I'd always kept my personal demon under control. The beast who lived in that hollow cave where I'd chained him always craved to break free and devour what it needed. I pressed a hand to my sternum, stunned by the stinging ache. I'd managed to live with and control my monster my entire life, but now it was pushing to escape.

Because of her.

The thing about grims was that our inner demons weren't simply psychological struggles or conflicting emotions. They were sentient creatures, given life by our ancestral curse. Not just dark magic, but black magic. Blood magic. It was sealed to our souls by our twisted, malevolent forefather and the things he'd done. The unbreakable spells he'd cast.

"Are you okay?" she whispered, reaching out to touch my chest.

I stepped back, my gaze snagging on her worried expression.

This was unexpected, but I'd always been able to manage it. Except that first time.

"Fine," I reassured her, pulling that cloak of cool control back around me.

Taking her hand, I led her through the throng back to the bar where her friend was flirting with Martell. Lavinia took the stool next to her, and I stood between them, nodding politely while Kaya waxed eloquent about the club and Martell's mixologist skills.

After a few minutes, needing to reassure Lavinia that my abrupt change in mood had nothing to do with her, I leaned close to her, wrapping my hand around her wrist in her lap.

"I'll see you at the Pin-up Photo Shoot tomorrow."

"Yes." She smiled sweetly, easing some of the tension tightening my chest.

With a brush of my thumb over her pulse, I gave her wrist a gentle squeeze then left. Nodding to my bouncer Blake at the door, I strode toward the parking garage on the corner at a brisk clip.

Tonight was…surprising. Shocking really.

My hopes were to see Lavinia and perhaps dance with her, lure her a little closer to becoming my lover. Not to kiss her, touch her, taste her. The mere thought had my blood burning again. But it was the other stirring that hadn't simply been surprising but disturbing. A touch horrifying.

She didn't only tempt me, but my monster as well. A creature that should never be unleashed and should never be fed. I blew out a breath in the cool night air, knowing I'd better keep the reins on him choke-hold tight. Because one thing was for certain.

There was no way I was giving up Lavinia.

CHAPTER ELEVEN

~GARETH~

In the corner of the studio, Willard was managing the live feed on our YouTube channel and posting comments when the photographer Jackson started with the first model. I'd double-checked that my software MIMIC had directed our ads toward the targeted traffic, but other than that there was nothing for me to do. My software did the job, and I wasn't the socially interactive type—in person or online—so I left that to Willard.

Not that he was the engaging sort either. But our team extrovert was Lavinia, and she was currently somewhere in the dressing rooms undressing down to a bathing suit for this little event.

I hadn't seen or talked to her since last night. My body thrummed with tension, craving just the sight of her. I wanted to look in her eyes and see if there was any regret there. Or perhaps longing.

After meeting the Jackson and checking in with Willard, I'd hung back, watching his assistants set up the lighting around the sleek and shiny black Harley—the prop for the models today.

The first one stepped in from a hallway entrance, not the way we'd come in through the reception area. A blonde bombshell padded toward the staged area in an intricately designed white bathing suit, multiple straps overlapped her breasts and crossed her shoulders, zig-zagging to reveal skin and tattoos on her hip, lower back, and one shoulder.

After twenty minutes of shooting, Jackson said, "Good, Melanie. Now let's get some on the bike."

Melanie posed herself in different positions, apparently used to this sort of prop. I couldn't deny the woman was beautiful, but my gaze kept darting toward the door she'd come through, waiting for who I truly wanted to see.

As Melanie left and another model stepped in—not Lavinia —someone else entered from behind me. I didn't even need to turn to recognize the black signature resonating in the room.

True to his word, Richard had come to *check out* our first fundraising event. But I knew that wasn't what or who he'd come to check out.

The darkness stirred again. So soon. Too soon.

I maneuvered closer to Willard along the right side. Hands in my pockets, I watched Richard flirt with one of the pretty assistants, Trisha, an Aura witch who'd been ensuring everything was perfect on set since I'd gotten here.

Jackson, a werewolf, glanced over his shoulder as model number two left and a third walked in. Not Lavinia. The young photographer's eyes rolled yellow-gold at the sight of Richard with his assistant. Then he called her over to allegedly fix something on the back of the model's bikini.

I couldn't help but let a smile slip. Jackson's wolf instincts told him that something was wrong with Richard. He may not be able to detect it for what it truly was like I could, but his wolf wanted his assistant far away from the likes of him.

About that time, Richard noticed me, his expression tightening. Not surprising. I'd been cold as fuck to him from the first. He gave me a terse nod then looked away.

Hmm. That wouldn't do.

I ambled over slowly, making a point to watch Jackson work with the new girl on set. As I stepped up beside him, I kept my professional demeanor in place.

"Morning, Gareth. How are the statistics so far?"

Ah, shop talk. Nice.

"Richard." I gave him a nod. "Better than expected. The online subscribers doubled overnight."

"Good to hear. Your team is working well together?"

He gave me a quick sidelong glance. I feigned an expression of respectfulness rather than the blatant hatred seething under my skin. He was the kind of man who expected respect and deference. I didn't mind pretending. For now.

Though I hadn't discovered his secrets yet, his mannerisms had already persuaded me he was a narcissist, which made complete sense. Most criminals able to evade getting caught tended to think rather highly of themselves. I knew he was of this ilk. He reeked of overindulgent self-importance.

"We're working very well together. We all have our strengths to contribute."

The third model exited just as the door opened and in stepped Lavinia.

"You most certainly do," were the words that slithered out of Richard's mouth.

A guttural growl reverberated deep inside me, my demon wanting to burst out of the cave and rip his tongue out. I quelled it easily enough, even while my attention was solely riveted on the raven-haired goddess walking across the room toward the set.

She wore her long black hair in silky waves that slid over bare ivory shoulders to the middle of her back. Her red bathing suit was cut to look like a spider web across her stomach, larger pieces covering her breasts. It left little to the imagination, but it was the spiderweb design that taunted me, reminding me of our dance at the club last night and what it had led to.

She glanced my way, her delicious mouth—highlighted by dark red lipstick—then slid into a smile. I believe she knew exactly what that swimsuit was doing to me.

I was so caught up in her, I almost missed the halo of malevolence pushing against me. Usually, it was my own darkness that spread to others, urging them toward their baser desires. But no, this had nothing to do with me. This was that same innate evil I'd sensed from Richard before. Except now, his focus was entirely on Lavinia.

I looked away and closed my eyes, inhaled a deep breath then exhaled slowly. I needed to remain calm, not lose my shit on him right here and now. I had no actual proof of what he was, but my instincts told me I was right. And I'd never been wrong yet.

Still, I decided to take the opportunity to test my theory. Obtain a little more circumstantial evidence until Peonie came through with a solid lead for me.

"Mmm. Sweet, isn't she?" I said softly where only he could hear, keeping my gaze on Lavinia as she leaned back with both hands on the seat of the Harley behind her, spectacular breasts jutting forward, sensuous smile for the camera.

"Darkside" by Neoni started to play, and Lavinia moved to the music, knowing exactly how to angle her beautiful body and face for the camera. Through the scooped sides of the swimsuit, there was a dragon tattoo curving up toward her shoulder where it disappeared under her hair.

In my peripheral view, I caught Richard staring at me, obviously wondering if I was messing with him. I pushed a second wave of coercion toward him and added, "Don't you think?"

"She is," he agreed, returning his gaze to Lavinia. "So sweet."

Clenching my teeth till I felt something click in my jaw, I

breathed out through my nose then added, "Too bad she prefers women."

That was a lie, of course. Lavinia was bisexual. But I was baiting him.

"Does she now?" he chuckled lightly. "That'll make things interesting."

"How so?" I asked casually. "I already tried. Trust me. Men don't stand a chance."

Richard's gray-eyed gaze turned menacingly predatory, roaming down her body and back up. It honestly took every ounce of willpower not to slide the pen out of Trisha's hand and shoot it through Richard's eye socket.

"Maybe for you," he huffed on another laugh, still not tearing his gaze away from her. "My chances are a given. No matter what she prefers."

Mother. Fucker.

Sweat beaded on my brow as I kept firm pressure on the mental door blocking my dark essence, which rumbled to be set free, shaking his cage with fury.

Then Trisha's pen popped out of her hand and speared onto the floor six feet away. "Oh," she mumbled, frowning at the pen as she picked it up.

I'd subconsciously actually started to shoot it toward Richard then dropped it to the floor, my monster fighting with my conscience. Vibrating with rage, I watched Richard pull his phone from his pocket and pretend to check something then subtly slant it toward the set. This asshole was actually snapping pictures of Lavinia.

I was going to kill him if I didn't walk away. Not figuratively. I was going to literally dismantle his skull and force the bone fragments inward till his brain turned to jelly.

"Excuse me," I mumbled stepping in front of him and lightly tapping his phone with my forefinger.

As I strode toward the door Lavinia had come through, I heard Richard cursing to himself. His phone had just stopped working for some reason. Probably because I'd melted the motherboard with a tap of my finger. My telekinesis was a special brand of magic. I could move microscopic components not even visible to the eye.

I smiled as I disappeared through the door and down the hall, satisfied that if I wasn't permitted to murder him—yet— then at least I could be sure he wouldn't have stolen photos of her to use for jacking off later.

I followed her scent down the hall, passing a few open doorways where other models were dressing. I didn't stop until I was standing in the doorway of a room where her scent was strongest.

Kaya was smoothing some lotion onto her skin, already in a black bikini. "Hi, Gareth. Lavinia is shooting now."

"Yeah. I know." I walked to the sofa behind the dressing table and vanity mirrors. "I'm just going to wait here."

"Suit yourself," she said, heading for the door, her sleek, black ponytail swishing behind her.

As soon as she was gone, I slammed the door shut with my TK and closed my eyes, letting my head fall back onto the sofa. Using the skills Aunt Lucille had taught me, I pictured the cave in my mind, shutting the giant wooden door and locking it with the skeleton key. Then I shut and locked the iron door with the rivets, then the outer steel door that was two feet thick.

The beast was secured and the cool wave of indifference swept away the boiling rage urging me to break bone and spill blood. I settled deeper, my muscles relaxing as I practiced the other meditation exercises, tricks of the mind that Aunt Lucille had taught me to keep me from becoming the murderous monster who lived inside me.

I'd wait here for Lavinia then calmly tell her she wasn't permitted to be anywhere around that fuckface, Richard Davis, when I wasn't around. I already knew how she'd take this news, but it wasn't open for discussion. She simply needed to agree that I was right.

Okay, apparently the beast was still riding me hard, those darker urges to dominate and master still lingering close to the surface.

If I knew she was out of harm's way, then maybe I could think straight long enough to figure out how to discover what Richard had actually done in his past. Something that whispered wickedly to my own demon, calling him out to play. Whatever sins stained his soul, he'd kept them well-hidden and secret. But he had no idea who was onto him. Or the lengths I'd go to find out.

I had my suspicions, but I needed proof. Until then, I had to keep him the fuck away from my woman.

CHAPTER TWELVE

~LIVVY~

It was so hard to focus on Jackson's direction when my attention was solely riveted on Gareth. Especially after he'd walked over to talk to Richard. They seemed to be having a cordial conversation from my small glances in their direction. But that was completely ridiculous. I knew that Gareth hated his guts. By the time I'd moved around the bike to try a pose Jackson wanted, Gareth was gone.

Strange. I hadn't expected him to abandon our first fundraiser midway through. Likely, he didn't want to be around Richard.

Still, that was weird. I figured after he saw this swimsuit I'd spent this morning cutting and adjusting just for him, he'd stick around a little longer.

"Okay, that's good, Liv. I think we've got it."

Kaya was already in the room, waiting to go on. She handed me a cover-up before tossing hers over the chair she'd been sitting in.

She grinned and opened her mouth to say something, but suddenly Richard was there.

"Terrific work, Livvy," he crooned, gray eyes devouring my breasts.

I pulled my cover-up tighter and tied it at the waist. "Thank you. Once I get changed, I'll check on the live feed on YouTube and interact with our subscribers."

"Brilliant idea." His gaze swept to Kaya, her slim body draped over the bike. "I can see why we've gotten so many followers."

He grinned, and though yes, I was well aware of the old marketing strategy *sex sells*, there was something in his greedy gaze that made me cringe.

"Glad you're impressed," I said tightly, easing back a step.

"Very impressed. I'd love to talk to you about your plans beyond this contest. You're an extremely bright young woman. Maybe we could talk it over when you're available."

"At the office, sure." My survival instincts were on full alert.

"Or over dinner." His gray eyes heated, and I was relieved to see they hadn't trailed back to my breasts but remained fixed on my face. He even wore a somewhat professional, guileless expression. It didn't exactly put me at ease, but it made me feel slightly more comfortable with this awkward conversation.

"The office would be better," I replied with emphasis.

"Whatever you wish. I'll catch up to you there."

I nodded my head toward the door. "I need to change."

Like, *don't try to fucking follow me, creeper.*

"Of course. Don't let me keep you. You and your team are doing great work." He glanced at his watch. "I'll check in with you all tomorrow for final results."

Then he walked away, and I could breathe easier. There was no mistaking that he had a thing for me. But just when I thought he was a complete lecher, he turned professional and polite.

Brushing him off, I headed down the hallway toward the

changing rooms. Carrie, a pretty red-headed witch, stepped from the first dressing room in a pink bikini.

"Smokin'." I gave her a wink.

"You too, spiderwoman."

I laughed as my thoughts swayed back to Gareth. It's not like I'd thought about much else since last night at the club.

Heaven save me, he turned me on so damn bad.

I'd never let a guy take my panties before. So pervy. But also, the fact that Gareth wanted them and wanted me to think about him all night when I realized I was panty-less was so sexy.

During our interlude in his office at the club, his cool veneer melted beneath the fucking hottest, hungry look any man had ever given me. Even under his controlled movements, there was no denying there was frenzied lust driving us both. Just thinking about it had my heartrate pumping faster.

So I was in a semi-aroused state when I stepped into my dressing room to find Gareth sprawled on the sofa, his head tipped back, eyes closed.

The cords of his pale throat and the way his veined hands were splayed next to him had my mouth watering. He was dressed in his usual tailored pants and starched dress shirt. Today's selection was steel-blue, his rolled-up cuffs revealing his sexy ink.

Slowly, he lifted his head, onyx eyes spearing me in place. They didn't waver, not even to take in my half-dressed state. I was all ready to tease him a little today, knowing he'd seen me in barely nothing at all. And yet, the look he gave me now spoke to deeper depths than lust or desire. It was jarring to say the least.

"Come here," he ordered. And it was definitely a command.

A melty sensation flooded my chest, dripping lower. I obeyed, enjoying the strange, foreign feeling of wanting to do what he told me.

His legs were set wide, his body relaxed, but his eyes weren't. They were fierce with an emotion I couldn't identify. I suddenly wished Clara was here, so she could tell me what was going on inside my grim reaper.

I stopped a foot in front of him.

"Closer," he rumbled low.

So I edged between his open knees till my own touched the sofa. He eased upright, his fingers sliding around the backs of my calves, stopping behind my knees, a sensitive spot that made me shiver.

His gaze finally dipped lower, but my cover-up hid my body. Still, he didn't lift his hands to open it as I thought—hoped—he would. No, he kept his grip firm and unmoving, not venturing higher.

"You wore this swimsuit for me."

I made it for you.

"Maybe."

He smiled, and my world tilted.

You have to understand. Gareth Blackwater was the broodiest, coldest, most untouchable man I'd ever met. Or so I'd thought. Now that I'd lifted that layer and stepped inside his private circle, a place he seemed not to allow anyone, I never wanted to leave. And when he granted me smiles like this one that struck me near mute, I wanted to kneel in front of him and do anything he asked. Or commanded. Preferably commanded, actually.

That thought both horrified and thrilled me in equal measure.

"Definitely for me," he murmured more to himself.

Deep breath in, then out. "Why'd you leave the studio?"

"So that I wouldn't kill Richard."

I laughed. He didn't.

"Are you being serious?"

"Deadly." His fingertips dragged across the backs of my knees then gripped firmly again.

"Why did you want to kill him?"

"Because he has plans for you."

"*You* have plans for me."

His black eyes darkened. I didn't think it possible but they so did. His irises were pure obsidian, actually bleeding into the white.

My God, what were grims truly?

His thumbs sculpted over the tops of my kneecaps, back and forth. "But you want what I plan to do to you."

"You're so sure?"

"Positive."

"So why don't you get started?" I nudged the side of his knee with mine.

"Not today," he said firmly.

I nodded, swallowing my disappointment. "True. We are on the job."

"That's not why."

"Then tell me." He was holding back, something I needed to know.

"Because my—" he paused and licked his lips— "I can't touch you the way I want when I'm in this state."

He wasn't toying or teasing me. He was telling me something important. Something he didn't share with just anyone.

"Explain that to me. What state is that?"

"I need you to listen to me and do what I ask." The deep baritone of his voice dropped even deeper. "Under no circumstances are you to be alone with Richard Davis."

I didn't comment that this was an order not a request as he'd implied. "You've already warned me about this."

"That was before I know what I know now."

"Which is?"

"The evil of this man is much greater than I originally thought."

"Do you have information on him or something?"

"Not yet," he growled through gritted teeth, the black of his eyes bleeding a little farther.

"Then how do you know this?"

"I've told you before."

"Because you're evil and can recognize it as a grim?" My mouth quirked in disbelief. "You aren't evil, Gareth."

"I didn't say that I was. I said it lives inside me."

"That doesn't make sense."

"I'm aware."

"Then *make* it make sense," I nearly shouted. "I want to understand. *Explain* it to me."

He was on his feet and across the room. "I can't!"

A crumpling metal sound pulled my attention to the left where a folding chair had been bent into a ball in less than two seconds. It rolled in a wobbly trail to the center of the room where it came to a stop.

Gareth's hands were on his hips and his head was down, hanging low. My chest heaved with deep breaths, my heart rate tripping faster at his burst of anger.

"We grims keep our secrets for a reason." He had his voice under control again, though it was still ragged and menacing. He was breathing roughly like me.

A heavy silence weighted the room.

"You can't explain it to me at all, Gareth?" I asked softly.

He looked up then, obviously hearing the plea in my voice. I wasn't begging because I needed to know all of his secrets. I was pleading for him to open up to me. I wanted to know more about him. I couldn't explain it, but my feelings for him had morphed beyond the scintillating desire and strained animosity always radiating between us. It was more tender now—fragile—something I wanted to explore and truly wanted to expand.

But if he couldn't open up to me, how could this go any further?

"Do you believe in monsters, Lavinia?"

Heart hammering, I held his gaze, well aware of his magic buzzing in the room. Something had set him off, and it wasn't my pushy questions.

"Even knowing about the supernatural world, I never

believed in monsters." I took a small step toward him. "Then they created Twitter."

His mouth quirked on one side, even while he remained statue-still, watching me carefully as I eased closer.

"You think you're a monster, Gareth?"

A sharp shake of his head, his eyes dark as he watched me move into his personal space. "No. But one lives inside every single grim."

"Do you mean the aura that all grims carry?"

"The aura is just a symptom. A halo effect of the demon we contain."

"What does this demon do?"

"It wants to feed. And without being contained, it will."

"What does it feed on?" By now, I was standing right in front of him. Those black eyes glinted with internal fire.

"Corruption. Power. But most of all...blood. Death."

I swallowed hard at that admission, trying to process the depth of what he was telling me. "Is yours contained?"

"Yes." Even while he answered, he clenched his jaw.

He wasn't lying but... "You're not telling me everything."

"I can't tell you everything."

I'd pushed him far enough. He vibrated with tension, fists clenched at his sides, the angle of his jaw sharp as a blade, gaze burning into me. I inched closer without touching him. He kept still as stone. It warmed me that he was this concerned on my behalf.

"I won't be alone with Richard," I whispered. "I promise."

A tangible wave of relief crashed over me like a tsunami. I inhaled a short gasp. Then his hands were in my hair, cradling my head, holding me still, and his mouth was on mine.

His lips coaxed and pressed till I opened wider, his kiss aggressive, persistent. I whimpered and he swallowed it down, clenching his fingers into my hair till my scalp stung, yet he kept our bodies apart.

When he sucked on my tongue then angled to bite my

bottom lip, I finally reached out to grasp his waist and press my body to his.

Suddenly, I was kissing air.

He was gone. I'd have thought he actually turned invisible if it weren't for the wake of wind pulling the opened door closed behind him.

I stood there, baffled by this entire interlude. Since when did grims move as fast as vampires? Vamps were the only supernaturals—the old and ultra-powerful ones, that is—who could move so fast they appeared invisible. At least, that's what I had thought.

Also, how could they be born with evil living inside of them? *What the hell were grims?!*

And why had the one whose mouth and hands I wanted all over me vanished the second things were getting hot?

I can't touch you the way I want when I'm in this state.

There was pain mingled with frustration and determination when he'd told me that. He had been protecting me.

Buzz, buzz.

I jumped, still standing where Gareth had left me. My phone vibrated again on the dressing table. I walked over and snatched it up.

JULES: FAMILY MEETING. ONE HOUR.

FROWNING, I TEXTED BACK.

ME: IS SOMETHING WRONG?
   Jules: No.
   Me: What's it about?
   Jules: Just come home after the shoot.

. . .

Sighing, I hurried and changed clothes. When Jules was in her laconic, maternal mood—which was ninety-five percent of the time—I wasn't going to get any information out of her.

In three and a half minutes, I had changed and lugged my bag to the front to oversee the last few models for the event. Willard was still in his spot on his laptop, and just as expected, Gareth was nowhere to be seen.

I couldn't even be mad at him. Not when I knew he wasn't in a good frame of mind to stick around and make small talk till the fundraiser ended. It wasn't like he could do anything anyway. His software was doing everything for him. For us.

After checking the tablet on the tripod which was feeding the live video straight to YouTube and interacting with a few of our subscribers, I had nothing else to do but wait.

I wondered what the hell caused Jules to call a family meeting. The last one we'd had was after Violet had dropped the bomb on us that she was leaving the family business and opening her tattoo shop, Empress Ink. We'd needed to discuss staffing and her transition to opening her own place.

But this seemed more urgent. Something was up. And while my mind pondered what it could be, it immediately drifted back to that fine grim reaper with a hot mouth and hotter kisses. How could I ever have thought him cold? I'd be lucky to not spontaneously combust the next time he touched me.

Funny thing was…I was more than happy to test that theory. More than willing to burn.

CHAPTER THIRTEEN

~LIVVY~

WE WERE PACKED INTO THE LIVING ROOM. A FEW CHAIRS HAD been brought in from the kitchen since it wasn't just my sisters gathered for the meeting, but also Mateo, Devraj, and Nico. Mateo had commandeered the club chair where Jules typically sat. He had Evie perched on his lap, an arm around her waist. This wasn't anything new. We'd all kind of gotten used to it. Alpha had been crazy protective ever since we'd found out Evie was pregnant.

We'd thought about doing some sort of intervention to get him to ease up, but Nico said it was normal and the best thing to do was to roll with his obsessive, psychotically possessive behavior. Nico said it would go away after she had the babies. Of course, then it would likely transfer to the babies, but we'd cross that bridge when we got there.

For now, Evie seemed fine with his overbearing attentions, and we just pretended it was normal. For the most part. Violet liked to poke the wolf every now and then, which was quite entertaining to us. All of us but Alpha, that is.

I squeezed between Clara and Devraj on the sofa. Clara passed me a bowl of popcorn.

"Okay, guys," said Violet standing in front of the fireplace, her half blonde/half purple hair twisted in a messy bun on top of her head. "I called this meeting—"

"*You* called this meeting?" I asked, confused.

I glanced over at Jules sitting on a kitchen chair beside Evie and Mateo, legs crossed, a glass of red wine in hand.

"Yes, I did," replied Violet. "Though I did get the okay from Jules. And Isadora and Devraj first."

"Why not me?" I asked.

"Or me?" asked Clara.

"Would you two shut your faces long enough for me to get it out?" asked Violet in her agitated voice.

Clara nudged me and I laughed. We mimicked zipping our lips in unison. Violet rolled her eyes.

"So! As I was saying before I was so rudely interrupted, I called this meeting today because we need to prepare for the arrival of Evie's babies."

"Babies plural? We know that for certain?" I challenged, knowing it would raise Vi's hackles.

"I predicted it, didn't I?" snapped Violet. "I already told y'all it's triplets."

"But that isn't definitive proof," added Clara.

I loved Clara. She could be as bad as me or Violet. She just did it with a sweet smile on her face that made you think she truly was innocent of malicious intent. Don't let her fool you.

I crunched on some popcorn and winked at Clara.

"I have proof," said Evie, raising a black and white sonogram photo with a weepy smile.

"What!" I jumped to my feet and ran over to her at the same time my sisters burst into exclamations of joy and excitement.

"Why didn't you tell us!" shouted Clara, jumping from the sofa.

"Oh, Evie, that's so exciting," said Isadora, leaning over where Evie showed her the picture.

"Me first." I held out my grabby hands.

Alpha growled. Not Mateo—definitely Alpha—then Mateo grumbled, "Be careful! I haven't blown the picture up for the fridge yet."

Evie handed it over to me with a smile, still firmly clasped in Mateo's arms.

"Why are you blowing it up?" asked Nico.

"So I can try to determine the sex of each."

"Still too soon," murmured Evie.

My heart squeezed at the sight of the little blobs. The photo actually had two sonogram photos with arrows pointing to babies one and two in one photo, then babies two and three in the other. It was hard to tell what was what, but I could see the definite outline of a small head and tiny leg.

"Oh, Evie," I cooed, letting it sink in that my dear sister was going to be a mother.

And I was going to be an aunt!

When I looked up at her, she blinked away some brimming happy tears.

"My turn," said Clara, taking the photo from me.

I took my seat again, grinning at how crazy it was going to be with three new babies around here.

"Holy shit." I leaned forward, catching Evie's face again. "Where the hell are y'all going to live with all those babies?"

"Dammit, Livvy." Violet heaved out a sigh. "That's why I called the meeting."

Clara passed the photo to Jules who got this achingly tender smile on her face as she looked down at it. Clara plopped next to me again and took the popcorn bowl.

"What do you mean?" asked Evie, genuinely confused.

"It's been decided." Violet clapped her hands together excitedly. "Isadora is moving in with Devraj."

"I thought she already had," said Clara. All eyes swiveled to her and her owlish sweet face. "I wasn't being sassy. I really thought she had."

"Not for my lack of trying, eh, love?" Devraj stared at Isadora like she was an angel fallen from heaven while he combed his fingers through her long, blonde hair.

Isadora turned so pink I thought she was holding her breath.

"No, she hasn't. Officially," said Violet. "But she is now. She and Devraj will officially move the rest of her things into his house next door this weekend."

Evie still stared in wonder, trying to figure out what this meant.

Violet barreled on. "I'm moving in with Nico. Not that my leaving the carriage house frees up room in the main house, but it does keep me out of the kitchen. So there will be more room for bottles and nipples and new baby machinery."

"Machinery?" asked Nico. "They're babies, not buildings under construction."

"Why are y'all moving out?" asked Evie, her voice becoming panicky.

Mateo squeezed her tighter against him.

Violet beamed at her. "We want you and Mateo to move in here. There's more space here. Isadora's old bedroom can be the babies' nursery. It was where we grew up." Violet's voice cracked. "It would be perfect for them."

Evie blinked rapidly, soaking this new information in.

Mateo had a thriving art gallery on Magazine Street, but his loft apartment above the studio certainly wasn't big enough for three babies. And I'd heard them debating what to do, since the housing market wasn't ideal at the moment. Nothing close enough to his studio or what they'd want for their first home together.

I scooted up onto the edge of the sofa. "I could move into the carriage house with Clara. Then there would be an extra bedroom for the babies. A playroom for when they start toddling around."

"Fantastic!" shouted Violet.

"Very generous of you, Liv," said Jules, giving me that proud mom smile that made me feel all warm and fuzzy.

Suddenly, Evie burst into tears. Like loud, ugly-crying sobs. The room fell silent, while Mateo shifted her on his lap, feeling her arms and legs as if looking for injuries, trying to find the threat so he could murder it.

"What happened? Did something hurt you?" he snarled. "Is it the babies?"

"No." Evie hiccupped, raising her tear-stained face. "I'm just so happy. Y'all are the best sisters in the whole, wide"—*sob*—"world!"

"Aww, Evie," said Clara sweetly. She rose and hurried to Evie's chair, then taking a seat on the edge, crowding Mateo and wrapping her arms around Evie. "We love you and the babies so much. We can't wait to meet them."

I laughed at the sight of Mateo still holding onto her, like she might go poof in a cloud of smoke if he let go. All while Clara hugged and rocked a sobbing Evie.

Jules stood and gave Violet's shoulder a squeeze. Vi was facing the other direction and slyly wiping a tear from her face. Nico stood and walked over, pulling her up against his chest. She clutched at his waist while he soothed her with a hand up and down her spine.

"I think we need food." Jules' smile was a little wobbly.

That's how Jules showed her love. She fed us.

"I'll say," said Isadora, her eyes shimmering as well.

That's when I noticed I'd let a few tears fall as well. "Bunch of watering pots, we are," I mumbled, rising to go and help Jules with dinner.

Jules had made a shrimp, oyster, and tasso gumbo. My favorite. I set out the gumbo bowls and spoons while she took the potato salad out of the fridge. Clara was already cutting the French bread. Suddenly, the kitchen was crowded and loud and wonderful. And while it honestly made my heart soar that we had such a big, loving family, it also twisted a knot in my stomach because I knew someone who did not.

While everyone served themselves, bumping around each other to make a zig-zag line to the rice bowl then the gumbo pot, I ducked out of the kitchen to get some air out in the back courtyard. The chatter and laughter was only slightly dimmed by closing the door. I found my way to Isadora's favorite bench under a heavy-branched live oak tree.

Tucking my knees up, I smiled at the pot of purple pansies at the base of the bench. Even though it wasn't even quite March, the weather had warmed enough for some flowers to bloom. Isadora might already practically live next door at Dev's —and soon would live there permanently—but she still came over to spread her love to our plants. And for us.

I sighed up at the clear sky. We were in that perfect Louisiana weather phase of spring. Once we hit late May or early June, it would be too hot to sit outside and enjoy the slight breeze as I did now.

Staring up at the stars, I thought of Gareth. I wondered what had happened to him in foster care. Even more, I longed to know about this dark monster grims lived with every day. And could Gareth's ever get out of control and hurt someone?

The problem was, I wanted to know everything about him, while a part of me wondered if I should. Was it smart to get involved with someone who purposely kept secrets because of the grim code or whatever? Was it wise to let my heart fall for someone who might very well end up breaking it?

The door leading onto the patio creaked open, and Violet stepped out carrying a tray with two steaming bowls.

"Hey. You're not first in line for your favorite gumbo? Something's up."

When she set it down on the bench between us, I noticed there was also two ramekins of potato salad and a small stack of French bread.

"Thanks." I picked up my bowl and dipped a piece of bread into the broth before taking a bite.

It was delicious, as always, but my appetite just wasn't as big as usual.

We ate in silence for a few minutes, Violet inhaling half her bowl before finally getting to what she came out here for.

"You know, something I learned in my relationship with Nico is to never put labels on people's potential prematurely." She snorted. "Wow, that was a lot of alliteration."

"I know, Vi." I took another bite then set my bowl aside on the tray.

"You can be kind of judgey, Liv."

It was my turn to huff out a laugh. "Thanks, you're so sweet."

"I'm being serious."

"I know, but look who's talking."

Violet set her bowl down and picked up the potato salad. "I'm just saying, don't push your grim away too soon." She spooned a mouthful.

"Do you know something?" Maybe her psychic abilities told her something she wasn't telling me.

"I know he's not your enemy."

Picking a piece of bread apart from the slice, I stuffed it in my mouth. "No, he's not," I mumbled around chewing.

"Ohhhh. This sounds interesting. You're holding out on me."

A click-clacking sound interrupted us as a little orange dog trotted right up to us, tongue hanging out. Archie. Isadora and Devraj's dog.

"How did you get out again?" Violet asked him.

He danced in a happy circle and sat back down, staring longingly at the food in our hands.

"I think he might actually be magic," I said, tossing him a piece of my bread. He danced around again, then I threw another.

"He's a goddamn flirt, too. Gets away with everything," muttered Violet. "Well, you can have free rein, Archibald," she sassed to him. "I'm officially moving out. Not that Fred wanted to come back anyway."

Fred was her pet rooster who she'd had to move to Nico's place after Archie kept getting out of Devraj's yard next door and terrorizing her ornery and territorial rooster.

"Is that his name? Archibald?"

"No. I just need a longer name when I fuss at him. I sound more serious."

"Yeah. He looks terrified."

Archie continued to hang his tongue out happily, his cute eyes sparkling from beneath his scraggly reddish hair hanging down.

"Okay, back to what you were about to confess to your favorite sister. What's going on with you and Gareth?"

I rolled my eyes, but honestly I wanted to talk to someone about it. After an agonizing minute where both she and Archie stared at me expectantly—Violet for my confession and Archie for more bread—I finally said, "I like him. He's not who I thought he was. I mean, he is. But also, he's not."

"Well, that clears up all the confusion," she snarked, tossing Archie the last scrap of her bread while she also stuck her tongue out at him.

Those two had a history, but no one could not like Archie.

"Do you know anything about grims? Their history?"

"Just the basic lets-fuck-or-fight aura they put off."

"They can do a lot more than that."

"Nice. Like what?"

"Well, Gareth can—" I stopped suddenly, realizing he might not want me to share what I knew.

Was I breaking his code if I shared information with her?

"Actually," she interrupted my thoughts, "I do know that they're telekinetics. Powerful ones. Or at least one of the Blackwater boys is. And Nico told me that they can move super-fast. Like vampires."

I smiled with relief. "When did you figure all that out? When the Blood Moon pack kidnapped you?"

"*Kidnapped* is kind of harsh."

"They knocked you out and took you by force. That is *literally* the definition of kidnapping."

"Yeah. But they didn't mean it."

I wasn't going to argue with her on this. The thought of that night still gave me nightmares, not knowing where she was and if she was okay.

"Anyway, yeah, one of them was using some high voltage TK that night and it wasn't me. I suspect it was Gareth, actually. So he's powerful? So what. If that's all that's got you worried, then let it go. I already know Clara told you that you need to date someone outside your comfort zone. I agree with her. Someone higher on the alpha food chain than you. If you like him, then date him. What's the big deal?"

I wanted so badly to tell her, *see, Gareth says there's a monster inside him that basically wants to crush and kill people, but he says he's got it all under control. Mostly. That's okay, right? I can still trust him?*

On the other hand, I didn't want to tell her for two reasons. One, this wasn't my secret to tell. And if I knew anything about grims, it was that they were militant about their secrecy. And two, I didn't want to tell Violet for her to say I was a damn fool to get involved with someone dangerous like that. That under no circumstances should I take a chance since this was early stages and my heart wasn't involved.

"You're right. It's no big deal," I lied.

"That's my girl. Go get you some grim dick." She picked up the tray. "Then tell me all about it."

I followed her inside to join my boisterous family, apparently batting around names for the babies.

"Bartholomew," said Nico.

Devraj laughed while Mateo shook his head, "No fucking way."

"What about Daffodil?" Isadora chimed in. "That's pretty."

"No flowers, Izzy." Evie protested. "No offense."

"None taken."

"How about Kylie and Miley?" Clara offered. "Oh, and the third could be Reilly!"

Violet turned to Clara. "As in Miley Cyrus?"

Mateo vetoed it instantly. "No rhyming names. Or pop icons."

"What about movie heroes?" asked Violet.

"We don't even know their sexes yet," laughed Evie.

"I've got it!" Nico raised his hand as if preparing the small audience for brilliance. "Frodo, Sam, and Merry. Or Pippin. Those could be either sex."

Devraj frowned. "Frodo could be a girl's name?"

"Sure, it could." Nico grinned.

"Y'all are all asshats," said Evie, laughing, while Mateo—or rather, Alpha—continued to scowl and growl at everyone.

I glanced at Violet wrapped in Nico's arms, her head against his chest. I exhaled a long breath, refusing to second guess my decision about Gareth. Because by lying to my sister, I'd certainly made it.

In that moment, I knew for certain that it was too late to turn back. My heart was already involved. And I wasn't going to walk away because of fear of the unknown. I just had to get Gareth to trust me enough to let me in.

Though I wasn't a gambling girl, I knew exactly what it would take for him to trust me. And damn, didn't that image inspire a heady dose of desire. All I could do was ask, and all he had to do was say no. My pulse skyrocketed at the thought of him saying yes. I couldn't wait to find out.

CHAPTER FOURTEEN

~GARETH~

I was almost across the Causeway Bridge, heading to Aunt Lucille's on the north shore of Lake Pontchartrain. Normally, the easy beat of Two Feet lulled me into a lazy, serene place. But I was still agitated over what had happened at the photo shoot. To be honest, I was overwhelmed.

No one had made my monster stir the way Lavinia had. Not since that first time when he'd roared to life and broken bones.

That flash of blood-stained tears and vacant eyes came to mind again. I pushed it away as I took the exit for Mandeville.

Aunt Lucille lived in a sleepy small town by herself, now that Uncle George had passed on. I glanced at the urn I had sitting upright in a box on the passenger seat, protected by foam so it wouldn't tip over.

Henry had insisted that I try one more time with Aunt Lucille before we finally put her husband to rest in a mausoleum. It had been two years. Aunt Lucille was a strange bird, and set in her ways, but maybe today was the day she'd relent and take him. Though I doubted it.

Aunt Lucille wasn't purposely estranged from her brother—my father—like Uncle Silas was. She'd simply lost track of him when he left New Orleans in his early twenties. That was the only reason she wasn't aware of me being put into foster care.

I learned later that the agencies had tried to contact her by mail and telephone, but Aunt Lucille said her phone was to call the fire department if she ever needed it. The only people that ever called were telemarketers and they could all *go to hell* as she so aptly put it.

She had been the only next of kin listed in my parents' insurance policies. My father had cut Uncle Silas out of his life completely. Of course, I don't think my parents foresaw the worst possible scenario of them both dying and the one relative who would've taken and loved me being so far off the grid, she never knew I was out there alone in the world.

Aunt Lucille had actually apologized to me when I finally came into Uncle Silas's care, realizing I'd been alone for so long, wandering from foster home to hellish foster home.

I never blamed her, especially when she loved me so unconditionally in those later teen years, when I was still angry and bitter about my lot in life. About the world. Besides Henry and Sean, she was the only person in the world I'd ever let get close to me.

Lavinia's curling smile and bright eyes filled my mind. I shook the image off, wishing I wasn't so off-kilter as I took one of the many country roads leading away from the center of Mandeville.

When I'd come to live with Uncle Silas, I'd met his eccentric sister Aunt Lucille through Henry. He and I would spend summers and holidays out here in Mandeville since Uncle Silas didn't do holidays. He hated his sister, which I gathered from the belittling comments about her wasting her talent and her embarrassing eccentricity, but he also knew that Henry needed a teacher.

Because she was a grim like Henry, Uncle Silas allowed it,

hoping to use Henry's gift to expand his power as the CEO of Obsidian Corporation. Unfortunately for Uncle Silas, Henry realized early on he wanted nothing to do with his power-hungry father. Not his own power. That's when he moved out and took Sean with him. Uncle Silas didn't seem to give a shit, calling both of his sons ungrateful and worthless.

Turning onto the gravel road, I drove up the winding drive through the several acres of woods that separated Aunt Lucille's home from the rest of the world. She ventured out to the farmer's market once a month where she bought vegetables and fruits from farmers she trusted or to take one of her beloved cats to the vet, but other than that she rarely left her house. She had a pretty severe case of agoraphobia and went out only to places she trusted and felt safe.

I pulled up to the Acadian style house built on brick columns, expecting to find her on the porch in one of her rocking chairs. But she was bent over a flowerbed out front, her wide-brimmed straw hat protecting her from the sun.

She glanced up when she heard my car, instantly smiling and straightening from her garden work. With both hands on her hips, she waited till I parked and turned off the car.

Heaving a sigh, I murmured, "Here's hoping, Uncle George." I picked up his urn and slid out of my car. My heels rang sharply as I walked along her steppingstones leading to the front of the house.

"Oh, hell no, Gareth Michael. You go put him right back in the car."

My heart stuttered as it always did when she used my middle name. My father's name. A man who'd loved me and left me far too soon. I'd gotten over my anger at my parents leaving me here alone, though unwillingly, in my late teens. But even the mention of his name, the mere thought that I might've had a better childhood, a less lonely life had they not gotten into that car that night…it still jarred me.

Facing off with Aunt Lucille, her expression now in a deep

frown, hands still on her wide hips. "Aunt Lucille, Henry told me he says—"

"I know what he says. He keeps comin' around all the damn time, and I've done told him not to."

"Please, Aunt Lucille," I pleaded.

Something about my expression softened her resolve. "He can sit on the porch while you visit. And that's it! Now come and get some iced tea. I just made a fresh pitcher."

I followed her up the porch steps, smiling at this monumental victory as I set Uncle George onto a small table between the rocking chairs. She'd never let me up the porch with his ashes before, so this was a big win.

"How are you doing, darlin'?" she asked in her sweetest auntie voice.

The smell of her house immediately seeped into my system, my body relaxing at once. A mixture of scents like lemon, honey, fabric softener, and cypress that made up every wall of this old house. The house Uncle George built for her. It was a comforting scent that had come to mean love when I'd finally accepted that she was safe, that she was one of my people. One of the few I could trust.

"Good."

Something delicious was cooking on the stove in a big cast iron pot. The spicy aroma blended with all of the other smells that made me feel like I was home.

"Mmhmm." She poured two tall glasses of iced tea and cut lemon wedges then put them on the lip of each glass. "How's that contest thingy going?"

Smiling at her description of the prestigious GMC public relations competition, I replied, "It's going really well actually." I couldn't help but wonder what Lavinia would think of Aunt Lucille. Instinctively, I knew Lavinia would love her.

"Oh, well now." She said, her crows' feet around her hazel-brown eyes crinkling as she smiled brightly. "Something's got you happy. Or is it *someone*?"

She had a touch of psychic ability. But she also simply knew my moods and could read them better than anyone.

"How do you know it's about a person? Maybe I'm just happy that I'm kicking the other contestants' asses."

She laughed and waved me to follow her back to the porch. The days were nice now that we were in March. A breeze filtered from the back of her property where there were no trees to block it and swept across the porch as we took a seat.

Her five sets of wind chimes tinkled in unison. To this day, that sound grounded me in a tranquility I couldn't describe. Aunt Lucille was the only adult, after my parents, who gave a shit about me. Her unconditional love was something I cherished more than anything.

I took a seat in the rocker next to the table and reached over to pet the orange Maine Coon cat now perched next to Uncle George's urn.

"Hi, there, Apollo." I gave the lion-looking cat a scratch on his head. He allowed it with an imperious look and a heavy blink of his orange eyes. "Where are Hera and Persephone?"

"Hunting, I presume. They like to bring Apollo dead mice and squirrels, proving their value as his concubines."

Smiling against the lip of the glass, I swallowed a sip before saying, "Aren't they all fixed?"

She huffed a laugh. "That don't make no difference. He still thinks he's king of the castle, and they still court him with dead rodents and such."

I glanced at Apollo, who gave me another superior blink before turning away to gaze out on his kingdom.

"He shouldn't have gone to work that morning. I told him so, but he didn't *listen*."

My heart sank, hearing words Aunt Lucille had said dozens of times since Uncle George had been killed in a factory accident. She'd had a sudden stirring of her darkness inside her that morning, an omen warning her that something bad would happen. She had told him so.

Uncle George wasn't a supernatural. He'd been human. And though he'd indulged his wife with her eccentricities, he'd never seemed to truly believe she had magic inside her. He'd loved her dearly, but he didn't heed her warning. And he'd died for it. She was still furious about it. And hurt, obviously.

Aunt Lucille was sitting in the rocker on the other side of the table where the urn and Apollo sat. She was staring at the urn with such deep sadness. Up until now, she'd only spoke of him with anger that he hadn't listened to her.

"He doesn't want to be put in a mausoleum," I said gently. "He wants to be here with you."

"I know what he wants," she snapped, taking a sip of tea. "He tells me often enough."

The breeze coasted across the porch, tinkling the wind chimes again.

"Now then, why don't you tell me about this girl?"

I flinched. "What girl?"

"The one you're all smitten with. The one that makes you smile. That's a rare occasion indeed for my Gareth." She chuckled, her plump cheeks rosy. "Lord, even when you were little, it took a lot of coaxing to get you to smile. But someone has been doing a number on you, I can tell. So stop stalling and tell me about her."

Holding the glass of tea between both hands, the condensation cool on my fingertips, I said, "Her name is Lavinia."

I was aware how I spoke her name. With reverence and awe. And hope.

"My, my, my." Her expression turned serious. "Pretty, is she?"

"Beautiful." I swallowed hard. "And smart. Funny. Kind."

My heart ached at the confession tumbling from my lips. I couldn't even talk to Henry like this, so openly. But Aunt Lucille had always been able to get more out of me than anyone else. Perhaps because she held no barriers in place or maybe because she spoke so openly and honestly or perhaps because I knew she

always wanted what was best for me, I always told her the full truth.

"You love this girl?" She asked it as a question, but it felt more like a statement. Like a definitive truth.

A surprised sound coughed out of my mouth. "*Love?* Who said anything about love?" What was she even talking about? I set my tea down and combed a hand through my hair. "We don't even know each other that well. We just met like two months ago."

Aunt Lucille stared at me, those all-seeing eyes making me uncomfortable. "You know that she's kind, funny, smart, and beautiful. But more than that, your heart is talking when you speak of her. Your soul too. I can feel it down to my bones."

My pulse raced like mad, jackhammering in my chest till I thought that quick-beating organ would burst right through my ribcage to shout a resounding *yes!* to Aunt Lucille's accusations.

"I know you're scared," she said gently. "And maybe you should be. It may not be love yet, but you're falling fast, Gareth Michael."

I sucked in a breath and leaned back in the rocking chair, gripping the arms with white-knuckled fingers. An old panic started to seize me. It wasn't the darkness that lived inside me, but the unwanted, rejected, and abused child trying to break free and run from this emotion sending me into a frightened panic.

"How do I stop it?" I whispered.

She chuckled and sighed. "I think it's too late for that. When a grim finds that special companion, their own lifeblood in another, the darkness won't ever let them go."

I stared at her in shock. She'd glanced at Uncle George's urn then lifted her gaze back to me. How could she say something like that when I hadn't even thought of Lavinia that deeply?

Liar, the monster whispered.

"Is that what this is?" My voice was rough and raw with

140

emotion, something that was terribly rare for me. "You think she's my…one? Without ever having met her. When *I* don't even know what I feel for her?"

"I know my psychic abilities are limited, son. I also know what I know." She glanced at the urn again before taking a sip of her tea. "But there's only one thing I really need you to hear."

"What's that?"

"Mark me well, Gareth Michael," she said, aiming one of her hard expressions at me. The one that told me she meant business. "You are worthy of love, dear boy. And you have so much of your own to give."

Swallowing the lump in my throat, I rasped, "I know. You've always been there for me. So has Henry. And Sean."

She shook her head and reached across the table to place her soft, wrinkled hand atop mine. "You clung to us as a child who needed a family. Who'd found your family. But since then," she shook her head, sadness in her eyes, "you haven't let in one soul. It's time you understood that you can trust others too. Especially the one who's meant to be your partner in life."

I turned my hand over to hold hers in mine, staring down at the stark contrast. "But how do I know she's the one?"

"How do you know she's not?" she snapped back. "Are you willing to let her go and never find out?"

A dangerous rumble vibrated deep inside me from the belly of darkness. My hand clenched on hers, the promise of *never* echoing in my mind.

Aunt Lucille's smile looked almost feral, her brown eyes darkening as she stared into mine. She looked more like a grim than ever with that look.

"You're going dark, Gareth. Your beast knows, just like I told you." She squeezed my hand again when I said nothing. "So do this old lady a favor, will you? Open the door to your girl. Let her in."

Clamping my jaw for a second, I finally said, "She wants to know more about grims. About what we are."

"Then tell her."

"But grims keep the code so—"

"Oh, fuck the code."

Aunt Lucille's harsh language made me laugh.

"The code was set in place by people like your Uncle Silas. I still love my bastard of a brother, though he doesn't deserve it, but he's of the old ilk of secrets and mystery. Wanting to garner power to be the superior race of supernaturals." She let my hand go and lifted her glass again to take a sip. "All that is bullshit. Especially when it comes to soul mates." Again her gaze strayed to the urn. "You share everything."

"I see," I said softly, lifting my glass to take another swallow and cool my racing blood.

"So make me a promise you'll do what I say. Let Lavinia in, my boy. It's what's best for you."

"Okay, Aunt Lucille. *If*—" I raised a finger, "you let Uncle George stay here with you."

She heaved a sigh and rocked back in her chair. "Suppose I've punished him enough." She eyed the urn. "It's a deal."

Right then, a silver tabby and a calico came trotting out of the woods, the calico carrying a small creature in its mouth.

"Look at that, Apollo. Looks like Persephone won the hunt today. Speaking of food, why don't you come in and have dinner. I've got beef stew on the stove. I'll make us some jalapeño cornbread."

"That sounds delicious, Aunt Lucille."

"Grab those glasses for me." She picked up the urn.

I walked ahead when she held the screen door open with one hand, the urn on her hip. "Persephone! Don't you bring that damn thing in my house! It stays on the porch."

Then she slammed the screen door shut behind us, gabbing about slicing some fresh tomatoes for a salad. I barely listened, marveling at this new sensation of lightness. There was no tension in my body, no tremor of darkness trying to sway my will. That was because I'd finally given in to the right path. I was sure of it. And that path led to Lavinia.

"And how's Sean? He still getting into trouble?" She set Uncle George next to some potted flowers on a table under a window.

"Afraid so," I told her, filling her in on his latest escapade at school, as I set the table.

"You need to talk to him, Gareth. He may be like you."

"I know."

Being a grimlock was rare. And a huge responsibility. I didn't have the guidance I needed in my teen years, until I'd come to Uncle Silas's home and had met Aunt Lucille.

As we settled into a meal that filled my belly and my soul with comfort food cooked by this woman who loved me, I realized I needed to go see Sean. If he was already acting out, he needed guidance sooner rather than later. And I might be the only one who could offer him what no one had offered me.

Sean wasn't an orphan, but his family unit was small. He didn't count his father in that unit. Though Uncle Silas had the resources to train Sean in whatever magic was manifesting inside him, he'd never paid attention to his sons as he should. I'd never let Sean suffer from a fatal mistake like I had.

"I'll go see him tonight," I assured Aunt Lucille.

"You do that. Now, tell me what your Lavinia looks like," she said a cheeky grin.

I couldn't help but smile. Then I proceeded to talk about my favorite subject all the way through dinner, wearing a stupid smile I couldn't seem to, and didn't care to, wipe off my face.

CHAPTER FIFTEEN

~LIVVY~

W‌ALKING INTO EMPRESS INK, I EXPECTED TO SEE SEAN AT THE front desk, but I found Violet propped on his stool behind the counter instead.

"Hey, there."

Violet looked up from the pad she was sketching in. Looked like she was working on a new tattoo—a wicked looking butterfly, one wing tattered and torn, the other perfectly formed.

"Hey, sis. What's up?"

I leaned both elbows on the counter as she continued sketching. "Just wanted to stop in and see how business was doing."

She snorted. "No, you didn't." She glanced up then tucked a tendril of her half purple, half blonde hair behind her ears and looked back down at her work.

"If you know so much, you tell me why I'm here then."

"You want to talk about a certain grim."

"No, I don't."

We'd just talked about him last night at the house where I'd finally decided I was going to give this thing between us a go.

"Yes, you do."

"I came to brainstorm ideas for our next fundraiser, if you must know. I'm totally stumped on what to do next."

"Okay, that's a plausible reason to drop in on a Saturday night when you're typically out with Kaya. But also, you want to talk about your man."

A fluttering filled my stomach. *My* man. He wasn't mine. Not yet. The very thought had me biting my bottom lip to keep from grinning too hard.

Violet laughed, pausing in her sketching. "I can't even express how happy this makes me."

"What?" I snapped, frowning and smiling at the same time.

"This sappy, googly-eyed look over a man like Gareth."

I didn't protest the look, because I was well aware. "What kind of man is he?"

"Super dark and broody. And delicious."

She had no idea.

"He's also fun," I added on a laugh. "And funny."

"That I would never guess. But I suppose he would loosen up with the right person. Very promising, sis." She nudged me with her elbow when I rolled my eyes. "Seriously though, I get really good vibes from this."

For Violet, the family Seer, to say so had my heart exploding with excitement and joy. And nervousness.

"We're not officially dating or anything."

"Mmhmm." She kept sketching. And grinning.

"We aren't. Not yet anyway."

But I wanted to be. Yes, I'd finally admitted it to myself, I really wanted to date Gareth.

"Don't worry," she assured me.

"You know something? Tell me, Vi."

She laughed. "No. Too much information is a hazard when it comes to these things." She patted my hand. "Just trust me."

Trust. Speaking of which, I realized that if I wanted more from Gareth, I'd have to make a deal to gain his trust. One he really wanted. And I was pretty sure I knew what he wanted. The thought both thrilled and terrified me. Especially since I realized he was packing a lot more magic than I was. Dangerous magic. A fact Violet did *not* know.

"Okay," I finally said softly, glancing around. "Where's Sean by the way?"

"He's in the breakroom." She went back to her sketch, her lips quirking into a smile again. "Needed to do something, so I said I'd cover the door."

"We're all done," came that familiar deep voice that sent a shiver from the top of my spine down to my toes.

Gareth walked into the lobby from the hallway ahead of Sean who looked pensive and a little sad.

"Hi," I squeaked out. "I didn't know you were here."

When I glanced at Violet, she was folding up her sketch book and grinning, avoiding my gaze. Sneaky witch. I prayed he hadn't heard our conversation.

Gathering my scattered wits, I plastered on a smile, hoping he didn't notice me melting at the sight of him in jeans and a black Henley. I was always aware of his fit physique in his tailored pants and dress shirts, but this offered a more defined outline of his body.

I wasn't a huge soccer fan, but I ended up getting sucked into the World Cup when Devraj parked on our sofa last November and watched every game. I was completely hooked on the excitement of the international competitions but also drooled over the lean-muscled, hard bodies of the players. As I stood there staring, Gareth reminded me of them.

His mouth tipped up on one side as he stared right back. We were doing that who-would-break-eye-contact-first thing, but this time I felt zero animosity or anger. Instead, I only felt the heat and weight of his dark gaze, devouring me with quiet perusal.

"How are you today, Lavinia?"

His calm veneer was back in place. Just the tenor of his low, rumbly voice sent my pulse into orbit.

"Good."

"You look good."

His head tilted ever so slightly as he took in my casual yoga pants—black with little pink polka dots, a pink crop top that left a sliver of skin showing on my stomach, and my denim jacket.

Sean moved behind the counter and leaned on both forearms. "You guys want to, uh, use the supply closet?"

I snapped a wide-eyed gaze at the deviant to find him snickering at his own joke. Gareth merely frowned since he *thankfully* had no idea what went on in that supply closet. Apparently, those four walls had seen quite a bit of action between both Evie and Mateo as well as Violet and Nico.

Then Gareth asked, "What happened in the supply closet?"

I almost passed out when Sean opened his mouth. "Shut it," I warned.

He laughed, and I was sure I'd have to knock him unconscious to keep from further embarrassment when the door opened and in stepped two werewolves.

Immediately, Gareth moved his body slightly in front of me.

"Well, it's about damn time," Violet huffed.

The taller one, Shane, waved a bank bag in front of him. "I told you I'd be by today."

"That's what you've been saying for a week."

"To be honest, we were waiting for payday," said the other one, Rhett, the auburn-haired hottie of the pack.

Shane grinned, revealing one of his best assets. Shane was the leader of the Blood Moon pack who took up residence here several weeks ago. Oh, after they happened to kidnap Violet and put us all through a night of hell. Nico gave him a good beating for it though, so I wasn't mad about it anymore.

Nico had mentioned to Violet the other day at the Cauldron that their accounts were in the red for all the magical tattoos she'd given the werewolf pack but hadn't been paid for yet.

Violet had calmed him, telling him Shane had promised to bring the payment this week.

And so he had. "Well, here you go, princess." He upended the bag, dumping dozens of twenties on the counter.

"Damn, bro." Sean immediately started counting and stacking.

"Where'd you get all the cash?" I asked, stepping around Gareth.

"Another lovely Savoie sister." Shane hit me with that dimpled smile, combing a hand through his dirty blond hair. "Lilly, right?"

"Livvy," I said, the same time Gareth growled, "Lavinia."

A pulse of grim magic sizzled across the room with an oppressive push.

Shane pressed a hand to his chest at the same time Rhett took a step back and growled, his eyes flaring wolf-gold.

"Ouch," laughed Shane, rubbing his chest. "Easy, grim. I get it."

"Gareth," I hissed, tugging on his sleeve.

Ice man was back, cold and forbidding. But it was directed only at the two wolves in the room. He broke his glare away from them to peer down at me, a line creasing his brow. My look of concern must've gotten through to him.

Suddenly, the heavy weight of magic evaporated, then Gareth did something I never could've imagined at that moment. He took my hand and laced our fingers tightly together.

Violet coughed out a laugh. Sean grinned but kept on counting the cash.

Shane glanced at our hands and nodded, easing away from us and closer to the counter. "It was easy money."

"How?" Violet arched a blondish brow.

"Stripping," said Rhett.

"What?" I laughed.

Sean stopped counting to look up. "Seriously?"

"Well, not exactly. But yeah, sort of," explained Shane. "A rich witch in the Garden District threw a fancy bachelorette party for her sister. She started chatting me up at Tracey's pub a couple weeks ago, wishing she had a couple of beefy werewolves to be the entertainment at her party. So," he shrugged, "we served drinks."

"Shirtless," added Rhett.

"A couple of us put on a show. Rich witches threw us lots of tips."

"Plus the actual fee," added Rhett. "Still can't believe she agreed to two grand for us to pass out drinks and do body shots all night. Something we do for free every weekend."

"Unreal. I'm actually surprised they weren't afraid you'd go all beast-mode on them or something," laughed Violet.

Rhett hooked a thumb in a front pocket of his jeans. "I think a couple of them were hoping we would."

"They were an open-minded group," said Shane.

"And horny," added Rhett.

"Bonus." Shane grinned.

Violet shook her head before glancing down at the stack Sean was still counting. "Well, I guess we're even. How are things going with the tattoos?"

Violet had been implementing a rare kind of magic, using charmed ink to create permanent spells for supernaturals. After realizing werewolves needed her brand of magic to calm their beastly side, she'd been steadily tattooing the entire pack plus some of their friends in Texas who'd been dropping in sporadically.

"Good, Violet. Thank you," he said sincerely.

Sean wrapped the stack of bills with a rubber band and wrote the final amount on a sticky note, shaking his head. "Next time, you guys call me if you need an extra."

"The fuck they will," said Gareth in his glacial tone. "Like you need another reason to get into trouble."

Sean held up his hands, forcing his expression into something almost penitent. "Okay, okay."

"Bet that was a show though." Violet crossed her arms and shook her head. "Doesn't surprise me a yard full of shirtless werewolves raked in the bucks."

They chuckled, then I gasped, accidentally squeezing Gareth's hand. He pulled me closer, jerking his attention to me.

"Holy shitsticks!" I turned to Gareth. "I've got it!"

"Got what?" asked Violet.

Gareth simply waited for me to find my words.

"The next fundraiser!"

"A strip show?" Sean clapped his hands. "I'm in."

"No." I laughed. "A werewolf wet t-shirt contest! Perfect for spring weather. Everyone's ready for summer. The neighborhood would come out in droves."

"The neighborhood?" Violet snorted. "I think all of NOLA would come out, especially if you put it on the SuperNet."

"Plus," I said excitedly, "it'll help bring awareness that werewolves are friendly, fun guys. Not so beastly after all."

"Jules would like that, I bet," said Violet.

I turned to Shane. "Would you guys do it?"

"What's this for?" he asked, the first serious expression on his face since he'd walked in.

I explained about the contest and our charity to raise money for supernatural orphans, to sponsor creating an agency specifically for them.

"Hell yeah, we'd do it," he answered with conviction, Rhett nodding next to him.

I turned to Gareth who hadn't said a word, but still kept my hand in his. "What do you think?"

His hostile gaze had grown darker, a definite frown marring his expression.

"You don't like it?" I asked.

"No." He heaved a sigh, which seemed like the most emotion I'd ever seen on him. Besides the lust-blazing fire in his eyes when we'd done sixty-nine in his office and the metal-twisting fury at the photo shoot. "It's a brilliant idea actually." He held my gaze, voice softer when he added, "Not surprising coming from you."

His praise made me feel like an Olympic sprinter crossing the finish first, a giddy joy swelling inside my chest.

"We could host right outside like we did for the shop opening." I still had all of my notes and details from throwing a big street party for Empress Ink. "What do you think, Vi?"

She smiled wide with a lascivious look. "You had me at werewolf wet t-shirt contest."

Suddenly, I was anxious to get home and get started on ideas. A familiar buzz of adrenaline zinged through me like it always did when a new idea took hold of me.

"I need to talk to Jules," I mumbled to myself.

"Let me walk you out," said Gareth, leading me by the hand. The one he hadn't let go during that entire conversation.

I said goodbye and told Shane we'd be in touch, then we walked out toward the street. It was already dark. As we stepped up to my car parked on the street, I noticed his Audi several spaces behind me, which I somehow missed when I'd gotten here.

Under the night sky and now that we were alone, I finally felt how strange—and wonderful—it was for Gareth to be holding onto me as he was.

"What's this?" I raised our laced hands.

His onyx eyes flickered to me and held. "You can let go if you want."

After a few seconds, I whispered, "I don't want to."

He swallowed hard and leaned back against my driver's side door, then tugged me closer, sliding his free hand onto my waist. His warm palm branded my bare skin beneath my crop top, his thumb sweeping up and down, sending delicious shivers down my body.

This felt so right. How did this feel so right? A few weeks ago, I wanted to kill him.

That was a lie. I wanted to tie him up naked and whip him for his constant asinine behavior, and then I wanted to fuck us both silly.

"I know you want to get home and get all your ideas onto paper, so I won't keep you."

"How do you know that?"

"I can see your brain spinning from here."

"You can keep me for a little bit." I eased closer.

His expression didn't change as he lifted the hand from my waist to cup my face and pressed his lips close to my ear. "Don't tempt me."

I fisted a hand in his shirt and leaned into him, nudging between his spread legs.

Our last kisses were mind-melting invasions with teeth and tongue and hot, heavy moans. Desperate and aggressive. This one was not.

He grazed his nose along the underside of my jaw, coasted his lips across mine with a soft sweep. He finally let go of my hand so he could press his hand to the small of my back and pull me entirely against his hard body.

When he finally slid his tongue along the seam of my mouth, I couldn't take the soft teasing anymore. Wrapping my arms around his neck, I crushed my body and my mouth to his, urging him to open wider and slipped my tongue inside.

A deep groan vibrated from his chest to mine then he slid both hands to my ass and hauled me against his hard body. The long pipe in his jeans pressed against my hip, dragging a whimper from my mouth. When I tried to kiss him deeper, he eased back, slowing the pace all while stroking and squeezing my ass gently, like he might be giving a platonic back rub. It was maddening.

Never in my life had I wanted to climb someone's body and

fuck them on the street, but his tender kisses and gentle licks and soft nips and slow strokes were setting me on fire.

"Gareth," I whined against his mouth, rubbing my breasts against his chest. "You're driving me crazy."

He cupped my ass firmly, giving me a tight squeeze, then hauled my body harder against his. Finally, he slanted his mouth to mine and kissed me deeper. Still torturously slow but with the possessive intensity I craved from him.

By the time I was a moaning, pliant mess in his arms, he gripped my hips and pushed me away. Standing upright off the car, he opened my driver's side door and nudged me at the small of my back.

"Get in."

That wasn't what I expected. Typically, the woman or man I was dating would be clawing at my clothes and ushering me to the closest place for privacy. The fact that I knew by the sizeable bulge in Gareth's jeans that he was in as much agony as I was had my mind spinning that he was sending me on my way.

"We could slip right around the corner into an alley, you know," I suggested.

He shook his head, one of those rare smiles spreading wide. "Get in the car, Lavinia."

When he used that authoritative voice, I could do nothing but obey. So I ducked into my seat. He reached in and buckled my belt, taking a moment to cruelly adjust the strap to fall between my large breasts.

"Now you're just being mean," I whispered.

He paused, his whole upper body leaning into my car. He braced one hand on the seat by my right hip, the other on the head rest behind me, and leaned close. Lost in glittering obsidian, I kept still as he swept another too-gentle kiss across my mouth.

"When I fuck you for the first time, Lavinia," another excruciating, slow slide of his lips over mine, "it won't be in a back alley. It'll be in my bed." He nuzzled into my hair and nipped my earlobe. "Where I can lick and suck every delicious inch of you." He trailed his nose along my jaw till his gaze caught mine again. "Where I can fuck you hard and long till you're exhausted and spent. And when you're finally too tired to move, that's when I'll fuck you nice and slow. You'll come harder than you ever have before." A soft, chaste kiss. "Goodnight, Lavinia."

Then he slammed the door shut, and crossed his arms like a cold sentinel, not like he hadn't just set my panties on fire. He waited for me to start the car and drive away. Completely in a haze, I did. All the while, I cursed him for revving my body so hot and sending me away cold and wanting.

Even so, as I made my way down Magazine Street to the house, I smiled at what he'd said, the things he planned to do to me. The ways he planned to fuck me. This was finally happening. And soon, if I had any say about it.

CHAPTER SIXTEEN

~LIVVY~

As I stepped out of the elevator, I practically vibrated with excitement about the new fundraiser idea.

"Good morning, Cynthia," I said as I passed the receptionist's desk.

"Good morning, Livvy."

I'd sat down with Jules for an hour last night and explained my idea. She listened patiently as she always did, agreeing that this would be a terrific way to get werewolves out front in the supernatural community, to showcase them in a fun way. It would also be a demonstration that Violet's charmed tattoos had a calming effect since the whole Blood Moon pack had been tattooed by Violet.

"Though this isn't exactly the venue I'd invite heads of the covens to," Jules had added with raised brows, "I do believe it's a safe start to open some minds and bring the community together."

Werewolves were ostracized and segregated from most parts of our community. They didn't even have organized covens to be a part of the larger supernatural community. There was a long line of prejudice against them for their violent tendencies. But Violet had discovered a way to counteract their curse. To give them control over their wolves with her magic. It was a beautiful thing.

Ruben and Jules were formulating an organized plan to bring to the High Witch Guild, to open the doors so long closed to the werewolves. So she'd ended up smiling at my playful fundraiser, a small step to open the arms of the rest of the supernatural community to them. I mean what better way than to parade hot, wet werewolves on a stage for everyone to enjoy?

Violet had even convinced Nico and Mateo to do it. I snickered to myself, remembering Mateo—or Alpha rather—giving me a wink and rumbling, "Don't worry. They'll come out in droves to check out a supreme wolf like me." Then he'd immediately apologized in Mateo's gentler voice.

I stepped into the office, first one here as always, flipped on the lights and headed to my desk. Once I'd pulled up the files I was working on last night, I sent them to the printer. Smoothing the flared skirt of my dress, black with a pattern of tiny red roses, I wondered if Gareth would like it. I'd specifically worn this one because it was shorter than my others for work, straddling the border of professional and party dress. I wanted to look especially pretty for him today.

That's what I was thinking while I stood at the printer then heard someone directly behind me say, "You look lovely today, Livvy."

I spun with a frightened gasp and pressed a hand to my chest. "Oh. Mr. Davis. You scared me."

"Richard, please." He was standing too far inside my personal bubble of space. I hadn't even heard him walk in, the printer was making enough noise to prevent it. "I didn't mean to." Then his smile slid wide, and I felt a distinct tremor of warning.

When his gaze dropped down my body, which was well-covered in today's attire, a slithery sensation coiled tight in my belly.

"I was just…" I pressed back to the table in the corner of the room holding the printer, gripping the edge of it behind me, "getting started early."

"You do that a lot, don't you? Cynthia mentioned that you're always early to work."

I gulped hard, knowing on instinct that he fished out that information from Cynthia, specifically to discover my comings and goings.

"We've got our second fundraiser to work on today." I turned away from him to pull out the papers from the printer.

Then he was there. Right behind me. One of his hands was braced on top of the printer, effectively blocking me into the corner, his body only inches behind me. I suddenly wished I hadn't worn my hair up, because I could feel his breath on my bare neck.

"Mr. Davis, I'm not comfortable with how close you're standing."

I didn't want to use compulsion magic on him, because that might make him angry. And he wouldn't do anything to me in broad daylight in the offices, I told myself. Would he?

"Do you know I'm an Enforcer," he said in a low, intimate tone, still standing too close as if he hadn't even heard me. His body heat creeped over my skin though he hadn't touched me.

"Mr. Davis—"

"Richard. Please." His *please* was anything but a request. "I could help you go a long way in this business. A man in my position with my level of power." Then I felt it. His hand on my hip.

I jumped and twisted around, breaking his hold by stepping back toward the wall.

"You could go far with me at your side." He stepped closer again, lifting both hands and wrapping them around my forearms.

This was not fucking happening.

He pressed me back to the wall. On instinct, I used my influencing magic, summoning it as I said, "Stop touching me."

The magic pulsed from me into him. He dropped my arms and took a step back but didn't leave, still staring with a wicked gleam in his gray eyes.

"I want you to leave," I bit out. My magic whistled, then evaporated into the air.

Dammit.

This had happened to me before, my magic not taking effect when my anxiety levels spiked.

When I was eighteen on a trip to Tennessee with a bunch of friends, one of the guys had lifted me to toss me over a small cliff into a pool of water as he'd done to the other girls. I was petrified, and no matter how many times I'd told him to stop and put me down, trying to use compulsion, it hadn't worked. He'd still tossed me over the cliff to my terrifying dismay. That's when I realized I needed to be calm and confident to use my magic. Something I was not at this very moment.

He lifted his hand again and gripped my hip.

"Richard, you're making me uncomfortable."

Instead of backing away, he squeezed my hip and pressed his body closer, his chest grazing my shoulders. Was I actually going to have to get violent with this douchebag? I was doing my damnedest to not make a scene, but what the fuck?

"Did you hear me? I'm an Enforcer."

"You already said that."

"You know what that means, don't you? I can take anyone's powers away whenever I want."

I gaped in shock. Who the hell did he think he was? *He was threatening me?*

"That's illegal," I told him, trembling from the implied threat that he could take my power away.

What? If I didn't become his fuck buddy?

Enforcers could only use their powers outside a sanctioned

order by a High Witch Guild if another supernatural's life was in danger. He knew this. Everyone knew this.

His gray eyes narrowed as he grinned wider. "Only if you're caught."

How could you not get caught? I'd report him in a millisecond if he ever tried that shit with me.

I wasn't having this shit. Deep breath in, I exhaled slowly. "Stop touching me and back away." I injected as much venom into my voice, summoning my magic again.

He dropped his arm but didn't back away. He was resisting my magic. He was an Enforcer after all, and stronger than I was.

"You should feel honored." His fingers wrapped around my arm again. "I'm an important man."

"I don't feel honored," I hissed. "I want you to—"

"Richard!" A powerful pulse of heavy magic sliced swiftly through the room like a guillotine.

I sucked in a breath, while Richard stiffened and straightened, his eyes glazing over. I stepped to the side and out of his reach. The magic was sharp and agonizingly oppressive. I whimpered even though the sizzle of glamour wasn't directed at me.

"Remove your hands from Lavinia," came the menacing command. Richard removed them. "Go back to your office and do not leave your desk until seven p.m."

Immediately, he took a step backward, turned robotically, and walked out of the office. I spun and put my back to the wall. Richard passed Gareth, murder in my grim's eyes.

When he was gone, Gareth asked in a grating, rough voice, "Are you all right?"

I nodded, swallowing hard against heavy emotion. I'd had men flirt inappropriately in office settings, but I'd never been a victim of sexual harassment. It left a slick of ugliness behind. Even though I knew I'd done nothing to deserve that treatment, it made me feel powerless and nauseated.

"My magic wouldn't work," I said blankly. "Not completely."

"You were frightened." Gareth's voice was cold and distant. "And he's a strong warlock."

He hadn't moved from the door, his frame practically vibrating with fury. His eyes blazing black, actually bleeding into the whites of his eyes.

Oh, shit.

His rage was growing, not diminishing. The room actually appeared darker, shadows lurking around his frame, smoke-like tendrils whispering around his ankles.

"Gareth," I said softly, walking toward him with slow, steady steps. I raised my hands in a calming gesture.

He didn't answer, apparently battling that monster he'd spoken of. His eyes were full black, swirling with obsidian ink, by the time I reached him and put both hands on his face.

"I want to kill him." His voice was guttural and menacing, his jaw clenching beneath my palms.

"You can't kill a man for touching me."

Those otherworldly eyes slanted toward mine. "Oh, but I can," he said almost sweetly, sending a shiver of fear down my spine. "I can do it from here with little effort at all. Without even laying a finger on him." His ominous gaze went back to the wall. "I've done it before," he confessed.

I blinked swiftly, tears pricking about something I wasn't sure he'd intended to tell me. He'd killed someone?! His beast was riding him so hard he trembled with the furious instinct to act. Then I knew what he meant.

"You mean that vampire in the foster home? In self-defense?"

His chin dipped just barely, his hard gaze holding mine. Somehow, I knew he expected me to react with disdain. I wouldn't, but now wasn't the time to dredge up the past. His beast was already trying to claw its way out of him. He seemed poised on a knife's edge.

"Gareth," I whispered softly before sliding my hands around his waist and pressing my cheek to his chest. "Please don't. You know the penalty if you take a life without trial."

The supernatural world had a different system of laws and justice. After a trial by peers in front of a head witch Enforcer who served as judge, and if the suspect was found guilty of killing another, the penalty was immediate death. Right there in the courtroom by the attending Enforcer. In this case, as Enforcer, my own sister would have to kill Gareth.

I suddenly wanted to vomit at the thought. Squeezing him tighter, I practically shook him when I said, "Don't you fucking dare. I'm fine. Snap out of this right now, Gareth."

Something in my voice made him shudder, then his arms were around me. He breathed heavier, his chest rising and falling quickly. A gentle hand slid to the nape of my neck.

"Are you all right?" he asked for the second time.

His voice was back to its normal deep but calm rumble, no longer shaking with unspent rage.

Pulling away, hands still on his waist, I looked up to find his eyes back to his normal shade of brown—warm mahogany— the black having receded.

"I will be." I gulped hard. Adrenaline still coursed swiftly through my limbs, heart still hammering hard.

His gaze swept over my face and body as if assessing to be sure I was in fact still intact and not harmed. On the outside, I looked fine, but I was aware that there were fractures in my confidence and sense of safety. Still, I held it together as best I could.

His expression turned to anguish. "I'm so sorry I wasn't here sooner." He embraced me closer, heaving out a hard breath.

For a moment, we were silent while he held me close and soothed me with firm strokes on my back. I eased into him, relishing the comfort he gave me. Then he said, "We need to go and report this to Victor Garrison."

The realization made me tense, because of course we did.

What would that do to the competition? Would it null the whole thing?

"We do. But not yet."

"Why not?"

"Richard is the liaison. An accusation would require a hearing in front of a coven jury and judge. It would mess up the entire competition."

"I don't care about the competition." He was back to clenching his jaw.

"But I do. Gareth—"

"Whoa," said Willard as he stepped into the room, finding us in each other's arms. "Sorry. Should I"—he glanced back down the office hallway then back at us— "leave or come back? I'm not sure what to do here."

He was so sweetly awkward, I laughed and stepped away from Gareth. He gave me that look that said this conversation wasn't over.

"No, Willard. Good morning." Remembering my earlier excitement that had been ruined by that fucktard Richard, I hustled back to the printer and grabbed the pages. "I've got a fabulous concept for our next fundraiser, and we need to get planning right away. But I do have a few ideas."

"Just a few?" Willard asked, eyeing the stack in my hands.

Gareth still wasn't back to his normal self yet. Rather than his customary grim-brooding, he was in a state of murder-contemplation-brooding.

"Let's have a seat at the conference table, so I can go over my initial thoughts."

Willard took his normal seat. After I sat down and shot Gareth a look, he finally heaved a sigh and settled on a chair, crossing his arms.

I couldn't blame him for being put out. Honestly, I'd have the same reaction if I'd found some woman in the office harassing him, but I needed to pull him out of his death stupor. I one hundred percent believed him when he said he could kill

Richard from here. How? I wasn't sure. But Gareth didn't lie or exaggerate his capabilities.

And on top of all the other things I now knew he could do, I had to add coercion and magical influence to the list. Was there anything grims couldn't do?

While becoming more fascinated, I also had this niggling worry about his admission that he'd killed someone. Who? How? Why?

I thought I knew Gareth enough to know that he wouldn't kill someone in cold blood, but was he always this controlled man sitting at the table now?

Controlled. I huffed a laugh to myself. He stared at the door as if he were about to run through it to find Richard and do something stupid. And sweet.

His violent reaction to finding Richard harassing me told me that he had strong feelings for me, at least. Not that that was the kind of declaration of his affection that I wanted.

"Find something amusing, Miss Savoie?"

Oh, we were back to this. His voice had a little bite in it. Anger was still riding him hard.

"No, Mr. Blackwater."

"I can't imagine you finding anything amusing at the moment," he snapped, furious that I could smile after an incident like that.

Of course, that made me smile wider. His scowl deepened.

"So what's the idea?" asked Willard, seeming to feel out of place with the conversation.

"We're going to have a werewolf wet t-shirt contest. I already have the full line-up of volunteers."

Even Nico and Mateo agreed to do it, and my sisters along with JJ and the rest of the crew at the Cauldron were going to help run the event.

"Werewolves?" Willard frowned. "Aren't they kind of…you know?"

He didn't complete the sentence, like he was uncomfortable

even mentioning it. I couldn't blame him. Werewolves kept to themselves, and unless you knew any of them personally the way I did, it would be easy—wrong, but still easy—to fall back on an old prejudice that ran deep in our community.

Before I could give Willard my spiel about judging people before you know them, Gareth said, "Werewolves are supernaturals. They deserve the same respect as anyone else. The violent tendency that makes you nervous is unfounded. Besides the fact that werewolves don't lose control of their beasts twenty-four/seven, Lavinia's sister has put a permanent calming spell on them via tattoos. There's nothing to worry about."

Willard's brow raised slightly but he nodded, and that was that.

"Great!" I clapped my hands together, "Now let's get back to the event."

I opened my planner with my calendar and started throwing out upcoming dates. We needed to do it soon, but not too soon that we didn't have time to plan. The contest requirements were to sponsor three fundraising events before the April deadline. As I was rattling off possible dates, Gareth huffed out a heavy sigh and combed his hands into his hair in an uncharacteristic sign of frustration.

"I can't fucking focus here today." His eyes darted to the doorway.

"Why?" asked Willard. "Did something happen?"

"Yes," snapped Gareth.

Willard flinched at Gareth's hostile response. "What?"

"Nothing." I aimed a hard warning look at Gareth.

Gareth scoffed. "*Nothing?*" He twisted to face me, his expression morphing back into murder mode. "You call that nothing?"

"I don't want to talk about it right now."

"And I don't want to think about it right now," he added, a pulse of furious magic billowing into the air.

Willard jumped again, glancing around. "Did you guys feel that?"

I rolled my eyes. "It's him." I pointed to Gareth then whisper-yelled, even though Willard could hear me perfectly, "Get yourself under control. I know you're pissed, but it didn't even happen to you." Oh, boy, that wasn't the right thing to say. His jaw clenched so tight I heard his teeth grinding together. Gareth's look of malice was now burning into me. "Stop it, Gareth. We have work to do."

"Fucking *fine*," he growled. Yes, growled like a goddamn werewolf. Then he snapped to his feet and slammed the chair back in place. "But we're not working at this hellhole today. We're working off-site."

"Um. Okay," Willard agreed immediately, jumping to his feet. The beta immediately obeyed the alpha in the room. "Where?" He grabbed his satchel off his chair.

Inwardly agreeing that was probably a good idea—Gareth obviously wasn't going to focus in the same vicinity as Richard —I gathered my papers and tucked them into my leather bag.

"I'd offer our house, but Mateo is moving in today, and Violet is moving out."

Gareth seemed to be about to ask me something about that but then Willard added, "I've got two roommates, and one works night shifts so he sleeps during the day. He'd be pissed if we woke him."

"We'll go to my place," said Gareth, charging through the doorway but waiting in the hallway for us to catch up.

Willard walked on ahead, while Gareth followed with me right beside me. His expression was fierce and glacial, the impenetrable ice man looking for a victim. When we passed the receptionist desk, I told Cynthia, "We're working off-site today."

"Oh, thanks for letting me know. I'll note it in case Mr. Davis asks."

"He won't be asking," Gareth murmured only loud enough for me to hear while we waited in front of the elevator.

His gaze swept toward the hallway on the other side that led to the upper administration offices. Then I remembered what he'd commanded of Richard.

I looped my fingers around Gareth's forearm and leaned closer, "Will he really not leave his desk for anything? All day? Until seven tonight?"

His gaze swiveled from the hallway leading to Richard's offices to me. I nearly gasped at the level of fiery emotion swirling in those obsidian depths.

"Not for one fucking thing. He's stuck in that chair. Hope he didn't have fiber this morning. As it is, he'll likely piss on himself at some point. But he won't leave his desk until exactly seven o'clock."

Okay, then. That level of persuasion was rare. Like *really* rare. I could plant thoughts in people's minds, even from a long distance. But coercion or persuasion, however you wanted to look at it, usually had a timeline. When we were kids, I would sometimes *persuade* Violet to do the dishes and I'd put the clean ones away, because I hated doing the washing part. She'd snap out of the spell an hour or so later and chew me the hell out for it.

"Gareth," I said with censure. "That's kind of cruel, isn't it? I mean—"

"Don't even fucking think about it. He deserves to sit there and suffer for what he did. To think about what he did. And wonder if I plan to report him to his boss, which I do."

I squeezed Gareth's forearm. "Not yet. Not in the middle of the contest. It'll ruin the whole thing."

"I don't give a flying fuck about the contest, Lavinia. I care about you and the way he mistreated and disrespected you. No telling what he would've done if I hadn't arrived when I did." His frown deepened when he glanced toward the elevator again. "Good thing my intuition told me to come in early today."

"Wait. Are you psychic too?" I whispered too loudly, catching Cynthia's attention.

He wrapped his arm around my shoulder, squeezing me

closer, apparently not caring what Cynthia thought about two contestants cozying up to each other. At this point, neither did I. The feeling of his protective arm around me was utterly divine.

He leaned closer to me and said low, "Ask me later. Just know that Richard's career is toast."

"Just wait," I begged. "Look, I'm angry too. I don't want him doing this to someone else and getting away with it."

His jaw clenched again, a sign he was holding something back. But I went on.

"I agree. We will go together and tell Mr. Garrison everything. After the contest is over. If we do it now, then there will be an interrogation, and it'll throw the whole thing off course. They might even cancel it. I'm not saying what he did isn't completely disgusting, but I'm unharmed." Though emotionally rattled, I didn't admit that. I placed a hand on his chest. "Think about the orphans. We still have work to do, Gareth."

His gaze locked on my pleading expression, but I could tell I was swaying him. The elevator dinged and the doors opened. Willard waited while I stepped in first then Gareth followed.

As the elevator dropped toward the parking garage, he took my hand in his and squeezed, letting out a relieved sigh. I think simply putting distance between us and that asshole Richard was helping him calm down.

"Okay," he agreed quietly. "After."

I squeezed his hand back and smiled up at him. He didn't react, his expression still hard, but there was a glimmer of light in those dark eyes that had my heart asking where he'd been all my life.

When we stepped out into the garage, I wasn't surprised to find a shiny Audi parked right next to my car.

"What's the address?" asked Willard, stopping to open his GPS on his phone.

I did the same. Gareth rattled off an address then we walked to our cars. Once I was safely ensconced in mine, he finally backed out, leading the way.

We lost each other in morning traffic, leaving the business district and heading into the Garden District, the houses growing bigger and bigger as we drew closer to his address.

Willard was right behind me as we turned down Prytania Street. Gareth's Audi waited in front of an iron gate that was opening by remote when I pulled up behind him.

"Wowza," I muttered to myself, staring at the old-style mansion that Gareth lived in.

I knew he had money, but I didn't imagine he had *this* kind of money.

We wound up a long driveway that circled at the front door, but Gareth drove around the back to the garage which opened as he approached.

Willard and I parked in the circular driveway dominated by a white marble fountain. I stepped out and stared at the work of art. It was a beautiful statue of a naked Medusa, holding the head of Perseus. The water spouted from Perseus's mouth. When I stepped closer, I noticed that Medusa's partially opened mouth revealed sharp, vampire fangs. Knowing Gareth, there was a story and purpose behind this. Like everything else about Gareth, I longed to know more.

Stepping up to the giant, intricate glass and wood front door, I stared. Willard joined me.

"Hot damn. Does he live here alone?"

"No," said Gareth when he opened the front door. Apparently, he'd traced vampire-fast through the house to let us in. "Queenie lives with me."

"Who's Queenie?" I asked before I could think better of it. There was no mistaking the jealousy-tinged-annoyance in my tone.

Gareth smiled. A bright, big one that made my insides melt and my knees wobble. "Come on in and meet her."

CHAPTER SEVENTEEN

~GARETH~

I was glad I had the drive from Garrison Media back to the house to completely calm the fuck down. It had taken every ounce of willpower to keep my beast at bay, to keep from acting on my first instinct when I'd walked into the office and seen Richard cornering Lavinia with his filthy hands on her. My first thought was to break his hand then break his neck and kill him.

My level of control had certainly come a long way. There was a time when I reacted with swift retribution. Richard Davis was a lucky man. I'd spent decades honing the skills Aunt Lucille had taught me, to corral the black magic living inside me that always wanted to be unleashed.

Rather than piddling on himself at his desk in his corner office where I'd confined him—and he would at some point today I was pleased to remind myself—he would have been a pile of broken bones, bleeding out of several orifices. Had I not had the patient tutelage of my caring aunt, Richard would now be dead.

But I had. So I'd managed to punish him in the mildest of

ways. I hadn't wanted to relent to Lavinia, that we not report his sexual harassment immediately. But she'd had a point. It would certainly upend this entire campaign, coloring it with the ugliness of Richard's behavior. There was a chance that the contest would come to a halt altogether.

Then Lavinia would've been right and we'd have to forfeit all of our hard work so far, not continuing the campaign so close to my heart. To bring awareness to the need for a foster program for supernatural orphans. Something direly needed by our community.

If I could've just thrown money at it to resolve, I would have. But grims didn't have the influence in the supernatural community the way witches did. The High Witch Guilds controlled the majority of laws and governmental programs for our international community. I needed their help to get this campaign off the ground, to bring witches and warlocks to the table to help those most in need of our help. Our children.

"Right through here," I told Lavinia and Willard as they crossed my doorstep. "We can work in the living room."

I led them through the foyer and down a short hallway, past the winding staircase and into the open living room.

"Whoa," murmured Willard as they walked farther into my home.

I hadn't looked at it through other people's eyes. The living space was large with cathedral ceilings, wooden beams soaring twenty feet overhead.

On the opposite wall of the brown suede sectional sofa and club chair was a river-rock fireplace that climbed to the vaulted ceiling. This room overlooked a spacious backyard and patio with a pergola. Beyond the living room was an open dining room, also overlooking the backyard.

"Make yourselves comfortable."

I turned to them, finding Willard staring out through the windows, Lavinia's surprised expression on me. For the first time, I felt a little uncomfortable with my wealth.

Though I'd accumulated all of it myself from working cyber security for Obsidian Corporation, the many apps I'd created and sold to the highest bidders, and the recent night club I'd opened, I'd not quite realized how this level of wealth was not the norm.

I'd once been penniless, alone, and unwanted. Though I could do little about the second two, I'd made it my goal to make sure I would never be without money again. I suppose, as in all things, I went a little overboard.

Swallowing against my discomfort, I'd asked, "Can I get you something to drink?"

Lavinia opened her mouth to reply, but then the click-clack of Queenie's toenails on the wood floor announced her arrival.

Lavinia's expression softened from shock to sheer joy. "Look at you, pretty girl."

She lowered to her knees and held out a hand. My three-legged dog immediately pranced over to the other pretty girl in the room.

"Oh, my goodness," crooned Lavinia as she stroked her back and pushed the loose white hair away from the dog's eyes to look at her. "What a sweetie you are." Then she looked up at me, smiling so wide my heart clenched at the beauty of it. "Queenie?"

A stiff nod. "Queenie."

Her head bent back toward my princess, lavishing attention on her. Lavinia had tied her long black hair back with a silky, red scarf. Hands in my pockets, I tried to hold myself together at the sight of a beaming Lavinia on my floor in her business attire with my dog in her lap, laughing and cooing softly. She was so fucking beautiful and perfect, I couldn't breathe.

Without another word, I left them and fetched some bottles of water from the fridge. I took a minute to collect myself, well, as much as possible. I think the fact that I was still riding emotions of fury all the way back to my house, that I hadn't prepared myself for what it would feel like to have her in my home.

If I didn't know there was research that supported the primal reaction of an alpha male who held his mate in his lair, I'd have thought I was coming down with the flu. But no, this feverish feeling, accompanied by an increased heart rate and almost sickly sensation, came from the fact that she was undoubtedly my mate and was making herself at home in my personal domain, but she wasn't mine. Yet.

She didn't even know that grims could recognize their true mates like vampires and werewolves. But how could she? She didn't know our ancestry?

Yet again, I felt compelled to tell her. I wanted to even while it had been drilled into me from adolescence upward to follow the grim code.

Fuck the code.

I smiled at Aunt Lucille's words ringing in my ear as I returned to the living room with three waters in hand. Willard had set himself up in the club chair, having dragged my oak coffee table toward him to prop up his laptop. Lavinia sat in the middle corner of the sectional, her tablet and stylus in her lap. She tapped her calendar open and scrolled. Queenie was curled up at her hip.

I closed my eyes at the longing that pierced through flesh and bone, to have her right there every day, every night, forever, looking so sweet and perfect. Then I cleared my throat.

"Here you are." I set a water in front of both of them.

"Very nice home, Gareth." Lavinia was still looking around.

"I'm pleased you like it." My pulse quickened which confused me until I realized how badly I wanted her to like my home. How much I wanted her to like being here. Hopefully permanently someday if I was lucky.

"It's very neat and clean, which doesn't surprise me." She smirked playfully.

"I like things in order."

She huffed a laugh. "I know, Mr. Control Freak."

She honestly had no idea.

"Okay," I changed the subject, "where do we start?"

"The date for the event," said Lavinia, petting Queenie absent-mindedly. "I say we do it the Saturday before St. Patrick's Day. People are ready to get outside, but we don't want to butt up against all the green beer parties and so forth."

"True," I agreed, sitting next to her and propping my feet on the coffee table before opening my laptop. "Though you know what would be cool to further promote the event?"

"What's that?" asked Lavinia.

"We could give a free green beer coupon from The Cauldron to everyone who buys a ticket to our event. I'm sure Jules would agree to split the cost of the promotion."

Lavinia's eyes brightened. "That's a fabulous idea. Jules would definitely go for it."

We were given a small budget to work with for the expenses with each promotion. But after seeing the sales from tickets to the online YouTube viewing of the Pin-up Photo Shoot plus the added donations during the event, we had more than enough to re-invest in the set-up of the wet t-shirt contest.

"Um, I kind of thought of another possible idea," Willard added timidly.

He was introverted by nature, but also he lacked the confidence in speaking with others. While a definite genius in graphic design and collecting trafficking data—so good, he'd make a fairly decent grim—Willard needed to be more aggressive with his ideas.

"Tell us," I told him.

He glanced at me then down at his lap as he always did, tapping the edge of his laptop nervously. "So, the Irish Channel Parade is a popular event."

That was an understatement. The St. Patrick's Day parade was more popular to locals than Mardi Gras.

"True," said Lavinia. "What were you thinking?"

Willard shifted nervously but went on. "Well, it goes right down Magazine Street past Tracey's, which is considered the original Irish Channel bar. What if we did a live event like we did for the photoshoot, covering the parade from right outside Tracey's."

Lavinia squealed with excitement. Willard jumped. Queenie simply lifted her head and licked Lavinia's wrist. I frowned, jealous of my own damn dog.

"That is a freaking fabulous idea, Willard!" She turned her shining excitement toward me, and I didn't even suppress my smile. Her enthusiasm and joy was contagious. "Can you imagine? Willard, I'll make us both some cute shamrock crowns."

"Crowns? We?" he choked out.

"Of course! We'll be King and Queen Shamrock, an honorary appointment only since we aren't actually affiliated with the parade, just to play up the fun of the day."

"I can't be in front of the camera." Willard's voice squeaked with anxiety.

Lavinia laughed. "Oh, yes you can. This is your idea. I'll be there to help you and guide the conversation, but you are one hundred percent going to be a part of the show."

"What would I say?"

I had to bite my bottom lip to keep from laughing at Willard's painfully terrified expression as he let it sink in that his idea was so great, we were not only doing it, but he was co-hosting it.

Lavinia tapped on her tablet, pulling up sites on the parade of course. "You'll research the floats that will be on, the history of the parade, why it's important to our community and so on and so forth. You're great at delivering facts."

"In a droll, dry manner. Yes."

Lavinia simply smiled in her encouraging way. "You'll be great. I'll be right there next to you. And Gareth will be feeding us info with event subscribers on the YouTube channel, giving us questions to answer from our viewers. Right, Gareth?" She looked at me expectantly.

I captured that look and stored it away for later. I was cataloging every one of her lovely expressions and hoarding them like golden treasures. This dragon refused to let even one of them slip away.

"Of course," I agreed.

"See? As a matter of fact, Willard, if you want to get started on research for that. You'll need to contact the manager at Tracey's first, so why don't you type up that email."

"Can one of you check it though before I send it? Sometimes, I don't come across the way I intended in emails."

"Sure," she said easily. "I think Gareth and I can handle planning the wet t-shirt contest. To be honest, I did a street party gallery opening for my sister Violet and Nico's tattoo shop several weeks ago. We should set up the exact same venue, except instead of a stage for a band, we'll need a longer catwalk. We can use the same rental company I used last time."

She kept jabbering about the gallery opening—the food truck vendors, the alcohol supplied by the Cauldron, the permits she'd gotten from the city to block off the dead-end street. I heard her, but my concentration had slipped altogether, my focus on that red silk scarf.

The way the silken cloth trailed over her pale shoulder when she turned her head. It was a teasing touch that made my fingers itch and my body burn. Paired with the thick, dark waves of her ponytail brushing along the soft skin of her neck and over her breast, it was a miracle I could focus on anything at all.

"What do you guys want for lunch?" I asked, standing up, needing to get out of the room.

"Is it that time already?" Lavinia glanced at her tablet. "It's only ten." She laughed, as if she knew my behavior was erratic.

"I'll find some menus."

I could hardly handle having her so close—the woman of my dreams—imagining all the ways I wanted her in my house.

Sitting at the kitchen bar while I cooked us dinner, stretching out on the sofa together watching television, playing with Queenie out in the backyard, spending night after night in my bed while I pleasured her.

Mark me well…you are worthy of love, dear boy.

"Think of something else," I muttered to myself, blinking away these overwhelming thoughts and emotions as I opened a kitchen drawer where I stored my to-go menus.

I couldn't walk back into the room with an obvious erection. It was only ten in the damn morning, for fuck's sake!

Combing both hands through my hair, I inhaled and exhaled a deep breath, willing my dick to behave.

"Get your shit together," I muttered.

Then I calmly shifted my half-hard cock in my pants and took the to-go menus back to the living room where I'd somehow force myself to think nothing but professional thoughts for the remainder of the day.

CHAPTER EIGHTEEN

~LIVVY~

T HE SKY WAS PINKISH-ORANGE AS THE SUN SLIPPED BEYOND THE tall trees in Gareth's backyard. Pizza boxes and to-go drinks from Reginelli's Pizzeria were still piled on the coffee table. We'd been working quietly on our own after Gareth and I had spent some time brainstorming party favors.

My favorite so far was promo t-shirts we'd sell at cost and buttons we'd give away. The design would be the Blood Moon pack logo which was a howling wolf's head at the center and the event title *Wolves Gone Wild Wet T-shirt Contest* and the date.

At first, Willard had butted into the conversation, reminding us that we'd have humans, not just supernaturals showing up at a street party, who would wonder what the title meant. But Gareth quickly explained we'd advertise that the event was sponsored by the Blood Moon pack, and humans would associate the wolf reference to the motorcycle club.

The supernaturals would know the truth of it, and that was what was important. To see werewolves in a friendly, fun manner, dedicating their time for charity. And not going all beast-mode in a wild, screaming crowd.

"And their muscles," I'd added. "Don't forget they're dedicating that too."

Gareth had frowned but made no further comment. I kept my grinning to a minimum, but I loved poking him. That's why I'd decided to play my favorite Depeche Mode songs on loop through his Bluetooth speaker.

He hadn't said a word. No one had in over an hour. But I could see his jaw clenching when "Never Let Me Down Again" came on for the third time. He glared at me, but I simply smiled sweetly back, then returned to my tablet.

He rose and stacked the empty pizza boxes then carried them into the kitchen, while Willard went to the bathroom. When Gareth returned, he had his phone in hand, and he looked like a man on a mission. He sat on the opposite part of the sectional sofa rather than next to me this time then reached over and tapped my phone with his index finger. The music immediately stopped.

How'd he do that?

Then he set his phone on the table and a new song came on. As soon as the opening lines with the craggy voice of Gordon James Gano, the lead singer of the Violent Femmes, came on, I knew what it was. It was an iconic, eighties song of the alternative punk era. Gareth's demeanor and expression transformed from annoyed to hot, aroused male in a millisecond.

His MacBook remained open at his side not propped on his thigh the way it had been the entire day. He leaned back against the cushion, his hands clasped in his lap, one ankle crossed over the other knee, toe tapping to the swift beat.

He was in a relaxed position of observation, but his body was tense, coiled. And I was the object of his inspection as Gano asked why he couldn't get *just one kiss.*

This wasn't Gareth being defiant and irritated from listening to my music. This was a serenade. And the song "Add It Up" was a plea, a command, and a countdown.

Suddenly, I couldn't breathe.

He hadn't taken his dark, predatory gaze from mine, and now he was mouthing the lyrics to me without missing a word.

Willard walked back into the room, becoming instantly aware of this stare-off Gareth and I were yet again embroiled in. Then Willard mumbled something about needing to get home while quickly snapping his laptop shut and heading out the front door without another word.

All the while, Gareth's focus hadn't moved from me as he continued to "sing" the aggressive mantra about a guy wanting to get into a girl's pants.

By the time he got to the part about needing *just one fuck*, I was squirming in place, turned on beyond reason. Still, I didn't break away from him and he didn't move an inch. Until Gano's voice got soft, leading to that hard sexy line. That's when Gareth moved one hand from his knee up his thigh and cupped his obviously hard package in his pants, all while singing about being between my thighs.

I whimpered, said thighs sticking together with sweat, my panties sticky for another reason. He stood and moved slowly around the coffee table, the alternative rock beat loud and aggressive. While sex radiated from the man, he didn't attack me and push me into the cushions like I thought he might. Hoped.

No. He bracketed his legs on the outside of mine and leaned forward, forcing me to push back into the sofa cushion. He braced both his hands next to my shoulders, easing his face close to mine as the song finally wound to a close, ending with a sharp snap. Then nothing. No sound at all.

The intensity of our locked gazes for the duration of that entire song plus the obvious frustrated desire building between us had my pulse throbbing so hard I could feel it at the base of my throat.

"I want to fuck you, Lavinia. In my bed. Right now."

Well, no mixed messages there. That's one thing I could always count on with Gareth. Direct and to the point.

I licked my lips, remembering the conversation with Violet and what I'd decided to do, to propose, in order to gain his trust.

"I have an offer. Or maybe a request."

He waited while I inhaled a deep breath, knowing I'd never once thought about letting someone do this to me before. But somehow knowing it was exactly what Gareth wanted and needed from me.

"I'd like you to tie me up."

Goddess save me. The brown of his eyes vanished behind liquid pools of black. He didn't move a muscle, but the glittering fire in his gaze melted me further back into the seat cushions.

"Will you obey my commands?"

On a ragged exhale, I whispered, "Yes."

"You said you'd never hand the reins over to me."

"I telepathed it actually, but yes. You're right. I did say that." It was on the day he'd first telepathed that erotic image that had kept me up many, many a night.

"What's changed? Why would you offer something like that to me?"

"Because I want something from you."

"What?" The black bled farther into the white.

"Your trust."

He was the one breathing heavily now. Still staring, still considering. Then he stood straight and held out a hand to me. I took it and let him help me to my feet. Before I could take a step, he turned me by my waist and held my face between his warm palms then he slanted his mouth against mine. I whimpered when his tongue touched mine, sweeping softly and sweetly.

Clenching my fists in his hair, I held him tight as he delved deeper. Then something tragic dawned on me. I broke the kiss.

"Oh, shit."

"What is it?" His brow pinched together.

I couldn't believe this. I didn't know I'd have this opportunity today, a workday, to be in Gareth's bed. My appointment to get waxed was in fact tomorrow afternoon.

I'd planned to ask him out on a date this weekend, and we'd finally do the deed. But the deed was totally happening right now. Except I liked my pussy nice and tidy for such events. I wasn't hygienically prepared, dammit!

"Tell me," he demanded.

Gareth likes direct. Okay then.

"I had an appointment to get waxed tomorrow."

That frown was back. "So?"

"I like to be trim down there."

He continued to frown at me like I'd lost my mind.

My hands now on his shoulders, I tried to put space between us, but he refused to let me move in inch.

"It's not a big deal," I told him. "If you'll let me borrow a razor, I'll take a quick shower and—"

"No."

Figures. Most guys don't like to loan their razors. I was about to suggest I go home, get a shower, and return after but he had other plans.

"I'll do it."

I laughed. "Come again. You want to shave…my pussy?"

"Yes." The frown was gone and that incinerate-my-loins look was back. He eased forward and brushed a feather-light kiss across my mouth. "I can be gentle."

He waited, patiently as ever, while I stared slack-jawed, trying to process his request. Then finally, "Okay."

"Okay?" His brow rose in a shocked expression I'm not sure I'd ever seen on him.

"You heard me."

"Close your eyes."

Immediately, he tossed me over his shoulder caveman style, and he traced up the stairs. I barely had the good sense or time to close my eyes as he'd told me. The movement was so fast, it might've given me motion sickness if I hadn't.

"Gareth!" I yelled as he tossed me off his shoulders and onto his bed.

I landed on my back, my legs splayed, knees up. His grin was nothing short of feral. "Take your clothes off and get back in that exact position."

His gaze skated down my body before he turned toward his bathroom. Luxurious bathroom with dark tile from what I could see. I took a second to catch my breath as he disappeared inside, not turning on any lights.

"I can just lift my dress."

He popped back into the doorway of the bathroom. "You agreed to do what I say. Are you going back on your offer already?"

I shook my head as his gaze watched my hand with my panties while I tossed them to his bedroom floor.

"Fuck," he growled, adjusting his dick in his pants before tracing downstairs then back again in ten seconds and disappearing back into the bathroom.

It wasn't in my nature to agree and go along so easily. I was always fighting back or the one who was doing the ordering around at the very least. I was used to leading. Following was new to me. But he was right. I'd agreed to obey.

The thought sent a new kind of thrill down my body, heat swelling between my now panty-less legs. To let go and let him take the reins could be exactly what I needed. That's what Clara and Violet kept telling me anyway.

Was I really doing this? Letting a guy wield a razor on my tenderest bits? Exposing myself so nakedly—literally—for his keen observation?

Yes, I loved taking a walk on the wild side, but my heart was racing with a lot of adrenaline and a touch of trepidation. Still, I wanted to do it.

So I stood and removed my dress, unzipping it down the side while I heard the water running in the bathroom. I quickly removed my bra and scooted back onto his king size bed. The comforter was gray, but I lifted the corner to find—yep—black, silk sheets. My pussy throbbed at the very sight of them.

"Oh, boy."

When I lay my head down, the knot of my ponytail bothered me. Untying the scarf from my hair, I removed it and the ponytail holder and set them on his nightstand, shaking out my hair before lying back and crooking my knees back in the position he wanted me.

Of course, when he walked out of his bathroom in nothing but black boxer briefs, a white towel over his arm, holding a razor in one hand and a bowl of steaming water in the other, my pulse stuttered again. I'd imagined his body and gotten to feel quite a bit of it under his tailored clothes. Neither of us were fully naked during our interlude in the bar, so I hadn't planned for the glorious eye candy before me.

Fair skin, tight muscles, just the right amount of sparse hair along his naval and across his chest. His thighs were thicker than I'd thought and the bulge in his boxer briefs was as big as I remembered. Suddenly, I wanted to skip the shave, but also there was something insanely thrilling about Gareth servicing me in this way.

"You look like a naughty waiter," I remarked with a smile.

"You look like my delicious dinner." His dark gaze was in fact eating me up with relish.

I squeaked when a kitchen chair came floating through the doorway. He grinned, having used his TK to summon it. He made it land right beside the bed then he set his bowl and razor there. A can of shaving gel came floating from the bathroom then.

I couldn't help but laugh at the insanity of the situation,

which of course made my large breasts bounce. His hot gaze caught all.

He closed his eyes, nostrils flaring, as he whispered something to himself.

"What's that? I didn't hear you," I teased.

"I was praying for patience." He maneuvered onto his knees between my spread legs.

"I didn't know you were a spiritual kind of guy."

"How could I not be?" he asked, unfolding the towel. "Perfection like this doesn't happen by chance." His gaze was on me again, everywhere. Then he spread the towel below me. "Lift your hips."

I did and he slid the towel under me so my bum rested on it. I must've been frowning in question, because he added with a quirk of his mouth, "It's going to get wet down here."

A nervous laugh belted out of me. Punny Gareth was unexpectedly adorable, trying to put me at ease. Then he was all business.

"Let your knees drop to the mattress. I need you wide open."

Jeez, Louise!

Another wash of heat swept over my skin at his business-like and authoritative manner. But I did as I was told and spread wide for him.

The lamp flipped on all by itself. Telekinesis, of course. Neither Violet nor Jules could do that, use their TK with such precision.

He took a washcloth from inside the bowl and squeezed out the excess water then he unfolded it and gently placed it between my legs, completely covering me. I winced a little at the sudden heat, then sighed at the lovely sensation. He pressed his entire hand over the cloth, making sure the heat softened my skin.

The weight of his hand there and the fierceness of his gaze

felt like a marking. Like he had every right to hold my pussy and drink in my naked body spread out before him.

Who knows? Maybe he did. Maybe the Goddess of Magic and Earth meant him just for me. Because one tiny word kept repeating inside my head. *Yes.*

His gaze held mine with infinite tenderness as he repeated the process with the cloth, making sure my skin was pliant and soft.

"Be gentle," I whispered. "I'm quite partial to everything down there."

Obsidian eyes held me in their thrall. "Trust me, Lavinia."

I swallowed hard at his plea, for that is what it was. And wasn't that the whole reason I'd offered to be bound? To show him that I did? I simply hadn't expected this intimate prelude. But here we were. I exhaled a deep breath and tried to calm my nerves.

"Is there meaning behind this?" He trailed a finger over the tale of the dragon tattoo that curled over my hip.

"No." I smiled, comforted that he seemed to be distracting me. "Like what?"

"Black dragons symbolize revenge." His expression never shifted, but the timbre of his voice dipped a fraction deeper.

"Yeah, I know. But it doesn't mean that for me. I just thought it was cool." I looked at the way the tail of the dragon curved along my waist, disappearing to my back where I knew the head roared across my right shoulder. "And I like the contrast of the black ink against my skin. Why?"

"I was wondering if there was someone else I needed to put on my hitlist."

"Don't tease," I told him firmly.

He lifted the rag, his dark gaze flicking to mine then away. "I wasn't." Then came the shaving gel.

"Good heavens," I hissed as he worked the lather with agile fingers in the crease of my thighs and along my pussy lips.

He didn't react except with a slight quirk of his lips at my obviously aroused reaction to his attentions.

"Have you done this before?" Again, I was annoyed at the jealousy I heard in my own voice.

"Shaved a girl's pussy?" His dark gaze darted to me then back at his attentively working fingers, rubbing the gel everywhere, even down my crack to my ass. "No, Lavinia." His voice was low and sonorous. "I've never done this before."

Satisfied, I relaxed as he took his razor and started higher up in the crease of my left thigh then went about shaving with precision and deep concentration. The sensation was soothing and relaxing. Definitely not the same as a waxing.

Closing my eyes, I let myself enjoy this odd but lovely experience. "I'm going to make an appointment with Blackwater's Parlor twice a month."

"I'm at your service," he said matter-of-factly, rinsing the razor and tapping it on the edge of the glass bowl. "What currency are you paying me in?"

Grinning without opening my eyes, I answered, "Kisses."

"I'll deliver kisses anywhere you want them."

"I meant I'd give *you* kisses." I cracked an eye open. "But I'll take them too."

He didn't even glance up at me, his professional look firmly in place. He started to shave lower, the fingers of his free hand pressing along the inner lip—and because he couldn't not, also my clit—to get a close shave. I bit my bottom lip to keep from moaning too loudly, but I couldn't keep silent altogether.

This was the strangest and yet somehow the most erotic foreplay I'd ever had.

"Do you like to keep a little strip or do you want it bare?" he asked, dipping the razor into the bowl and moving to the other side.

"Whatever you want."

He paused, which had me opening my eyes in a sleepy, aroused state. He shook his head on a small laugh.

"If this is what it takes to get you compliant in my bed, then I'll shave you for free for the rest of your life."

He was all concentration and yet a line creased his brow for a second then was gone. He'd said it offhandedly. Did he mean to imply we'd be together for the rest of our lives? The thought had been laid out there, nevertheless.

Me and Gareth, forever.

I tested the waters, playing right back. But also, not playing.

"I'll put it in the prenup," I teased him. "I won't take your millions of dollars, and you will shave my pussy with tenderness and affection twice a month."

He sat up straight, setting the razor aside. "Deal, Lavinia."

There was no teasing note in his voice or his expression, but the intensity amplified when he gripped my ankles and placed my bare feet on his shoulders.

"Keep them there."

He lifted the razor again after swirling it in the warm water. He refreshed the shaving gel farther down my crack and went back to shaving with gentle yet precise strokes. He went *all* the way down, being as proficient as if this were an important job.

I had a feeling this was how Gareth did everything. With utmost care and deep concentration. Whether he was analyzing data for the campaign or researching for a new app or shaving my pussy, he was going to give it all of his attention. Something loosened inside my chest, that melty sensation flaring back tenfold.

We hadn't even had sex yet, and I was pretty sure that I was falling for this enigmatic man. One who had yet to truly open up to me.

Baby steps, I reminded myself.

Suddenly he was on his feet. "Don't move," he commanded. So I didn't.

He carried the bowl back to the bathroom where I heard the faucet going on and off. He returned with the cloth, rinsed and heated again as I could see the steam. He pressed it to my pussy and let it sit for a moment, holding his hand there, looking down at me. I remained still, looking back.

After a moment, he removed it and set it on the chair then picked up a bottle he'd brought from the bathroom. He poured some lotion into his and warmed it between his palms. Gentle heat caressed my skin as he started at my thighs and massaged up and at the creases, then slid one hand over my pussy and between the lips, sliding the pad of his thumb around my clit.

I made some unintelligible noise, part grunt, part moan as my hips came off the bed, wanting more of his attention. I was so loose and aroused and hungry for his touch. For his everything.

He massaged the lotion with smooth, perfect motions but not hard enough.

"Gareth," I whispered, rocking up into his questing, exploring fingers. "Please."

Magic sparked in the room. For once in my life, I didn't know if it was mine or his, my body heating and coming alive with remarkable speed.

He removed his fingers from my slit. I whimpered in distress. He gripped my thigh and leaned forward, placing an entirely too chaste kiss on my freshly shaved mound. Then he stood up at the end of the bed, towering over me.

"Hand me your scarf."

I couldn't think for a second, arousal humming through my body. I rolled partly over and lifted the scarf from the nightstand then held it out to him. He took it, his forearms and biceps going tight as he stretched it between both of his hands.

"Now get up on your knees facing the wall, hands behind your back."

I stalled, my brain trying to catch up. He was definitely tying me up.

He angled his head and asked, not harshly but definitely with a thread of dominance, "Are you going back on your word?"

"No."

Quickly, I obeyed his command, breathing erratically at the level of arousal pooling between my legs and the heat coursing through my blood from obeying his commands. Strangely, handing over my will to him had never made me feel more powerful. Or free.

CHAPTER NINETEEN

~GARETH~

In all my fantasies of getting Lavinia into my bed, I never thought it would start with me shaving her pussy. It had been a strangely erotic experience. And intimate. By the scent of her arousal, it had revved her up as much as me.

But it wasn't even that intimacy that had melted a layer of ice around my heart. It was her offer to be bound. To be at my mercy. Especially after that incident with Richard fucking Davis. A man who wouldn't be drawing breath easily very soon if I had my way.

Before my blood could start boiling, I slammed that door shut on my mind, pushing that problem far away. He had no place in this room right now.

Lavinia had done exactly what I'd asked. Currently, she was nude, on her knees, on my bed, facing the wall, hands behind her back.

Gently, I wrapped and tied one wrist with the red scarf. Then I bound it with the other, tying it firmly but softly into a bow.

Kneeling behind her on the mattress, I wrapped an arm all the way across her chest to her opposite shoulder. "Ease forward to rest your cheek on the bed. I've got you."

She did. She trusted me, giving me her weight, and allowing me to position her on the bed, face down, ass up.

Her submission meant everything. She had *no* idea what this was doing to me. I'd played games in bed with other partners, but that's all it had been. A means to an end. Arousal and release.

But Lavinia knew me better than anyone, better than any woman before her. She possessed information that would give most supernatural women extreme pause, would not only make them refuse to be bound in my presence, but would likely make them run screaming from my home. Then promptly report me to the closest High Witch Guild.

She'd witnessed firsthand a touch of the dark magic that lived inside of me, how it could escape my control if I wasn't fully focused. She'd heard me admit that I'd killed another person. And she was aware that my magical power was greater than hers and anyone she knew. Even an Enforcer, which was—according to records of the witch and warlock guilds—the most powerful supernatural in our world.

Now, she knew better. She'd watched me overpower Richard without any effort at all. Though she hadn't witnessed the destruction of his entire being that was taking place in my mind in that moment, she was a smart woman. She knew there were few, if any, limits to what I could do. What I would do if provoked.

And yet, she'd offered herself to me. Like this.

After combing her long black hair aside to smooth across the covers, I placed a palm at the base of her beautiful, slender neck and slid it down her spine. She curved under my touch like a contented cat, exhaling a slow breath, her eyes closed. She trembled.

"Don't be afraid."

"I'm not." And she meant it. The trembling wasn't from fear.

I straightened, one hand gripping her soft hip, the other still traveling its slow trek down her spine, over her bound hands, to her sweetly curved ass. Smoothing my hand in a circle on her right cheek, I said, "You are so unfathomably beautiful, Lavinia."

Then I reared my hand back and spanked her hard. She jolted and grunted, likely not expecting the sting.

"Have you ever been spanked before?" I asked her, voice losing some of its control.

"Never."

"Mmm. My handprint looks so perfect right here." She tensed when I moved to the other side. "Relax."

She choked out a laugh, but I smacked her again, stopping that altogether.

"*Fuck*," she muffled into the mattress.

I soothed the sting with soothing circles.

"Do you want me to stop?" The question, the offer, took a monumental level of surrender on my part, because every ounce of my body rebelled against the idea of stopping.

After a few heavy breaths, she whispered, "No."

"All you have to do is say *stop*. At any time, say that word and I will."

"I'm not saying it," she bit back with intent.

I could hear every level of her emotions. Frustration, arousal, denial of the arousal. That made me smile.

I let my hand slide lower, gliding a finger along her slit. As I knew already from her scent, she was slick and soaking. She moaned when I swirled over her clit.

"Good girl."

No.

Her thought popped into my head. She'd opened a telepathic channel. Another thing that made me smile, because she was giving herself to me in so many ways.

No? I asked her back. *Do you mean* stop?

I never said that. Don't try to force me to use your safety word.

I chuckled at her defiance. *Why did you say no then?*

I meant, why does this feel so good?

Stop thinking so much, I ordered her. *Let me take care of you.*

She visibly relaxed, releasing another breath, eyes still closed. I reared my hand back and smacked her again on the opposite side then three times in quick succession on the left.

She jumped every time, crying out and cursing again. I soothed the reddened skin immediately with soft, slow circles. She breathed more heavily. Her pussy glistened with arousal, but I gave her one last rap on the other side.

She jerked forward. "Gareth," she groaned into the covers, twisting her wrists but the scarf held.

The sound of her begging me, the sight of her bound for me, compliant and submissive, the reddened marks of my handprint on her ass. Fuck, I'd never been this hard in my life.

"Shh," I soothed, crouching behind her. Lifting her ass higher, I whispered against the heart of her, "I'm going to make it all better."

Then I licked her from clit to her entrance, kissing her deep, thrusting with my tongue. She made soft mewling sounds, squirming beneath me, while I kept her as still as possible. She rocked back, trying to ride my face, but I held her tight.

This is torture, her soft words filtered into my brain.

What do you want?

You know what I want?

Say it.

Fuck me, Gareth. Please.

Out loud, I demanded.

You want me to beg?

Yes.

"Please, Gareth. I want you to fuck me so hard. Like you've never fucked another woman. Like I'm all you want, all you ever need. Please, fuck me...so, so hard. I *need* you."

I honestly didn't think she would do it. Lavinia wasn't the begging kind of woman. She was the one who'd make others beg, crawl, become slaves to her whims and desires. Which is why my vision hazed with lust when the words started pouring from her mouth.

I'd used my TK to open my nightstand table and fly a condom through the air to me after her first *please*. I suited up and squeezed my cock with one stroke before I slid the head through her silken slit. It wasn't just the words that were unraveling me one syllable at a time. It was the truth I heard in them. *Felt* in them.

The *need* was a beast all its own, hers for me, and mine for her. Something I'd yet to ever experience. It was terrifying and wonderful at once. And fuck, if I wasn't going to feed this monster till it was good and sated.

Pressing against her opening, I gripped her hips. "I need you, too," I confessed, fucking into her one inch at a time till I was seated fully, hissing at the glorious feeling of finally being inside her. "Need this sweet, tight pussy. Goddamn, Lavinia."

She moaned, arching her back further, letting me go deeper. "Yes," she cooed. "Now, fuck me hard. Gareth. *Please*."

Without fail, I started to fuck her with hard, fast strokes, flesh slapping flesh, the slick sound of her wetness driving me mad. She felt so goddamn good. I couldn't believe the level of ecstasy pouring through my veins, burning through my body while I pumped her good and deep.

Groaning, I gripped her rounded hips and drove home with the hard thrusts she'd asked for. Begged me for. My body, mind, and soul narrowed to the visceral pleasure she was giving me, taking me the way I wanted her. Her moans grew louder as she rocked back in rhythm with my body.

She was so fucking perfect. I was losing my mind—and so much more—with every drive. I knew with crystal clarity that I'd never be the same after this. After one night in the arms and inside the body of Lavinia, I'd be reborn a different man. One who lived and breathed for only her.

"Coming already?" I marveled aloud when the flutters escalated to grasping pulses around my dick, her loud wail hardening my cock even more. "Fuck, baby," I growled.

Still inside her, I stopped thrusting while her orgasm continued to squeeze me tight. I untied the scarf, one side still wrapped around her wrist. Her arms fell limply to her sides, and I heard her sniffle.

"Fuck."

Pulling out, I rolled her over and lowered between her legs, holding my weight on one forearm ,and cupping her face with my other hand. A tear slid down her cheek into her hair, her eyes glassy with post-orgasm bliss and some other emotion I couldn't identify.

Her spirit seemed to be floating in sub-space from the minimal pain and being bound, which was unexpected. It had also made her come far faster than I imagined.

"Did I hurt you?"

My gut clenched, pain lacerating my heart at the thought that I had. I didn't think I had physically, but if I had or had caused her emotional distress, I'd kick my own fucking ass.

She shook her head and smiled as another tear fell. I wiped it with my thumb. "No, Gareth," she whispered. "Now, fuck me slow. And kiss me softly."

Realizing I was the one taking orders now and not giving a damn that I was, I immediately obeyed her, sliding in deep. I crushed my chest to hers, wishing I'd made time to give attention to her beautiful breasts. Later, I told myself, right before I pressed her mouth open with mine and slid my tongue along hers.

I swallowed her moan and spread my knees wider so I could hit her at a better angle and fuck her the way she'd told me to. The way she deserved, worshipping her with my body, grinding deep.

Some part of me marveled that I had no problem taking orders from Lavinia. I'd never taken orders from anyone. Ever. Not after I'd killed the last person who'd ever dominated me in any way.

But obeying Lavinia didn't feel like being oppressed or pushed or smothered. It felt...right.

Lifting enough so that I could watch her face, our lips brushing with each tender thrust of my hips, I stared in amazement.

"You're the most beautiful woman I've ever seen."

She smiled. "That's just sex endorphins."

"I haven't come yet."

Her smile faded, because she knew. I wasn't hiding anything anymore. Not from her. I kept the world at bay behind my cold mask. But she saw in my eyes what I'd known for a while now.

I was in love with her. So fucking deep.

She wrapped her legs around me, her heels digging into the backs of my thighs as she fucked me back harder. It spurred me on, and I couldn't go softly anymore, pounding her with increasing speed.

I coasted my hand down her neck to her breast—more than a handful—then moaned at the feel of her lovely flesh in my palm, her body writhing beneath mine. She was all softness and sweetness, and I was everything hard and cold. Yet, she took me inside her—not just her body. She let me inside her mind. She'd let herself be vulnerable, knowing it could've been dangerous. That I was dangerous.

She trusted me instead. And she fucked me not like a submissive—because she was certainly not that—but like a woman who'd finally found her equal.

That lightning rod of electricity buzzed down my body. I dropped my head into her neck and bit her shoulder as I spurted and pulsed inside her, holding myself deep and groaning, grinding harder.

"Ah!" she screamed, climaxing a second time and shuddering beneath me, her nails digging into my back.

I hope she made me bleed. I wanted her marks on me. Marks. I lifted my head enough to see teeth imprints in her fair skin.

What the hell was wrong with me?

I was panting. So was she.

She coasted one heel up the back of my thigh then lowered her hands to grip my ass.

"So firm," she teased. "Do you work out?"

I blinked a minute, trying to come back to myself. "What? My ass?"

"Feels like buns of steel back here."

I couldn't help it, I collapsed with laughter, my head buried in her hair. She giggled and gave both my ass cheeks friendly slaps.

"Maybe I could spank you next time."

My cock twitched inside her.

"Oooo. He likes that idea." She clenched her pussy around me.

"Stop that." I nipped her neck. "He's sensitive now."

She snort-laughed. "After the torture you've put my vagina and ass through, you have no room to complain."

Lifting my head, I pushed her hair away from one cheek so I could see her well. "Who's complaining?"

Then I lowered my head and kissed her. For a long time. Long enough to stir my cock again. Long enough to feel my heart pound even faster, synchronizing with her own fluttering beat.

"How about a shower?" I asked softly.

"Yes. Then you feed me."

"Anything you want."

And I meant it. She could've asked for all of my wealth, my house, even Queenie—well, maybe we'd have to share Queenie —and I'd have given it to her.

I continued to comb my fingers through her long hair, growing addicted to the silky texture. Who was I fucking kidding? I was already addicted, obsessed, with all of her silky textures.

"I've never come so hard in my entire life," I admitted.

"I rocked your world, didn't I, Blackwater?"

"You have no idea."

She really didn't.

Then she reached up with both hands and cupped my face. I had never let anyone do that to me before. Ever. And I hadn't even flinched. She brushed the pad of her thumb across my mouth, her scent utterly intoxicating.

"The feeling's mutual," she said with heartfelt sincerity, her blue eyes darkened with desire and another, much headier emotion.

The feelings were mutual. I could hardly believe it.

I'd spent an inordinate amount of time in my life cursing the heavens, cursing fate, for yet again shitting all over me. But in that moment, I said a silent prayer of thankfulness. Never had I been more grateful or felt more blessed than in this place and time as I held Lavinia Lenore Savoie in my arms.

CHAPTER TWENTY

~LIVVY~

"Sorry, I just really expected black ravens or maybe *Nevermore* tattooed somewhere."

"Because of my middle name?" I laughed yet again. I couldn't help it. I was giddy at this playful side of Gareth.

We'd taken a shower, where he'd yet again fucked me senseless, then he'd dried me, and tucked me back into his bed. He left only long enough to fetch a few bottles of water and order delivery. After eating cheeseburgers and fries on top of the covers, which also shocked me because he was a bit of a clean freak, we'd snuggled back in and...talked.

We'd been talking for the better part of an hour. About his cousins Henry and Sean, who I learned were more like his brothers. But also his Aunt Lucille who he wanted me to meet. My heart melted into goo when he asked me softly, tentatively. Then the smile he'd rewarded me with when I told him I definitely wanted to meet her injected me with another shot of endorphins.

It was like Clara had zapped me with one of her happy

spells nonstop for hours. I couldn't explain this euphoria. Just looking at him made my heart speed up, and warm.

"Okay, I'll admit my mother had a thing for Poe. And yes, I am a tad Goth."

"No way," he said with seemingly genuine shock.

I slapped him playfully on the shoulder. He grabbed my hand before I could pull it away and laced our fingers. We were both on our sides under the covers, facing each other, still naked. Like it was the most natural thing in the world. And now our hands were entwined between us.

"If I'm going to be totally honest," I continued, "I did have a little Poe fixation through my teen years and into college."

"What was your favorite? 'The Tell Tale Heart?' No. It was probably 'Cask of Amontillado.'"

"Why would you think that?" I asked, sounding fairly offended. "You think I'm into horror?"

His grin was wicked. "I think you're a ruthless female who in her teen years with amplified hormones might've enjoyed a bit of brutality."

"Well, you're wrong, Mr. Blackwater," I sniped haughtily. "My favorite was his love poems. Very specifically 'Annabel Lee.'"

"Wasn't that the one about his dead wife where he cried on her grave every night?"

"Yeah. So."

"Super romantic."

"Obviously, you don't understand because you're not a romantic."

"Obviously."

"Gareth, the poem isn't about grief."

"It's completely about grief."

"No, it isn't!"

"The poem says, *and so, all the night-tide, I lie down by the side of my darling—my darling—my life and my bride, in her sepulchre by the sea, in her tomb by the sounding sea.* He is literally mourning her every single night, weeping on her grave. If that's not the picture of grief, I don't know what is."

He rattled off an exact quote so matter-of-factly, I was stunned.

"Eidetic memory," he reminded me.

"Wow," was all I managed to say, wondering how long ago he read the poem and still retained it word for word in his big brain.

Damn, I was getting turned on again, thinking about his big brain. His mouth slid into that naughty smile.

"Impressed?"

"Don't try to change the subject. Yes, he's mourning, but that's not what the poem is about. It's about everlasting love, even beyond the grave. I don't have a photographic memory like you, fancy-pants, but I do know he says their love was more than a love. That the angels in heaven and demons in hell—"

"Under the sea."

"What?"

"He says, *under the sea* not *in hell*."

"Whatever. That none of them can separate my soul from her soul."

"*Dissever* not *separate*."

"Stop being a know-it-all, Gareth. I'm trying to explain that the central meaning of the poem is that even death can't separate them. Their love for each other is too great even for that. It's not about him moping about and crying. It's about the fact that they *loved with a love that was more than love* as he states early in the poem."

"You're right."

I snort-laughed. "You're admitting it? Excuse me while I go into shock."

"I mean you're right, that's the exact quote. Good job for someone without an eidetic memory."

"You're irritating."

"You're adorable. Especially when you get angry. I love that flush of pink crawling up your neck right now."

He glanced down to my throat then back up to meet my gaze. We started our staring game.

It felt different this time. Yes, the charge of sex was still there, though dimmed after multiple rounds over the past several hours, but that wasn't what dominated the exchange this time. I wanted to know more about him—everything actually—about his interests, his past, everything. But I also didn't want to break this lovely spell. Whatever it was.

Finally, it was Gareth who spoke first. "Ask me."

"Ask you what?" I huffed out a little laugh.

He didn't smile. Not at all. He'd turned rather pensive. Usually, he wore his aloof gaze void of introspection, simply examining the lesser underlings who surrounded him with either indifference or distaste. Of course, his looks for me had shifted into a much hotter region than the ice man expressions.

But this wasn't any expression I'd ever seen him wear before. Yes, pensive. Thoughtful. Perhaps even a sliver of hope glittered in those dark eyes I'd come to adore.

"Ask me anything, Lavinia. Anything at all."

Anything? I asked him, mind to mind.

His only response was a careful dip of his chin.

Trust. Here it was. He was letting me in the inner sanctum not only of the grim reaper but of himself. This guarded, enigmatic man who kept his secrets well-hidden and locked away, had just opened the door to me.

I snuggled into the pillow, inching just a little closer. He watched every infinitesimal move I made, that softer mien still there.

"Why is it that grims have the power to use telepathy, telekinesis, and can trace as fast as vampires?"

He was silent for a moment, watching me. I waited patiently.

"Not all grims can."

"Why can you then?"

"I'm a grimlock."

I frowned at a term I'd never heard before. Jules hadn't either because she'd have educated us on it. She felt it her duty as the most maternal sister to give us any new information about the magical world. And this is something I'd never heard before. Before I had a chance to ask what that meant, he went on.

"It's probably better if I go back and tell you how grims came into existence."

My eyes must've bulged out of my head, my heart tripping faster. Now this was something no one I knew had ever known.

His mouth quirked at my obvious shock. "Yes, Lavinia. I'm telling you one of our most well-kept secrets."

"You're not going to have to kill me after you tell me or something," I teased, referring to the old adage I can tell you but then I'd have to kill you.

I was trying to make him laugh, but he scowled instead.

"I'd never hurt you. And I'd kill anyone else who did."

Whoa there. He wasn't kidding. Our elbows were bent so that our clasped hands were laying upward between us. I squeezed his hand and tucked both of ours under my chin, against my upper chest.

"My ancestral forefather was a Varangian, a name the Romans called Vikings from what's now Norway. He was also a warlock. In 873, he and his clan raided the state of Kievan Rus'—modern Russia—and later became a Byzantine Varangian Guard."

Fascinated, I didn't move or say a word, soaking in the rolling melody of his deep timbre.

"This Guard was fierce and an unparalleled force serving the Byzantine emperor, but they were also still Norsemen and used to their pillaging ways. At least, that's the way my Aunt Lucille told it to me." He paused, looking at our linked hands then went on. "He saw my ancestral foremother when she was cleaning linens for her master at the communal well. She was a vampire and a slave. Her name was Izolda. He took her that day, paid the slaveowner though her owner hadn't wanted to give her up, and took her to be his wife."

"A warlock and a vampire? So long ago. I hadn't known there was intermarrying that long ago." I thought about that a second. "Most children of intermarried supernaturals have either the mother or the father's gifts. Not *all* of them."

And that didn't explain the darkness of grims, what Gareth had told me was a monster living inside all of his kind.

"If he'd been a normal warlock, then yes, their children would've simply been either witch, warlock, or vampire. But he wasn't. He practiced forbidden, dark magic."

This was not simply forbidden in the modern world, but highly illegal. A practice that could get a witch or warlock stripped of all power permanently by an Enforcer. Or even sentenced to death, depending on what crimes they committed using the forbidden magic.

"In his practices, he had no problem using blood sacrifices to cast heinous, dark spells."

"What was his designation?" I asked hesitantly, though something told me I already knew.

"Enforcer," he admitted quietly.

The most powerful of witch or warlock-kind practicing black magic. Blood magic.

"It wasn't just the dark magic he was practicing but what he was trying to do that made it unforgiveable. And had such lasting effects." He graced his thumb lightly over mine, no longer looking at me at all. "He was trying to raise the dead."

I inhaled sharply but said nothing at all.

"He attempted to bind them to him, to use them to do his will. And he was making progress." He exhaled a deep breath then caught my gaze again, seeming to want to read me as he told the rest. "One night, he performed a blood sacrifice on an altar in the woods, using an innocent child as his blood sacrifice," his voice became raspy, though still steady, "casting a spell on a new moon and using his skills in numerology and astrology to find the most potent witch sign and the most auspicious night where stars had aligned. Legend says, he awoke an army of the dead who he successfully bound to him. A legion of ghosts with corporeal spirits that could hurt and harm his enemies.

"But his wife, Izolda, came upon him in the woods. The innocent child he'd murdered for his spell was in fact her own son she'd had by her first master. In a rage, she attacked him and ripped out his throat. He didn't even have time to use his dead army to stop her if that was possible.

"In her killing of him, she'd also swallowed his blood. Blood that had been filled with the power of black magic and the dark spell he'd cast. She committed the worst of crimes and ingested the blood of the most evil and most powerful of men." He stopped for a minute before adding, "She had unknowingly fed it to the unborn child in her belly."

Good goddess above!

I clenched my fingers in his, a reflex at the realization.

"Gareth," I whispered softly. "And that was the first grim reaper."

"Yes."

"The warlock, my ancestral father's name was Grímkæll. A combination of the words grim and *ketill*, which means helmet or more accurately cauldron. But that may not have even been the reason we earned the name grim reaper."

"What do you mean?"

"The child born to our vampire foremother Izolda was like me. He contained all the darkness and all the power. His children and the first few generations were given the name grim reapers because wherever they went they left a trail of death. They couldn't control the monsters inside themselves. Yes, the Black Plague killed many humans during the middle ages, but another factor for so many deaths were the first grims who gave into the darkness they wielded, killing indiscriminately. For gain of riches and land or simply because they enjoyed it."

He tried to tug his hand free, his frown deepening, but I held tight, keeping them tight against the warmth of my body.

He gazed at me in wonder. "Aren't you disgusted by me yet?"

His voice didn't tremble or resonate with fear or shame. Steady as always, my grim.

"Why would I be disgusted by factors that you had no control over? This may be your history, Gareth, but it is not *you.*"

Then he truly gazed at me in amazement, a glint of admiration glittering in those dark depths.

"Go on," I told him. "If you think this will scare me away, then you don't know me at all."

He swiped his tongue over his bottom lip as if he were about to kiss me. Instead, he soldiered on with the harrowing story of his ancestors. "Some grims were born with only some of the abilities, and a few with new ones. Like my Aunt Lucille and Henry."

"What are their abilities?"

He didn't answer my question but explained something else. "Each generation, a few carried the powers of both the Enforcer Grímkæll and his vampire wife. Minus the blood-drinking. Interestingly enough, none of the offspring of future generations required blood as sustenance or grew fangs."

He tugged his hand again and I let him have it this time. He gently swept a long lock of my hair off of my face and over my shoulder, his fingers trailing down my arm then back up, seemingly mesmerized.

"Don't get distracted. Or try a stalling tactic."

Without a hint of a smile, he continued. "So these particular grim offspring held great power. Telekinesis, telepathy, extraordinary strength and speed, heightened senses, strange gifts with numbers and highly advanced IQs, and of course the ability to strip any supernatural of power. To kill with a single thought."

He'd been tracing the pads of his fingers along my lower arm but now pulled his hand away and met my gaze. "These types of grims who are very few in the modern world are called grimlocks."

That's what he was. My heart tripped at the realization.

"How rare are grimlocks?"

"There are a handful living in the United States."

"And worldwide?"

"Twenty-seven that we have on record. There may be some born who haven't developed full powers yet." He looked away, that pensive expression fixed in place. "All grimlocks are required by our laws to register their designation as soon as it's revealed."

"When did you know?"

"At eleven."

"Register with who?"

"Though grims don't assemble with the witch and vampire covens, we do have our own. There is an Office of Designation within our order of grims who monitors all of us."

"Monitors?"

His gaze lifted from the bed back to me. "We have to keep our own under control. Keep track of…incidents."

Crimes, he meant. Because of the darkness.

"So you're one of twenty-seven grimlocks in the world?"

He nodded, his lips thinning with strain.

Wow. So Gareth was special on *that* kind of scale.

Swallowing hard at something I needed to know, I asked gently, "Is the darkness more powerful or more…evil in grimlocks?"

Those black orbs delved into me, knowing. "No more evil than any other grim but certainly more aggressive, more *willful*. And more dangerous considering what grimlocks can do. Which is why it's so imperative that they are taught early how to master it. To lock it away."

Scooting closer, I spread my fingers over his chest, feeling the rapid beat of his heart which belied the calm, cool mask he currently wore for me.

"Will you tell me the rest?" I meant about who he'd killed.

"I will. Just not tonight." His hand covered my own. "Please?"

My heart melted at the soft vulnerability and acute pain seeping through his veneer. He was scared to tell me. Afraid of what I might think? But he didn't realize that my intuition as a witch was akin to my sisters in that I knew what my heart and soul told me was undeniably true. I wanted to assure him that he had no reason to fear, even if we didn't talk about this anymore. It was obviously hurting him.

"You killed someone," I said aloud, getting that elephant out there on the table.

His heart rate quickened under my palm, his eyes widening subtly. He was good at holding his masks in place.

"But it was self-defense. You can tell me whenever you're ready, but I already know what I need to about you, Gareth."

I skated my hand up and around his nape, tugging him closer.

"*You* are not evil, no matter what darkness you hold inside you. I know that with every beat of my heart. And if you never tell me what happened, that's fine too. I admire the man I see." I traced my fingers up his sharp, clenched jaw and across his intelligent brow and down to his succulent mouth. "And I see a lot more than you think." Cupping his jaw, I brushed my thumb over his bottom lip. "I want what I see. Now more than ever."

Suddenly, I was beneath him, his hard body pressing me down, his muscular thighs spreading mine wide. His hands combed into my hair until he cupped the back of my head with both hands, holding his torso up on his forearms.

He didn't say a word. Simply looked his fill while he slid his thick, hard cock along my slit. I coasted my hands softly up the tight muscles of his back and hugged him closer. His mask vanished, revealing all the longing tenderness of a man who'd lived without this for far too long.

"Oh, Gareth." I swallowed the lump of emotion swelling inside me. It wasn't pity but the need to assure him he was wanted. And should be cherished. "Kiss me."

He did. With infinite care and sweet passion.

After he'd put on a condom and before he'd slid inside me, he whispered, pleaded, "Stay the night with me."

"Yes."

Then we had sex for the final time that night.

No. We made love.

After we'd both come and he was still inside me, kissing my swollen lips, I whispered, "I'll stay as long as you want me."

Those words were offered freely and with great sacrifice on my part. To submit not just my body, but my heart too. He understood exactly what I meant, because he lifted his face from mine, examining me with complete and utter awe.

"Then stay forever. Never leave me."

It was both command and request rolled together, his gaze serious but also soft and warm.

"Okay, Blackwater," I mumbled casually. "That sounds nice."

Understatement of the century.

His body shook with a laugh as he pulled out of my body. "Nice," he whispered, seemingly to himself as he went to the bathroom to take care of the condom.

I'd had tenderness and made love before with other women. Other men. But something told me that he never had. This was his first time. Whether it was my witch's intuition or simply a deep knowing after the secrets he'd shared, I wasn't sure. What I was sure about was that I wanted to give Gareth everything he'd been without. The tenderness and care and yes, the love, that he deserved.

The thought made my heart skitter with fear. I'd been in love before, once or twice maybe. But this felt deeper somehow.

The risk of loving a man like Gareth was high. Because I couldn't simply own him like I had other lovers in the past. He'd own me too. And handing that power over to someone else was more than terrifying.

What was more frightening was walking away from something, someone like this. I wasn't going to.

When he returned to the bed, he instantly scooped me closer onto his chest, his arms tightening into an unbreakable embrace. His mouth brushed the crown of my head as he exhaled a shaky breath.

Sighing, I remembered the statue in front of his house. "The fountain out front. That's a tribute to Izolda, isn't it?"

"Smart woman" he whispered into my hair, his fingers playing loosely with a lock of it. "I imagined Izolda triumphant after she'd killed her husband, the man who murdered her innocent child. Much like Medusa should've been triumphant after being cursed by Athena when she *dared* to be violated by Poseidon in one of her temples," he said sarcastically, his tone taking on a lazy lilt. "I liked the idea of immortalizing Izolda and Medusa into one victorious statue. Monsters who served justice to their aggressors."

I traced the ridges of his abs, my eyes growing heavy, my smile dreamy. "You're quite the feminist, Gareth."

He squeezed me tighter. "Don't tell anyone."

"Why? Because you'll lose your hard-hearted, cold-blooded reputation?"

"Exactly." He pressed a light kiss to the top of my head.

"Your secret's safe with me," I whispered.

Then we both drifted off into blissful sleep wrapped in each other's arms. Where we both belonged.

CHAPTER TWENTY-ONE

~GARETH~

Just after I'd arrived at Ruben's night club, Henry slid into the booth across from me. The Green Light, was a den where vampires could socialize and enjoy nightly entertainment. It was also a spot for them to meet a potential blood host, then partake of them in the rooms behind the red velvet curtain in the back corner.

Ruben ran the finest vampire den in the city. The ambiance was art deco elegance with small crystal chandeliers over the tables surrounding a dance floor. A stage area was set up for whatever singer was hired for the night.

While many vampire dens were typically shrouded in the dark, Goth décor, Ruben created a lighter, more sophisticated ambiance for his customers. The booths and club chairs, all over-sized and covered in velvet or brocade, gave the place a luxurious vibe. Small gas lanterns cast a warm glow to the windowless club.

It wasn't open yet, but it was Saturday afternoon, so the bartender was stacking clean glasses behind the bar and servers were bustling around setting up tables with clean linens and votive candles.

"Why did you want to meet here?" Henry combed a hand through the longish hair on his crown, mussing it further. He was chewing that gum again. "I could've met you at your house."

"Ruben wanted to see me about something. He mentioned you were working, so I figured I'd just meet you here." I glanced toward the hallway near the bar leading to his office. "He's in a meeting right now."

Henry worked for Ruben at a number of tasks. Though many supernaturals probably thought he was no more than a recruiter of human blood hosts simply by standing near the entrance, he was more than that.

It was true that a grim's shadowy essence would lure humans and other supernaturals toward the doors of The Green Light, urging them to explore their baser urges in a vampire den. But it was a grim's ability, especially one like Henry or me, to detect evil in others which Ruben valued most.

Henry was as attuned to the malevolent depths of others as I was, and Ruben wanted to keep the filthy elements out of his club. More than that, he wanted them on his radar so he could keep tabs on the vampires who may not be following the rules.

As vampire overlord of New Orleans, it was his job to keep all of them in line. So if one happened to stroll into The Green Light, Henry would simply text the man's description to Ruben and tell him what level of evil the man carried—because there were levels—and Ruben and his men would keep vigilant watch.

"Visited Aunt Lucille," I told him. "She finally took Uncle George into the house."

"Did she?" He looked as shocked as I'd felt that day when she carried the urn inside with us.

I nodded. "Finally."

Henry shook his head, looking relieved. "Good for Uncle George."

"Mm," was my grunt of agreement.

"So what is it?" asked Henry, his typical scowl back in place. "I know this isn't about Aunt Lucille and Uncle George."

While I presented a cold, indifferent mask to the world, Henry bristled with frenzied annoyance most of the time. Of course, if he'd make peace with his magic, I knew that some of that anxiety would ease. But I'd talked him to death on the subject. He'd have to come to his own conclusions in his own time.

"I spoke to Peonie," I told him. "She gave me some names." I texted the screenshot with the information I had to him.

Henry's phone buzzed on the table. He opened the file and scanned it, his jaw clenching.

"I need your help, Henry. I need you to use your gift."

He snorted in disgust, setting his phone back down. "It's not a gift."

I wouldn't argue this point with him for the hundredth time, but I let him hear the emotion behind my desperation. "I *need* you, Henry."

"For Lavinia?"

Whereas my eyes shifted in color, from brown to black depending on my mood, Henry's remained the deepest ebony most of the time. But I remember when we were teens that they would shift to hazel-gold sometimes, as they were right now.

"She means something to you," he said definitively. Not a question.

She means everything to me.

"Yes," was my succinct, guttural reply.

He looked at me, realizing, tapping his fingers nervously on his jeans under the table. He glanced away toward the bar, swallowing visibly.

"You know what you're asking?"

"Yes. And I wouldn't do it if I didn't believe—no, *know*—that Lavinia is in more danger than she realizes."

"So this isn't just some paranoia or alpha bullshit because you're obsessed with her."

I laughed and shook my head. That made him frown deeper.

"Henry. Listen to me. I know what I know."

He winced, hearing the dominance leak out of my voice. He also knew good and well that I was in far more control of my beast than he was. My darkness and I were in sync, so I knew I was fucking right about all of this.

"Why not get Aunt Lucille to do it?"

I knew he'd ask that. "Because what she discovers will be very unsettling. And if it comes to a court hearing, she may not be able to come. As a matter of fact, I think we both know it would be too hard for her."

Henry knew as well as I did that Aunt Lucille's agoraphobia was crippling. She only ventured to places very close to her house that she trusted. Besides, I had a feeling this assignment would be good for Henry. It was about damn time that he re-opened the doors to his magic. What he was meant to do.

He tapped his fingers on the table, getting fidgety simply thinking about it.

"Let me put it to you this way," I added with all seriousness. "Imagine it was Clara instead of Lavinia in the line of sight of a dangerous, possibly lethal, predator."

Henry stopped tapping, went deathly still, his eyes glinting with fury. After a brief pause, he said with serious intent, "I'll do it."

Leaning back against the seat cushion, my hands clasped on the table, I said, "Thank you. When can you do it?"

His brow pinched as he combed a hand through his hair again. "It may take a while." He heaved a sigh, the anxiety returning. "I haven't used the magic in a long fucking time."

"Henry," I said in a low voice, "I know what I'm asking. And I'm sorry, but please don't take too long."

Sure, there were others like him I could call on, those who

hadn't put a permanent block on their magic for over a decade. But I needed someone discreet. Someone I trusted to keep my investigation secret. I needed proof before I did anything further. Plus, there was a part of me that wanted Henry to confront his own demons. Perhaps, this would be a baby step toward that end. Toward the path he was meant to be on.

"Of course." His voice was raspy, pained. "I won't let you down."

"Thank you." I finally exhaled the heavy breath it seemed I'd been holding since I'd stepped in here. "I know you won't."

Right on time, Ruben appeared from the hallway with Jules Savoie right behind him. Ruben was impeccably dressed as always—tailored dark pants, white starched shirt, and a navy-blue vest. As he drew closer, I made out the intricate pattern of a beautiful Medusa's head woven into the vest. His cufflinks winked under the warm light of the chandeliers.

Jules looked austere and regal as ever. It certainly wasn't her clothes—khaki pants and white polo shirt. It was in the authoritative demeanor she carried like a queen. It was also the ripple of power she wore like a cloak. She was a powerful Enforcer. For a split second, I thought of telling her about Richard Davis, but held my tongue. Not yet.

"Good afternoon, Blackwaters," said Ruben, sounding both formal and pleasant at the same time. "Thanks for coming, Gareth."

"Hi. Uh, I'd best be going." Henry exited the booth and turned to me. "I'll let you know when I have what you need."

"Thank you, Henry."

Again, he understood my level of appreciation with those simple words. He gave me a tight smile and strolled toward the exit.

"He didn't have to leave," said Ruben, gesturing toward the booth for Jules to sit first, opposite me. "What we wanted to ask isn't top secret."

Jules slid into the booth. Then he settled in beside her, but not too close, I noticed.

"He's got some angsty brooding to do over a favor I needed."

Ruben gave me that knowing nod and smile. He knew Henry's moods as well as I did.

"So what is it you needed from me?" I asked.

Jules and Ruben both started to speak at once then stopped.

"You go ahead," he told her.

"No, you," she said tightly, frowning. "It was your idea."

I thought they might bat the ball back and forth in this over-polite and strained cordiality they were playing at. Right before Ruben took the lead, the manager and barista of his bookstore sashayed up to the table.

Beverly was a blond bombshell and a vampire. Her perfect features and hourglass figure, currently encased in a red pencil skirt and silky white top, were made to lure.

"Excuse me, Ruben," she said in her naturally sultry voice. "But that package you've been waiting on finally came in." She presented a padded envelope about the size of a book.

I didn't miss the annoyance that crossed Jules expression.

Ruben frowned, his mood seeming to turn annoyed as well. "Leave it in my office on my desk, Beverly. Thank you."

"Of course, sire. I'll take care of that for you."

The way she said *sire*, a common term for vampires to their overlord, was a tad too worshipful. Jules's face pinkened, while Ruben turned back to me. He smoothed a hand down his tie and vest, clenching his jaw. There was always tension squeezing the air tight when these two were in the same room together. I wondered how long it would take for this agreeable, convivial cooperation to break when they'd either tear each other's clothes off or kill each other.

"You know that we're working on a presentation for the High Witch Guild of the southern region. For the werewolves."

Of course I did. I nodded.

"We plan to start there first, since it's our own region where we have the most influence. But we'd like to add something that would give assurance to them that the werewolf community is making strides on their own. I was thinking we needed something like the grims have."

I didn't flinch or move a muscle, keeping my exterior cool. "Like *what* that we grims have?"

"Your registration and tracking program."

"How do you know about that?" I asked, surprised though I shouldn't be. Ruben was a very resourceful, influential man.

"I have my own sources who I won't betray," he said with an amiable smile.

Ruben was so similar to me in demeanor. Except whereas my unruffled manner came with a touch of aloof coldness, his came with charm and calculation.

"Let me guess, you want me to develop this computer program for you."

His smile widened. "Exactly."

"Are you sure werewolves would submit to this sort of invasive tactic? I suppose I can mention, since it seems you already know, that tracking is part of the grim world. We are born knowing it's for the safety of our community. But werewolves have always been independent, even without their own supernatural race. Most live as loners."

"We've talked to Mateo and Nico," added Jules. "They admitted that some might be reluctant because of the exact reasons you're mentioning. This would be on a voluntary basis. But they also agreed that once word spreads, more will want to get on board."

I shifted forward, interested. "You mean once word spreads about Violet's charmed tattoos."

Ruben nodded. "That's what we want the program for, honestly. Not to track them like criminals, mind you, but to trace who has been given the tattoos and who else needs them. But we'd need a database of all werewolves worldwide. Our hope is that we will start local and win the approval of the High Witch Guild of the Southern Region to include a Werewolf Clan to the interracial supernatural gatherings. Then we will spread outward from there."

Tapping my forefinger on the table, I added, "And you'd present to them data from this program of the werewolf populace receiving the charmed tattoos, who'd shown no signs of outward violence in their communities. This program that I'll write will help you prove in your presentations that they deserve a place in the larger supernatural community."

I usually hide my disdain, but it was difficult. Grims chose to be left out of the greater supernatural community. We had leaders of covens, too, who reported to the High Witch Guilds simply to keep a place at the table in case we ever needed it. And our reports were minimal in providing information, at best. It was mostly to appease witches and warlocks who sat at the highest places of supernatural government, so they felt like we were doing our part in keeping our own in line.

But werewolves were never offered a seat at the table. They'd been cast out long, long ago because their magic was the result of a curse put upon them by an angry witch centuries earlier. She had had a right to be angry, but her hatred morphed into prejudice that still held true today. Time can erode many wounds, but it can't erase bone-deep intolerance that's taught from birth.

Jules tucked a strand of her sleek, dark auburn hair behind one ear. It was short, off her shoulders, exposing most of her slender neck—a no-nonsense cut for a no-nonsense woman and witch. Still, it suited her, revealing her delicate and noble bone structure.

"I understand what you're thinking," she said resolutely. "That their clans deserve a place at the table no matter what."

"Don't they?"

"They do," she assured me. "But we're fighting more than injustice here. With your intelligence, Gareth, you understand that reason and logic and justice do not always go hand in hand. We need persuasive evidence that now is the time to let go of the old intolerance."

She was right, of course. Hatred could do great harm. I'd spent too much time wallowing in my own, hating all vampires after Dennis. It took a year of Aunt Lucille teaching me that not all vampires take without consent and hurt anyone whose blood they crave. It finally dawned on me that hatred only hurts me.

The lore of the witch Ethelinda, who'd cursed Capitán Ortega to become the werewolf and offered her own death as a blood sacrifice, had been taught to every witch and warlock as a child. And even grims, vampires, and werewolves. Everyone knew that Ortega had hunted and tortured and burned witches relentlessly in the middle ages. Ethelinda became a legend, somewhat of a hero, when she cursed him and his entire male line into infinity to become the beast that he was.

It would be hard to break that stigma, especially for those who'd kept to the code and avoided mingling with werewolves, who didn't acknowledge that they felt joy and love and hurt and pain just like everyone else. Ruben and Jules had a difficult road ahead of them, but I believed the stigma could be undone. Just like I'd stopped hating vampires because of what one of them had done to me, the world could open its eyes to the kindness, creativity, and compassion that so many werewolves had to offer.

"Of course I'll do it," I finally said.

"Terrific," breathed Ruben.

Jules smiled, the first one I'd ever seen on the Enforcer actually. She was quite beautiful when she smiled. "Thank you, Gareth."

"We should discuss your fee," said Ruben. "Something similar to the last contract for the iBite app?"

Jules rolled her eyes at the mention of the app I created for Ruben which was basically a blood-host matching site for vampires and humans. I knew instinctually her disdain wasn't for me or the app in general, but because of Ruben's off-the-charts ratings and stalkers as a "swoony vampire" women would be lucky to get bitten by.

"No need," I added. "I'll do this free of charge." Before they asked me why, I added, "Because it needs to be done. If I can help in your cause, I will."

"That's very generous," said Jules. "I know your time is valuable."

"So are the lives of every werewolf who lives in isolation and apart from society," I said, with sincerity this time not the bite of bitterness. "I'll keep you updated with my progress."

"Thank you again," said Jules.

I stood. "You're welcome. I'm glad to help."

Ruben rose with me. "Still on for Monday night?" he murmured as Jules scooted out behind him.

"Of course. Same time as usual?" I asked.

"Yes. Bring more of that whiskey you brought last time."

"No problem."

"What are you guys up to?" asked Jules, her gaze on Ruben.

"Oh, just our usual guys game night."

She huffed a small laugh. "Poker night?"

"Something like that," agreed Ruben with a smile.

I hid my own. We weren't poker players.

"Don't bet too much money," Jules warned me, pointing to Ruben. "That one is sneaky and *highly* competitive," she said with emphasis as if she knew from experience.

"Thanks for the advice," I said as she walked toward the exit.

Ruben's eyes never left her until she was out the door.

"She's got quite a chip on her shoulder for you," I observed.

"It's been there quite a while," he agreed, then faced me with a glint of determination in his cool, blue gaze. "But I'm knocking it off, whether she wants me to or not."

"Good luck."

"I'll need it." He clapped me on the back. "I'll see you Monday."

CHAPTER TWENTY-TWO

~GARETH~

"Come on, come on," growled Mateo. Or Alpha rather. "Get your drinks and let's go!"

On our game nights, Mateo's subdued personality took a backseat to Alpha's bloodthirsty, competitive side. It was Mateo's idea to start these game nights shortly after we'd helped him and Nico save Violet from the Blood Moon pack. Our weekly game had quickly become a welcome routine for all of us.

For me, it was nice to hang out with like-minded guys. To not feel on guard as I so often did out in the wider world. I was learning to loosen up quite a bit and widen my circle of friends.

I sat in my usual spot, the brown leather club chair in front of the giant, square mahogany coffee table in Ruben's living room. Devraj was already settled on the left side of the sectional sofa next to Ruben, both of them sipping the salted caramel whiskey I'd brought.

"I could drink this all damn night," said Dev, smiling at his half empty glass.

"Where's your cousin?" asked Alpha. "We're not waiting on him."

"Here," said Henry, walking straight through the living room toward the kitchen.

Ruben lived in a house not far from mine in the Garden District. He'd renovated as well, but with less modern touches, keeping to a more classical style. A giant, dark wood mantle framed the fireplace. The furniture and walls were painted with muted, warm hues, and accent pillows and artwork provide splashes of color to make the room striking.

On the wall opposite the fireplace hung a crimson tapestry with a beautifully detailed rendition of Hades capturing Persephone in a field of wildflowers. Hades was coming out of a dark hole in the earth in a chariot with a team of black horses and had one arm around her waist, pulling her into the carriage. It didn't escape my notice that Hades had blond hair and Persephone was petite but fierce looking.

"Hurry it up! I can't play all night. Gotta get back to Evie."

"She's not going to have the babies five months early," said Ruben, kicked back in a pair of gray joggers and a white t-shirt.

I had to admit, seeing him without his armor of an expensive tailored suit, complete with vest, always jarred me a little. This is the only time I ever saw him completely relax and let down his guard. I suppose the crown of being overlord for such a large vampire coven was quite heavy. It had me thanking the universe *for once* for letting me live my life without the weighty responsibility shouldered by so many others.

"It's not because he's worried about Evie that he needs to get home," commented Nico from his place in the twin chair like mine, drinking a Killian's Red. "It's because his wolf gets anxious and can't stand to be more than five feet from her for more than a couple hours."

Alpha growled, while Dev and Ruben chuckled.

"Evie and I are leaving town for the new moon, and I've got packing to do," he argued.

"We always go out of town. What makes this time so special?" Nico asked.

"You just sit over there and keep your mouth shut. I don't need your input in the game tonight."

Nico never played as this was more of a four to five player game. But he liked to come and tell Mateo what to do, how best to fight and get out of battles alive.

"You would never survive without my input," remarked Nico as Henry took a spot on the sofa next to Mateo.

"We'll see. Let's get started." Mateo leaned forward, straightening his cards on his side of the board game Gloomhaven.

At first, I didn't think a Dungeons-and-Dragons-like board game would hold my interest. I'd joined in because Henry said yes right when Mateo asked us, and I didn't want to come across as rude. Besides, I liked hanging with these guys. We were all quite different as supernaturals but also the same, if that made sense.

We were several play sessions into this specific campaign. The overall objective of the game was to kill our enemies and win as a team as we moved across the board.

We each played as a different class or character. I'd chosen the Mindthief who was more tactical and used his cunning and calculated moves to win fights. Ironically, we'd set our own rule that no one could use actual magic. That was considered cheating.

"Damn," said Devraj, after turning over a move-action card. "Vermlings again."

"Bad luck," I muttered.

"I hate those damn things," said Ruben, shivering.

Vermlings were rat-like creatures who were hard as hell to kill.

"Okay," Henry leaned forward. "I can throw a net here."

He was our Tinkerer, a class that was constantly on high alert and could scramble to distract, attack, or heal. A bit of a manic character, which seemed to suit Henry's personality just fine.

"I've got the most XP," growled Alpha, reaching for a fighting-action card, "I'm going to crush these fucking Vermlings."

"I'm coming too," said Dev, turning a fighting-action card. He was our Scoundrel, a character who could sneak in and do serious damage.

XP was lingo for experience points. Mateo was our Brute, which meant that he could take a beating and still survive. Which he did with the Vermlings.

Once the Vermlings were killed, and we'd all escaped mostly unharmed, it was my turn. My move-action card made me smile. "Another coin," I called to the table.

"Damn," said Nico. "Aren't you amassing quite a fortune over there?"

"Sounds familiar," said Henry with a sly grin.

"Actually, I'm going to take some of my coins and level up with armor."

"Don't you have enough?" Dev asked. "Seems like you have an entire armory over there."

"Look, my personal objective is to deliver this box all the way over here." I pointed to the far corner of the board. "I don't want to die before I get there. Don't get your panties in a bunch because I'm always prepared."

"Boy Scout, that one," said Mateo.

Ruben let out a bark of laughter. "Don't count on it."

I gave him a knowing smile then turned back to the board.

We all had personal objectives to achieve besides the big campaign to win. I was meticulous and observant. I couldn't help but plan for every eventuality on the board. Just like in life. But nothing prepared me for the next scenario when Henry turned over his move-action card.

"Oh, shit," he mumbled.

Alpha leaned in close to read it. "Goddamn frost giant!"

"Fucking frost giants," muttered Dev.

"Again?" I picked up my drink and took a swig. "How many of those fuckers are on the board?"

Ruben and I almost died last week fighting one off together.

"Guess I'll have to save your asses again," said Alpha, voice full of the wolf.

It was true. Last week, his Brute character had managed to defend enough then Dev's Scoundrel crept in and gave the killing blow.

"Alright. Here I come," said Ruben, turning over his fighting-action card to help us, now maneuvered closer to Henry on the board.

Ruben was our Cragheart. He didn't have one fighting style, a jack-of-all-trades. Like the rest of us, he'd chosen a Gloomhaven class that reflected his character in life. He was resourceful on the game board and off of it.

All of us had to get in on this one, but we managed to escape the frost giant just barely.

"Good thing I bought that armor," I murmured when we came out alive.

"Drink and piss break," announced Mateo then hopped off the sofa and headed for the hallway. "But ten minutes tops!"

"Another drink?" I asked Ruben.

"I'll get it." He took my empty glass.

I stood and stretched, then wandered over to the buffet near a window. There was what looked to be an antique vase painted with cherry blossoms. I speculated it was authentic, because this was Ruben's house after all. He didn't like anything fake.

On the other end of the buffet sat a large figurine, more like a small sculpture about a foot in height, not counting the cherry-wood mount. It was another couple from Greek mythology. A winged Eros embraced Psyche, her nude form waking in bed, her arms reaching around his neck as he leaned closer to kiss her.

Ruben stepped up beside me and handed over my glass of whiskey.

"Seems you have an affinity for the Greeks."

He stared at the small sculpture. "Some of them."

"Do I detect a theme?"

Ruben arched a brow at me in challenge.

"Yes, you do," said Devraj, joining us, his glass in hand.

"Let me guess," I said to Dev. "The girl is resistant to the monstrous god, but he woos her any way."

"Woos is a kind interpretation," added Dev. "Kidnapping is more accurate."

"You're both complete asses." Ruben gulped down his *sipping* whiskey in two swallows.

Dev and I both laughed. You'd have to be a complete idiot not to see how badly Ruben wanted Jules Savoie. How he seemed to surround himself with visions of getting her.

"Don't be angry," I told him, still smiling. "In the case of Eros and Hades, they both get the girl."

"And live happily ever after," Dev added. "Of course, you'd have to actually *start* wooing the girl in order to get her back."

Ruben flinched, and I was sure it was because of Dev's slip of the word *back*. He'd had her once before, and then lost her.

"Sorry," muttered Dev, realizing his hit stung a little too much.

"Not at all." Ruben sighed, staring into his empty glass. "You're right, of course."

Dev and I shared an anguished look. Then I asked, "How's the campaign for the werewolves going?"

Ruben chuckled, a true smile tilting his lips. "Better than I hoped. Jules and I will travel together to Houston to present to the High Witch Guild. We're proposing to gain a spot for the werewolf clans on the regional Guild Coven first. Getting their foot in the door as an equal is our first endeavor."

"And then?" asked Dev, curious.

As was I.

"If all goes well in Houston, Jules will petition Clarissa Baxter to pick up the campaign in the US, and then Jules and I will go to England where the guilds have the most influence over the UK and Europe."

Swirling the ice in my glass, I said, "Seems like that will be quite a long campaign."

Ruben's gaze returned from whatever distant point he'd been focusing on and looked at me. He had that fierce look of a vampire on the hunt.

"Oh, yes. Weeks and weeks. Months, even." When he smiled again, wider this time, I caught a flash of his fangs which had descended.

Yes, he was definitely on the hunt. I wondered if Jules had any idea what was coming for her.

"Good for you, brother." Dev squeezed his shoulder.

"How about another drink?" I asked Ruben, taking his glass. "Definitely."

"How about we get back to the fucking game!" bellowed Alpha, back on the sofa, ready to go. "I'm ready to kill another frost giant and protect you weaklings."

I laughed as I headed back to the kitchen. Right as I refilled our glasses with ice, my phone buzzed.

It was Lavinia.

LAVINIA: I wanted to officially invite you to Sunday dinner this weekend. I know I'll see you tomorrow at work, but I just thought of it and couldn't wait.

"Something wrong?" asked Henry, making a Sazerac with Rye whiskey, brandy, and bitters on the island.

"No." I glanced at him before texting back, suddenly uncomfortable. "It's Lavinia. She, uh, invited me to Sunday dinner this weekend. With the family."

Henry paused then shook his head on a smile. "Good for you, G."

We finished making our drinks and headed back to the table, pretending everything was normal. But it wasn't. Or at least, not my normal. The one where I kept everyone at a distance except for a very select few.

Returning to the game, I realized that this foreign feeling that made me feel easy and relaxed without being locked inside my fortress of a home was contentment. And that warmth in my chest was spreading further at the thought of being seated next to Lavinia and eating dinner with her family.

No one had ever asked me over to a family dinner before. Never had a woman asked me to meet anyone in their lives. Perhaps that was my fault, since I'd never put off the vibes that I wanted anything more than sex and kinky bedplay. To be honest, I'd never wanted more. Or perhaps, I hadn't wanted it with them.

But Lavinia…

"What's that goofy smile for?" asked Devraj, laughing as if he already knew.

"I'm going to take a wild guess," said Nico, "she has long black hair and blue eyes."

Without answering, I scowled down at the board, "Are we going to play this fucking game or do I have to feed you all to Vermlings on the next round?"

"That's what I'm talking about," Alpha growled while reaching across the table and giving me a high five. "Someone who's finally on my side. Now let's play!"

CHAPTER TWENTY-THREE

~LIVVY~

"Ooo, you look pretty." Clara came up behind me while I set the table for Sunday dinner.

Well, tables actually. We'd started having our Sunday dinners at the Cauldron since we could put together several four-tops and include whoever wanted to come that day without being overcrowded. Jules always cooked for our Cauldron family, me and my sisters and our significant others.

Today was the first day I'd have a significant other, and my stomach fluttered with nervous energy every time I heard the pub door open and someone else walk in. A "Closed" sign hung in the window and regulars knew we stopped serving at two on Sundays, but we waited till everyone was here. And I'd told Gareth just to come in the regular door. My sisters usually came in through the back courtyard and the kitchen.

"Thanks," I said, while placing forks and knives at each place setting.

"Is someone special coming today?" Clara wore her innocent, sweet expression. The one she used to convince me she had no idea what was up, when she totally did.

"Why do you ask that?" I played along.

"Because you're using the fancy holiday linens and you're setting the tables. And you're wearing that dress and *that* lipstick."

True, we typically set plates and silverware on the buffet table and let people serve themselves. And yes, I usually wore pencil skirts and professional dresses and never to Sunday dinner. But this one was bright red with a black rose pattern. It was flowy from the hips down and short. When it swished, it showed the perfect amount of lower thigh. And I did have the matching lipstick, Cherry Bomb.

"I invited Gareth," I told her.

"I know."

I rolled my eyes. "Then why'd you ask?"

"Because I wanted you to admit that you're into him."

True. Of course, all I could think about all week was how many times he'd been into me. I had been so busy with work and, well, hightailing it to Gareth's when I could that I hadn't had any lengthy conversations with my sisters about him.

"Hold the phone," said Violet, setting a bowl of Spanish rice on the buffet table, "Livvy, you're blushing. What the fuck did I miss?"

"Her boyfriend's coming to dinner." Clara grinned, straightening one of my place settings.

"He's not my boyfriend. Officially."

Was he?

"This is exciting." Violet clapped her hands, steepling her clasped hands beneath her chin and wearing that maniac mastermind look on her face, complete with evil grin. "I can't wait to torture you in front of him."

"Like how? Violet, don't meddle."

"Who do you think I am?" She snorted and headed back to

the bar where Nico and Charlie sat talking to JJ. "Of course I'm going to meddle."

"Goddess save me," I mumbled, my stomach doing a fluttery twirl when the door opened again.

It was Devraj and Isadora, laughing about something as they walked inside, hand in hand. Those two were the ideal couple, always touching and making googly eyes at each other. I couldn't imagine Gareth looking at me like Devraj looked at Iz. Like he worshipped her. Adored her. Would die for her.

Not a full minute later, Gareth walked in the door, and all air left my lungs. I don't know why seeing him in casual clothes twisted me into such lusty knots.

He stood just inside the door in worn jeans and a fitted navy-blue t-shirt that did lovely things for his biceps. I bit my inner lip to keep from smiling at the adorably awkward expression plastered on his face.

I walked over, his gaze devouring me from top to toe.

"Hey," I said, beaming and more than breathless.

When I took his hand, he immediately laced our fingers together and tugged me closer. Then he did something I'd never imaged the stoic ice man would ever do. He cupped my face with his free hand and kissed me tenderly.

"Hey," he returned, swiping his index finger along my jaw, certainly noticing the blush heating my face.

Clearing my throat, I stepped back and led him toward the bar where everyone was gathered, except Jules in the kitchen. Our only Cauldron family members who'd stayed for dinner tonight were JJ, Charlie, our line cook Sam, and foodserver/bartender Finnie.

"Everyone," I announced to the eight pairs of eyes watching us approach, "this is Gareth Blackwater." Then I gestured toward each of them, "Gareth, you know Violet and Nico, of course. This is my sister Isadora, her boyfriend Devraj, JJ and his boyfriend Charlie, Finnie, and my sister, Clara."

"We know each other," said Devraj with a friendly smile, "Good to see you, Gareth."

"We've met, too," added Clara. "Hi, Gareth. Welcome."

I don't know why I even bothered. He likely knew everyone here with his grim information hotline or whatever.

"We haven't met, but I've heard about you," said Finnie, leaning in and shaking his hand.

"Really?" asked Gareth, sounding interested.

"Yes, Livvy has told us all about your first meeting," chimed in Charlie.

I glared at him which only made him grin wider.

"Ah." Gareth dipped his chin in a stiff nod. "Let me guess. She gave me glowing reviews?"

"Super glowing," chimed in Charlie.

"Actually, if I recall correctly," Violet emphasized with dramatic flair and my stomach dipped. "She called you a cock-waffle. Or was it a twatwaffle?" she asked Charlie.

My cheeks flamed. "You're dead to me, Violet."

Gareth squeezed my hand and peered down at me, his expression warm. Not a hint of anger at all. "Whatever she said," he held my gaze, "I'm sure I deserved it."

Holy hell. I could not handle this version of Gareth.

Cold, antagonistic asshole was so much easier to manage than this man who made my knees wobbly and my stomach fluttery.

"Dinner's served!" shouted Sam, carrying in a giant Magnalite pot.

The others headed for the table except for JJ. "What'll you have?" he asked us.

I turned to Gareth. "What would you like to drink?"

"Guinness would be great." His eyes lingered on my mouth.

"Go grab a seat. I'll get it for you."

His gaze roved over my face one more time, then he reluctantly let me go. Clara ushered him over to sit next to her.

"JJ, can I get a Guinness? And a Xanax please?"

He chuckled, his gruff, bearded tough guy exterior softening at my obvious fretfulness.

"A glass of your favorite Pinot Noir will do, I think." He handed over the bottled import and a glass of wine for me then winked. "I think this one will keep you on your toes."

That was an understatement.

"I think so, too." Then I frowned. "Wait, you just met him? How would you know?"

He poured a draft beer, obviously for himself since he took a deep gulp before rounding the bar to join me.

"I hear everything through Charlie who hears everything through Violet and Clara."

"And what do you think?"

He smirked and sipped his beer as an answer. "I just met him, but I like him." His gaze swiveled to Charlie. "Even if he's giving off that grim vibe that keeps making me want to drag Charlie out of here so I can fuck his brains out."

I coughed on my sip of wine. "JJ!" Then I noticed the way he was ogling Charlie sitting over at the table. "Hmph. It's weird. I'd forgotten about the grim aura. Things have shifted with us, so it's, I don't know, different."

As our true feelings grew for each other, his aura didn't have the same impact on me. I mean, I still desired him like mad, but it was tempered with more tender feelings. A euphoric emotion that had less to do with lust.

"All I know," added JJ, "is that I think I'll need one of Clara's spells to counteract the next time he comes for dinner."

"I'll let her know," I told him.

Gareth had taken a seat across the table from Charlie and Violet. Charlie suddenly glanced over his shoulder, giving JJ a blistering come-hither look.

"Whoa," I said. "I suppose everyone who can't block grim auras will need one of Clara's spells next time."

"Come on," chuckled JJ, tossing an arm over my shoulder.

"I can withstand it for a meal." He sipped his beer. "But Charlie and I will be ducking out right after dinner."

I laughed as we walked over to the table together.

Clara and Violet laughed at something Gareth said, which made me smile. He wasn't exactly the charming type. And yet, he was, in his own way. He charmed me, that's for sure. It was just an aggressive, forceful sort of charisma as opposed to the magnetic appeal of Devraj or the subtle allure of Ruben.

I leaned over his shoulder and took the plate from in front of him. He inhaled sharply when my breast brushed his arm.

"I'll fix you a plate," I said quietly, feeling shy.

Yes. *Me*. Feeling shy! It was ridiculous. This man turned me inside out and upside down.

"You don't have to," he said, catching me gently around the wrist.

"I want to."

It was so strange. One day, we were at each other's throats, ready to annihilate the enemy—aka, each other. Then we were reluctant but cooperative partners on the campaign. And somehow, we had transitioned into smitten lovers. It all happened so fast. But at the same time, it simply felt so right. I couldn't get over the fact that I was as comfortable with him as I was with my sisters who were the dearest people in the world to me.

I served us both a plate from the buffet parallel to our dining table. Jules had made her spectacular spicy crawfish enchiladas with a creamy cheese sauce. She'd entered from the kitchen with a plate of pico de gallo, shredded lettuce and fresh guacamole.

"Welcome, Gareth. It's good to have you," she said as she headed to her spot toward the top of the table.

I set his plate in front of him and sat beside him with my own.

"You know my sister Jules, too?"

He nodded, glancing at Nico still in line with Violet

"Ruben and Jules asked me to develop a program to help with their campaign," he said in a low voice.

My heart melted a little more, noting that he was being discreet to spare Nico's feelings on the sensitive subject of the werewolf intolerance issue. That reminded me.

"Where's Evie and Mateo?" I asked down the table to Jules.

Violet sat across from me. "They should be back by now. Nico and I got back two days ago."

It was the full moon earlier this week. Evie and Violet had taken to going away with their men into the woods when it was that time of the month.

Violet nudged Nico with her elbow when he sat beside her. "You heard from Mateo?"

"No. Was I supposed to keep tabs on him?"

"I'm just surprised," added Violet, scooping a spoonful of salsa from the bowl on the table and plopping it onto her enchiladas. "Mateo has practically put Evie on house arrest. I didn't think they'd travel all the way to their cabin right now."

"I think you mean *Alpha* has her on house arrest," interjected Devraj.

"That's the truth," added Violet.

"So Gareth," Clara asked on the other side of him, "how's your cousin, Henry?"

"Subtle, Clara," laughed Violet.

"I'm just asking about the well-being of Gareth's cousin. There's nothing wrong with that."

"He's fine," Gareth assured her. "Any particular reason you ask?"

"I noticed that he's been rather grouchy the last few times I've run into him."

Gareth wiped his mouth and took a swallow of his beer. I was suddenly enraptured by the bobbing of his Adam's apple and the working of his throat.

He set his glass down, saying, "I think that's due to the fact that he's trying to quit smoking."

"He is?" her blue eyes lit up and I could feel her happy spell zapping the air.

I felt a giddy sensation to my bones without her even touching me.

"I didn't think he would." She ducked her head, trying to be more subdued but the cat was out of the bag.

"Did you suggest that he quit smoking, Clara?" I forked three crawfish tails that had fallen out of my enchilada.

"Um, I didn't suggest it, no," she said nervously, playing with her food. "I did however tell him of the dangers of smoking."

"But we can't die of disease," said Nico, already devouring his third enchilada.

"True. But there are other negative factors of smoking besides disease."

"Such as?" I glanced across the table and shared a knowing look with Violet. She grinned right back.

"Well, you know. It can still hurt a supernatural's breath stamina."

"Breath stamina?" asked Violet, looking confused when I knew she wasn't.

"Yes. For vigorous exercise." Clara seemed to be creating an abstract artwork out of her enchilada and pile of lettuce.

"Well, we wouldn't want him to have a reduced ability for breath stamina and vigorous exercise," I agreed.

Gareth turned his head at that, arching a brow at me.

Then Violet finally dropped the bomb. "Clara, correct me if I'm wrong, didn't you date a smoker a few years ago and complained that he tasted like an ash tray every time you kissed?"

Nico nudged Violet with his shoulder. "Leave your sister alone."

Clara turned a few shades of pink but then she lifted her head and said matter-of-factly, "That's true. And since I plan to eventually kiss Henry Blackwater, quite often, I want to be sure the experience will give us both pleasure."

Gareth coughed, choking on his last bite of enchilada.

"You okay?" I asked him.

"Fine." He cleared his throat and took a gulp of beer.

"But, Gareth," whispered Clara, "you can't tell Henry of my plans. I don't think he's quite ready to be wooed by me."

Gareth's eyes met mine, widening at Clara's confession, sheer astonishment blatantly pasted across his face. Then he turned back to her. "How can you know he isn't ready now?"

"My magic tells me so. I'm just biding my time," she said sweetly. "Till he's ready for me."

Violet leaned forward, "Then you're going to pounce, aren't you, tiger?"

"I'm not really a pouncer, to be honest."

"Stalker?" I asked, teasingly.

Clara gave me a glowering look. "Stalking is just rude, Liv. And wrong. No." She glanced up thoughtfully. "I'm really more of a trapper than a hunter."

Gareth cleared his throat again, not quite having recovered from his coughing fit. "And you plan to trap…Henry?"

He was completely baffled. It was the most wonderful state I'd ever seen Gareth in. In total shock and awe. If anyone could do that to a person, it was Clara.

"When the time is right." She was still in her thoughtful reverie but then turned a bright smile to Gareth. "But you have to promise to not say anything."

"I won't say a word." And I could tell he meant it.

Suddenly the door burst open and a squealing Evie was being carried in by Mateo, bridal style, both of them laughing.

"Oh, my," said Clara. "Their auras are golden."

"Isn't that for joy?" asked Violet, more attuned to Clara's color interpretation of emotional auras.

"That's mutual, complete bliss." She beamed at them.

Then Mateo was standing at the head of the table where he carefully put Evie onto her feet. He instantly wrapped his arms around her middle, one hand gently molding the tiny bump of her growing belly.

"We have an announcement," said Mateo, pure pride beaming on his face.

"We got married!" screamed Evie, showing us her wedding band.

A clamor of noise rose all at once. I clapped with a *whoop*, Violet jumped out of her chair and ran to hug her, Charlie cheered, JJ clapped, Jules smiled.

But Clara yelled as the initial shockwave died down, "No, Evie!"

Everyone turned to her. Evie's face fell.

Clara's pout was prominent. "Now I can't plan a wedding shower or the wedding. I have so many ideas."

Evie escaped Mateo's grip. He begrudgingly let her go. She rounded to Clara and pulled her out of her chair and hugged her tight. "But now you can plan my baby shower."

Immediately, Clara beamed again. "Yes! I can!"

They hugged and swayed. Nico rose and walked over to give his cousin one of those man hugs where they pounded each other's backs too hard.

"We need champagne!" boomed JJ, rushing toward the bar.

"And one apple cider," growled Mateo/Alpha, "for Evie."

I watched Evie glowing with pure joy as she chatted with Clara about the baby shower she wanted to give. Then I felt a large, warm palm slide onto my leg and grip gently.

Gareth stared at me with a question in his eyes.

"What?" I asked.

"Are you okay?"

That's when I noticed I was crying. I laughed and wiped the back of my hand across my cheek.

"Yeah. I know I'm weird, but I tend to cry when I'm really happy."

His small smile was so tender, so dear. He lifted a hand and tucked a lock of my hair behind my ear. "What do you do when you're sad?"

"I get angry and want to break things."

"What about when you're angry?"

"I bake something chocolate?"

He smiled wider.

"I know. I'm weird," I admitted with a huff.

He clasped my neck and drew me close. "You're wonderful," he breathed against my lips before placing a soft kiss there.

Someone tapped their fork or spoon against glass, getting everyone's attention. I thought it would be Mateo about to give a speech. But it was Devraj who rose from the table, holding onto Isadora's hand.

"We weren't sure when would be the right time, but I suppose this is a good time as any." He stared down at Iz, swallowing hard and apparently unable to get the words out.

"Well, what is it?!" Violet squealed.

Isadora stood with her own soft smile for Devraj. "We're engaged."

A round of overlapping *congratulations* filled the room.

"That's wonderful, Iz," I called to her, another tear slipping free.

Isadora laughed and smiled up at Devraj.

"Yayyy!" yelled Clara. "More showers!"

JJ walked over with a round tray of champagne flutes filled to the top. One was darker, obviously the cider for Evie.

Isadora turned to Jules. "We know you're busy, so we don't want to interrupt your work with Ruben. But we really wanted a winter wedding."

Devraj wrapped a hand around Isadora's waist and pulled her against him. "We just can't wait much longer."

Jules smiled, looking happier than I'd seen her in a long while. "Don't worry about anything. Ruben and I will wait to travel till after the wedding."

"And after the babies are born," added Evie, having moved closer to the head of the table.

Actually, we'd all stood and drifted in a cluster closer

together. Gareth laced his fingers with my hand again. I looked down at them.

"To Evie and Mateo! And to Isadora and Devraj!" I shouted, holding up my glass. "May your love always be as strong as it is now."

"Hear, hear!" yelled Violet.

"And their babies," added Clara.

"Hear, hear!" echoed Charlie, smiling up at JJ who'd thrown his arm around his shoulders.

Everyone drank, then it grew quiet as Jules raised her glass, her eyes shimmering with emotion. "To Evie, our sister who is always there to selflessly help anyone who asks. I am so grateful for that day when you dragged a grouchy werewolf into our house and demanded that we help him."

Laughter filtered across the room. Mateo pulled Evie closer and nipped her on the neck. Alpha was more aggressive and possessive than he'd ever been before she was pregnant. We all knew it was simply the werewolf way and accepted it.

"And to Mateo," Jules added quietly, "thank you for finding Evie. She needed you as much as you needed her. I don't think I have to ask before I say for everyone here that the Savoie family is proud to have you as a brother-in-law."

"Hear, hear." Violet's cheery voice was watery, her tone lower.

We all drank, and another tear slid down my face.

Jules turned to Isadora and Dev. "Congratulations to you two. I never thought any man would penetrate the wall Isadora kept around her heart."

"Devraj definitely penetrated her," whispered Violet.

Nico pinched her ass. She squealed, then he covered her mouth as she laughed and he whispered something in her ear.

Jules arched a maternal brow at Violet then went on. "But again, I'm glad you did. I'm so happy," her voice cracked on the last word and she had to exhale a deep breath to go on, "that my sisters have chosen so well. I'm proud to have you all in the

Savoie family." Her gaze slid to Nico and then to Gareth. My heart hammered against my rib cage, wanting to beat right out of my chest. "Cheers!"

More laughter rang around the room as we drank again, my throat tight with emotion. Gareth seemed stunned into motionless silence, barely touching his glass to his lips.

"Come on," I told him, dragging him over to talk to Evie and Mateo. "I want you to get to know my family."

He was wearing his armor again, his mask back in place. But he was cordial and interested in every conversation as we mingled with my family. Someone had put on some music, and we drank a few bottles of champagne before it was time to clean up. Jules had asked me to come and help.

"Will you walk me out first?" asked Gareth.

"Of course."

His Audi was parked right across the street from the Cauldron underneath a streetlight, lit now that it was dark. Rather than walk across the street, he pulled me against the outer wall of the Cauldron, somewhat shadowy in this spot.

"I could walk you to your car, like the gentlewoman I am," I teased.

He shook his head. "I don't want you to cross the street back to the Cauldron at night without me."

I almost laughed, because I was very capable of crossing the street safely by myself. But he wasn't joking. His protective instincts were showing loud and proud. I couldn't laugh at that. It was in his nature. He descended from a vampire, and they were as animalistic as werewolves in their protectiveness.

He leaned his back against the wall and tugged me against him, sliding his hands around my waist. Yet again, I was struck by how easily he was with his affection in public. This was a shocking and wonderful revelation about the ice man.

I suppose I shouldn't call him that anymore. He no longer wore that persona. Not for me anyway.

"I hope you had a nice time." Again, I was feeling shy, a very unfamiliar sensation for me.

He lowered his head to my neck and huffed a hot breath against my skin. "Besides Friday night, this was possibly the best day of my life. I didn't know families could be this way. I thought it was a fairytale."

"Oh, Gareth." I wrapped my hands around his neck, hugging him closer.

I tilted my neck to the side. He swept his mouth along my skin, not kissing or nipping, simply brushing his lips, exploring, lingering on my flesh. I shivered.

"Cold?"

"Not at all." I pressed my body closer. "Quite warm actually."

His hands slid lower. One palm rounded my left cheek, the other drifted lower till he could grip my thigh under the skirt of my dress.

"Come to my place?" he asked, stroking his hands and his mouth.

"I want to, but I know we won't sleep. And we only have five days left before the next event."

The wet t-shirt event was next Saturday. I figured he'd try to coerce me into coming over, but instead he said, "You're right." He lifted his mouth from my skin, his eyes glinting with that fire that made my knees buckle. "When I get you back in my bed, I'm going to want to fuck you all night." His palm on my leg slid around under my skirt to my ass, his fingers grazing the soft skin of my inner thigh.

"Uhn," I grunted, pressing my forehead to his chest. "You're going to kill me, Gareth."

"No, indeed, Lavinia. I'm going to take care of you." He removed both of his hands and cupped my face, tilting it up to look at him. "For as long as you'll let me."

I grasped his wrists to keep his hands there, not to pull them away. "Okay," I said softly.

"Okay?" He arched that dominant brow, using that commanding voice.

"For as long as you want me."

He stilled, watching me with such deep concentration and then examination, then finally reverence before he lowered his mouth to mine. It was soft at first before he angled my face to the side where he wanted me and pressed my mouth wider with his own, stroking in with his hot tongue, fucking my mouth with complete abandon.

I moaned and rubbed up against him, shivering at his hard, jeans-clad dick rubbing against me in my soft dress. After a thoroughly mind-hazing kiss, he pulled back, biting my lip as he went. He tongued it one more time then he walked me back to the door of the Cauldron.

"Sweet dreams, Lavinia," he growled.

"It will be." I turned at the door, "After I masturbate to thoughts of you tonight."

His smile was pure devilry. "As I have been to thoughts of you every night since we met."

I gasped. He winked and crossed the street, folding into his sleek car, watching and waiting for me to go back inside. Only then did he drive away. Gareth was all beautiful, sharp lines and sensual grace and devastating intelligence.

How did I ever not know he was the most perfect person in the world for me?

CHAPTER TWENTY-FOUR

~LIVVY~

"ALL GOOD, WILLARD?"

I sat next to him at the private table I'd set up directly in front of the door to Empress Ink, farther back from the crowd and the stage so we could monitor the online subscribers to the event. I'd even commandeered Sean to handle the video via my tablet on the tripod set up on a small dais down center of the stage next to the DJ.

Gareth had handled a lot of the set-up for the day—permits, food truck vendors, and selling large numbers of subscriber seats on the SuperNet. As well as acquiring the DJ from his night club for the event. I'm not sure how Gareth did it, but he'd quadrupled our online presence from the Pin-up Photo Shoot event. When I'd asked, he simply said, *"A lot of grims owe me favors."*

With today's subscriber tickets online and the entrance fee at the gate farther up the street—manned by Ty and one of his werewolf friends, two of the younger guys of Blood Moon pack who'd opted not to perform on stage but wanted to help—we were already in the five figures for this event. I was beaming with delight.

"All good," said Willard, tapping in welcome comments on our now streaming YouTube channel.

"Awesome. I'll see you after then."

My job was emcee. I wove through the crowd and behind the stage. We had a makeshift bar set up on the other side just like we had for the Empress Ink gallery opening. Hopefully, this one wouldn't include a kidnapping like last time.

JJ, Finnie, and Sam were working the bar. Gareth was talking to Nico behind the stage. He was dressed down again, but not quite as casual as last Sunday. Today he was in those dark, designer jeans and a button-up gray shirt. It wasn't the starchy kind, but one of a softer, lighter material. Still, he looked professional and fancy and delicious.

My mind wandered back to Wednesday night, the only night I'd had the time to stay over at his place. My toes curled at thoughts of him eating me out on his staircase, because we simply couldn't make it in time to his bedroom.

He didn't tie me up that night, but he had blindfolded me and tortured my body with so much erotic pleasure that my screams had actually made Queenie bark in fright downstairs and come running to my rescue. We'd laughed, then we had to pause so Gareth could go calm her down and give her a treat.

"Love seeing that smile on your face," he said when I was finally right next to him.

"Well, you put it there," I told him.

He slid his hands around my waist and leaned close, whispering in my ear, "And I love what you're wearing though I have to admit I'm a little jealous all these guys will be checking you out."

I wrapped my arms around his waist, hugging him closer. I was wearing a black vee-neck *Empress Ink* T-shirt and cut-off denim shorts. I rarely wore anything this casual—or this conventional—but I figured I should fit in with the wet t-shirt contest crowd as emcee. Plus I wanted to help out Violet and Nico with a little promo on their shop since we were using their street corner.

Fortunately, the days and nights had turned balmy and warm. The weather fluctuated with cool fronts this time of year, but the sun was setting and it was still comfortable in the mid-seventies. Perfect for a wet t-shirt contest. While New Orleans loved a good day-drinking event, I'd wanted to attract the night crowd of the neighborhood which tended to be more active. I wanted our street party packed, and it had certainly worked.

Gareth's mouth drifted to my neck, one hand skating down to my ass.

"No need to be jealous. You know I'm going home with you," I reminded him.

His hands squeezed tighter, a hum rumbling in his chest as he licked along my pulse. "Let's go now."

Laughing, I pushed him back. "Impatient."

"Greedy." His content smile was so unusual and stunningly beautiful, it nearly knocked me over.

"Livvy, here's the list you wanted," Clara popped up right beside us.

I extricated myself from his arms and glanced at the printout of the performance playlist. "Oh, great. Thank you."

"Can you do me a favor?" Gareth butted in. "Can you bring that list to Bentley?"

He pointed to the DJ who worked regularly at his club. Gareth had donated Bentley's time. In other words, he'd paid for his services today, but had paid him out-of-pocket rather than use campaign funds.

At the moment, Henry happened to be talking to the guy. When Clara's gaze swiveled across the crowd to the DJ set-up on a small dais at the foot of the stage, her smile and eyes brightened with excitement at Henry standing next to Bentley.

"Of course, Gareth," she agreed, striding back through the crowd.

"Playing matchmaker?" I asked Gareth.

"So what if I am. You don't approve?"

He gave my waist a squeeze. "It's not necessary."

"Oh, really?" I leaned in, tilting my head back to gaze up at him. "Does Henry have a crush on her already?"

His smile warmed, his eyes shimmering darker. "Something like that."

I was about to ask for more information, but then his soft expression hardened to flint, his fingers curling into my denim. He straightened and turned to look over his shoulder behind him. That's when I noticed Richard Davis was here, and he was smiling jovially to the crowd, making his way toward us.

"Shit," I muttered. "Don't do anything, Gareth."

He didn't respond, his stance was like a stone-cold sentinel at my side, a possessive arm wrapped around my waist, holding me tight.

Richard's amiable look dropped to something more penitent when he caught my eye. I could feel the anger vibrating off of Gareth who'd pressed my body to his. Richard stopped in front of us.

"The event looks to be a success."

Neither of us replied. Richard gave a tight nod.

"Right. So I should've come to see you this week." He glanced at me then Gareth. I was unsure who he was talking to, me or both of us, but then he addressed me. "I wanted to apologize for the misunderstanding at the office."

"It wasn't a misunderstanding," I clarified with cold professionalism, the best I could manage. "You made an inappropriate and unwanted advance on me."

I hadn't told Gareth everything that Richard had threatened me with. I knew that if I had, I'd have a hard time keeping him from killing the bastard. And while we hadn't spoken yet about the fact that he'd killed someone in his past, I knew that the darkness inside Gareth could urge him to kill again. Actually, I felt a seething rage humming through his body right now. Not his usual cool demeanor at all.

"I did make an advance," admitted Richard, looking somewhat penitent but that did nothing to calm the man next to me. Richard looked away, and then back to me. "I was under the impression you were receptive."

"Bullshit," snapped Gareth, obviously unable to hold his tongue any longer.

Richard clenched his jaw, slashing a quick glance at Gareth but returning his gaze to me, trying for an apologetic demeanor.

"I wanted to sincerely apologize for being out of line. I can assure you it won't happen again."

"Got that fucking right," muttered Gareth, still holding me in an iron grip.

"Gareth," I hissed, warning him to settle down. I could handle this without him losing his damn mind.

Richard didn't even look at him though his mouth thinned into a line. "I hope that we can move past this incident and work professionally from here onward, Miss Savoie."

Gareth trembled beside me, giving Richard the scariest death-glare I'd ever seen.

"Thank you for the apology," I finally managed to say. "We can."

"I don't think we need to drag GMC into this." His gray eyes weren't repentant at that moment but shimmered cold with a slight warning. "It could throw a wrench into the contest. Might keep you from advancing if we got embroiled into a he said/she said report with Victor."

I blanched, realizing he was insinuating that I was somehow in the wrong. I could see it now. If I went to Mr. Garrison with what had happened, he would counteract with words like *she wanted it, the way she dresses, the way she smiles and looks at me, she led me on.*

I gulped hard at his implication, for a split-second wondering if I had ever given him mixed signals. Even though I knew I hadn't. Men like him were so good at gaslighting women beneath them in the workplace, making us feel like it was our fault they were lecherous, handsy assholes.

I opened my mouth to respond, but Gareth had already unwrapped his arm from around my waist and had placed a palm on my abdomen, gently pushing me behind him.

"Mother fucker. Hear me now," he growled. "I saw what you did, so don't even think about implying that she wanted what you were doing." His voice had dropped into a terrifying register that sent a cold chill down my spine. "What you were *about* to do."

Richard's cordial demeanor had vanished. He was staring right back at Gareth. Still, I wasn't prepared for what he said next.

"If you think to slander my name to Victor Garrison or to anyone at GMC over *nothing*, I'll be happy to explain that you're only defending her because you got inside her pussy first."

I flinched, both at his blunt, offensive words and at the pulse of rage that sliced out of Gareth. I grabbed Gareth's arm, noting his eyes were bleeding black.

"Gareth. Don't," I whispered.

He wasn't listening to me, and Richard wasn't backing down. I swear, I thought I saw a misty shroud of black smoke emanating from Gareth but then it vanished before I could determine if my eyes were playing tricks on me. It had happened before, that day Richard had accosted me in the office. Gareth inhaled a deep breath then let it out slowly.

"Get the fuck out of here. *Now*," he growled.

A jarring push of persuasion pulsed outward to send Richard on his way. Before the asshole pivoted, he glanced at me and where I was clasping Gareth's arm, then abruptly left, snaking back through the crowd toward the exit.

"I'm sorry," he rumbled, turning to pull me into his chest, one hand coasting up my spine.

"Why are you sorry?"

"For reacting...badly. And that you had to listen to that piece of shit's fake apology and what he truly thought."

Pressing my cheek to his shoulder, I whispered, knowing he could hear even over the crowd, "I knew he was an asshole, but not that big of one."

"Now you know."

"At least he'll leave me alone now. He won't bother me at the office after this."

Gareth remained silent, stroking his steady hand up and down my back soothingly. I pulled away to look up at him. His eyes were storm-black. I wrapped my arms around his neck, scraping the nails of one hand over his nape.

"If he does, he'll have to deal with you," I teased with a smile, trying to bring him out of his funk.

He shook his head, gaze roving my face. "I don't know how you do it."

"What?"

"You're perfectly pleasant and sweet after what that prick said."

Shrugging a shoulder, I admitted, "I already knew he was an asshole. I mean, yeah, I was a little shocked he actually said what he was thinking aloud, but I've had worse said to me."

He clenched his hand on my hips. "Who?" he growled, a deep frown creasing his forehead.

I laughed. "No one in my life now. Don't worry about it."

He kept still, seething down at me.

Rolling my eyes, I said, "Let's just say, I rejected a guy or two who felt the need to insult me in return. But that was a long time ago."

"What the hell kind of guy would do that?"

"Heavens, Gareth. Where have you been living, under a rock?"

"I'd never treat a woman like that."

I snuggled closer. "Which is why you're the kind of guy who actually is welcome in my bed."

"I'm the only guy welcome in your bed," he grumbled, sliding his hands to the small of my back and pressing me closer. "Or girl. I don't share."

My smile widened. "Are you saying you want to be exclusive?"

His frown vanished and he arched an eyebrow, adding with a heavy dose of sarcasm, "What do you think?"

"That's what I'm asking you." I grinned.

He dipped his head low to my ear, "I want to be the only one to ever lick your sweet pussy, to hear the intoxicating sounds you make in bed, and to feel you come around my cock." He nipped the sensitive skin below my ear then teased with his tongue.

"That sounds like you're asking me to be your girlfriend, Gareth."

"I'm demanding it."

"Or what?" I laughed.

He lifted his head to look down at me. "Or you'll break my heart."

No teasing at all then. Nothing but hopeful sincerity and a hint of pain shining in those obsidian eyes. My heart thrashed against my ribcage, pushing me to respond in the only way I could.

I lifted onto my toes, holding his gaze as I pressed a soft kiss to his lips. "Then I'm yours."

His eyes slid closed on a groan. He took my mouth with crushing need, one hand coming up to cradle the back of my head so I wouldn't go anywhere.

I wasn't going anywhere. I was right where I wanted to be. At the center of the universe of my grim reaper.

"Livvy!" called Violet from behind us.

He made a sound of frustration in his throat when I pulled apart, which only made me laugh. Violet was back behind the stage. She tapped at her watch.

"When is this over?" Gareth asked, his hands roaming up and down my waist and hips greedily.

I laughed again and pushed out of his arms. "You go hang with Willard and help him interact online. You know he's just as socially awkward online as he is in person."

He nodded his agreement and heaved a sigh, combing a hand through his perfect hair and mussing it up, looking so much like his cousin Henry for a moment. With a gusty breath, he wove away from the stage toward Willard set up in front of Empress Ink.

The crowd had grown as it was almost three o'clock, the time to kick it off. People milled around getting food and drinks and lining up around the stage. There were tables in a semicircle around the raised platform, but there were already dozens of women standing for a closer look.

I'd posted head and torso shots of our "contestants" around the neighborhood as well as online, advertising the event. Sure enough, the NOLA ladies had come out in droves as well as quite a few men.

We'd advertised the event locally as an MC club—the Blood Moon pack—providing entertainment for charity, to raise money for the Louisiana foster care program. We'd emphasized that the money would go toward providing the services our foster care children needed, so it wasn't a lie. We just didn't explain that the money would go to supernatural foster children, because of course most humans had no idea we existed. And those who did kept the secret to themselves.

The online subscribers were all supernaturals, but I spotted a mixture of both in the crowd today. Time to get the party started.

Heading toward the back of the stage, I heard the rumble of deep voices and laughter before I spotted our entertainment for the day gathered together.

Heaven have mercy!

"Whoa." I stood and blinked as the group of them turned to me.

They weren't even shirtless yet, but the threadbare, tight-fitting white t-shirts I'd ordered for the occasion left nothing to the imagination. They each wore different swim trunks—all of them werewolf themed. They varied in pattern—tiny moons, claw marks, wolf prints, wolves howling. I belted out a laugh when Mateo turned to me—black swim trunks with one word in bold lettering across his crotch—ALPHA.

"There she is," crooned Shane, incorrigible flirt, pulling me in for a side-hug.

Smiling, I shoved out of his arms. "Best not get your scent on me."

"Why? You got a werewolf boyfriend that might get pissed?"

Nico grinned. "No. But she's got a grim boyfriend who will rip your head off without even touching you."

"Which one?"

"Gareth," answered Nico.

"Yikes. Yeah, I remember him. Scary fucker." Shane ran a big hand down his chest and took a step back. "I'm attached to my pretty head."

I have no idea why but Shane—big, bad leader of the Blood Moon pack—being intimidated by my grim had me beaming with pride. I wasn't aware that Gareth had done anything to obviously demonstrate his strength in front of Shane back when Gareth and his cousins helped get Violet back from them. But I also knew that werewolves had the most highly attuned senses. They'd sense a dangerous threat a mile away. And Gareth Blackwater was a threat to anyone who got in his way. Or touched his girl.

My tummy fluttered with giddy excitement at the fact that I was indeed *his girl*. Not a shred of doubt or wonder. Funny, because this is the moment in a relationship I typically analyzed if getting attached was the right course for myself and whatever girl or guy I was dating. But with Gareth? All I felt was the repeated word in my mind, my heart, my soul...*yes*.

"Okay, gentlemen," I spoke up, "if you haven't seen it already, I've got the line-up with the songs you've chosen on the poster board here." I pointed to the poster I'd filled out last night and taped to the back of the stage this morning.

We'd built a PVC pipe scaffolding to hold the curtains that ran in a horseshoe shape along the back of the stage so that the audience couldn't see and gawk at those waiting to go onstage.

"After I give my opening remarks down front of the stage, I'll announce each of you one at a time. Just come out when your music starts and do your thing."

"I say we toast to Livvy for putting this together," said Nico, raising the Abita beer he was holding.

They all raised their own, which I hadn't really noticed. I suppose some liquid courage would loosen them up for their performance.

"It wasn't just me," I admitted. "My whole team and, quite frankly, my sisters helped out."

Nico stepped forward and held my gaze, the gorgeous man giving me the kindest, softest look. The one he gave to my sister Violet quite often. "Maybe. But it was you who made it possible. Who thought that this might help us find our place in the community, as well as help out supernatural orphans who can't find good homes. Many of whom are wolfkind."

The supernatural community, he meant. He glanced to the others, all levity wiped from their faces.

"You and your sisters have done more for us in the last few weeks, and I suspect in the coming months, than anyone, any witches, have done for our kind in our living history." He raised his bottle to the suddenly serious group of men. "Here's to the Savoie sisters."

"Hear, hear!" they chorused, clinking bottles and drinking together.

I swallowed the lump in my throat, wishing I could squeeze

them all in a big bear hug. Then again, Nico was probably right that Gareth wouldn't like a bunch of manly werewolf scents all over me.

"Thank you, guys," I managed to say sweetly without my voice breaking. "Don't forget that we appreciate what you're also doing for the supernatural foster program we plan to create. Y'all are awesome for doing this for us."

"Okay, okay," growled Alpha, not Mateo, "let's give these people a show." He glanced at the poster board then winked at me, "Saved the best for last, I see. Smart woman."

Mateo was last on the list, by chance, but Alpha's typically over-the-top confidence just had me laughing as I walked up the back steps to the stage. A roar of mostly feminine applause and cheers erupted when I walked out with a big wave. Violet handed up the mic from the foot of the stage. I'd be emceeing from the platform down there which we'd roped off for the DJ as well.

"Good afternoon, NOLA!" Summoning my magic, I pushed out a wave of influencing glamour, the kind that pulled eyes to me like a magnet. I wanted everyone watching and cheering as our guys put on a show. "Who's ready to see a wet and wild show tonight?!"

~GARETH~

The crowd screamed. Lavinia looked like a wet dream sashaying across the stage in her short shorts and t-shirt tied in a knot at the waist, all her insane curves on display. The men in the audience seemed to appreciate their emcee. Strangely, I didn't have a big urge to rip their eyes out of their skulls. Well, maybe a small urge.

It was the breathy words she gave me just a few minutes ago that had me settled and content.

Then I'm yours.

The intensity of emotion surging through my veins threatened to undo me altogether. I'd only just experienced this heady feeling of belonging to her, of her belonging to me, and I was already addicted. It was both foreign and familiar at the same time. Perhaps a thread of what I remember when my parents were alive. When I had a home and knew bone-deep that I was loved.

Lavinia hadn't used such deep words of attachment, but I felt them shining from her eyes. It was…world-changing. With a few little words, she had suddenly become the center of mine.

Trying to distract myself from the fact that my life's course had just altered to follow wherever Lavinia led us, I glanced down over Willard's shoulder to check out the traffic on our live stream on YouTube. Willard was actually interacting with the early comments easily enough.

"Good job, Willard."

He nodded without looking up. "It seems our audience is mostly female, and they are extremely excited about this event."

The surprise in his voice that had me smiling. Willard was very smart when it came to computers and data. But when it came to people, he couldn't quite figure out what made them tick.

When Lavinia had demanded that he co-host our next event on St. Patrick's Day, I thought it was a bad idea. Then I realized that Lavinia was always seeking the best in people, to push them toward their boundaries to become better, to broaden their horizons as they say.

I was never that kind of selfless person. In fact, I made a point to disconnect from others. Besides my cousins and Aunt Lucille, I pushed people out of my sphere. Always seeking to amass my achievements and security by way of income instead of friends or relationships. I'd sought to ensure that I had a home, a fortress, no one could take away from me.

Yes, I understood my nearly manic selfishness stemmed from

belonging nowhere and to no one during my formative years in foster care. The care that had allowed me to become a victim of abuse by a fellow supernatural. The care that had driven me to murder out of fear and rage. Since that moment, I'd done my damnedest to push the world out, to build my empire of financial security.

Strangely, the thought of allowing Lavinia close, to give her the opportunity to cut me deeper than Dennis ever had, than the rejection of countless foster care parents or my Uncle Silas, than even the death of my parents, somehow didn't send me into a panic. Quite the opposite. I wanted to open my arms wide. And if she sliced my heart open, I'd happily bleed. For her, I'd do anything.

The crowd roared after Lavinia welcomed them, thanked everyone for coming out in support of our fundraiser, then announced the first contestant.

"Rhett enjoys jogs in the park, slow dancing, working on his bike, and pretty much anything where he can work with his hands."

A scream erupted as the beat of "Bounce" by Missy Elliot announced his entrance. He did one runway walk then strutted back to the middle where Violet met him and splashed a bucket of water on his chest. The audience went insane as he did that whole Magic Mike thing before tearing off the t-shirt, revealing a perfectly sculpted body.

"Damn," murmured Willard. "The audience is excited," he said in that unaffected voice.

I shook my head, smiling at Willard's way of pronouncing the biggest understatement. The comments were popping up faster then he could read them.

I watched Lavinia laughing at the crowd and Rhett's enticing performance. He danced downstage then back to center where Clara dumped a second bucket of water on him.

"What do we think of Rhett, y'all!" screamed Lavinia into the mic.

Another uproar as Rhett did a spin with his arms up, showing off his body one more time, then he hooked an arm over Clara's shoulder and walked back toward the exit.

Sure enough, Henry watched with a murderous glare from where he stood next to Bentley even though Clara had untangled herself from Rhett before he left the stage. She was blushing as she refilled her bucket from the hose laying at the back of the stage, her own blouse clinging to her torso where Rhett had rubbed his wet chest against her.

Yeah, that wasn't going over well for Henry, watching from near the DJ. But he needed to get his head out of his ass and do something if he didn't like it. He'd been grumpier than usual when I greeted him this morning, which was my fault. He still hadn't done the favor I'd asked.

I knew why. I got it. The part of his magic he'd blocked off pained him. But it *was* a gift, no matter how he tried to pretend it was a curse. It could do good in this world. It could help me, and Lavinia, not to mention countless others.

But I didn't push him when I'd asked if he'd started for me yet and his response was a grumbled, vehement, "No."

Suddenly, I sensed powerful witch vibes off to my left. Jules was walking toward me with another woman. It took me a split second, but I placed her in my memory of studying the witch guilds. Clarissa Baxter.

"Hi, Gareth," said Jules, "I wanted to introduce you to someone. This is Clarissa Baxter, President of the Coven Guild."

President of the Coven Guild of the United States to be more precise as well as one of the international High Witch Guilds, which was comprised of the president witches and warlocks of thirty countries globally. She also presided over the southern region of Texas where she was based in Houston. The Coven Guilds supervised all supernaturals, while the High Witch Guild was specific to only witches and warlocks. Still, they were a powerful force of influence among all supernatural communities.

Tapping into my memory of my study of Clarissa Baxter, she had been in power for fifteen years, reelected every three years by the regional heads of coven. While she was fifty-three, she appeared thirty-five, and would likely not age physically for another fifty. She was a somber-looking but benevolent witch of the Enforcer designation. And according to my dark essence, she had no skeletons in the closet, so I greeted her with a cordial smile.

"Nice to meet you." I shook her hand.

"This is quite the event," she gestured to the crowd. "From what Jules tells me, you and your team have done an outstanding job."

"Thank you."

I waited for her to perhaps mention something about werewolves being the headliner of this event, knowing that Jules was in league with Ruben to introduce their campaign for the werewolves to Clarissa first. So when she spoke again, it actually took me by surprise.

"I wanted to let you know that we've received the portfolio from your team and rest assured that we have taken notice of the issue."

Confused, since I hadn't sent a portfolio of any kind to her and wasn't aware of one, I shifted my gaze to Jules who still wore her typically unreadable expression. Yet her chin tilted higher, a small smile of pride playing at the corner of her mouth.

"The one Livvy sent to Clarissa," Jules added.

Before I could try to digest that, Clarissa went on. "It was your testimony that actually roused the interest of the Coven Guild most of all."

My heart thumped harder though I kept my expression neutral as usual. "Oh?"

"Yes. The fact that a grim of your distinction and family

connections would offer such a," she paused, almost uncomfortable, "personal account of your struggles in the human foster care program."

My pulse thrummed so hard, I could feel the quick beat in my throat. I didn't let my expression betray the myriad of emotions somersaulting through me. In my testimony, I had simply elaborated on the difficulties of being a grieving supernatural thrust in homes where I was unwanted and where the humans couldn't help me as I transitioned into my magic. I hadn't mentioned Dennis and what had happened, only that the experience had caused tragic circumstances before I was taken in by my uncle, head of the grim reaper coven in New Orleans, who had the resources to help me through the transition into my magic safely.

"Your account got the attention of the entire Coven Guild here in the US," she continued. "I hope you don't mind that I felt the need to share the portfolio. We'd like to meet with you and Lavinia after the GMC contest is over."

Just to be clear, I had to say what I suspected she was telling me aloud. "You would like to meet on establishing a supernatural foster program."

"Yes," she smiled wider, obviously sensing my unease and shock despite my attempts at hiding what I was feeling. "It's apparent from the research Lavinia sent to us along with all of the testimonies that the current agency hasn't been doing justice to our youth. And that is unpardonable." Sincerity was written all over her face. "We would like to institute a larger foster care program that includes representatives from all races of supernaturals."

"Including werewolves?" I couldn't help to ask.

Her gaze roamed to the stage where one of the Blood Moon pack was tearing off his drenched t-shirt while dancing to "Birthday Sex."

"Including werewolves," she confirmed with a small smile. "Their children would suffer just as much as any other supernatural in the human foster care program when they came into their magic without guidance."

"I agree." I clasped my hands behind my back, trying to keep my emotions in check and come across harmless. "It's a tragedy no child should endure."

With a tight nod, Clarissa said, "I'll set up a meeting for June so we can discuss the details."

"Thank you."

And I meant it. This was what I'd planned and hoped for by entering this contest, by persuading my team to adopt my cause for the campaign. I'd thought that I'd need to win the contest to gain the attention needed to attract the awareness of the Guild Coven. But no, Lavinia had done it without me even knowing.

I leaned back against the brick of the Empress Ink building and watched her introducing Nico to the stage. This beautiful, brilliant woman had fulfilled my dream of saving supernatural orphans from the tragic fate I'd endured. She'd done it without me asking it of her, but because she saw the need, compelled by her heart to act. To do what I'd never been able to.

I fucking loved her.

My chest ached at the intensity of it. Closing my eyes for a moment, I listened to her stirring up the crowd for Nico, suddenly needing her all to myself. But I could be patient. Perhaps.

I settled in, arms crossed, and watched her, biding the time till this was all over so I could take her home. The need was almost feral now, tendrils of my dark essence testing my walls to keep it in place.

It was a strange sensation this time. Abnormal to the usual cravings of the beast lurking inside me. It didn't want to hurt or crush or kill. It wanted to seduce and own and dominate. I let that feeling ride, fantasizing of the ways I'd fulfill the monster's yearning desires. And in doing so, sate my own.

Lavinia belonged to me. The monster wanted to stake his

claim with animalistic and carnal finality. For once, I was in complete agreement.

With a shuddering breath, I came to a conclusion. Something I needed to do. To be sure of her. I'd show her the beast tonight. If she welcomed him, the basest part of me, then she'd truly, wholeheartedly be *mine*.

CHAPTER TWENTY-FIVE

~LIVVY~

I COULDN'T STOP LAUGHING. NICO WAS WORKING HIS BODY TO "Grind With Me" by Pretty Ricky, singing the words to Violet who was currently sitting at the edge of the stage, her water bucket empty and forgotten beside her. She'd decided she'd take a seat for the show when her ripped, gorgeous werewolf boyfriend strutted onstage.

Frankly, I was shocked that Nico even knew this song. When he played gigs with his guitar in the Cauldron or other pubs around town, it was always croony, soulful songs from the nineties and beyond. Not this sexy, hip-hop beat that he was moving his body to perfection to, making the audience scream and lose their minds. I'm sure some of these ladies were the broken hearts he'd left behind when he finally knocked some sense into my sister.

He tore the t-shirt off, which got the same reaction every single time the other guys had done the same thing. But rather than show off for the audience, he was now grinding slowly close to Violet who reached up and clawed her purple-painted nails down his abdomen. The crowd loved it!

He did one of those Magic Mike moves then had her pinned to the stage floor beneath him, doing those sexy, roll-your-body push-ups on top of my sister. I seriously thought the girl beside me was going to faint.

"He's so fucking fine," she yelled to her friend.

Nico kissed Violet with open mouth, tongue, and everything, causing the mob to erupt into manic screams yet again. Then he scooped her up, tossed her over his shoulder caveman style and waved to the audience before sauntering off. Violet pushed off his ass to raise her head and waved to the audience from upside down.

"And that was Nico Cruz, my friends." I opened my phone to my notes and surged ahead. "Next up, we have the president of the Blood Moon pack, Shane Morgan. While he loves keeping fit in the gym and riding his Harley on nice days, his favorite thing is custom-designing bikes. He also loves to party, ladies. All night long. Let's hear it for Shane!"

The opening notes of "Stroke Me" by Mickey Avalon lit the audience on fire. Shane took a wide-legged stance, combed both hands through his hair, flexing his biceps, and rolled his body with a pelvic thrust at the end.

Clara was there, tossing a bucket of water on him, then he really went to work. The spotlights, now glowing since night had fallen, caught the water droplets and made them glitter on his skin.

He was definitely channeling Channing Tatum. But the biggest surprise of all was when he ripped off his apparently Velcroed on swim trunks and revealed his impressively large package in a black speedo.

Hand on his crotch, he swung his trunks around his head, nodding and winking at Charlie who sat near the bar, laughing. Then he tossed the trunks to Charlie, who easily caught them. JJ wasn't working at the moment, but apparently enjoying the show. Except he wasn't enjoying Shane's flirting with his man.

When Violet slid a folding chair onstage, Shane used the prop for some sexy grinding moves. JJ put his hand over Charlie's eyes at that point, pulling him back to his chest and whispering something in his ear.

As the song wound down, I lifted the mic. "What do y'all think of Shane?"

Another eruption of cheers, then I glanced down to see Mateo was up next for our last performance.

"Last but not least, ladies, we have Mateo Cruz. By day he's a talented metal work artist, devoting his time to creating sculptures of Greek gods, goddesses, and other amazingly cool subjects. But his most important job, he says, is being a good husband to his wife, Evie, and future father to their children."

As I was introducing him, he'd strolled out and swaggered down the middle of the runway toward me. When I finished, he plucked the mic out of my hand, his eyes flashing gold with the wolf's presence.

"Evening, ladies," his barrel-deep Alpha voice resonated into the mic. He rubbed a hand, fingers splayed, over his muscular chest and abdomen, his tight t-shirt revealing all. Several women squealed. "Just wanna let you know, you can look all you want but you can't touch. This strong, fit body belongs to my mate."

He winked toward the bar area. Sure enough, Evie was perched on a barstool next to Charlie. My sister's growing baby bump and fuller breasts were more prominent in her fitted t-shirt with Deadpool saying, "Did someone say Chimichanga?" She blew him a kiss as "Closer" started thrumming a heavy beat.

Violet meandered up next to me since Clara was being the water girl for this last performance. Violet smiled a sassy smile as she maneuvered up next to me and wrapped an arm around my waist, her mouth close to my ear.

"I'm taking over." She took the mic from me.

"Why?" I frowned, wondering what disaster happened that I needed to take care of.

She waggled her eyebrows. "Trust me." Then she nudged her chin toward Empress Ink.

Gareth leaned back against the wall near where Willard was working, his arms crossed, his body posed in his typically indifferent, I-don't-give-a-fuck posture. But his eyes.

Holy fuck, his eyes. They could incinerate me with the feral desire burning in their dark depths.

Taking Violet's advice, because I couldn't seem to do anything else, I pushed through the crowd going ape-shit crazy over Mateo's moodier performance to Nine Inch Nails. Gareth shoved off the wall when I cleared the crowd and stepped onto the sidewalk by the shop.

Night had settled in, but the perimeter of the spotlights on the stage haloed the outskirts of the street party. Here under the awning outside Empress Ink, it was quite dark. Willard didn't even look up, tapping away at his laptop. Not that I noticed much, my attention riveted to the sexy AF man in front of me.

"Close your eyes," he whispered huskily.

I knew what he was going to do, and I was ready for it. As soon as I closed my eyes, he tossed me over his shoulder, a firm hand on my ass, then traced lightning-fast around the corner and down the shadowed driveway leading to Nico's house. It was attached to the tattoo shop and separated by a gated courtyard.

Before I could ask where we were going, he jumped over the gate. Yes, *jumped*—with the help of TK, that is. The sensation of magic tickled my stomach. Laughter bubbled up my throat when he righted me.

"I didn't know you could do that."

"There's still a lot you don't know about me."

"Like what?" I backed up till my shoulders hit concrete—the wall that was the back of the tattoo shop.

The moon shone bright tonight. Even though it wasn't full, the humped waning gibbous orb cast a cool glow on the court-yard. A fountain trickled nearby, the roar of the crowd and blaring music dimmer here.

"My monster wants to play with you." His voice had drifted to that deeper, huskier register that made me think of sex.

His hands were relaxed at his sides and yet there was a tight rigidity to his stance. He was holding onto control, but barely it seemed.

"Do you mean the darkness that lives inside you?"

"Yes."

"The one you told me is evil."

"Yes. At its core, it is. But it is also a part of me, driven by my lower, baser desires." His eyes were bleeding into black now, the whites of his eyes slowly disappearing.

My pulse quickened, goosebumps raising on my skin at the sensation of the fierce, powerful magic vibrating from him.

"What does your monster want to do?" I whispered, begin-ning to tremble in the presence of something otherworldly.

"Own you. Fuck you. Make you submit."

My knees would've buckled and dropped me to the stone courtyard if I hadn't been leaning back against the brick wall, my palms flat against it. My nipples pebbled beneath my bra, my body responding to his magic with quick, sharp arousal.

He tilted his head, gauging my response. I couldn't come up with a witty or sassy rebuttal, my body humming with sensation and need like never before. Like I wanted to be *owned* by his darkness.

"I'd like to meet your monster," I finally whispered. "I want all of you to know all of me."

It was a heady thing to put my body in the hands of someone as powerful as Gareth. It was daring, risky, and Jules would say stupid, to willingly put my well-being in the hands of a man who housed a creature of darkness inside him, born of black magic.

Gareth's body tightened as he shook his head, his telepathic voice resonating with doubt in my mind. *We'll see about that.* It was a dare. Then he straightened as if preparing himself for something dangerous, something that could change our current course. That could break us apart. Or weld us so tightly that nothing could ever tear us apart.

"Take off your clothes," he ordered in that deep, seductive lilt.

I didn't even think. I just stripped as fast as I could, kicking off my Vans first, then dropping my shirt, shorts, panties, and bra in a pile in front of me. His gaze licked over my breasts, down my torso, and between my legs.

"On your knees."

I slowly dropped onto my pile of clothes, giving my knees cushion from the concrete.

Finally, he lifted his hands and cradled my face, long fingers spearing into my hair. With a thumb under my chin, he tilted my face up. I could barely make out his features, the silvery moon a halo behind him, leaving his face in shadow. Nothing but those fey eyes glinting like black glass. His hands held me with soft affection, a complete opposite of the words that came out of his mouth.

"I'm going to fuck this beautiful mouth. And I'm going to come down your throat." He let his thumb at my chin stroke down the center of my throat, illustrating his point. "It's going to be a lot. You'll want to choke and pull away. But you better fucking not," he said with infinite tenderness and firmness at the same time. "You're going to drink me all down and lick my dick clean after."

I clenched my thighs at his insanely offensive, perverted commands, getting more aroused by the second. His nostrils flared as he cradled my jaw with extreme gentleness, stroking that thumb back up to my mouth, pressing down on my bottom lip.

"Yeah, that's what I thought. Your pussy is getting good and drenched for me. But you've got work to do first. Be a good girl and do your job well. Then I'll let you come."

He released my face and waited, his otherworldly, full-black demonic eyes watching me. Waiting to see what I would do.

The normal Lavinia would've told a guy to go fuck himself for telling me what I was going to do, much less for threatening that he'd only let me come if I gave him head the way he wanted it. But for some crazy reason, my body ached to do every single thing he demanded. Not only that, I wanted him to keep talking, to defile my senses with his naughty, filthy commands.

He tilted his head again, voice impatient and rough. "What are you waiting for?"

Rather than go straight for his belt, I unbuttoned his shirt first, spreading it open with my palms and scraping my nails down his chiseled abdomen. His muscles tightened, but other than that he made not a move. Then I unbuckled his belt, pulled down his zipper and his briefs, his big dick popping free.

Wrapping a hand around the thick girth, I leaned forward and licked the tip. His hips jerked, but he didn't make a sound.

"Suck me good," was the dark command from the shadows above.

When I parted my lips over the crown, he rocked his hips forward, filling my mouth. I made a surprised sound but opened wider, taking all of him that I could. I stroked him at the base with one hand and cupped his sac with the other.

He hissed in a breath. I looked up while I took him deep, his dick tapping the back of my throat with each thrust. He combed a hand gently into my hair then fisted it at the base of my skull, holding me still while he fucked my mouth.

"You look so perfect," came his deep rumble, "on your knees, bare for me, taking my cock like a good girl."

The words were demeaning, but his voice rang with a worshipfulness I couldn't describe. I spread a hand on his bare abdomen, watching him unravel slowly as I sucked harder. He might be guiding the pace well enough now, but I was doing my best to make him lose that stellar control.

Then that black smoke I'd seen before drifted outward from his body. My pulse pounded harder as it solidified into snake-like tendrils, sinuously weaving through the air toward me. That electric intensity of primitive magic sizzled along my skin, raising goosebumps on my arms. I started to pull off of him, but he held me hard and kept thrusting.

"**You want the monster**," he grated, a foreign wildness in his voice. "**You're going to get him**."

Two vines of black coiled around my wrists, the cool touch of dark magic shivering into my skin. Strangely, it didn't feel evil or malevolent. It didn't give me the urge to do something sinister as I thought it would. Rather, it both soothed and tantalized me, sending a shiver of pleasure down my body.

I moaned as two more vines snaked out and encircled my thighs, holding me still. For him. Another traced a cool finger of black smoke from the base of my throat, down and round one breast, licking a peaked nipple with cool smoke before descending between my thighs to whisper over my clit. I whimpered, humming around Gareth's thrusting cock.

The gruff voice of Trent Reznor echoed into the courtyard, singing about fucking his girl like an animal, all while I came apart on my knees at Gareth's feet with his dick down my throat.

Gazing up, I watched him as I moaned, my orgasm coming closer with his dark essence teasing, touching, and shackling me on the ground before him, chaining me *to* him.

Gareth tilted his head back, his fist tightened in my hair, the cords of his throat and beautifully carved chest bathed in moonlight as his cock thickened in my mouth, just before he came down my throat on a feral groan.

I swallowed as he'd commanded, and yes, I started to choke. He let me ease back a little to take it better, but I continued to suck the tip till the pulsing rush of his seed stopped. On a panting gasp, I pulled back, letting his dick pop free. My jaw ached, but I still licked him clean. Again, as I'd been told.

There was a twisted pleasure humming through my body at doing what he'd commanded me to do, my body still primed for an orgasm that hadn't come yet.

The tendril of his essence between my legs had stopped teasing my slit and was now fully wrapped around my waist. His monster held me captive by wrists, legs, and torso. Not that I was planning on going anywhere. Not until he told me what to do next.

Gareth's expression, half hidden in shadow, was more primal than I'd ever seen. Though he'd just come, his dick was still half hard and getting harder by the second.

He reached out a hand, his fingers lightly tracing my jaw, a thumb brushing my cock-swollen lips.

"**Good girl**."

I blinked heavily at his praise, a whimper escaping my mouth.

"**On your feet**."

Before I could even try to stand up, I was being lifted, either by the TK or his dark essence, then I was spun around. I sucked in a breath, holding my hands out to brace myself, but he didn't let me fall. He wouldn't.

"**Bend over. Hands on the wall**."

I complied, feeling completely exposed and needy beyond reason. I wanted him to fuck me like an animal. Apparently, that was the same thing on his mind.

He leaned over my back, bracing one hand outside my own on the wall, his mouth at my ear.

"**You're so fucking perfect, mate**."

He cupped my breast and pinched my nipple, mounding the globe roughly as he continued to pour dirty, possessive words into my ear. My brain hazed at the strange inflection of his voice and the word *mate* in his guttural tone.

"**This is mine**," he squeezed those long fingers around my breast before sliding away, pinching the tip as he went.

His hand slid between my legs, dipping two fingers inside me then spreading my cream around my clit.

"**This pussy is mine**."

His voice had gone to that deep, dark timbre, the one where I knew he and his monster were one and the same.

He pinched my clit lightly, causing me to jump and cry out.

"**Be still**," he growled. "**Tell me what you want**."

He circled my entrance, spreading my wetness, teasing me till I made a sound of frustration.

"You know what I want," I breathed out heavily.

"**Tell me**."

"Your cock, Gareth," I breathed out shakily.

He lifted off the wall and gathered my hair from both sides till he could wrap it around one fist. The other gripped my hip then he pressed at my entrance and slammed home with one thrust. So deep and fast that the stretch was painful at first, rolling into pleasure when he ground inside me.

His fingers bit into my flesh, his hold in my hair stung my scalp, and my pussy quivered at the erotic pain. Then he really started to fuck me.

A throaty growl vibrated behind me as he pounded in deep and hard, and I knew that if his darkness had a voice, that was what I was hearing. The thought that Gareth was letting his essence drive him as he fucked me with savage thrusts was both frightening and thrilling.

If he'd done this, thinking I'd use our safe word *stop* and end this, he was out of his mind. I wanted everything his monster would give me.

In the distance, Lada Gaga's "LoveGame" drove the crowd, but here, the only sounds were of slick wetness, flesh slapping flesh, my breathy grunts he pounded out of me with each near-violent pump of his hips, and the dirty words he kept whispering with that husky, unearthly voice.

"Your pussy was made for me." An inward hiss then a guttural hum of pleasure. **"Mmm, how you squeeze my cock. Yes, just like that. This body was made for my use, for my come. I'm going to fill you till you burst, till my scent is coming out of your pores. Going to fuck you till you know who you belong to. Who owns this beautiful, fucking body. This tight, wet pussy. No one else will dare touch what is *mine*.**"

Dazedly, I realized he hadn't used a condom, but it was a hazy, distant concern knowing I was on the pill. The monster apparently didn't give a fuck about proper sex etiquette. All I could do at the moment was hold on for dear life as he drove into me with relentless, bruising speed.

Wanting to see him, I craned my neck and looked over my shoulder. His eyes were full black, shadows surrounding them, veins of black creeping across his face, down his chest, and up his arms.

"You have this beast in your thrall, woman," he said, sounding very little like Gareth.

The tendrils on my body tightened, making sure I couldn't break free of him. He grinned, looking feral and inhuman. He pulled my hair, turning my head to face the wall again, then he arched my neck and spine till it hurt. It felt so goddamn good at the same time.

What was this madness?

I'd never been into kink or pain. If anything, I'd chosen gentle, languorous lovers. But I wanted the pain, craved it... from him. Only him.

He reached around and slapped my clit with enough sizzling sting, I went up onto my toes with a cry.

"Be quiet and take it."

He slapped me again, harder. I flinched but bit my lip to keep from making a sound of complaint. He rubbed my clit with the pad of his finger, soothingly, keeping up his relentless pounding of my pussy. The tentacles of black smoke snaked up my arms and around my legs, squeezing me tighter, keeping me imprisoned and locked in place so Gareth could fuck me like a madman.

"**Good, beautiful girl**," he crooned, sounding less and less like Gareth and more like something else that was not of this world.

Even so, every time he praised me, my pussy clenched and gushed.

"**Look how wet you get for me. Need to see more**." He slid his hand away from my dripping slit, planted his palm on my ass and spread one cheek wide. "**Mmm, yeah, look at you**."

He adjusted his grip, spreading me wider, then massaged his thumb right where we were joined. Then he circled my tight hole in the back and slid the tip of his thumb inside.

"Ah!" I cried out, arching my spine at the shocking pressure, especially when he didn't stop at the tip but kept pressing in. I'd never explored anal with previous partners. The sensation was shocking and stung more as he slid in deeper.

"**You wanted all of me**," he grated out with biting ferocity. "**Then fucking take me**."

He pounded me harder, his dick swelling and stretching me further, pounding me mercilessly with his cock and his thumb in my ass, going so deep, my vision started to haze. He fisted my hair tighter, the pain resonating through my body, tipping higher than the pleasure.

And I loved it. I fucking loved it.

What was happening to me?

My neck and spine arched higher, my gaze on the stars in the night sky, my body being used with relentless hammering, my breasts bobbing, nipples erect, palms scraping on the brick wall. The tentacles on my arms wound farther up till they circled my breasts then my nipples, squeezing till I cried out at the sharp sting, torturing me with its cool touch of pleasure and pain. Yet another tendril slid up my spine and encircled my throat, gently but firmly gripping, the cool smoke squeezing just enough to show me who was master.

"Gareth!" I was begging, but for what, I wasn't sure. I couldn't think.

His coils slid tighter over my skin, keeping me perfectly bound, my thighs spread wide for him, my body bent for his master's merciless fucking. So he could use me just like he wanted to. It was wrong, but I whimpered at the thought, my juices slicking me more.

"**Yessss.**" Another deep, loud hum of approval. "**Come for me, mate**," came the eerie, gravelly command. "***Now.***"

Like every single time, I couldn't resist his order. But when the orgasm spiraled through me with painful eruption, my body convulsed, and I lost all control. I cried out on a sob. Suddenly, I was jerked upright into his arms, still speared on his cock, a hand possessively across my chest squeezing one breast, the other mounding my pussy.

As I drifted into a dreamlike euphoria tinged with pain, my sex still clenching his dick, feeling exquisitely raw and frighteningly vulnerable, I heard his savage voice in my ear.

"*Lavinia.*"

My name rang from man and beast with awe and longing and misery. I barely whimpered, unable to even lift my arms as he bit the slope of my shoulder and came inside me, growling his pleasure, emptying himself deep with slow, grinding pumps. I didn't even respond to the agony of his vicious bite, my mind floating elsewhere in sub-space.

The rest was a dizzying haze. I was propped on a bench, a hand holding me steady. My shorts were being jerked on. Then my shirt, arms limp, sliding into the sleeves like a puppet. Someone was crying. It was me.

"*Fucking Christ.*" I was being lifted gently into strong arms. "I've got you, baby." A soft, sorrowful voice, laced with despair and regret. A press of lips to my forehead.

Darkness.

CHAPTER TWENTY-SIX

~GARETH~

I'D NEVER BEEN THE KIND OF PERSON TO SELF-HARM. AS A child, I was a fighting survivor. As an adult, I was a selfish, ambitious asshole who quite frankly loved himself. But right now, I was considering options of how I could seriously punish myself for how I'd just treated the precious woman laying beside me in my bed.

After I'd gotten her here, I'd texted Henry and asked him to help Willard wrap up the event, refusing to tell him why we'd left without a word. Henry being Henry, he didn't ask.

I'd tucked her under the covers and kept to the outside, knowing how she'd feel once she woke. Still, I couldn't be parted from her until I was sure she was okay. I managed to get her to swallow two Advil in her dazed, altered state after I'd fucked her like the monster I was. There was no question I'd caused her pain. I was a goddamn animal. Remorse churned the acid in my stomach.

I cocooned her body under the covers and tucked her body close to mine, combing my fingers gently through her hair, giving her as much tenderness and gentle care as I could even while she was still unconscious. Knowing full well she wouldn't want or accept my touch when she woke.

What the *fuck* had I been thinking?

You know, the demon whispered from the depths where I'd caged him back behind solid, supernatural walls.

Yes, I'd thought to test Lavinia. To show her what she was asking for in knowing *all* of me. I'd used her body for my own pleasure, pushed her to the brink, dominated her physically and emotionally. I'd let loose the darkest part of me, craving her full submission to the beast beyond reason. The need to invade, conquer, and overcome her drove me tonight.

A need ingrained so deep, it came from my Varangian bloodline, I was sure of it. From the one who'd sacrificed innocents upon blood altars, who'd cast black magic spells to amass more power. To take whatever he wanted by foul, brutal force.

I'd shown Lavinia what the monster in me truly wanted from her. I couldn't get past the fact that she'd given me the most soul-shattering pleasure I'd ever experienced. But it was at the expense of her well-being. I tried to regret it. I wanted to regret it, for fuck's sake. But I was a twisted bastard.

If I could wipe the memory of it away, I knew that I wouldn't. I'd always cherish the way she made me feel in that moment. While I'd subdued her with brutal force and told her every thought I'd kept hidden deep, she wasn't the one bound and chained. I was. I'd worship her for eternity for giving me one heavenly moment of full acceptance.

To be a grimlock like me—who'd known keen loss at an early age, repeated rejection, and brutal abuse at the hands of one who should've shown me kindness and compassion—I never thought to know true belonging. The closest I'd ever felt was with my cousin Henry. But still, even he had never seen what my beast truly was. I never let anyone that close. Until tonight.

And now, she would leave me. There was no question. She

would wake and realize what had happened. She would know the filthy creature that I was deep inside. Not the mask of control and power that I showed the world, but the ugly demon who wanted her still. I could only be grateful he hadn't wanted her blood. Just her body on the most primal level.

Still cuddling her close, facing her, I eased the edge of her t-shirt collar aside to examine the bite mark. I hadn't broken the skin somehow, but nearly. It was already purpling with detailed indentions of my teeth. I traced a finger over the mark, stomach churning with acid. Not because I hated my mark on her but because I loved it. I couldn't regret it. And if she stayed with me, I'd want to do it again. A rumble of approval vibrated in my chest.

Fucking hell. I hated myself.

Lavinia made a soft noise in her throat, eyes blinking awake. I withdrew quickly and sat facing her, one foot on the floor then reached for the glass of water on the nightstand. Her brow wrinkled in confusion when her eyes met mine.

"Where are we?" she rasped sleepily.

"Here. Sit up and drink this." I gently helped her into a sitting position.

She winced in pain, and again I wanted to stab myself in the chest. Five thousand fucking times.

I tipped the glass against her mouth. She drank half of it, her hand over mine. I couldn't help wishing she wouldn't remember. That she'd touch me trustingly like that forever. But I'd never take away what I'd done, not even through a glamour, which I could. There would always be truth between me and Lavinia. Even when we parted. Even when she hated me.

"Mm." She tapped my hand on the glass, so I set it back on the nightstand. She still seemed confused, glancing around.

"Do you need anything? Advil? A cool bath, maybe." Though I doubt she'd want to get naked anywhere near me, I couldn't help but offer.

Her brow creased in a question. "What's wrong?"

Swallowing against facing what I'd done, frightening away the best thing that had ever happened to me, I said, "Don't you remember?"

"What do you mean?"

Heaving out a breath to find the courage, because this was harder admitting aloud than I thought it would be.

"You're still sleepy. You don't remember yet?"

I reached up to touch her hair then pulled my hand away, clenching a fist in my lap. She frowned, so I went ahead and told her. Best to rip the Band-Aid off quickly. Get this over with.

"When we were *together* in the courtyard, I let my darkness out. He—no *we*—because I'm responsible too. We were too rough, too violent." I wanted to vomit at what I was dancing around, but I confessed it anyway. "We were abusive to you. I apologize for any pain I caused you, but I don't apologize for what happened. I can't lie to you. I wanted you to know all of me. Even knowing you'd hate me after, I needed to show you."

The darkness needed to be seen, and I couldn't have stopped it if I'd tried.

Her frown deepened. "What?"

Christ, this was torture. I had to say it again? "It will come to you in a minute, what I did—"

She snort-laughed then winced again, touching the bite-mark at her shoulder tenderly. I was definitely going to vomit any minute now.

"Gareth," she said gently, reaching out to put her hand over mine in my lap. There was ring-like bruising around her wrist and forearm. The monster's marks. *My* marks. "I remember everything. I didn't forget one second of it."

My pulse sped with sickening speed, the ache in my chest winding tighter. "I should've known you'd be gentle like this."

"Huh?"

"When you left me."

"Gareth." She laughed. Actually *laughed*. Sweetly and with tenderness in her eyes. "What the hell are you talking about? I'm not leaving you."

"I *hurt* you."

"No, you didn't."

Huffing out a sound of disdain, I grabbed both her hands—gently—and flipped them over, stretching her arms toward me. The crisscross of rope-like bruising went all the way up to her biceps. Her palms were pink with rough abrasions from the brick wall. I'd washed them clean and applied lotion several times while she was sleeping. But there was still evidence of what I'd done.

She stared down at the bruises, turning her arms to look at them more closely.

"They're kind of cool, aren't they?"

I choked. "Are you fucking mad?! I hurt you, Lavinia. You should be slapping me, spitting in my face, cursing my name while storming out of my life."

She laughed again, but it died quickly. She shook her head. "I'm not going anywhere."

I couldn't even process what she was telling me. "Are you a masochist?"

"No." She rolled her eyes. "Well, I don't know, maybe I am." She shrugged. Shrugged! "And maybe you were a little rough." Whatever expression I made had her laughing harder. "But it wasn't abuse, Gareth. It was just your monster loving me, the only way he knew how."

I shook my head in complete disbelief. "I can't even believe what I'm hearing. You're in pain, and you're…forgiving me?"

Again, she rolled her eyes like *I* was the ludicrous one. "You're so dramatic, Gareth. I'm not in pain. Not much. And there's nothing to forgive. I'm on the pill, too, by the way." She turned sideways and propped herself up on a pillow and grunted in pain.

"See!" I lurched from the bed, paced away, and turned, staring at her with clenched fists.

I'd imagined every possible reaction when she woke and *this* was none of them.

"Okay, so I'm sore. But I knew what I was getting myself into." She gave me those wide blue eyes that made my heart soften, my resolve wilt, my soul stumble.

"You couldn't have possibly known."

"I know you're having a hard time grasping this, but I am a very intuitive witch."

"I know that you are."

"So you're saying that after all you've told me about yourself, about being a grimlock, about the darkness," then she added more softly, "about killing someone else, that I had no idea what I was allowing to be unleashed. Is that what you're saying?"

"No." Again, I swallowed hard, emotion thickening my senses. "You're the most brilliant, beautiful woman, witch, I've ever known."

Her blue eyes shone with tears standing in them. "Then hear me now, Gareth Blackwater. You've shown me your worst. And I'm still here." She lifted a hand to me.

After a few seconds of agonizing over this new reality where she welcomed me into her arms rather than run screaming from my house—from my life—I stepped closer. Tentatively. Incapable of stopping myself, I lay on top of her, very gently, and pressed my face into her hair, inhaling the sweet scent of her.

"God, you're remarkable."

"It's goddess, actually. And I *am* remarkable."

Lifting to look at her lovely face, I added, "I'm not sure there's a definitive answer on whether the grand creator is male or female."

"Says the male who thinks he knows everything. Also, every creature on earth who creates life is female, so there's that," she pointed out then frowned. "Except seahorses, that is."

I laughed, completely blown away by her generous and resilient spirit and sweet temperament. "I'm never letting the beast out again. I'm going to get Violet to come up with a spell to trap him for good."

She traced a finger across my forehead, down my left temple and along my jaw. "No. You won't do that."

"I can't let that happen again."

Her eyes widened. "I think that's up to me. And I most certainly would like that to happen again." She waggled her eyebrows. "If you hadn't noticed, I came so hard I passed out."

"And then you cried," I reminded her.

"I've told you before that I cry when I'm happy. I was most definitely blissed out. Fucked senseless, yes, but in the best kind of way."

My senses told me she was telling me the truth, but I simply couldn't wrap my mind around it. This was going so differently than I thought it would. Infinitely better, but she'd struck me dumb.

"I love this speechless side of you, Gareth. No witty or snarky come-backs?"

"We'll wait a year and maybe revisit this idea of letting him out."

"Don't be ridiculous. A month will do."

Frowning, I needed clarification. "Wait. Do you mean we're not having sex for an entire month?"

She laughed, her neck arching, which had me cataloguing all the places I wanted to worship with my mouth.

"No, dummy. We can get back to regular sex in a few days, a week max, I'm sure. But monster sex needs to be spaced out."

"Monster sex." I grinned.

A flush of pink colored her cheeks. "It was delicious," she whispered. "Also, just so you know, I'm anemic. I bruise really easily."

Disgruntled, I took her delicate wrist in my hand, turning it over to look at the purplish lines again. "I'm getting you on a strong iron regimen starting tomorrow."

"Yes, Daddy."

My gaze shot to hers. She blinked sweetly at me.

"Don't even toy with me." My dick was half hard at her teasing.

She laced her fingers with mine. "How often does your, you know, darkness do that? Come out like that?"

"This is only the second time I've allowed it to fully possess me."

"When was the first?"

Yes. It was time to tell her all.

I heaved out a sigh, shifting to lay on my side, head propped on one hand, our entwined hands on her belly.

"In my fourth foster home, I was left alone a lot. I'd gotten used to that. Like most foster parents, the Wexlers, gave up easily when they couldn't reach me. I was withdrawn after my parents died."

"They should've tried harder."

"But the real problem was that the Wexlers were human. I'd started to feel the dark essence at a very young age."

"It doesn't happen at puberty for grims? I know for werewolves, their wolf doesn't show up until then."

"Actually, it is different times for grims, but yes. Most of the time, it's around that hormonal change from child into adolescence. For me, it was much sooner. Shortly after my parents died. I was afraid of the dark thoughts it was giving me, so I went cold and silent. They tried to get specialists to work with me, but I refused to open up. I knew something was wrong with me."

"But it wasn't you. It was just your grim magic."

I smiled at her sweetness, raising our clasped hands to place a kiss on the back of hers, where there was no bruising. No need to explain yet again that grims, by birth, are unnatural. If she accepted who I was, then I wouldn't contradict her.

"Do you remember me mentioning the new boy that came to the house? Dennis?"

"The vampire?" She gulped hard. "What happened?"

"I was so happy. I realized he was like me. I didn't want to eat raw meat, but I'd already begun to trace through the woods behind their house. It felt exhilarating. Freeing, to use the magic. One day, I saw Dennis heading into the woods after school. I followed him and called out to him."

Pausing, I remembered the way Dennis had stopped and turned at my approach, the eerie way he'd glared at me. He was already near feral. Something that happened to vampires and even werewolves sometimes. To be fair, to grims as well. The three supernaturals who held animalistic tendencies inside themselves. Only witches were free from this curse. This was the reason that the Coven Guild was presided over by witches and warlocks.

"I told him I was happy he would be my brother and that I was a grim reaper. A supernatural like him. My parents had told me about other supernaturals, but I'd never met a vampire. When I approached him, he reached out his hand as if to shake it." Heaving out a breath, I went on. "When I did, he jerked me into his hold and sank his fangs into my neck. It was painful. So painful."

She squeezed my hand. "Oh, Gareth. I'm so sorry."

Every supernatural knew that the vampire bite could give great pleasure, even erotic pleasure, depending on the vampire giving the bite. But from a feral creature whose mind was already poisoned, it could bring nothing but pain.

"Once he'd drank his fill, he dropped me to the ground, grinning at me with my own blood staining his teeth. He told me I'd better wear a hoodie, because it would be my fault if the humans found out we were supernaturals. Then he'd have to do something about it."

"Stars above," she whispered. "He was threatening to kill you or your foster family?"

"Yes. Though I wasn't close to them, I still didn't want them to die because of me."

"It wouldn't have been because of you."

I smiled down at her again. "I know that now. But when you're a child, you believe whatever someone tells you. I'd decided I'd stay away from Dennis and keep quiet, try to keep the family safe."

"Go on, Gareth. Tell me." Her heartbeat was picking up speed, fear scenting the air.

"He started visiting me at night. I'd be completely asleep, then I'd wake to his weight on top of me, pinning me to the bed while he ravaged my neck, my shoulders, my arms if I tried to beat him off."

"No, Gareth." A tear slipped from her eyes.

"Don't cry." I cupped her face and wiped it away. "I'm okay now."

"So your monster came awake one of these nights."

I nodded. "There was a two-year-old boy, Robbie, in the family's care who I liked to play with. Dennis would torture me by saying he'd kill the baby in his sleep if I didn't let him drink his fill any night he wanted to. Robbie's crib was in our room." I exhaled a slow breath, remembering that night. "As I've said before, there was something wrong with Dennis. I believe he was a serial killer in the making. And a vampire on top of that. There'd been a local boy who'd gone missing and was never found. When our foster parents talked about it, Dennis just smiled at me. The neighbor's dog was found dead, savaged by a 'wild animal' the adults said."

"Dennis."

"Yes. So one night, I heard Robbie crying in the crib. I awoke to see Dennis laying Robbie down on his bed, pulling off his little onesie at the shoulder. I," I wished I didn't have an eidetic memory because the picture was still seared into my brain— "I knew what he was going to do, so I leaped on him and started beating him. He left the baby and attacked me, tearing into my shoulder through my pajama shirt, and the monster came alive. All I felt was rage and pure hatred. That was the first time I saw the black smoke shoot from my body. It grabbed Dennis's arms and legs and broke him in multiple places before breaking his neck and dropping him."

"Gareth. I can't even imagine." She had pulled her hand from mine and was cupping my face now.

"It happened very quickly. When our foster parents came into the room, I was holding Robbie, bleeding from the shoulder, and Dennis was crumpled on the floor, dead, blood on his mouth. Mine."

There was also blood pouring from his ears and eyes, but I'd not upset Lavinia anymore with that gruesome part of my past.

"So, the Wexlers called the cops and paramedics. It had been ruled that a brain aneurism had killed Dennis though no one could account for how he'd broken his own arms or legs. I remember one of the paramedics staring at me very hard, her magic humming in the room."

"She was a witch?"

"A grim, actually. That's how word got back to my Uncle Silas, how the memories of all those involved were erased, and how I flew under the radar as a grim having murdered at eleven years old."

"Your Uncle Silas took you in because you'd murdered someone?" She looked aghast.

"When it was told to him that Dennis had been killed because his bones had been pulverized in two hundred places, my uncle knew that I would be a powerful grim. I'd showed signs of being a grimlock at a very young age. Since there were others in our family's history I later learned, he decided to take me in." Sighing, I tucked a lock behind her ear, smiling at her look of disgust. "Uncle Silas covets power and nothing else."

"But Henry. And Sean. They're not like that."

"No. They and my Aunt Lucille are my only family I care

about." Pausing, I trailed a finger along her jaw. "Well, cared about until now. Before you."

We sank into staring at each other, something that had become so common between us now. In the beginning, there was tension and animosity then later came loads of lust. Now, it was a look of recognition, of connection. Hearts and minds meeting, communing, and belonging. A jolt of adrenaline shot through me at what I read in her eyes. Or hoped that I saw.

"What are you thinking?"

Her lips parted but she paused. Then finally, "I'm afraid to tell you."

"Never be afraid to tell me anything." I trailed my fingers along her jaw, savoring the sensation of touching her silken skin. "Tell me," I whispered.

She smiled, her eyes glassy. "I love you, Gareth."

My heart did indeed skip a beat. I heard it, felt it, as if my very soul held its breath.

I closed my eyes, breathing in her lovely scent and this newfound grace, wondering how I ever deserved it. When I opened my eyes, I leaned over her, sweeping a gentle kiss against her mouth.

"I love you, Lavinia. More than you could possibly ever know."

Her arms wound around my neck, pulling my weight more fully on top of her. "I know, Gareth."

I laid my head down on her breast and wrapped my arm around her waist. Her hands combed through my hair. We lay there in silence, petting and holding each other. I was taking in my new reality. That I loved and was loved in return.

"Thank you," I whispered. I couldn't explain the level of gratitude I felt for finding her, getting her, keeping her.

Her laughter rolled under my ear, making me smile at the sweetest sound on earth.

"Silly, Gareth," she sighed, pressing a kiss to the crown of my head.

I chuckled to myself. Never in my life had I ever imagined someone calling me silly and living to tell about it. But Lavinia? She could call me anything, say anything, do anything, and I'd remain right where I was. At her side, where I finally knew down to the depths of my jaded soul, I belonged.

CHAPTER TWENTY-SEVEN

~LIVVY~

HE HAD TO STOP THIS. IT WAS GETTING RIDICULOUS. WILLARD hadn't noticed, but he never noticed anything so what was new.

I had my head down, jotting down Willard's ideas on my notepad as he rattled them off and was trying to ignore the besotted grim staring at me like I hung the moon and the stars. He hadn't stopped giving me those sappy, smiling looks all day.

When I glanced up from my notepad, I realized delightedly that he was still grinning like...well, like Devraj looked at Isadora. Like I was the center of his universe.

My tummy fluttered, watching him twine my red hair scarf around his hand dreamily. Gareth didn't fidget or toy or play with things. He did everything with definitive purpose. That meant that he'd brought that damn thing to the office to remind me of our first night of hot sex, and I knew it.

He knew I knew it.

While I was fully healed after our courtyard sexcapade—especially after several sessions with Isadora, bruises all gone—I hadn't shared that fact with him just yet. I couldn't help it, but it was fun torturing Gareth.

He enjoyed torturing me too, because all he'd done the whole damn day was gaze at me with hearts in his eyes or seduction playing at his lips. He was imagining all of the things he wanted to do when I said the word go. I couldn't help watching those clever fingers toying with the scarf. He was torturing me on purpose.

"Sounds great, Willard. What do you think, Gareth?"

His eyes rounded in surprise, his hands halted in their twining of my silk scarf. "What?"

I bit my lip because I'd never seen Gareth completely baffled and unprepared. He usually had ten opinions about any one question.

"About what Willard was saying about the parade commentary intro."

He straightened in his seat. "What was that again? Can I see your notes?"

I placed the pen on the notepad and slid it across the table to him. He stared at my diligent bulleted talking points that Willard and I had batted around all morning while Gareth daydreamed like a smitten schoolgirl.

"Oh, I see."

His face tightened in concentration. This was what I was accustomed to viewing across the table at our office at GMC. Gareth in complete businessman mode. He took my pen and scribbled his own additions. Of course. Gareth couldn't let one thing pass him by without giving his two cents. Neither could I, so I wasn't complaining, just noting how similar we were. In some ways.

He was far too serious for his own good. Even now, seconds after he had spent the last several hours woolgathering about us in bed, I have no doubt, he was able to snap back into his austere Grim Gareth persona like flipping a coin.

He made a lot of circular patterns, probably marking the

points he wanted highlighted the most, and dotted an "I" or something with a hard stab at the paper and then slid it back across to me.

"See if that meets with your approval."

Picking up the notepad, I stared at the doodle he'd made at the bottom, reading *Gareth loves Lavinia* inside a scribbled heart, outlined like ten times. Then there was an arrow pointing off to the side. *P.S. He also wants to fuck her brains out as soon as possible.*

My heart swooned. So did my pussy.

"Do you think we could add that to the agenda?" he asked seriously, not a single sign of playfulness on that fine face of his.

"I think this could be arranged."

"Let me see," said Willard, holding out his hand.

Not on your life, Willard.

"Um, let me type these up for you first then you'll have a clean list to work with."

"Clean?" asked Gareth, arching a brow.

"I mean, you know, typed and organized." I clutched the pad to my chest.

"Good idea," said Willard, turning back to his laptop. "I'll want to add my own notes to it to flesh it out when you're done."

"Sure thing." I hopped up and headed to my desk.

Gareth followed me, hot on my heels. As soon as I sat in my desk chair and moved my mouse to wake the computer, he was behind me, both hands on the arms of the chair. He dipped his head low and nibbled at my neck.

"When can I fuck you?"

My thighs clenched. "Tonight, I should think."

He half-groaned, half-whimpered.

I angled my head to the side so he had better access, enjoying the lovely shiver along my skin. "Are you telling me that you've never gone a week without sex? I find that highly unlikely."

"I've gone way longer than that."

"So what's the problem?"

"I've never been in love before," he whispered before biting my earlobe. "I can't help it. You're all I think about."

"I've been in your bed every night."

"And it's driving me crazy, because I can't touch you every-where and in every way that I want." He licked the sensitive spot below my ear. "I want *in*, Miss Savoie."

"You know, you haven't even taken me on a proper date yet." I tried for haughty and indifferent, but Gareth's aggressive and needy attention was drenching my panties.

"I'll take you to dinner tonight."

"And not Daisy Dukes."

"Not Daisy Dukes." His arms crossed my chest and he squeezed me in a hug, still with the chair between us. "Only the best for my lady."

"Stop it," I hissed, looking up at him over my shoulder.

"Stop what?"

"Being so ridiculously mushy. I can't even think straight when you're like this."

He let out a bark of laughter then pressed a kiss to my cheek and stood up straight. He wiggled his fingers and tucked his hands in his pockets to show me he was being a good boy.

"I'll let you get back to work."

Then he swaggered off back to the conference table where his own laptop was still sitting unused for the entire day so far. I couldn't help but let my gaze stray to his tight ass. Mmm. He was delicious. I squirmed in my seat.

Gareth looked over his shoulder and winked. "You like watching me walk away, don't you?"

I stuck my tongue out at him and turned back to my desk-top, butterflies doing some kind of crazy dance in my belly. All it took was one hot look and he sent me into a spiral.

There were several reasons why Gareth was currently competing with Clara for happiest supernatural in New Orleans. One was that we were finishing up our last fundraiser for the competition, Willard's idea to host commentary and live-stream the Irish Channel Parade for St. Patrick's Day.

This parade was an old tradition of NOLA's. The Irish Channel was a neighborhood within the Lower Garden District that was home to the first Irish immigrants who flocked here during the Potato Famine in the mid-1800s. For decades, NOLA has celebrated St. Patrick's Day with this parade that winds down Magazine Street and through the old neighborhood. Willard's idea presented a fabulous way to showcase the neighborhood history and traditions that still run so deep.

The second reason Gareth was so chipper was, of course, that he and I had finally confessed our feelings for each other. Falling in love was strange and wonderful and mind-boggling. You think there's a finite level of love you can feel for a person, but then it keeps growing every day.

Like just now. He looked over his shoulder and winked with one of his cheeky remarks and my heart expanded even more. It was utterly magic. That's when I realized something.

Love is the best magic in the whole world.

And the last reason Gareth seemed high as a kite was that Richard Davis had been MIA since the wet t-shirt contest. Cynthia at the front desk mentioned he had business out of town, but for us to call him with anything we needed.

Pfft. We would not be calling him for anything. I was glad he was gone. Not only was he a grade A douchebag, but even the mention of his name made Gareth's eyes wash from brown to black in a millisecond.

Gareth and I agreed to wait till after the contest was offi-cially over before we met with Mr. Garrison about the incident. I certainly wasn't going to let this slide so he could prey on someone else, but I didn't want it interfering with the contest either. And it was almost over.

Needless to say, knowing Richard wasn't around made it much easier to relax and work at the office. The hours zipped by, then Gareth was standing beside my desk, holding my purse. He looked adorable.

"It really doesn't match your outfit," I remarked, standing and checking him out.

He glanced down at my pink bag with red lip kisses all over it. With a wry grin, he slid the strap over my shoulder and took my hand. "Time to take you on a date, but let's drop your car at my house before."

"Aren't you going to let me change first?"

"Why? You look great."

I was wearing one of my more comfortable A-line dresses. It matched my purse but it was black with a red kiss pattern. I should argue that we could manage being separated for an hour or so before dinner, but who was I kidding? I didn't want to be apart from him for a single minute.

Hand in hand, we made our way out of the GMC building and to our cars, then I followed him back to his place. As soon as we walked in the door, I scooped up Queenie and gave her a cuddle. She wiggled happily in my arms and licked under my chin. Gareth gave me one of those heated looks.

"Jealous of your dog?"

"Yes." He smirked and held out his hands. "Let me feed her. You go out on the patio. It's a nice night. I'll bring you some wine."

Handing Queenie over, I rose up and kissed him on the cheek. And goddess above, the man blushed! A swath of perfect pink crossed his cheekbones. It was lovely.

As I walked through the kitchen and living room to the patio sliding glass door, I stopped and stared, my mouth falling open.

Under the pergola, his patio table—the height of a coffee table—was covered in candles and covered trays of food. There were plush red pillows strewn around the table and more candles as well as tiki torches surrounding the pergola.

Gareth was behind me, skimming his hands around my waist, dipping his head low.

"Dinner for my girl."

"How did you do this?"

"I paid Sean a lot of money."

I laughed. "Did he cook for you too?"

"Hell no. That boy can't cook. I did. Henry helped with dessert actually." He slid open the door. "Go on. I'll bring the wine."

I strolled across the stepping-stones to the pergola. The structure was covered in wisteria vines that gave the area a naturally intimate vibe.

He'd added a few more pillows since the last time we'd been out here. I blushed at the memory as I settled on a pillow by the table.

Gareth had shared with me earlier this week that Clarissa Baxter had met him at the wet t-shirt contest and invited us to meet with her on organizing the supernatural foster care program that was so obviously needed. She'd even admitted that the current agency run through the Coven Guild was unsatisfactory.

Gareth had thanked me for sending Clarissa Baxter that portfolio, under this very pergola, with me spread out on the rug beneath these extra cushions, on his knees and with his head between my thighs. Heat crawled up my neck at the way he'd treated me that night. I'd been still too sore for *sex* sex.

After he'd kissed me with languorous, almost reverent, sensuality and I'd come with a low cry, he'd placed a kiss to my thigh and pulled my skirt down. When I'd reached for his belt buckle, wanting to reciprocate, he stopped me then pulled me into his lap sideways. "I just wanted to say thank you." He'd pressed a soft kiss to the crown of my head and tucked me closer, hugging me tighter against him. "Let me hold you."

I liked the way Gareth said thank you. I loved it actually. *Loved him.* I grinned at the wallpaper on my phone, a sleepy pic of Gareth I'd taken right after he woke up. His mouth was slightly tilted up on one side, giving the camera that private look of affection only I had the privilege to see. The rest of the world saw only the ice man, and that was fine by me.

"Here," he was standing next to me, handing me a glass of red wine.

The click-clack of Queenie's nails on the stone patio announced her coming my way. Between her teeth, she was holding something.

"What do you have, girl?"

She pranced closer onto the rug and dropped it into my lap. It was a dark red velvet box. A jewelry box. Before I could wonder another minute, Gareth was settling on the rug beside me. He stretched one leg out under the table, leaning on one hand and angling his body toward me, giving me a subtle smile.

"For me?" I asked dumbly. Because of course it was.

He didn't say a word. Just watched me.

My heart was in my throat as I opened the square jewelry box. Inside was a silver necklace. On the chain was a nickel-sized locket which was a beautifully crafted eye of medusa. Where the blue stone for the iris should be was a round sapphire, the eye rimmed in tiny diamonds. It was stunning in design.

"Gareth." I simply held it and stared.

"I was wondering if one of your sisters could cast a protection spell on it." Then he added in a lower, softer voice. "I want to keep you safe. Even when I'm not around."

"You know protection spells aren't like bullet-proof shields, right?"

"Yes. But a protection spell might give you some warning of danger or veer you onto a safer path." He smiled when I looked up at him. "I'll do anything to protect you as best I can." He still remained quite still, watching me with tenderness. "You are my heart, Lavinia. Without you, there is no life worth living."

"Gareth." A tear streaked down one cheek.

He frowned. "Happy tears, right?"

I nodded.

"Look on the back."

I flipped the pendant over to find the scripted words in quotation marks. *"We loved with a love that was more than a love."* *Gareth & Lavinia*

I breathed out a sigh and a sob at the same time. Then I jumped up onto my knees, wrapping my arms around his neck. He caught me of course as I kissed my way up his neck to his mouth.

"Thank you. It's so beautiful," I whispered against his lips.

"As are you." He settled me sideways on his lap, coaxing me closer with gentle hands.

Then the kiss deepened, as did our love.

He was the one to finally come up for air. "Let me put it on you."

I turned and lifted my hair, shivering as his fingers lightly grazed my nape.

"There." He placed a kiss to my nape. "And now dinner."

I let my hair down and turned to face the table as he lifted a serving dish cover.

"We have shrimp linguini with a white wine, garlic sauce."

"Yum. *You* cooked this?"

He feigned an offended look. "Lavinia, I'm more than a pretty face and body. I do have other abilities outside the bedroom."

Laughing, I served the salad. "I apologize if I offended your sensitive feelings."

"Apology accepted."

We were both grinning as we settled into eating. It was delicious. But my hands kept wandering to the locket at my neck. His gaze softened every time they did.

After we'd finished, he stood and collected our dishes.

"I can help." I stacked my fork and salad plate.

"I've got it." He took it from me. "Stay here. I'll bring out dessert."

While he carried his plates then lifted the rest with telekinesis, the dishes following him like in a Disney movie, I fluffed the pillows and spread them out so we had a bigger area to lounge.

The stars were coming out, twinkling between the vines on the pergola. Bright and beautiful, making the night even more perfect. Right as I settled back into our nest of cushions, he returned with two plates.

"I have to admit I asked Clara what your favorite was."

I bolted upright as he settled next to me, handing over a big slice of Black Forest cake, complete with a top layer of whipped cream, cherries, and finished with a chocolate drizzle.

"Gareth!" I snatched it away none too lady-like. "Black Forest chocolate cake and jewelry? You're the best boyfriend ever."

He chuckled and lay down on his side, propped on an elbow, eating with his free hand. He ate slowly, watching me devour and hum on every bite.

"Henry made this?"

His grin widened. "My cousin has some secrets, my cousin."

"Speaking of, I still have questions about yours." I leaned back against my pile of cushions, half-laying down, my plate on my stomach.

He cut a piece of his cake but instead of eating it, he fed it to me, his gaze intent on my mouth. After I'd chewed and licked a bit of whipped cream off my bottom lip, he finally met my gaze.

"Ask away."

"No distracting me with the sexy looks."

"Who's distracting? I'm just feeding my girl." He acted innocent but I could see his wheels turning about ways we could use this cake in bed play.

"Okay, question one. How old are you?"

He grinned. "Sixty-five."

I frowned.

"What? Don't like being with an older man?"

"How old do grims live?"

Everyone knew that witches generally lived into their three hundreds, sometimes longer. Werewolves lived about a half a century.

His smile turned serious. He used TK to lift both our plates out of the way and set them on the table then he wrapped an arm around my waist and pulled me sideways till my body was pressed to his.

"We have vampire blood and that seems to have taken hold in our length of life."

Vampires lived well close to a millennium.

"Why are you sad?" he asked, his fingers tracing the necklace at my throat.

"Why do you think? I'll grow old and die long before you."

He frowned. "No, you won't. Mates age together. You know that."

I remembered something but wasn't sure if it was true. "Your monster called me your mate. You believe we truly are?"

"I *know* we are." He wrapped his hand around my waist again, squeezing softly.

Witches and warlocks didn't get that definite *knowing* about mates the way the other supers did. We just fell in love the old-fashioned way.

"How do grims know they've met their mates? I've read that vampires smell and taste the calling in their blood. For werewolves, it's a wolf thing. They just seem to know. Witches and warlocks don't have that sort of thing."

"Wrong again," he corrected gently, his fingers skimming up my arm back to my throat, constantly moving and trailing lightly over my skin.

"My mother and Jules told me so, Mr. Blackwater. There is no such thing as mates for witches and warlocks."

"Not like vampires, werewolves, and grims. Not an instinctual or animalistic calling of the blood, the scent, or the essence of another. For a witch and warlock, it's more a match made by the magic in the soul."

"Soul mates," I added.

"Right. But hear me now, Lavinia." He leaned forward to press a chaste kiss right below my collarbone. "You *are* my mate. I sensed it from the start. Though I couldn't identify why you were driving me near madness, the monster knew. And when you gave yourself to him, to me, I was sure of it."

I combed my fingers into his black hair, scraping my nails along his nape. "So if we're true mates, that means I'll live as long as you?"

He lifted his head to gaze down at me. "If we're blessed, yes."

He was thinking of his parents who died in a car accident, never able to live out their full lives together.

"Do grims always mate with grims?"

"Yes. It's part of our code. To keep our dark secret within our race."

"Because any child of a mixed marriage could be a grim."

He nodded, his expression serious but still open.

"So you're basically breaking the grim code or laws or whatever to be with me?"

"Lavinia. I'd break the whole world to be with you."

He crushed his mouth to mine, devouring me with sweet, invading kisses that rolled on and on and never stopped. I was lost in him, immersed in bliss and a euphoric kind of magic.

He *was* my mate. I felt it, soul-deep.

When he stripped me down to nothing but my necklace and made love to me under the stars, I smiled up to the heavens, thanking the universe for giving me my grim. My dark, gentle monster to love me for a long lifetime to come.

CHAPTER TWENTY-EIGHT

~LIVVY~

I FINGERED THE PENDANT AT MY THROAT WHILE I SAT AT A RED light. I smiled, thinking about my sisters' faces when I showed it to them last week. Jules was the best at protection spells. She was going to cast one for me tonight, a sort of witchy blessing.

Since there was a new moon tonight, it was the most auspicious time for casting. And since I hadn't bothered to spend one night at home lately, I promised Jules I would be there tonight. After we finished with our event, covering the St. Patrick's Day Parade and wound up our last fundraiser, we'd head to my house.

I'd actually invited Gareth to come with me and watch. We'd do a witch's round with all my sisters in our little garden gated off for just such an occasion. The look of awe on his face when I'd asked him was priceless.

"Come on," I murmured. "Besides, you are a kind of warlock, aren't you?"

He'd smiled at that. It was true. Grims were actually a

special designation of witch and warlock. That also had me smiling.

Traffic was moving but barely as the Lower Garden District filled up fast with parade-goers. Tracey's, an original Irish Channel bar, was on Magazine Street but not close enough to my house for me to walk.

I'd stopped in this morning to shower and change. After breakfast in bed at Gareth's, that is, he had told me to bring some of my clothes over and shoes and shampoo and toiletries. Especially whatever razor I preferred. He'd said the last with a wicked grin.

"Aren't you going to ask me rather than tell me to move my stuff in?" I'd asked, while sprawled on top of him and kissing his jaw.

"I just did," he'd said before rolling me over and making me even more late this morning.

The man didn't know how to actually *ask* me for anything, so used to being in command, but there was time enough to teach him. I was patient. Especially where Gareth was concerned.

I was in the absolute best mood. Not even heavy traffic could wipe the smile off my face. Still, I was wishing I'd taken an Uber over. That would've been smarter, then I could've ridden home with Gareth.

A group of neighborhood locals passed in front of my car, all dressed in their green. One guy wore a green top hat and two of the girls wore boas, the rest sporting strings of green Mardi Gras beads. The to-go tumblers they were sipping on undoubtedly held alcohol. It was nearly eleven, a perfectly acceptable time for day-drinking to get going in New Orleans.

The parade started at one, but the live stream would begin at noon, getting in some pre-parade interviews with the owner of Tracey's and locals at the pub. Even with the current traffic, I still had plenty of time to make it there, find a parking spot, and get ready for the broadcast to begin.

My phone rang and made me jump. I smiled at Willard's name, knowing he was probably in full-on freakout mode. This was his baby, I'd reminded him, though I'd help him every step of the way.

"Hey, Willard."

"*Where are you?*"

Yep. Freaking out.

"About three blocks away."

"Damn, I really screwed up."

"Stop panicking. What's wrong?"

"I left my copy of my interview and agenda notes on my desk last night. I don't know how I could've done that."

"It's okay," I assured him. "I have a copy too."

"You don't understand. I'd made my own hand-written notes in the margins. I just don't know if I can do this without them, Livvy. I'm not used to talking to people so I had additional items to talk about if the conversation goes silent, and now I'm going to freeze on camera and not know what to say. I'm going to ruin the whole show."

"Calm down." I tried not to laugh. "I will be there, but if it makes you feel better I'll run by the office and get them."

I knew that Willard's notes were his safety blanket, and this was a big step for him to be out front and center.

"You don't mind?"

"Not at all. It'll take me another thirty or forty minutes to get there though. Good thing I said we should arrive an hour early."

I laughed. He didn't.

"Stop worrying. Besides, Kaya should be there shortly. She can take over if I'm not there in time for the live stream to start. Today is going to be fantastic. I'll zip by and get your notes and be back in a flash."

A heavy, frustrated sigh breezed through the phone. "Okay. If you say so."

"I do."

"Thank you, Livvy. You're the best."

After ending the call, I shot a quick text to Kaya to be sure and be on time, explaining quickly that I'd be late. I was so glad I'd had the foresight to ask Kaya to help out, just in case we needed an extra hand.

Then I took a left, using my shortcut toward the business district. Fortunately, GMC was in one of the high-rises not too far away from the Lower Garden District. It only took twelve minutes to zip into GMC's parking garage, which was mostly empty on a Saturday. Time was still good. My phone buzzed with Kaya's reply.

Kaya: I've got you covered. Currently standing next to your terrified business partner.

I smiled and told her I'd just gotten to GMC and would be there soon. Then I took a second to text Gareth while riding the parking garage elevator to the first-floor lobby of the building.

Me: I hope you're not running late. I'm making a quick stop for Willard but won't be long. Kaya is already there. See you soon. Love you.

I slid the phone in my pocket and exited the parking garage elevator.

"Hey, Perry." I waved to him at the security guard station.

Perry looked up from his phone, a little surprised. "Oh, hi, Miss Savoie." He smiled wide. "Dressed for the parade today, I see."

"Yeah." I laughed. "We've got our last event today over at Tracey's."

"Damn, I wish I was off today."

"What time does your shift end?" I asked, knowing Saturdays must be a long, lonely workday for him.

"I'm off at five."

"Perfect." The elevator dinged and opened. "I'll swing by and bring you a green beer and some shamrock beads."

"Thank you, Miss Savoie." He beamed with a little blush.

I waved as the elevator doors shut. I had of course gone

casual today in black jeans and a green scoop-neck t-shirt that read: *Kiss Me, I'm Irish.*

Of course, I was only a tiny percentage Irish on my mother's side, but this was more in celebration of the day and the festive mood for the parade. I pulled my phone out and glanced at my texts. Gareth still hadn't read my last one. Unusual for him, since he typically read and responded within seconds.

Stepping out of the elevator, it was weird to hear absolutely nothing. No phones, no Cynthia at the front desk typing away at her computer, no voices muffled beyond the lobby. An eerie buzz washed over me as I walked through the darkened area, lit only by the sunlight through the windows. There were minimal lights on in the hallways, but it put me a little more at ease. It was just creepy because no one was here, I told myself, hurrying to our office.

I flicked on the light and thankfully saw Willard's notes sitting on the corner of his desk where he'd left them. When I rounded the conference table and leaned down to pick them up, a jarring, electric sensation made me lose my breath.

"Ah!" I cried out in pain, clutching one hand to my chest, the other on the desk.

What's happening?

An overwhelming sense of nausea followed that sensation of…loss. That's all I could feel. Was I having a heart attack? I was so stunned by this strange harrowing feeling, trying to figure out why I suddenly felt weak that I didn't notice someone had entered the office behind me.

"It'll go away in a minute."

I whirled around at the sinister lilt of Richard Davis's voice. He stood only a few feet away. I hadn't even detected him entering the room. My mind immediately caught up to what was happening.

"You," I shook my head, tears pricking at the sudden agony and fear barreling through me, "you took my magic away." My voice broke at the heartbreak of it. The empty, gaping hole where my magic shone like a beacon only a minute before.

He took a casual step closer, but there was nothing casual about the cold hunger in his eyes. "I can give it back, sweetheart. For a price."

His eyes traveled to my breasts, and he licked his lips, leaving no mystery as to what he wanted.

"What you've done is illegal. How do you think you can get away with this?"

I tried to keep my voice calm and to reason with him before he went too far. But my instincts were telling me he planned to go much further. His gray eyes roved my body, not hiding his obvious lust, before finally meeting mine again.

"That's not what you should be asking." He stepped closer.

I pressed back against the desk.

"What you should be asking," he murmured softly as if to a lover, making my stomach roll with nausea. "Is how you can get out of this room unharmed."

Adrenaline and terror shot through my bloodstream, my legs wobbly with realization that he wasn't toying with me. He wasn't playing. Or maybe he was, and he was much more of a sick fuck than I'd realized. Gareth had realized it. He'd known from the start.

I reached out for my magic again and said, "You should walk away right now."

Nothing happened when I tried to push persuasion into my words. No zing of power slid through my voice and out to him.

A rumble of low laughter shook his chest as Richard eased closer, less then a foot away now.

"It's gone, Livvy." He lifted a hand and traced the scoop neckline of my t-shirt, trailing his fingers along my skin. "You have to pay the toll. And keep your fucking mouth shut," he growled with an edge of fury. "You spread your legs for that grim. Why is it so hard to do the same for me?"

He was out of his goddamn mind. "There are cameras everywhere in the building."

"There are." He gripped my shoulder and leaned forward, whispering in my ear. "The monitors are in my office. That's how I knew you were here. Alone. That's why I shut the cameras off right before I came to find you."

Panic seized my entire body. I thrust my knee up toward his crotch, but he blocked me with a hard hit of his palm to my thigh. He grabbed me by the hair as I kicked and clawed, raking my nails hard down his neck.

"Fucking *bitch*," he growled.

Then I felt a jerk at my neck as he ripped open the collar of my shirt.

"No!" I screamed, reaching out with everything inside me, sending Gareth my anguished pleas for help through our telepathic link.

Nothingness. My terror grew when I found only an empty hollow where my magic should've burst forth with power and life.

"Don't!" I kicked and flailed as he wrestled me around until I was facing the conference table, my arms and body bound and squeezed tight to his much stronger one.

"Stop struggling," he hissed in my ear, grabbing me by the throat.

"If you think I'm going to let you get away with this, you're out of your *fucking* mind."

His laughter vibrated from his chest to my back as he squeezed my throat till I couldn't breathe. "You can't tell anyone anything if you're dead, little Livvy."

Then he slammed my torso forward, bending me over the conference table.

❧

~GARETH~

. . .

I TEXTED BACK TO LAVINIA AS I WALKED FROM MY CAR.

Me: Where did you have to stop? Parked one block from Tracey's. Walking up now.

I hadn't intended to be so long at Henry's this morning. When he'd called me after Lavinia had left to change, he sounded like death warmed over. When I got to his house, I found him in his super Goth bathroom, all gray tile, white marble floors and black, freestanding bathtub—yes, black. He was hunched over the toilet like he'd had an all-night bender.

I'd gotten him some pain pills and water and a wet rag to cool him off. He looked pale and exhausted. Freezing cold but feverish.

"What happened?" I'd asked him.

"I found them," was all he'd said, pausing to gulp down the water I'd brought him. The entire glass, panting when he'd finished. "They were far away and it took me awhile to reconnect with my magic. But I found two of them. The third one, the niece, wouldn't come at first. But I waited. She finally did."

"Fucking Christ, Henry. How long were you suspended, trying to get her?"

"I don't know." He looked up at me, dark eyes blinking, pain etched in every line of his face. "You needed her. You needed all of them."

"Yes, but not at the expense of you, Henry. For fuck's sake." I lifted him from his bathroom floor and with one arm under his, around his shoulders, I practically carried him to his king-sized bed.

He was barefoot and bare-chested in a pair of jeans. His eyes slid shut and I stripped him of the jeans, then tucked him in and texted Sean to get his ass home. He'd protested that his shift at Empress Ink didn't end till this afternoon.

ME: I don't give a flying fuck. Tell Violet or Nico

you have to leave. Family emergency. Henry needs you. Get your ass home.

SEAN: On my way.

That done, I sat on his bedside and watched him. He'd pushed himself too hard. For me. I swallowed the guilt and held my hand on his chest, measuring his heartbeat which was steadier than when I'd found him.

My pale hand was stark against the large black raven tattoo, its wing cresting up to his neck, my thumb touching the newest tattoo that connected to the raven. His ink had nothing to do with Poe but with the netherworld symbolism of this bird. Glancing around his room, I noticed the giant new artwork across from his bed. He'd told me he'd commissioned something new from Mateo. The subject not surprising. I sighed.

"Just rest, Henry," I told him, though he was already out.

I didn't think he was in real danger, but I couldn't leave him alone. By the time Sean arrived, some of the color had returned to Henry's face and he was resting easily. And I was running late to get to Tracey's.

As I jogged up the block, dodging people who were making their way to the parade route, I glanced down at my phone again. Lavinia hadn't responded to my text.

Frowning, I pushed through the crowd toward the front of the pub where Willard sat on a tall stool. Lavinia's friend Kaya was standing beside him, the tablet on the tripod next to her, ready to go for the live stream. Lavinia had asked for Kaya's help to man the tripod and interact with the subscribers live on YouTube. I'd happily relinquished that job over to her, because I wasn't really the friendly banter kind of guy.

Glancing at the bystanders, I didn't see Lavinia.

"Thank God you're here," said Willard.

Kaya rolled her eyes, while adjusting the tripod facing Willard and his empty stool. "I've got it all under control."

Nodding, I kept scanning the crowd. "Where's Lavinia?"

"She stopped at GMC to get my notes."

I froze as my blood iced. "When?"

Willard's panicked look turned to fear. "Why? What's wrong?"

I grated out, "When did she go there?"

Kaya stepped forward, checking her phone. "She texted ten minutes ago that she'd just gotten to the building. She should be headed back now."

I could barely breathe. Without giving a shit that we were in the presence of a shit ton of humans, I traced faster than I ever had, faintly hearing surprised gasps and grunts from people I nudged to the side as I wove through the crowd in hyper-speed. They'd see nothing at all, possibly a faint blob in their peripheral vision that would be gone by the time they turned to look for who had knocked into them.

Bypassing my car, I streaked through the streets at top speed, unable to quell the nauseating fear swelling inside me. That's when I realized the fear wasn't just mine. It was hers.

My beast roared to life, climbing from his cage and to the surface of my mind and body.

Lavinia! I bellowed through our telepathic link, knocking into a solid wall, that felt like impenetrable ice.

He was there. That mother fucker had nulled her powers.

Lavinia!

My scream echoed into a hollow chasm in my mind as I rounded the street corner to the GMC building.

A faint, desperate cry reached me, as if from miles and miles away.

I'm coming, my love. I'm coming.

The monster growled with furious malice. I didn't try to stop him. We were one and the same at the moment.

I didn't know if she could hear me, but I couldn't help but scream out to her into the darkness where our thread had been cut. I hoped not entirely. Or permanently. I prayed she could hear me coming for her.

I crashed through the glass door, unable to slow my speed

even for a second. The guard leaped to his feet, staring past me at the shattered glass on the floor. I ripped the metal door off the stairwell, throwing it across the lobby then I shot like lightning up thirty floors to our office.

Her scent grew stronger, rancid with fear and pain, my heart practically thudding right through my rib cage and out of my chest. I barreled through the staircase door leading into the top floor of GMC.

Zig-zagging through the empty lobby, I could hear the struggle taking place in the office. I roared aloud, like the monster that I was. When I saw him restraining her on the conference table, Lavinia on her back, kicking helplessly, his hand on her throat as he groped with her jeans, trying to force them down her legs, the world was suddenly drenched in black.

Kill.

My lethal arm shot from my host's body and wrapped around the enemy's throat, jerking the puny warlock off my mate. I suspended him in the air, his feet dangling helplessly, turning him to face his executioner.

Yes, you fucking piece of shit. Look upon your doom. I will erase you from this world for what you have done to my precious one.

I relished and basked in the joy of watching his face purple, oxygen unable to course through his body. I loosened my hold so that he wouldn't fall unconscious, wanting, needing to extend the pain, bathing in the bliss of his agony.

"Gareth!"

My mate clung to me. Yes, woman. Watch what we do to our enemies. Watch his blood pour from his body for daring to touch you. I am here now to set the scales right.

"Gareth! Don't!"

She is soft-hearted, our mate. It is not her fault she

has no stomach for what I am about to do. I tighten my hold, swirling my tentacled arm further around his throat. He kicks helplessly, trying to gain air.

I savor his struggle, watching the veins in his eyes bulge and bleed. One crimson tear falls from an eye. Not enough. I want all of his tears of blood to rain. I want to bathe in them before I rip his spine from his body and tear every limb from him.

"They'll kill you! You can't do this without just cause! Please stop!"

No one will kill me, darling one. No one can. I don't try to explain but gather her close to my chest with my host's arms, reassuring her all is well. I will watch our enemy die slowly and painfully.

He touched my woman. He gave her pain and fear. He will not die until I've given him ten times the pain and fear he bestowed upon my mate. Then I will hang the pieces of his body from this building, so that all can see what happens to those who dare to harm what is mine. My precious one.

"Gareth." *She grasps the face of my host and forced me to look away from her prey and down to her.* "Please hear me now. If you kill him like this, without a trial, they will kill you. We will be parted forever."

I cannot help the bellowing growl that escapes and frightens my mate. Can they take her from me? Is what she says true? No creature is powerful enough to kill me, but could they separate me from her?

"Please hear me. Please do as I ask. He will get what he deserves. But it must be done the right way, my love."

I flinch. Yes. I am her love. She proved this true with her prostrate obedience. She let me subdue her in the open air under the stars. She submitted to me and let me mount her in the proper way, completely yielding to my power and strength, bending before me and taking me till she cried out her pleasure. My precious one asks me for a boon. But I cannot let the enemy go free.

A jolt of magic punches me hard. My host wants control again. I cannot fight against him for long. My host is powerful, like me, as it should be.

I look back to our enemy, the spineless woman abuser. I smile tears of blood streak down his face. With a quick snap of my tentacle, I crack his skull against the glass wall. The glass shatters but also does its purpose in knocking the enemy into unconsciousness.

"Yes. Thank you, Gareth. Thank you."

My mate kisses my host's face, my vision growing blurry as the host regains his control. I cannot go back into the cage without making my power known. Sliding the tentacle down the arm and the hand that held our precious one by the throat, I snap several bones in the arm and all twenty-seven of them in the hand.

The enemy flinches but does not wake. As I'm being pushed back, far and deep, I snap both his legs for good measure, smiling at my mate, now safe from harm. He can't hurt her now. He will never touch her again.

"Gareth," Lavinia cries. "STOP!"

Instantly, I froze, obeying her command. I shook my head, pushing back the beast, coming back to myself with her in my arms and the crumpled body of Richard Davis a few feet away.

"Fuck. Did I kill him?"

The nausea that swirls in my gut is my own now, remembering this same feeling of coming to when I was eleven and seeing the broken, shattered body of Dennis.

"No. He's breathing," she reassures me.

I reached out with my senses, hearing his pulse beating frantically. As well as Lavinia's.

Cradling her face, I take quick inventory. Her shirt is torn, exposing her bra, her jeans unbuttoned, and there is a nasty red mark around her slender throat. I close my eyes against the rage, needing to contain the monster. If he gets out again, I know I won't be able to keep him from murdering Richard.

"Are you okay?" Lavinia whispers, tears streaming down her beautiful face.

"Am *I* okay?" I huff out a disgusted laugh and haul her into my arms.

She's shaking. So am I.

"Please tell me that you're all right," I muffle into her hair, unable to loosen my embrace for even a second.

"I am now, Gareth." Then she sobbed against my chest, her small cries muffled by my shirt.

"Shh." I stroked my palm from her head down her back, over and over, letting her cry it all out.

I'd gotten here in time, but I needed to hold her longer to reassure myself and the monster still rumbling deep in his dark cave that all was well again. I didn't take my eyes off of Richard for one second.

"I think," she whispered so low I could barely hear her, her fists twisted in the back of my shirt, "I think he was going to kill me."

"Shh. I've got you now."

I didn't bother to tell her that I knew that he would have.

When she'd calmed enough that her breathing had evened out, I stepped back and sat in a chair, pulling her onto my lap. She tucked her head against my chest, still clinging to me.

I texted Jules with my arms still around Lavinia. That was the legal requirement when a supernatural-on-supernatural crime had been committed. But also, she was Lavinia's sister.

Then I texted Ruben. While Jules was the head of all super-naturals in the region, Ruben was overlord of the vampires. He was the muscle used to obtain and hold criminals in custody until their trial. I knew he'd text Devraj immediately and have a team here within minutes.

I needed to get this piece of fucking filth out of my sight.

My control was threadbare, the need to eviscerate him still skating along my subconscious, seducing me to murder for what he'd dared to do to Lavinia.

"Don't worry, my love," I whispered against the crown of her dark hair. "He'll never hurt anyone again."

Of that, I was certain. My monster and I had both wanted to kill him on sight. But executing a supernatural for attempted assault wouldn't have been sanctioned by our order.

As punishment, his powers would've been nullified so that he couldn't use them against anyone ever again. He'd likely be given a ten-year sentence in a supernatural prison, nowhere anyone wants to be. And upon release, he'd have a permanent trace charm put on him to track him and ensure the guilds would watch his every move until his death. But killing him for what he'd done to Lavinia would've put me in danger. That, I couldn't allow.

Once the trial had taken place and I gave my evidence, I knew my monster and I would both get our wish. I held her close and kept watch on the soon-to-be dead man on the floor and forced myself to be patient. To wait. Soon, I'd have justice.

And my revenge.

CHAPTER TWENTY-NINE

~LIVVY~

"I just want to fucking kill him," growled Violet for the third time, pacing at the foot of my bed.

"We all do," said Evie, sitting quietly on my other side, holding my hand and petting my arm softly.

"Violet, if you can't calm down, then you have to leave," Isadora chastised.

Iz had one palm on my neck, the other on my heart. She was pushing her healing spell into me, her moss-green eyes serious but compassionate.

I knew that I was safe, but my insides were a viper's nest of fear, worry, and shame. Though I knew what had happened and what had almost happened was all on Richard Davis, not me, it's much harder to explain that to your mind in the midst of trauma. The avalanche of emotions pummeling me were still wreaking havoc, even while I focused on convincing myself I was safe.

Thankfully, Isadora and my sisters' presence was easing me minute by minute.

"Can you feel the magic yet?" asked Isadora.

"A little," I admitted, recognizing the tiny, familiar thread of power whispering through my body, embracing me like an old friend.

"It will take some time, but it will be back fully soon enough," Isadora assured me.

Clara opened the door and entered carrying a cup of hot tea. She set it on my nightstand. "It's got my special infusion of herbs in it."

That meant she'd used her own spelled tea and herbs, most likely a witchy dosage of anti-anxiety.

"Thank you, Clara. Is Gareth here yet?"

Violet stopped pacing. "Livvy. If Gareth was in this house, do you think we could keep him out of this room?"

I swallowed hard, both happy and sad. He loved me and would do anything for me. I knew that. I'd watched him nearly murder a man for me.

"No, don't cry," Violet whined, her face falling. "Please don't cry, Liv."

"You can cry," Isadora assured me. "All you want."

Then Jules stepped in, her expression black and furious but also composed somehow. She eased up somewhat when her gaze caught mine.

"What happened?" I whispered.

Everyone else remained silent and waited.

"Richard Davis is in custody. Ruben has him under guard. I've contacted Clarissa in Houston. She will come for the trial at once."

"They better not be getting a healer for him!" yelled Violet.

"Violet," Jules warned. "Calm down."

Suddenly, Violet burst into tears, covering her face with her hands. "I should've seen it. I should've stopped him."

"Oh, no," said Clara, jumping up and wrapping her twin in her arms. "It wasn't your fault, Vi."

Jules walked over and pulled Violet's hands away from her

tear-streaked face. "Stop blaming yourself. You can't see every-thing. You know this."

"Still," she hiccoughed on a sob. "He could've..." She looked at me with the most agonizing pained expression.

"But he didn't," I told her. "Gareth was there. It's all okay. I'm going to be okay," I promised her.

And though I didn't feel okay at the moment, I knew I would be in time.

"I love that grim reaper." Violet sniffed and wiped the back of her hand across her cheek.

The door opened and Gareth walked in, his gaze on me when he said, "I'm afraid I'm spoken for, Violet."

I smiled at him, more tears falling.

"Let's give them some privacy." Jules waved her hands to usher my sisters out.

Isadora leaned over and kissed my forehead. "How do you feel now?"

"Better." I gave her a nod of reassurance.

"I'll come back in a little while." She glanced up at Gareth.

"Thank you, Iz."

When they left, Isadora shutting the door behind her, Gareth stood beside the bed, hands clenched at his side, agony in his eyes. Very similar to the look Violet wore a few minutes ago.

I reached out. "Come here."

Instantly, he took my hand and sat gingerly on the edge of the bed. He cradled my hand with both of his.

"I'm so sorry, Lavinia. I should've foreseen this."

"How could you? You're not a Seer too, are you?"

He shook his head and licked his lips, nervous. "He was supposed to be out of town. I didn't know he'd come back."

"No one did. And we certainly didn't know he was lurking at the offices alone, like he was waiting for me or something."

"He *was* waiting for you." Gareth's brown eyes flushed black.

"What do you mean?"

"He put a spell on Willard."

"How?" I sat up and pushed back against my headboard. "When?"

"Willard had his notes the whole time. I learned through his roommate that Richard had shown up at his apartment that morning. The roommate didn't know what they'd said, but apparently Richard had put a glamour spell on him to make him believe he needed those notes and to send you to get them. Willard still doesn't remember Richard coming to see his apartment this morning but the roommate was positive it was him."

I shook my head, baffled at how badly we'd underestimated the malevolence of that man. "Poor Willard. Don't let him feel guilty about this. I don't want him to blame himself. Violet is still beating herself up that she didn't have a vision about it."

"Kaya is hanging with him tonight, to make sure he's okay."

I laughed, imagining wild Kaya hanging with introverted Willard.

Gareth cleared his throat, stroking his thumb over the pulse in my wrist. "I spoke to Victor Garrison. Told him everything."

I nodded. "Good. What did he say?"

"He told me that we should've come to him the first time there was an incident." He gave me a slight I-told-you-so look.

"Probably so." I sighed, no fight in me left. "What about the competition?"

"He said not to worry about it. He told me to tell you to get well and that's all."

Gareth looked at the tea, then picked it up and held it out to me. "Drink this."

Again, too tired to argue, I did as I was told. "I'm a bit zombified."

"You be however you need to be. And I'll do whatever you need me to do."

After taking another sip, I set the teacup on the nightstand and scooted over toward the middle of the bed. "Come lay by me."

His brow pinched. "You need to rest."

"You just promised to do whatever I needed." I swallowed hard, laying my head on my pillow. "And I need you." I patted the space on the pillow. "Right here."

He lay his head down on my pillow, facing me, and laced our fingers together. "You have me, Lavinia." He pressed a kiss to the back of my hand. "You always will." He brushed my hair off of my face.

We started our staring game, our faces inches apart. This one full of quiet tension and vast relief. His eyes shimmered a warm brown now. We didn't say a word. Not at first.

Then I felt it, a touch of magic in my mind. A gentle brush as Gareth opened a telepathic link.

I love you, Lavinia.

I sucked in a breath at the shock of feeling, the tingle of my magical link that Richard had cut being restored, and the tenderness Gareth poured into his mental caress.

Pulling our clasped hands up to my mouth, I pressed my lips to the back of his hand and spoke to him in our secret way, mind-to-mind. Richard hadn't taken it away after all.

I love you, too.

He smiled. *Go to sleep now. I've got you.*

I didn't think it possible to sleep after all I'd been through. After the maelstrom of emotions and adrenaline. After losing my magic then slowly regaining it back. But having Gareth close and hearing his promises of love seemed to put everything back in its proper place.

Close your eyes, he told me. *I'll be here when you wake up.*

And though I was soul weary, I quickly slipped off to sleep, my body and mind finally resting, now that I was safe in my mate's arms.

CHAPTER THIRTY

~LIVVY~

I SAT ON THE CUSHIONED BENCH OUTSIDE THE COURTROOM— one of the properties that Ruben had converted into the guild courthouse for our region. This had been an old Catholic church that had been abandoned and condemned for destruction by the city. Ruben had bought and renovated it to serve their uses for trials.

The décor was uncharacteristically elegant and comfortable for a courthouse. On the other hand, I'd expect no less from Ruben.

The hallway, once an atrium that had opened through double doors, had polished wood floors with silver and blue rugs. A silver chandelier at the center lit the room and the comfortable sofas and benches in the waiting room were covered in sky-blue brocade. It was all meant to soothe those who had to wait here to be summoned into the nave where the trial would take place.

Right now, I was calm and quiet. Strangely so.

Actually, not so strangely when I looked around at my sisters all around me. Evie stood to my right with Mateo at her side. Violet stood to my left with Nico. Clara sat on the bench next to me, holding my hand and breathing her essence of light into me. Isadora held the other, pushing her healing spell into me as well.

I was fully healed now. Physically. There were no marks at my throat. Pictures had been taken and my statement written down last week after Richard had been hauled unconscious from the premises by Devraj, Sal, and Roland, Ruben's right-hand men.

In the last week, Gareth had basically moved into the carriage house with me and Clara, not once sleeping anywhere but in my bed. He'd brought Queenie over who'd quickly become queen of the castle. While I couldn't wait to go back to our sleepovers at his place, my sisters, particularly Jules, wanted me at home until this was all over.

Richard was safely behind bars in Ruben's custody, wherever that was, but my sisters wanted me close to home. Besides, it felt good to be surrounded by family while my body and mind healed up. Evie and Mateo had already started decorating the nursery upstairs. I found it comforting to sit and help Evie pick out paint colors and fabric patterns for the crib bedding. Clara baked me everything chocolate you can possibly imagine. My favorite was a recipe from the Great British Bake Off star Paul Hollywood, which was a delicious devil's food cake.

Gareth had wrapped up all of our statistics and data, including a total of $75,603 we'd raised in our campaign to start the supernatural orphan program. I had no idea what would happen with the competition now. We were finished with the campaign, but now there was this strange cloud hovering over the whole contest.

If Mr. Garrison chose me as the winner, would it be seen as only making up for what had happened under his roof? If he chose Willard or Gareth, would it be seen as prejudice against me since I'd brought on a black stain against his company?

Gareth nearly lost his mind when I mentioned that, stating emphatically that it was Richard Davis who stained the company's reputation, not me. But still, I knew how the world worked and how people could twist any situation to fit what they wanted to believe.

Right now, I didn't care about any of that. I was solely focused on giving my statement in front of the judge and jury today.

The judge would normally be my sister, but since we were related, Clarissa Baxter was called in to give an unbiased judgment. Jules still sat on the jury as head of the witches and warlocks of New Orleans. Ruben served on the jury as overlord of vampires. Devraj was his second, but since he was also a part of my family, he couldn't serve on the jury. Ruben had chosen one of his trusted men, Sal, a cool, dark-haired vampire, as the second vampire on the jury.

As was the custom, Victor Garrison would serve as a representative of the offended party, as the crime took place on his property. Though I was the actual offended party, it was decided that the owner of GMC and the employer of both the accused and the victim would serve on the jury. I had no idea what Victor Garrison thought of this whole thing, whether he thought me a liar or not. But I didn't care.

As long as Gareth was at my side, I'd be fine.

Right now, he stood with his back to the wall across from me, arms crossed, wearing his full ice man façade. I couldn't help but smile, knowing the fierce exterior he wore now was all for me.

The final two on the jury were representatives of the grim covens. Silas Blackwater, head of their coven, and another grim I'd never heard of, Jane Kingston. Gareth had told me she was a grim he knew and would deliver fair judgment. But I was captivated by Silas, the ornery and neglectful uncle I'd heard so much about. He looked stern, powerful, and somewhat menacing. All that I'd expected him to be.

When I'd asked if his Uncle Silas could be unbiased, he said it didn't matter. That it didn't matter what any of them thought because he had irrefutable proof to share with the jury. When I'd asked what, he changed the subject. I'd noticed but didn't care. If Gareth said he had it all taken care of, then he did. I'd find out soon enough.

That was the jury of seven. In addition to the jury, there were always two Auras to serve as well, to determine the truth of what both the accused and the victim said. Jules had told me that Clarissa had brought a warlock from her region, an Aura named Gideon Bates. She had met him once before at a Summit and assured me he was a good man, a kind warlock, who would see justice done. He would serve as the chief Aura, since he wasn't related to me or biased.

Clara would serve as his second. I always knew Clara could read emotions so well that she knew if one of us was lying. I'd just never thought much about an Aura being used in this capacity in the courtroom, or maybe I'd just not bothered to know. Never thinking I'd step foot in one.

The double doors to the courtroom opened and out stepped Sal, Ruben's man. "Miss Lavinia Savoie and Mr. Gareth Black-water, you are both called forward. Miss Clara Savoie, you may enter as the Aura's second."

Gareth shoved off the wall, still frowning furiously, and held out his hand. I took it and stood, exhaling a heavy breath.

"You're safe, Lavinia," he murmured as he guided us through the door.

"I know."

I glanced back at Clara who gave me that encouraging, sisterly smile, as she followed in behind us.

Gareth squeezed my hand and held it as we walked up the center aisle. The front of the church where the altar once stood had been transformed into a dais for the judge and jury. The witness stands were on either side of the sanctuary facing one another.

Richard Davis was already in his seat on the right, alone. After a week, his throat was still mottled purple. I can imagine that Gareth, or maybe Ruben, had made damn sure the healer had given minimal attention to him on my behalf. His entire right arm and hand was in a cast. So were both his legs, and he was in a wheelchair. I didn't feel sorry for him at all.

Thankfully though, he wasn't looking at me, but at Gareth, his eyes round with fear. Gareth wore his cool, indifferent expression, but his irises were black as pitch. I squeezed his hand, wanting him to stay calm.

"Richard Davis," Clarissa intoned, "you have been accused of illegal use of magic, attempted assault, and attempted murder. How do you plead?"

"Not guilty," he stated, eyes pleadingly on the jury.

"We have statements by both Lavinia Savoie and Gareth Blackwater about what took place. Though the cameras were conspicuously turned off and did not record the events on March seventeenth of this year, the statement of Lavinia Savoie was deemed truth by a local Aura."

"Her sister, Your Honor," Richard protested.

"Which is why," added Clarissa, "I have brought an Aura outside the Savoie coven's jurisdiction. An unbiased Aura."

Gideon was a handsome warlock with brown hair and kind eyes. He stood from the bench in the audience next to Clara and stepped toward our side of the courtroom. Jules watched me, concern obvious in the pinch of her brow. I smiled to let her know I was okay. Ruben sat next to her, his stern expression much colder than was the norm for him.

I understood everyone's concern. The outcome of this jury could decide to strip a man of his supernatural powers, excommunicate him from our community, and track him all the rest of his living days so that every step he took would be watched.

Gideon stood beside me. "May I have your hand, Miss Savoie?"

Gareth flinched, but I squeezed his hand with the one I was

still holding to reassure him before setting my other in Gideon's. He didn't need to touch me to know what I was feeling, but everyone knew that touch amplified an Aura's abilities.

Gideon took my hand gently and said, "If you will please recount what occurred on March seventeenth."

I recounted the events in as brief but accurate and detached a manner as I could. Gareth was beginning to vibrate with fury at my side, but somehow kept it all in check by the time I said, "That's when Gareth came in and subdued Richard."

"You mean broke both my legs, my arm, and my hand after he'd rendered me unconscious by strangling me," Richard protested in a weaselly voice.

"You're lucky I didn't kill you," said Gareth.

Clarissa pushed a pulse of power into the room, effectively getting everyone's attention. "That will be enough of sudden outbursts, Mr. Davis and enough of threats, Mr. Blackwater." She gave Gareth a hard stare that obviously didn't affect him in the least, because he was still staring murderously at Richard across the room.

"Now, Mr. Davis, what do you have to say to these accusations since you have declared yourself not guilty? Wait for the Aura before you speak."

Clara rose from a front bench seat in the audience, which was empty other than her. Supernatural courtrooms tended to be much more private than the public displays in the human world.

She stepped toward Richard Davis, which had me stiffening with anxiety. Gareth had moved his hand to my back, brushing me lightly for assurance. I didn't like my sweet sister anywhere near that asshole. But he wasn't about to do anything crazy in this room. He knew he'd be dead in a blink with the number of powerful people around him.

When Clara touched his shoulder, he said, "You have to understand that Livvy Savoie has been making flirtatious advances at me since the day we met. With the clothes she wears and the looks she gives me, she's made it obvious that she wants me."

Was this douchebag seriously going to blame the victim? He might as well have said, she asked for it.

"Clara," Clarissa interrupted before he could go on, "Judgement?"

Clara, serene but for the slight pinch in her brow, said, "He believes this to be true."

Of course he did. Fucking prick.

Gareth had somehow remained entirely calm, his gaze on the double door entrance.

"Go on, Mr. Davis."

"I was sure that she'd come up to the office that day, hoping to find me alone as well. Her boyfriend has been more of a jailer, keeping me from getting to know her in a professional or a personal manner."

"You do realize that it is unprofessional to get to know an employee in a personal manner, do you not?" asked Victor Garrison.

Before Richard could answer, the doors burst open. Henry Blackwater strolled into the room, scowling with extraordinary fierceness. Especially when his gaze caught on Clara standing next to Richard with her hand on his shoulder.

Gareth stepped from behind the banister where we were and took two steps into the room.

"Stop, Mr. Blackwater!" shouted Clarissa, coming to her feet.

Gareth and Henry had both stopped in their tracks, probably not knowing which one Clarissa was speaking to.

Silas Blackwater stood as well as Jules and Ruben.

"What is the meaning of this, Henry?" Silas rumbled in a deep, gravelly voice. Apparently, the baritone register ran in the family.

Henry didn't look at his father.

My heart hammered faster, because I could feel power

surging in the room. I wasn't sure if it was from Gareth or Henry or both, but something was coming. My skin tingled with the rush of magic.

"Excuse me, Ms. Baxter," said Gareth, calmly clasping his hands behind him. A disarming pose.

"What is this about?" demanded Silas.

"Please, Silas," said Clarissa. "Let's follow proceedings properly."

I couldn't help but smirk. Gareth had moved into his I'm-harmless stance, but he was anything but.

"I would like to lodge another accusation of the accused, Richard Davis."

In the supernatural court, this was legal. Once a man or woman was on the stand, any accusations could be lodged, but must be proven without doubt for punishment.

"Make your accusation," said Clarissa, seemingly mollified since he appeared non-threatening and Henry had stopped moving into the open courtroom, standing next to the last bench.

"I accuse Richard Davis of the murders of Winnie Pryor, a witch of the designation Hex-breaker, Melinda Fairly, designation Seer, and his niece, Priscilla Davis, Healer designation."

Richard's face blanched, and no one said a single word for a full minute. A prickle of magic rippled over my skin. Clara shivered. She felt it too. Something huge was present with us.

"These are grave accusations, Mr. Blackwater. Punishable by death if proven."

"Indeed." He stepped forward to the center of the room and faced the jury. "As you are aware, I am a grim. And because this is a closed courtroom, anything revealed here must be kept strictly confidential."

"Yes." Clarissa glanced toward the other jurors. Everyone nodded but Silas who was glaring at his nephew with a hint of fury and dread. She stared at him specifically and said, "Whatever is revealed here must never be shared outside this room."

Basically, the supernatural courtroom was Vegas. What happened there, stayed there.

"Gareth—" warned Silas, but Gareth cut him off.

"Uncle, we've cultivated and sequestered our power for far too long. We will use it to benefit the world of all supernaturals. Not just the grims."

That seemed to shut Silas up, though he appeared more furious than ever.

"If you will please allow my cousin Henry to use his magic, he will show you the irrefutable proof that you desire."

This was an unconventional request, because the use of magic inside a courtroom—besides the Enforcer who served as judge and the Auras detecting truthfulness—was illegal. Clarissa leaned forward, staring at Henry who vibrated with magic, his gaze on Clara.

Clarissa didn't seem to care if it was illegal. She was the judge and could decide whatever she wanted, within reason.

"I grant permission to see this proof."

"Step aside, Clara," said Henry.

She did so immediately, retreating toward the dais.

The fact was, no one knew what grims were capable of. I did. Or so I thought. Until Henry Blackwater stepped to the center of the room and opened his arms wide like a crucifix.

A thump of power punched into the room with a resounding echo. Someone cried out—Clarissa, maybe? I wasn't sure.

But the entire room went dark. Not because the lights were doused, but because a shroud of black smoke emanated from Henry, covering the entire room in a giant, black halo. I'd seen this black smoke before. When it came from Gareth, it was the monster who lived inside him, intent on doing something wicked or foul. There was no malevolent presence in Henry's shroud. But there was a heavy darkness.

Whispers—overlapping and indecipherable—filled the

room. Like hissing secrets. A whir of wind pushed the oppressive yet powerful magic into the room, swirling in a vortex.

I gasped and clutched my chest. A white light appeared beneath Henry's arms, so bright I had to shield my eyes. So did the others. Except Gareth, who stood next to Henry, nodding to him with assurance. Henry's eyes were full black like I'd seen Gareth's before, when his monster took hold. Black veins streaked Henry's face and neck, down his arms.

"Come forth, Winnie." Henry's voice hummed with otherworldly power, an unnatural voice driven from the well of magic inside him. "Melinda. Priscilla. I call you now."

Above Henry's back, wings of black smoke, a deeper hue than what filled the room, opened wide. The glimmer of white light shone beneath the wings.

"Goddess above," said Jules, standing to her feet as a shimmering ghost stepped from beneath Henry's arms, from within the tunnel of light.

She was a young woman in her twenties. Next came another woman with lighter hair. And finally the smaller frame of a teenager, looking terrified as she emerged. All three looked solid as they must have here on earth except for the halo of white shimmering around them.

Henry spoke again. "Do you see your murderer in this room?" His voice rippled with magic, a fey sound, otherworldly and ethereal.

The three ghosts were busy surveying the people around them, swiveling to me then to Gareth then to the jury and then to Richard.

Priscilla's ghost visibly cowered away from Richard, closer to the dais. The other two remained close to Henry. I think they felt protected by him.

"He is there," said Winnie's ghost. "He took me from a club in San Diego on my twenty-third birthday. I was an intern at Forrester Media Company. He took my powers away, used me, then killed me that night."

"Thank you," said Henry, his voice dark and rough but also gentle, droplets of sweat beading his brow. "You may rest now, Winnie. I will not call you again."

She turned and smiled at Henry whose arms were still raised, holding the gateway to the next world open, black wings stretching wide. She touched his cheek and vanished inside the golden light.

Melinda shared a similar story from when Richard had worked a summer in L.A. But it was Priscilla who broke my heart. She was his sister's child. It was unfathomable. And while Melinda seemed at peace when her ghost hugged Henry and went back through the gateway. Priscilla still seemed frightened.

"You may rest now, Priscilla," said Henry.

Before she took a step, Clara came forward. Rather than shrink away, Priscilla turned to her bravely.

"May I hold your hand?" asked Clara.

Priscilla stared at my sister and no one breathed until the ghost of the girl put her hand in Clara's. I could feel the wave of bliss sweeping through the room. It was meant for Priscilla alone but Clara was a powerful Aura. Her joy and serenity flooded through my veins until a tear slipped free.

Priscilla smiled and laughed, the ethereal sound tinkling upward and vibrating up to the Cathedral ceiling, filling the room with only what I could call hope.

"Thank you," she whispered to Clara, then the ghost girl walked back to Henry and touched his arm before ducking underneath and disappearing into the otherworld.

Henry dropped his arms, hauling in deep gulps of air. Gareth stepped forward to help him but Henry waved him off and stood straight. The way he looked at my sister—with awe and reverence and need—stole my breath away.

There was utter silence in the court room, and ultimate terror shining in Richard's face as he stared at Henry in shock.

"As you can see, I've provided three witnesses to the murders of these three young women who went missing between one and four years ago. Richard Davis is a serial killer. If not punished properly, he will do it again."

I vaguely heard Clarissa sentencing Richard to death, my attention focused on the man with a mission standing dead center of the courtroom. My man. My monster.

"I request the duty to execute the sentencing," he said to the jury.

Everyone nodded. Even his Uncle Silas, apparently gloating at the grim power on display now. Henry had stepped over to Clara, blocking her from view, looking over his shoulder at Gareth.

Rather than turning to Richard, Gareth—black smoke unfurling from his body—turned to me, the monster wholly in his eyes.

"Turn your eyes, my love."

I nodded and closed my eyes.

A low, unearthly growl rumbled and filled the room. My monster was here. All else was frighteningly silent. A chill zinged down my spine, raising gooseflesh on my skin.

"Please don't," whispered Richard. I imagined his victims said much the same thing. Begged for mercy, for their lives, while he ignored them.

At the first crack of bones, Richard screamed in agony. I flinched but kept my eyes squeezed tightly shut. The crunching of bones continued and then a wet sound that made me jump. I covered my ears right as Richard's cries faded, right after I heard Henry say, "It is done, Gareth."

A little late, but I didn't want to see or hear any more.

Then familiar, strong arms were around me and lifting me. I kept my eyes closed, my face pressed to his neck as he carried me away from whatever was left of Richard Davis.

You're safe now, he assured me, mind to mind.

I know, I told him.

I wrapped my arms around his neck and nuzzled closer,

sensing bone-deep that I always would be now, with him by my side.

~GARETH~

"Would you like a beer? Wine?" asked Jules.

"No," said JJ. "He'll take a Maker's Mark on ice, if I remember correctly."

"Yes, please."

Jules nodded and disappeared into the kitchen.

I turned to Lavinia, almost speechless at this amazing woman. It had been a mere three hours since we'd left the courtroom and she was smiling like nothing had ever happened. Jules had shut down the Cauldron early so we could have a private celebration. Or recuperation. Whatever you might call it.

She'd kept her word and hadn't mentioned anything of the events to the Savoie sisters or Nico, Mateo, or anyone about what she'd witnessed inside the courtroom. She'd simply pulled me and Henry aside next to the others waiting in the anteroom and said, "We're going to the Cauldron. Let's go."

I couldn't keep from touching Lavinia, making sure she was okay. I'd executed Richard Davis for his crimes with a swift telekinetic snap of his neck, holding my monster barely at bay. He'd wanted to display his prowess and spray the room in blood, but I was fairly certain that wouldn't have gone over too well.

At any rate, the nightmare was over. Lavinia was safe, and justice had been served for those three poor women who he'd killed. He wouldn't hurt Lavinia or any other woman ever again.

"Can you believe what Victor Garrison said?" Her eyes glittered with excitement.

"Yeah. I think it was the right call, to be honest."

Victor had pulled us aside outside the courthouse and declared that the contest winnings would be split between all three of us. Due to the circumstances and according to his notes on our teamwork, he said we all deserved the accolades. I didn't bother to tell Lavinia that I informed Victor to split the money between Willard and Lavinia. I didn't need it. I'd gotten everything I wanted.

And more.

"You're remarkable," I whispered to her, skating a hand along her lower back to her waist.

She turned that brilliant, beautiful smile on me. "So are you."

"How'd we come to this?"

"What? From rivals to girlfriend/boyfriend?" She rolled her eyes as if I were ignorant. "Because we're just alike. In some ways. And opposite in all the right ways. We're just," she laced her hands together, "the perfect fit."

I kissed her jaw and whispered in her ear, "I'd like to perfectly fit later on. If you're up to it."

A blush of pink flushed her pretty face. "I was wondering when you were going to touch me again."

"What are you talking about? I *never* stop touching you."

She sipped her Flaming Gin Dragon, one of JJ's concoctions, "I just mean that since this whole mess happened, you haven't wanted sex."

Taking her hand, I placed it on my very hard dick. "I always want sex with you. But I was trying to be a gentleman since you'd gone through a trauma."

She squeezed her hand over my crotch, making me grunt. Then she grinned. "Thank you for being a gentleman. Tonight, I need you to be very ungentlemanly."

"Done."

"Here you go." JJ set my whiskey in front of me and I drank half in one gulp.

"So," said Ruben, taking a seat on my other side. "You've been holding out on me."

Lavinia stealthily removed her hand from my lap, then turned to Clara on her other side.

"Don't take it personally," I told him. "It's against the grim code to show our true natures, our magic, to outsiders."

Ruben huffed out a laugh. "I'm not an outsider."

"Yes, well, that's for certain now because you're one of the few non-grims who's seen what we can do."

And though the dark essence that lived inside all grims wasn't revealed in all of its hideous glory, I'd determined that we needed to become more a part of the supernatural world than we'd been in the past. Always sequestering our power for our own use. Uncle Silas was probably going to put up a fight, but I was ready for it.

"You did good today. Putting down that monster."

I winced at his terminology. "He just came up against one worse than he was. Fortunately, my own monster has one goal only these days. To keep her safe." I nodded toward Lavinia now laughing with Clara.

Ruben glanced toward her then me, his gaze snagging on Jules who was setting out a giant pot of jambalaya for us all.

"We've all got a monster inside us, Gareth. That's nothing new. It's just how you use it that matters."

I suppose vampires knew enough about monsters. Were-wolves were animalistic in nature, reacting out of fear or anger like an animal would. Witches and warlocks were the most human, the most civilized of supernaturals. But grims and vampires obeyed a deeper calling, submitting to more sinister origins. Only monsters craved blood and evil. In that, Ruben and I were very similar. Perhaps that's why he and I always saw eye-to-eye.

I raised my glass to him. He raised his own bourbon.

"To holding the monsters at bay," I said, clinking my glass against his.

"Indeed." He drank deep, his predatory eyes following Jules around the room.

"Dinner is served!" she called, and everyone moved from the bar at once.

I grabbed a hold of Lavinia's waist and turned her around to face me. "Are you truly okay?"

"Yes." She cupped my face. "If Clara and Isadora don't stop pumping me with their magic, I'll be the silliest, goofiest, happiest witch that ever lived."

"That wouldn't be so bad." I pressed a soft kiss to her lips.

She arched a brow. "But I don't want to be the silliest. I want to be the sexiest."

"To me, you will always be the sexiest." I kissed her beneath her jaw. She leaned her head to the side to let me kiss her there again. "And the sweetest. The loveliest." Another kiss, then I whispered into her skin, "The other half of my soul."

"We love with a love that is more than love."

Lifting my head, I caressed her soft cheek, staring into those sapphire eyes. "That we do, Lavinia." I clasped our hands together and brought them up, pressing a kiss to the back of hers. "And we always will."

EPILOGUE

Five Months Later...

~GARETH~

Violet paced to the window of the waiting room then back again. "If Mateo wasn't such a stubborn ass."

"He can't help himself," said Nico. "I'll likely be the same way."

"Ha! No one will be as overprotective and paranoid as Mateo."

"Alpha, actually," I corrected, standing against the wall next to Lavinia.

"True," she agreed, smiling up at me.

Mateo had only allowed Isadora and Jules in the room, nearly biting the heads off anyone else who came in. Literally. Including the poor nurses and doctor.

"You wanna know what I was just thinking?"

"No, Sean," snapped Violet, still pacing. "We don't want to know what you were thinking."

"I was thinking about pussies."

"Sean," warned Nico.

"No, seriously. People use the word pussy to insult someone for being weak. But pussies are strong, man. They can take a pounding all night. They can squeeze out a baby the size of a watermelon. But you just graze a nut sac and a man is down. We should be saying, 'Dude, you're such a ball sac,' when we want to call somebody out for being weak."

Clara laughed.

Violet lifted her hands to the sky. "Why me?"

I slapped Sean on the back of the head.

"Ow!"

Lavinia patted him on the knee. "You've got a point, sweetheart. I agree."

"That's actually quite true, Sean," added Devraj, propping up the other wall opposite me.

Sean rubbed his head, frowning at me. "Why'd you hit me?"

This kid, I swear. It was impossible to teach him good manners.

"Did we miss it?" Charlie and JJ rushed into the waiting room.

"No." Lavinia stood, giving Charlie a hug. Then JJ. "Did y'all have a nice time?"

"The best," said JJ, pulling Violet into a hug.

JJ and Charlie had taken another one of their trips. This one was only to the west coast, wine country, rather than abroad like the last one. They'd cut it short when Evie went into labor two weeks early.

"They're here!" Isadora burst into the waiting room. "Two boys and a girl."

"I already told y'all that." Violet ran past Isadora. The others filed quickly after her. Lavinia grabbed my hand and hauled me with her, bringing up the rear.

I couldn't explain my hesitance. Not until we were in the crowded room.

Jules held one bundle in her arms next to Evie's bed. Evie held a small, pink-faced babe. Mateo held the third. My heart clenched at the blissful domestic scene, the entire family crowding in to get a peek at each of them.

A nurse walked in and froze, her eyes bugging wide with all the people crammed into the small room. "Um, some of y'all are going to have to leave. Like ten of you."

"That won't be necessary," said Devraj, reaching over and tapping her on the wrist lightly. "It's perfectly fine for all of us to be in the room and we won't cause any problems."

"Oh." Her face brightened, eyes glazing with that dreamy look of someone who'd just been glamoured by a vampire. "Of course, it's fine." Then she turned and left.

I kept to the back, watching Lavinia lean over and kiss Evie on the forehead then sweep her delicate fingers over the soft tuft of black hair on the baby in Evie's arms.

"Did everyone wash their hands? Hand sanitizer!" growled Mateo, pointing to the bottle on the tiny table below the TV on the wall, scowling furiously. "Now!"

The baby in his arms squirmed and let out a tiny cry. Mateo instantly softened his voice and whispered sweetly, "There, there, baby girl. Daddy's got you."

"Um, everyone," said Evie, her voice watery with joyful emotion. "Jules is holding Joaquin. Mateo is holding Celine, and I've got little Diego here."

There was a hubbub of joy and adulation at the presentation of names of these tiny newborns, everyone hovering and peeking and petting the little supernaturals.

Again, I felt a pressurized strain on my chest, like it was difficult to breathe. I couldn't quite understand at first, then it hit me.

This was what a loving family looked like. This was what I'd never had and always longed for. I rubbed the center of my chest as I surveyed the scene.

Then the door popped open and an older couple I'd never seen before stepped in. But I instantly recognized the shape of the woman's eyes and face that matched Lavinia's. She was a lovely middle-aged witch, likely in her eighties though she looked in her forties for human years. The man behind her was tall and lean, a kindness and contentment to his face that I actually envied.

"Mom!" shouted Violet.

"Dad!" yelled Clara.

The Savoie sisters attacked the couple with hugs and kisses, and overlapping, excited questions and comments: *Why didn't you tell us? You have to meet Devraj. When did you fly out of Switzerland? Mom, this is Nico. Where's your bags? Dad, how's your knees?*

Devraj, Nico, and I shared wide-eyed glances, pressing back to the walls so the family could move around and hug each other. Mrs. Savoie scooted around the bed.

"Mom." Evie cried while laughing up at her mother, still holding one of her sons. "I'm so glad y'all came."

"We wouldn't miss this for the world, baby girl. Besides, I hear we have a wedding to plan, too."

Isadora beamed at her mother before turning to Devraj who was taking the baby from Mateo. The babies were being passed from one to another, or more like taken from one person's arms by another, the children so well loved already.

They'd been alive less than an hour, and there was no doubt that they'd be raised with safety and joy and love.

Mr. Savoie shook Mateo's hand, congratulating him on his sons and daughter. I think Mateo grew another foot from pride.

"Gareth." I turned to find Lavinia standing next to her lovely mother. "This is my mom, Serena Savoie. Mom, this is my boyfriend, Gareth Blackwater."

"It's a pleasure to meet you." She shook my hand. "A grim, eh?" She arched an eyebrow at her daughter. "Doesn't surprise me that Liv would take a walk on the wild side."

"Mom!"

"It's a pleasure to meet you too, Mrs. Savoie."

"Serena, please."

"Serena. I'd say that Lavinia is taming me pretty well."

Serena laughed. "I'll bet," she said without an ounce of truth in her words. She leaned closer and squeezed my shoulder. "Nice to have you in the family, Gareth. Thank you for taking care of our girl."

Then she moved on to Nico and Violet. And Lavinia was standing there, beaming up at me, making me feel like a king.

Clara popped up next to us with one of the baby boys in her arms.

"This is Joaquin." She handed him over to me without even asking. "You two are going to have the most beautiful girls," she said, tucking the blanket around the infant's head. "Even the ones you adopt."

"Girls?" My pulse jackhammered ten times faster all of a sudden.

Lavinia looked at me in shock, laughing.

"Yeah," said Clara. "Violet told me."

Clara moved on, leaving me with a baby in my arms. I glanced over at Violet who winked back.

"Girls?" I repeated my inane question. "What do I do with girls?"

Lavinia put her arm around my waist and placed a kiss on Joaquin's head. He gazed up, silent and unusually watchful, his eyes a deep blue as most newborns.

Lavinia looked up at me. "You're going to raise them. In a loving home." She kissed me on the cheek. "Because you'll be a loving, wonderful father."

She pressed her cheek to my shoulder, looking down at baby Joaquin. My heart nearly burst with the combination of hope and love I never dared to even dream I'd experience in my own lifetime.

Before Lavinia, I never would have. But this woman and her family had shown me what life could be like. What a true family could be like.

That heaviness in my chest eased. Then vanished altogether. I glanced around at the extremely loud family who would definitely get us kicked out of this hospital very soon. Smiling, I pressed a kiss to Lavinia's head, her face still turned down at her little nephew, his tiny fist wrapped around her finger.

"I love you," I murmured into her hair.

She tipped her head up then. "More than love," she replied sweetly.

Yes. *More than love.*

That was the emotion filling my heart and my soul as I held Lavinia and this new life in my arms, ready for whatever our tomorrows would bring.

THANK YOU SO MUCH FOR READING! IF YOU'D LIKE A SNEAK PEEK at the Prologue for RESTING WITCH FACE, turn the page.

SNEAK PEEK: RESTING WITCH FACE

PROLOGUE

~JULES~

"How was your date?"

Like a lit match, a burst of joy stretched my mouth into an instant smile. I felt ridiculously like Clara for a second.

Mom's returning smile was smaller. Sadder. "That good, huh?"

"Yeah," I admitted on an exhale of giddy feelings I'd never felt about any other man. "I think he could be the one, Mom."

She was folding towels. Zombie Cat was curled up next to her. It was midnight, but she was doing laundry, the domestic chore she loathed the most. As a matter of fact, Dad usually did the laundry just so she didn't have to. Not that we weren't all grown women in the house now and usually did our own. Except for Violet.

The fact that Mom was still up and folding and smoothing a kitchen towel into a perfect square in her lap told me she was anxious about something.

About me.

"What is it?" I sat on the sofa, my hands folded in my lap. "Is it because he's a vampire?"

She looked at her hands, unmoving on the kitchen towel, her mouth quirked in that tight, maternal expression.

"Not exactly," she said softly. "The transition of power ceremony has been set."

It might have seemed like she'd changed the subject. But she hadn't. These two topics were linked.

"I'm ready," I admitted with confidence.

"I know that you are." She met my gaze now, pride shining in her eyes. "The ceremony will be on the winter solstice. Your father and I will leave the day after. Unless you want us to stay a while longer."

"No, Mom. You and Dad have waited long enough."

She'd been training me and teaching me for three years, taking me on every guild meeting, every coven trial, every Summit, letting it be known she was confident that when she and Dad retired abroad, I would be well prepared to take her place. Moving overseas had long been their dream, and I wouldn't keep her from it.

Besides, I *was* ready.

"A vampire, a powerful one, could be a good partner for me," I said into the quiet.

The house was so still, as if it too was listening and waiting with dreaded anticipation.

When she didn't say anything, but simply set the folded kitchen towel to the side, her hand absently stroking Z, I had to go on.

"I know it's not normally done, mixed-magic couples. But I don't see why not."

Again, she didn't respond right away, seeming to gather her thoughts.

"I'd like to tell you a story…about your Aunt Penelope."

Aunt Penelope was Mom's sister who left the US years ago

and married a warlock in England. They never had children and always sent us quirky Christmas presents, but she never returned for a visit. Our house was in fact the house she grew up in with Mom.

"You know that Penelope is also an Enforcer. Like me."

"Yes," I answered.

Mom had told me this years ago, pointing out that her sister had never wanted to rule over New Orleans. Even though Penelope was the eldest, she deferred to her little sister, my mother, and then left to live abroad. I'd never know the circumstances that made her want to leave her home so completely.

"Before she left, and after I'd become Enforcer, she was in her twenties," Mom continued. "She was a ridiculous flirt. And so beautiful and charming that every man fell at her feet." She smiled at some memory then the light in her eyes dimmed almost as quickly. "She fell for an unbelievably handsome man. A vampire named Broderick. He was the overlord of New Orleans then, actually. Before Declan."

Two months ago, Declan had been promoted to a larger realm and coven, overlord over all of Massachusetts, Connecticut, New Hampshire, Rhode Island, and Vermont. He would rule from Salem where the vampires had first settled here in America, a place of their past with deep vampiric roots. It was a good promotion for Declan who'd served well with my mother for many decades.

The new overlord of New Orleans set to take Declan's place was a powerful vampire who'd come directly here from New York. Ruben Dubois. The man who'd dropped me off ten minutes ago. My heart thrummed faster, not wanting to hear the rest of my mother's story.

"Broderick wooed my sister with such persistence. He was incredibly handsome and charming. As most vampires are," she said gently, almost with regret. "Mother had already started her walkabout the world, leaving me in charge."

My grandmother, Ma Maybelle, was a wild witch, all too

eager to dispense with her role as Enforcer here. She'd started traveling the world almost as soon as Mom had taken her place, I was told. She visited home from time to time, but usually kept roaming from country to country, going on adventures with a new warlock wherever she landed. She might be in her two hundreds, but she only looked about fifty. A well-groomed, beautifully aged fifty.

"My mother," she started again, "had always told us to stay away from vampires. That it wasn't wise to let them drink from us. *Take them as a lover*, she used to say, but *never let them drink from you*."

"Why not?" My heart was beating like a hummingbird's wings now, though I kept calm and still.

"Back to the story. Broderick seduced my sister. So much so that she ignored my grandmother's warnings and let him feed from her. Again and again."

"What happened?"

"You have to understand, Broderick was an old vampire, in his four hundreds. Very powerful. When vampires reach a certain age, past their second century when we call them elders, their strength grows, their magic makes them nearly god-like. They amass more magic as they age."

"Except Enforcers are still greater, right?" I asked.

That was because Enforcers held the magic to null and strip any supernatural of their powers.

"Exactly. What my mother hadn't been clear about was why we shouldn't let vampires feed from us. She'd said something about old stories of vampires going supersonic or some nonsense. Penelope and I had never even dated anyone but warlocks, so I suppose Mother hadn't been all that worried. I love my mother, but she was always a bit reckless." She sighed. "And unfortunately, the stars had aligned for the worst possible scenario. An elder vampire drank from not just any witch, but one with the power of an Enforcer. And he himself was corrupt with a lust for power."